MURDER HANDED DOWN

MURDER HANDED DOWN

A Novel

Jay Zimmer

A Severn Book

Novels by Jay Zimmer

The Peter McDermott Adventure Series

Dry Terror

Code of Theophilus

Murder Handed Down

The Color of Dark

MURDER HANDED DOWN

A Severn imprint

This is a work of fiction

ISBN: 0983019509

Printed in the United States of America

**For S. J. Z. As Always
My Biggest Fan and
Gentlest Critic**

"A newsroom is a crucible. In it we burn away irrelevancy until we are left with a single product – the truth for all time"
—Austin Edmondson, 1975

And to the members of the Craft of Journalism and their heroic daily quest for the truth, this book is lovingly dedicated.

PART ONE

Washington, D.C., February, 1946

I

....suddenly a shot rang out.....

The body had been on the floor only a few seconds, but already others were milling around it, creating shadows in the garish stage lights. They looked down at the body, their eyes conveying a cross between kinship and revulsion, just as all creatures feel before a dead body. He had been a young man, certainly no older than 35. He was muscled and fit, and of medium height, with sandy hair that was beginning to recede at the temple. Death had come with devastating and unexpected swiftness, evidenced by the spreading red stain on the body's starched shirt-front.

Name: Chance Caine.

Occupation: Musician.

He had wandered into the club just the week before, accosting orchestra leader Mr. Bigalow, passing himself off as a trumpet player. Bigalow noticed that the stranger carried his horn bare, no case, no bag, with the mouth piece affixed in its place. He held the horn casually, but in the correct way. Bigalow didn't ask many questions, he needed a new bugle-boy, so he had the stranger blow a few lines from the first sheet of music he could find, just to make sure he actually *could* play, then put him on the bandstand that very night.

Chance Caine was an enigma from the beginning. He came in when he was told to, played the music he was given, and left immediately after the last show, saying little to anyone else in the thirty-six piece orchestra.

And now he was dead.

All that could be determined in those first moments – a time when his body was still warm – was that he died by a single, small caliber gunshot that came from the audience.

From the audience.

But who? And why?

Someone bent down next to the body and felt for a pulse, first in his neck, and then, apparently finding none, his right wrist, where the person lingered a moment. But finding no pulse there, either, the woman in the red evening gown straightened, took a long lingering look at the cooling corpse on the stage floor and disappeared into the crowd.

Bigalow elbowed his way through the human wall and looked down at the late trumpet player, a twinge of regret in his eyes. Quiet, enigmatic, reserved, those things this strange man was. But with all, he was a top-notch trumpet player who was capable of much better than the stock arrangements that stood on his music stand. For a moment, Bigalow wished he could have heard the man play his talent.

The crowd closest to the stage apron parted like the Red Sea and a flashbulb popped. A news photographer who had been in the crowd at the tables muscled his way in and snapped a flash picture of the body – quickly popped out the used bulb and snapped in another in a single motion and took another, this one closer. Bigalow grabbed the photographer by his arm and hustled him back toward the club floor, off the front of the stage.

"Have a little respect, will ya," Bigalow growled. "They guy's dead."

The photographer waved him off, then turned and walked toward the club's main entrance at the other end of the room. As he was going out, a uniformed D.C. policeman came in, ordering the crowd back. They moved on command.

The blue-suited figure arrived at the stage and took a look at the red stain on Chance Cash's starched shirt front. He spent a moment taking in the scene, then looked around.

"Who's in charge here?" he demanded.

Bigalow stepped forward.

"Arnie Bigalow," he said in a low voice.

"Call the station house," said the cop. "Tell them there's been a murder and we need some detectives here."

Bigalow stepped off the stage and whispered instructions to his bartender, then returned to the scene.

"Who's he?" the cop asked, indicating the stiff.

"Goes by the name of Chance Caine," Bigalow said. "He was my trumpet player."

"Hmmm," the cop mused, stroking his stubbly chin. "Well he ain't no one's trumpet player no more."

2

II

...it was a dark and stormy night...

It was raining in the Capital City – the kind of rain that washes the rats out of the sewers, and ripens the stink blowing inland from the Anacostia River, across the Washington Navy Yard.

This was the side of town where people lived, where people went to for cheap fun with others of their ilk, those with a secret to keep, those with a secret to share. Here a person could find a drink, a meal, a bed and perhaps someone to share the bed with. Here could be found a new identity, and old enemy, information on just about anything and any one. All for a price.

Here the liquor flowed and the jazz blended with the foul air.

Here those from Northwest Washington came to get in touch with their evil sides, to rub elbows with the denizens of the dark, whose day started when the sun went down. It was where the affluent came to feel earthy and crude and to take as their example those who *were* earthy and crude, but who tried with limited success to emulate their up-town cousins.

The Blue Heron was the newest night spot to spring up in metro-Washington. It rose from the phoenix of a hundred other businesses with a hundred other, long forgotten names, in the red clay building that adjoined the obscure and unused Metropole Hotel.

The owners of the Blue Heron tried harder than most. They spent a fortune on new lighting, new furnishings, a new kitchen and an ornate bar with intricate carvings which they hoped would get people talking. They didn't.

The Blue, as its workers and regular customers called it, also had the finest orchestra on the Eastern Seaboard. It was obtained by raiding the bandstands of other clubs from New York to Atlanta.

The Blue opened nine months ago to great fanfare, and for a time its orchestra reverberated far enough to bring the more genteel clientele from Northwest D.C. and Montgomery County, Maryland, and the Blue Heron boomed despite being in the forlorn shadow of a long forgotten hotel. Every night, Sundays included, the tables on its tiered floor were filled with the rich, the famous, and those who wanted to be. And those whose lives required darkness, and who came here to spread their own brand of morality to those who should know better.

That is until this rainy night.

The crowd was already thinning when Hank Baumert arrived. He was the epitome of the '40's pulp-fiction detective; tan trench coat turning brown as raindrops dotted its surface, its fit spoiled by the outline of a gun beneath his left armpit; gray Homburg with the brim tilted sharply down in front, and pulled low over his bushy black eyebrows; a day's growth of beard, eyes devoid of color and expression, and unfiltered cigarette dangling from the left corner of his mouth.

For a moment he surveyed the entrance to the club, its garish neon signs piercing the Washington night like a needle. He shoved his hands deep in his coat pockets and ambled to the entrance.

The uniformed cop at the door recognized him and stood aside.

"Anybody leave?" the detective asked.

"Yeah," the uniform said. "A few people who could make a good case for scramming out of here. None of the main characters in this little drama."

"Yer readin' too many books, kid," the detective said, making an unsuccessful attempt at a smile. He stepped through the door and sidled past the vestibule and into the main club room. Without preamble he sauntered to the stage and took in the scene.

Baumert, with the look and air of a sloven, was in fact, a first rate detective. His keen eyes quickly noticed everything about the dead man on the floor of the stage, even as he mentally worked out the trajectory of the bullet that had killed him. He looked at the dead man, looked at his face, his hair, his clothes, the dented trumpet that now lay on the floor a few feet from where the body had fallen. He looked at the sheet music that was scattered about on the floor, where it had fallen when the music stand in front of Caine, was overturned.

Then Baumert began to study the people who had milled about the stage.

Most were club employees; their clothing betrayed them. There were the waiters in their tuxedo pants, shirts and tiny vests, no jackets, along with the bar staff, men in dress slacks and gartered long sleeves. There were the women who shilled for the house, in short skirts and peasant blouses that showed a great deal of breast. Here and there were members of the audience; women in gowns and men in pressed suits and shirts with unwilted collars.

4

"Anybody see anything?" the detective asked out loud. Several in the throng about the stage looked up at him in annoyance. Noting that, he flipped open his wallet to display the gold badge and card identifying him as Detective Third Grade Henry Baumert, of the Washington D.C. Metropolitan Police.

The sight of the badge changed the mood on the stage. Many of the rubberneckers tried to work their way off the platform and out the door unobtrusively. Others raised their hands in front of them and backed away, and other just seemed to melt into the woodwork.

"Figures," Baumert thought. "And if I asked them individually, every one of them would say, 'I didn't see nothing.' Even the person who sat at the same table with the shooter would say that."

He didn't bother.

Instead he walked into the audience and lined up the table from which he thought the shot had come. He called the Maitre 'D and found the waiter for that section of club floor.

"Who was sitting here," he asked the waiter. "At this table, when the shot was fired?"

The waiter thought a moment.

"Big man, black pin-striped suit, brown hair, slicked back. Tall, wore wire-rimmed glasses. Perhaps 45 or 48. The woman with him was a good deal younger, not older than thirty. Blonde hair with black roots, red gown, good figure, and a gold necklace."

"How do you remember that so exactly?" Baumert asked.

"One remembers when the man gives you a twenty-dollar tip," the waiter said. "Besides, observing the people who come into this kind of place is kind of a hobby of mine."

"You ever see them before?" Baumert inquired.

"The man, yes, the woman no."

"You know who the man is?"

The waiter shook his head.

"I've served him two, three times. He is always polite and considerate and always leaves a big tip."

"Kinda like he wanted to be remembered," Baumert mused to no one in particular.

"Yeah, I guess so," the waiter answered, confused.

"Either of them do anything unusual? Like when the shot came?"

"The woman went onto the stage," the waiter told him.

Baumert's waning interest suddenly peaked again.

"She did?"   The waiter nodded. "I saw her almost run to the stage, you know, she picked up the hem of her skirt and kind of sprinted up there."

"What'd she do?" Baumert asked.

"She felt for a pulse on the dead guy, it looked like – she touched his neck and then his wrist, and then she ran off the stage again."

"To where?" Baumert demanded.

The waiter shrugged.

"She ran toward the back of the room. She might have gone out the door for all of mine."

"Did she have a wrap?"

"A what?"

Baumert spat.

"A coat, a stole, something."

The waiter thought a moment.

"No, not when she ran out of here. She might have something in the check room, though. And as fast as she was moving she might not have stopped to get it."

Baumert thought a moment, then turned back to the waiter.

"Thanks," he said in dismissal.

He called a uniformed policeman over.

"I want you to supervise the cloak room," he told the officer. "No one gets anything without a claim check, and you have them write their names and addresses on the checks when they turn them in. And if there's anything left in that cloak room when everyone checks out, don't touch it, just come find me."

The officer nodded and moved off.

Baumert returned to the stage and knelt to one side of the body. The clothes he had noted before; same as the other orchestra members were wearing – black tuxedo, no tails, starched white shirt with small collar-turn, and a bow tie. The shoes, though, didn't fit. They were scuffed. And worn. And brown.

The face was composed, the shot had come unexpectedly and death was so fast he didn't have time to react. There were blood spatters on his chin and neck, and a few droplets had found their way to his cheeks and nose.

Chance Caine had worn a single gold signet wring with the initials "C.C." etched into an onyx square. Baumert could see a chain around the man's neck but could not see what it held. There was a cheap silver wrist watch on his left wrist, and marks from some kind of bracelet on his right, but no jewelry there. That caused him to raise an eyebrow.

6

Something had been on that wrist that now was missing. Who took it? Was it in the band room? Did someone who had milled about the body right after the shooting take something from it? Who could it have been? Was it the woman in the red gown?

Baumert chewed on his fingernail until it bled.

III

... why don't we give 'em the gunsel?...

There were times when Detective Hank Baumert hated the public. Most of them listened to too much "Dragnet" on the radio. But would Sergeant Friday pick up a gun outside a crime scene And take it somewhere? Baumert doubted it. But that was what happened here.

The man that approached the detective had a look of triumph on his face, a look that said he himself had found the main clue that would crack the entire case.

He was a mousy, skinny, frail man in a too-big tuxedo, a thinning head of retreating hair and tiny hands with tapered fingers. In his right hand he held a small, shiny object.

"I found the gun," he said to the detective triumphantly.

Baumert's face clouded over as he looked at the weapon. He recovered quickly.

"Where did you find it, show me," he said quickly.

The mousy little man shrugged and led the detective out into M street and pointed to the gutter.

"It was there," he said. "I saw a flash from the street light and I picked it up.

"I wish you hadn't," Baumert said under his breath.

"Huh?"

Baumert waved him off and took the gun, looking down at it. It was clean.

"Did you wipe this off?" he asked.

The mousy man nodded with a thin little grin.

"I couldn't hand it to you with mud and dirt all over it, could I? I wiped it clean with my handkerchief.

Baumert was seething inside. He turned and beckoned to a uniformed patrolman who was standing nearby.

9

"Arrest this man," he told the cop. The face of the mousy man dropped.

"For what?" he demanded in a too-loud voice that attracted the attention of many of the lookers-on.

"Tampering with evidence," Baumert told him. "Don't you listen to the detective stories on the radio? You never, *never* touch something that might be evidence. You go and get an officer and you show it to him where you find it."

The man's face clouded over.

"Oh," he said "I wiped off fingerprints, didn't I?"

Baumert nodded, giving the officer the eye and jerking his thumb over his shoulder. The officer led the gun-finder away. Baumert looked at the gun for a moment.

"Baretta 7.65 semiautomatic," he mused aloud. "Eight shot clip." He pressed a button and the clip dropped out. He counted six shells in the magazine, which meant one was chambered for firing, and rammed the clip back where it belonged. Dropping the gun into his pocket, he went back inside the club to reconstruct what happened.

Baumert sat at the table from which he believed the shot mush have come. For long moments her merely sat and stared at the stage and the music stand behind which Chance Caine had been sitting. It was a direct line-of-sight trajectory at a distance of perhaps 30 yards, or roughly the distance from the pitcher's mound to home plate at D.C. Stadium a few blocks away. The detective pulled the weapon from his pocket, checked to be certain that the safety was on, and sighted down the barrel.

For anyone with even the slightest experience with guns it was an easy shot. For someone who really knew what they were doing with this kind of handgun, there was almost no way to miss. Leaning back, and clasping his hands behind his head, Baumert began to figure out what must have happened.

IV

...hell hath no fury...

They had entered the club as a couple but in truth they barely knew each other.

He was big, topping out at two inches over six feet with broad shoulders and thick, muscled arms that ended at beefy, well-manicured hands. His hair had a wet look, slicked back from the front and perfectly in place. His clean-shaven, oval face, devoid of any decorative facial hair, was perfectly set off by the almost invisible wire rim glasses he wore.

His suit was black, with the pin stripes just now coming into style. His shirt was of soft white linen, immaculately pressed, with a paper collar free of smudges or crumples. His tie was fastened to his neck with the latest knot, set off by the gold watch chain that stretched across the front of his vest and disappeared into the special pocket. He walked with his feet shod in expensive, impeccably shined wing tips, and costly Burberry socks imported from England.

The ornament clinging to his arm was every bit as elegant as he was.

She was blonde, at least from a distance,

She wore a yellow hat with a partial veil, tilted at a jaunty angle, one side touching the gold loop earrings. Her face was made up perfectly, eyebrows plucked to within an inch of their lives, cheeks rouged lightly and lips a screaming, pouty red. So was the gown that puffed out at the padded shoulders, which were the style of the time. Below the shoulders it plunged to a deep "vee," inches below her breasts, then clung to her belly and hips like a second skin before draping to the floor. She carried an oversize clutch-style purse of patent leather. Her arm entwined in his, she watched as the maitre 'd summoned a waiter who escorted them to a ringside table where they sat side-by-side facing the stage.

They ordered drinks, but beyond that they spoke not a single word to one another. They declined an offer to order dinner by shakes of their heads, and for the next several moments they stared straight ahead. Not at one another, not at the other people in the club – straight ahead, toward the stage with the closed curtain.

This was the Blue Heron, the first nightclub to make a go of the location next to the cursed – and still closed – Metropole Hotel. The owners, whose names were lost in a multi-leveled sea of corporate deceit, poured thousands into the club, and advertised it as the place to go for returning soldiers coming home from post-war, for sailors on pre-discharge duty at the nearby Washington Navy Yard; the Blue Heron was becoming the place to see and be seen among the Washington elite, where people of substance and affluence could rub elbows – among other things – with their opposites, those whose lives began after dark, and who slept when the sun came up, those whose morals and method of living were questionable. At this club, the corporate CEO and the mob don sat at the same table and shared the same bottle of Bollinger '23. It was here that the Washington lobbyist and a capo from La Cosa Nostra could meet in convivial fraternity, and join their two worlds in covert business, liberally lubricated with greenbacks and sex.

Twenty minutes after their arrival, the orchestra struck up from behind the heavy curtain. The two people at the ringside table didn't change their expression, they didn't join in the perfunctory applause, they didn't blink.

The curtain rose and the rotating stage turned clockwise, revealing the orchestra, playing away with Arnie Bigelow waving his baton.

The two people at the ringside table sat in stony silence for the first number, declining with a tiny shake of their heads, the offer of a second drink.

The second song started, a catchy popular tune of the time, with the brassy female singer pouting into a ribbon microphone. It was at this point that the male member of the mysterious duo took his right hand off the table, reaching down to hike up his right trouser leg. From a band just above his sock garter he took a small, lightweight blue steel pistol. Beneath the table he passed it to his right, into the gloved hand of the woman next to him. In a moment, the singer would step to one side of the grand piano that was situated well downstage, and the trumpet player on the opposite side of the stage – and in the upper tier of the orchestra platform – would stand and begin blowing his solo.

Just eight bars from now.

Under the table, the woman's fingers tightened around the grip of the gun, her index finger curling around the trigger, waiting, her eyes hardening, her lips pulling themselves into a thin, determined line.

The singer tossed her platinum hair and extended her arms in the way of countless nightclub canaries, singing the last sustaining notes of the chorus as she spun away from the microphone. Simultaneously,

12

Chance Caine rose from his seat and brought the golden trumpet to his lips, closing his eyes on concentration.

He blew his intro, counts three and four of the last bar the singer warbled, then leaned back to begin the first of his eight bars of solo. The woman let him get to the third bar, when the trumpet player came out of his back arch and stood upright basking in the notion that all attention on the tiered floor was on him. It wasn't of course; some were talking, some were sizing up their chances of getting lucky later in the evening, some were plotting some plot or another, oblivious to the sounds from the stage, and still others were indeed watching, riveted to the trumpeter pouring his talent into brass tubing and valves.

In a single fluid motion, the woman raised her hand above the table, pointed the weapon and squeezed the trigger.

Chance Caine toppled off the bandstand without even taking his horn from his lips, landing with a thud below the drummer's throne twelve feet below.

Dropping the gun into her bag, the woman stood and hiked up her skirt slightly, sprinting to the stage even as the crowd recovered from the shock of what it had collectively just witnessed and began converging on the stage.

She wasn't the first to reach the scene, but she was the only one not squeamish around the body on the floor with the red stain dead-center in his shirt-front.

She bent to the cooling corpse and feigned searching for a pulse in the arm then in the neck – with her free hand working a bracelet over the dead man's right wrist. Her mission complete, she deftly dropped the purloined item into her handbag and, hiking up her skirt again, she dashed off the stage past her table and the man sitting there, and out into the night. As she stepped off the curb in front of the club her bag opened accidentally and the gun slipped out, falling into the gutter with its rainwater runoff and mud. She rescued the item that was also in the bag, and kept going, losing herself in the darkness.

A block from the club, she hailed a taxi and vanished.

The gun, Baumert would later learn, was of Italian manufacture, a Baretta model M1935, made for the Italian troops in the Second World War. The weapon Baumert regarded was one of about 525,000 such weapons manufactured by Baretta. The Italian military was becoming more and more enamored of the superior Walther pistol being produced in Germany, and not wanting to lose their biggest contract, they designed a gun along German lines with the same reliability and accuracy. The

13

gun was so well thought of that it was issued to German forces as well between 1944 and 1945.

As for the two people at the ringside table – Baumert's expert detective methods would run the man into the ground. The man, one Enoch Chalmers, would be found in a down-scale Washington brownstone apartment, with no apparent means of support. He would claim that the elusive Lady In Red was merely a hired escort for the evening; that he had never seen her before that night nor after, a statement Baumert was nearly certain was false. But he couldn't – or wouldn't – shed any light on who the woman was. The escort service, whose name Chalmers supplied, had quietly gone out of business, and the former manager could not recall a female escort matching the description Baumert had.

Dead end.

And it stayed dead. No trace of the Lady in Red was ever unearthed.

The case remained open, but the investigation was as dead as Chance Caine.

PART TWO

Chapter One

The clanging bell was like a blade that cut deeply into his dream. The more he tried to shake it off, the deeper that invading sound cut into the flesh of his sleep. He tried turning over, but it persisted in its urgent summons. Reluctantly, Rodney Pitcher opened his eyes and focused for a moment on the red numbers on his bedside alarm clock.

3:15AM.

Pitcher steeled himself as he reached for the phone. No one calls after midnight with good news.

"This better be good," Pitcher growled into the phone, his tongue and throat feeling gritty.

"Pitch this is Fred Mattingly."

Pitcher was instantly awake. Fred Mattingly was the lead homicide detective for the Washington D.C. Metropolitan Police. Pitcher knew him well, from his years as a reporter on the Metro staff of the *Washington Post*, and still dealt with him occasionally as he plied his craft as general assignment reporter for Baltimore's *North Bay Times*.

"Can you come to the Blue Heron?" Mattingly asked.

Pitcher shook his head to clear it.

"The what?"

"The Blue Heron. It's an old nightclub adjacent to the Metropole Hotel in Southeast Washington."

"Oh, OK. That place is closed and boarded up, isn't it?"

"It's supposed to be," Fred Mattingly said somberly. "How soon can you get here?"

Pitcher looked at the clock again.

"Half an hour," he said.

"Make it twenty minutes," Mattingly said, and clicked off.

Pitcher hung up and rolled over on his back, looking at the sleeping figure in the bed next to him. Samantha Parker hadn't stirred in the course of the conversation. She lay on her side with her back to him, her breathing deep and easy. Pitcher felt a pang of regret because he was feeling amorous again, and Samantha Parker never objected to being awakened for a romp. But Fred Mattingly's voice sounded urgent. He sighed heavily and heaved his body out of the bed, reaching for his boxer shorts as he stood.

He padded barefoot across the carpeted floor of his Baltimore apartment, into his bathroom, halfway down the hall between his bedroom and the second bedroom that served as his office. He splashed some water on his face and gave his pits a sniff. He frowned into the mirror and smeared deodorant under his arms. He examined his face critically in the mirror under the dim night light, and decided that he didn't have time to shave.

Back in his bedroom he stepped into a pair of faded jeans and a ratty Georgetown Hoyas sweat shirt, plus a pair of soft moccasins. He kissed the sleeping Samantha Parker on the cheek as he left the room. She sighed and turned over.

In the foyer of his home he slid his arms into a gray winter jacket. He picked up his keys from the table just inside his front door and let himself out into the cold, pre-dawn morning.

Even with little to no traffic, it took Pitcher nearly forty minutes to drive the Baltimore-Washington Highway. Finding the ancient, decrepit night club took longer. Pitcher thought he knew where it was, but found himself turned around in the maze of streets and avenues that was Southeast Washington.

He finally stumbled into it, noticing the faded sign on a dark, eerie building sitting on a three-way corner in the glare of the neon lights from a Rexall drug store a half-block down the street. He parked at the curb and tried the dusty front door, half-surprised to find it unlocked. He pulled a penlight from his pants pocket and bathed its tiny glow on the foyer of the ancient building. He could see a light beyond the club-room door, a light that barely pierced the enveloping darkness. He pulled the door open with his fingertips and stepped inside.

The room was filled with uniformed police officers, and, here and there, a few men and women in plain clothes, but, because of the way they dressed and carried themselves, Pitcher knew they couldn't be anything other than cops. They were surrounding something indiscernible lying on the filthy stage floor.

As Pitcher approached, Mattingly stood up from a half crouch and noticed him, beckoning for the reporter to come to the stage.

It was a body. Pitcher knew that before he even approached the stage, because why else would a homicide detective be calling him in the middle of the night? She lay on her back in the dust of decades on the

18

rickety stage, almost in a fetal position, mouth agape, a congealed pool of blood mixing with the dirt. Dark, shoulder length hair was askew, limbs akimbo, her eyes were open, staring upward as if trying to see the blue hole in her forehead. She wore a dark T-shirt and nearly-new jeans over simple slip-on shoes.

Mattingly came off the stage and approached the reporter.

"Morning Pitch. I hope you've had your coffee."

Pitcher looked past Mattingly and frowned.

"Nothing like a body before breakfast," Pitcher said,

"Especially this one," Mattingly replied, grimly. "Did you get a good look at the face?"

Pitcher shook his head.

"Maybe you'd better."

He gestured for Pitcher to ascend the stage. The reporter approached the body with a sense of foreboding. In his career as a journalist he had seen many bodies, the remains of people who had met death in various ways, but he was not prepared for what was to confront him in this dank, dusty memorial to a bygone era.

"My God," Pitcher breathed.

"So you know her," Mattingly said a statement, rather than a question. He walked up behind the reporter and looked over his shoulder.

Pitcher only nodded.

"You OK?" Mattingly asked in a sympathetic voice.

Again Pitcher nodded.

"Her name is Reesa. Reesa Lowe. She is a distant cousin."

"So you know her," Mattingly said again.

"Not well. I only see her at family reunions and Christmas and such, and then only sporadically. I've met her; I've had dinner with her at a table filled with other relatives I could care less about. We've talked about various worthless things. That's about all."

"Do you know what she did for a living?"

Pitcher shook his head.

"She used to be a lab assistant somewhere, but I think I remember hearing that she went back to school to learn something else, I don't remember what. That's the last I have heard of her."

"Married?"

"Divorced last I heard," Pitcher said. "Her husband was a louse. Drank his paychecks and was physically abusive, or so the family grapevine had it."

The two men stood silently for a moment looking down at the woman on the floor.

"How did you know to call me?" Pitcher asked.

Mattingly reached into his coat pocket and took out a folded sheaf of papers which he handed to the reporter.

"She had these with her," he said. "It's notification of inheritance from one Albert Lowenstein, and it lists a small amount of cash and a few personal items that she was bequeathed."

Pitcher riffled through the papers.

"I see," he said laconically.

"You know anything about this guy Lowenstein?" Mattingly asked.

Pitcher shook his head.

"Not a thing."

"You're a big help, Pitch."

Pitcher grinned for the first time since arriving in the club.

"That's what my boss says."

"Oh, really? Why does he keep you around?"

Pitcher snickered.

"Comic relief."

He chuffed Mattingly on the shoulder.

"Thanks for the call, Fred. I appreciate it."

Mattingly nodded, and Pitcher turned on his heel.

Pitcher left a message on Samantha Parker's cell phone voice mail explaining what happened and telling her he would call her when he could. He knew she would huff and swear, but she would be OK with it. Since their first meeting during the hunt for pirate treasure in the Chesapeake Bay region, they had been something of an 'item.' Samantha was learning the demands on a reporter's time, his sometimes instantaneous departures. She didn't like it, but she thought Pitcher was worth not liking one thing about him.

He found his car where he left it and drove back the way he came. But once in Baltimore, he changed direction and drove not to his apartment complex on the northeast side, but to his office in the Inner Harbor.

The offices of the *North Bay Times* were in a converted warehouse near the harbor. At the piers nearest the office were a permanently moored Coast Guard cutter, a submarine, and a clipper ship. Pitcher had worked nearly four years in Baltimore and had never visited any of them.

He pulled his press card from his coat pocket and swiped it through a slot next to the door. There was a soft click, and he pushed the door

20

open, sprinting up the stairs to the glass doors. His key fit in the lock and he passed through the portal, walking to his own cubical in the main newsroom.

He waited a few minutes while his computer booted up, looking through his card file and his palm pilot phone list to see who he could call to find answers. He glanced at his desk clock. 5:45AM. Too early to call too many people but he knew one he could call right away. He lifted his desk phone and punched a number in speed dial.

Peter McDermott stabbed at the snooze alarm on his bedside clock, but the incessant buzzing wouldn't go away. And he hated to come all the way awake, especially since he was facing a long day at the office.

The managing editor of the *North Bay Times* finally realized that the intermittent buzzing wasn't the clock, but was his night-stand telephone. Ruefully, he remembered his long standing intention – never realized – to replace one or the other so his sleep-befuddled mind could distinguish easily between the two. Often when he was called in the wee hours the caller would hang up before he figured it out and got the phone to his ear. Not tonight, though, so he knew the caller was someone who knew him.

"McDermott!" he barked into the phone, his voice taking on an air of irritability, married to the slurring that often is a sign of someone hammered awake prematurely.

"Pitcher," came the voice in his ear.

McDermott sighed.

"Pitch whatever it is, it'll wait till morning," he mumbled sleepily.

"This *is* morning," Pitcher reminded him.

McDermott surrendered and sat up in bed, wiping his eyes.

"OK, Pitch, what's on your mind?"

In a few sentences, Pitcher outlined all that had happened that night. As he did so, McDermott turned on his nightstand light, and opened the plastic bottle of Diet Pepsi he kept there; swishing some of the carmel-colored liquid around in his mouth, and hoping the caffeine would jolt him awake. It almost did. Not quite.

"So anyway," Pitcher concluded. I came on into the office to try and make some sense of all this, but I couldn't wake anybody else up at this hour."

"So naturally, you thought you'd wake me up just to have someone to talk to."

"Sure," Pitcher said casually but with perfect seriousness.

"Sorry about your cousin," McDermott said, with what he hoped was a voice replete with the proper amount of sympathy.

Pitcher ignored the sympathy, lean as it was.

"Thanks," he said flatly. "All that aside, I'd like to find out more about the inheritance, and why she was killed for whatever she was killed for."

"And why she was in a long-closed nightclub in the middle of the night," McDermott chimed in.

"Right, there are so many angles to choose from here, I don't know which one to tackle first."

"Well," McDermott offered." You might search the *Washington Post* and *Baltimore Sun* obit pages and see if you can find the Lowenstein notices. That might give you an early clue."

"Doing that as we speak," Pitcher said sharply, a bit nonplussed. McDermott was teaching Journalism 101 to a veteran reporter. Checking the obits was basic, and Pitcher was already using the internet to do that.

"If you find him, give me a call," McDermott told him. "I'll stop by the probate court's offices on my way in and see if I can get a copy of the will."

"They don't open for another three hours, Mac." Pitcher told him, a smile tugging at the corners of his mouth. "Don't tell me you're going back to bed!"

On the other end of the line, McDermott smiled thinly.

"OK, I won't tell you," he said, and hung up. He laid back down and tried to make his mind throttle down. But that old reporter's sixth sense, the strong feelings he'd learned over the years never to ignore, swept the sleep from his eyes and the cobwebs from his brain. With a heavy exhalation of breath he gave up and stood, reaching for the robe he kept on the end of his bed. He padded into the kitchen and ran some water in the pot for coffee, but then thought better of it, left the half-full pot in the sink and walked to his study.

The desk lamp glowed as McDermott crossed into the book-lined room in his waterfront condo. Beyond his desk, through the sliding glass doors, he could see the lights of Eastport Marina. He sat in the padded recliner next to a small table and stared at the lights. Coming into this room often made him think of the road it took to get here.

He'd begun his career in a "Podunk" radio station in Indianapolis while still in high school. He'd worked his way up, and finally landed in a major radio newsroom where he won his first spate of awards, before crossing over into television.

Like radio, television was a ladder. You worked at a job until you could go no farther in position and pay, then you looked for another job in a bigger market.

McDermott had made it to the upper-middle markets, and had risen to a position of trust among colleagues, bosses and viewers, the awards on his wall multiplying. Then he peaked and was on his way back down the ladder. His next job was two markets below the one he left.

It was about that time – after stints in California, Illinois, and three different Louisiana cities, and Texas, where he had been instrumental in solving an abduction and murder that had almost proved fatal to him, that this opportunity arose.

He'd met a newspaperman named Charlie Hume and then two had become friends. When Hume bought an ancient, bankrupt weekly newspaper in a tax sale, he'd called McDermott and asked him to run the editorial side of the business. McDermott, in turn, had picked up top flight Metro reporter Rodney Pitcher from the *Baltimore Sun*, along with other high-end editorial writers, and the three of them had transformed the weekly *North Bay Times* into a major regional voice in Maryland and Washington D.C. Their honors included a Pulitzer Prize for hunting and finding the treasure of 18th century pirate Theophilus Turner.

McDermott averted his eyes from the lights of the harbor beyond his glass doors. He turned on the table light and tried to read, but he couldn't concentrate.

Giving up yet again, he snapped off his reading lamp, dog-eared the page he was trying to read and left the room, leaving the desk lamp aglow.

McDermott hated to enter a dark room. He had an obsessive like habit of making sure he always left the light on.

He took his time in showering and dressing, then picked up the keys to his Jeep, and stepped out into the waning night.

Chapter Two

Doctor Hidashi Itsoku stood back and took a long, long look at the body on his stainless steel table. As always, in cases like this, he found himself becoming a little sad. Sad that the end of a life could be spoken of in the expressionless, clinical words he had spoken into an overhead microphone

White female, 42, height five feet five and one half inches, weight, 151 pounds, brown hair long as the shoulder, blue eyes. No discernable health problems. Missing the appendix and two lower teeth, replaced by a partial plate. Cause of death: GSW. Gunshot Wound.

Itsoku had carefully pulled the fatal bullet out of the woman's brain and dropped it into an envelope which he had an assistant mark for ballistics. The bullet was battered and flattened, the result of having passed through the skull and the occipital lobe of the brain, where it slowed down considerably, and fragmented, the largest portion coming to a stop in the medulla oblongata. He was about to close the wound and consign the body to the refrigeration cubicles in the next room – the cause of death was obvious enough. But something wouldn't let him do it.

He re-gloved and stepped back up to the table, taking another look at the body. He started at the head, then palpated the neck and began to move down.

He almost missed it. He was feeling around on the torso, looking for bumps and lesions or any other sign of trauma or disease when his fingers found an indentation in the right armpit. He moved the arm and probed further. His finger found a small hole with very little blood. Intrigued, he pulled a probe from the sterile pack near the table and carefully inserted it into the wound. It penetrated not quite two inches before encountering something hard obstructing the pathway.

He had found another bullet.

Reaching to his side without looking, he dropped the probe and picked up a long, thin pair of forceps. He went back into the wound, this time grabbing the bullet with the forceps. He tugged lightly but the tiny missile wouldn't budge. Another tug, harder this time, and he was able to turn it a tiny bit at a time. Patiently, he rotated the bullet until the suction of the tissues and musculature surrounding it surrendered its grip. At that point, the bullet came smoothly out of the wound.

"Interesting," he said to no one. "Bullet trauma but not enough blood to capture anyone's attention. I couldn't have been *that* focused on the head wound."

He was putting the bullet into a tiny manila envelope when Marv Bent came in.

Bent was balding and nearly 60, his belt disappearing into enormous folds of fat above and below. He was white-haired and scruffy, wearing jeans and an incredibly wrinkled polo shirt, his police-issued gun hanging on his side butt forward, handcuffs dangling out of the hip pocket of pants that seemed to sag in desperation.

But for all his rumpled appearance, Marv Bent was the best ballistics man on the Eastern Seaboard.

Bent smiled at Itsoku through gapped, yellow teeth.

"Mattingly said you might have something for me," he said in a friendly, but businesslike tone.

Itsoku nodded and held up the envelopes.

"Two somethings," he said, passing them to the detective. One is a pretty badly mangled slug from the head wound. The other is a slug I found in another wound under her right arm. It's in very good condition. I marked the envelopes."

Bent nodded.

"You got a cause of death?" Bent asked.

Itsoku smiled.

"GSW, left occipital traveling through the brain into the medulla oblongata," he recited.

"Must have hurt," Bent observed.

"For a second," the pathologist said, laconically.

"If you've got the report and all the photos you can release the body," Bent said. "Mattingly is done with it."

"What's not done will be by close of business today," Itsoku told him.

Bent nodded and smiled again, stepping back out of the room.

Marv Bent's work room was an untidy, dust-covered, ill-lighted cave in the basement of the police building, a half-block from the city morgue. He threw the two manila envelopes on his work bench and draped his suit coat haphazardly over the back of his desk chair. He changed into a lab coat that one might imagine had been white at one time, but was now a brownish-yellow, thanks to a total lack of attention by a washing machine. He poured a cup of tepid coffee and looked at his case load list, a growing pile of envelopes like the ones he had brought over from the morgue; every one awaiting his professional scrutiny, everyone an open case involving violence, and, in most instances, death.

The items on his desk were in no particular order. Normally he would take the two cases from the bottom of the stack and do them first. But today something told him that the new ones would be the most interesting. With a sigh, he took the first of the envelopes and upended it into his free hand.

He recognized the slug as a 7.62 round, despite the fact that it was flattened and badly marred. He placed the damaged lump of lead under his comparison microscope and turned on the base light. For long moments he peered into the eyepiece, turning the lump with a pair of wooden photographic tongs.

"Hmmm," he mused aloud to no one. "It's German, by the look of it." Bent was referring to the composition of the metal that made up the misshapen pellet on his microscope table.

He removed the slug and returned it to its envelope, then replaced it under the microscope with the whole bullet from the other envelope.

To one entering the room moments later, it might have looked like Marv Bent had fallen asleep with his eye to the eyepiece. He sat motionless, only the sound of an occasional raspy intake of breath broke the near-absolute silence in the room.

Bent wasn't asleep; far from it.

Despite his slovenly appearance in body and environment, Marv Bent was a first class investigator. Adding to his value to law enforcement, he possessed an encyclopedic knowledge of firearms and ammunition. He kept his files in his head, where he claimed – with demonstrable accuracy – to have a photographic memory concerning bullets and the guns that fired him.

That was what occupied his mind as he stared intently at the bullet on the scope table before him. There was something stuck in the back of his mind, something the object he was looking at triggered, but he was damned if he could put his finger on it.

Without taking his eye from the eyepiece, he pulled a pencil from his shirt pocket and made a sketch of the lands and striations from the bullet on a pad of drawing paper he always kept next to the scope. Despite drawing "blind," his sketch was handsome art, and represented a perfect depiction of the bullet he was looking at. When he finished he pressed a button on the scope – also without looking – that took a digital picture of the slug.

Finally raising his eyes, he put the bullet back into its envelope and stored it in a locked file cabinet toward the back of his work room.

Taking a last slug of the day-old, dead cold coffee, he sat down behind his desk and pulled his computer keyboard to him.

Peter McDermott sat down on a bench outside the offices of the Clerk of the Probate Court. He loosened his suede jacket and did a quick speed-read of the sheaf of papers he had just received from one of the deputy clerks at a dollar a page. The stack of papers was thick.

Albert Lowenstein. McDermott went back to the beginning of the papers and began to read, slowly this time.

When he died, eight weeks before, Albert Lowenstein had been 94 years of age. He was a joiner by trade and had retired and lived in a modest home that he left to one of his many relatives. His wife had preceded him in death and several of his children had also passed away. His will named several nephews and nieces and distant relatives scattered about, mainly in the Baltimore area.

There wasn't much. A modest house in Towson. A car. His clothing and piles of assorted bric-a-brac, power tools, personal effects and some costume jewelry of his late wife's. Those items were scattered among relatives on a come-and-take-what-you-like basis.

The woman who lay dead on the stage of a long-closed night-club was specifically named in the will – along with about a dozen others – as heir.

He stood, scratching his head, and walked down the hall to the Health Department. He paid the five dollars and asked for a death certificate for Albert Lowenstein.

There had been no autopsy. Cause of death was listed as congestive heart failure. He had died in his home and a part-time care-giver had found the body.

Again he scratched his head.

One of the things his mentor had taught him all those years ago in Vincennes Indiana was to be thorough. At the moment, his self-imposed assignment was the death of Albert Lowenstein. He pulled his palm pilot out of his pocket and looked up the number of the coroner. He dialed as he walked toward the building's employee break room where he could hit a wireless hot spot.

Ten minutes later he was studying the coroner's report on Lowenstein's death.

The body had apparently been on the floor of his bedroom in his home for several days before the care-giver found him. He had been dead most of that time but the date and time of death could only be estimated. The body had been released for burial to a local mortuary where Lowenstein had a pre-need package all paid for.

Nothing here. Dead end. Routine death of an old man whose body simply wore out on him.

McDermott sighed heavily. He knew Pitcher was back at the office pounding the computer looking for a thread. The editor hated the idea of telling his colleague and friend that if there was anything remotely resembling a "routine" death, this was it.

McDermott closed and cased his laptop, pulled his keys out, and walked to the parking lot where he turned his Jeep into the early morning Baltimore traffic.

But the routine death of Albert Lowenstein did nothing to explain why Reesa Lowe was dead on the stage of a night club in the seedier side of Washington that had been closed for decades. Pitcher, too, had found Albert Lowenstein's death pitifully routine. The murder – and it's location – were pieces that didn't fit.

In the offices of the *North Bay Times*, the reporter threw up his hands in disgust. He was becoming convinced that there was no link between Reesa's murder and the death of her elder relative.

But Pitcher, like many reporters, was obsessive-compulsive. – he couldn't leave a matter alone while there were still some loose ends. Reesa on that ancient stage was a very loose end. And she was unraveling, revealing other strands that needed to be resolved.

Obviously, the reason she was on the dusty stage of a long-closed night club was strand one. Around that one, all the other ones hedged.

Another strand: Was her death connected at all to the death of Albert Lowenstein? If so, how? Why? Certainly murder was a senseless act, but almost no one killed without having a good reason. Almost no one. Could her murder have been just a random thrill for some sicko?

There were far too many unanswered questions.

Maybe Mac came up with soemthing, he thought as he absently dug the point of his pencil into the palm of his hand.

Marv Bent stared again at the whole bullet taken from the body of Reesa Lowe, hoping something inside the lens of the comparison microscope would jar his memory. He was certain he had seen the striations and lands on that bullet before, but unlike other cases, he couldn't put his finger on this one. He leaned back against the tattered chair and stared at the ceiling, trying to remember. Giving up, he returned to his desk and stared once again, this time at the computer screen. He hoped that the germ of a thought would force its way into his mond and he could come up with at least a key word to search by.

"Hmmm," he mused to himself aloud. "That slug is a 7.62. Not many of those around these days..."

He took a stick pen and made a note in the margin of a long-forgotten report on his desk. From another pile there, he took a book of weapons and looked up a reference.

"Baretta," he said, aloud again. "Old type, pre-Korean war. Interesting."

He turned back to his computer and placed the cursor into the 'search' field, where he typed, "7.62, Baretta," and for good measure, added, "unsolved." He pressed Enter.

He could hear the hard-drive buzz and whirr in the dead silence of his work room. Then he heard the computer shift from the local tower into the police records server – a large common-drive that contained millions of bits of information. That meant in the years Marv had been in the forensics and ballistics offices, he had never handled what the computer was looking for. That was very unusual.

But before he could ponder the matter further, the computer came up with its answer and displayed it on the screen.

Marv Bent stared open mouthed at the computer's answer to his queries. He jotted down the case number, made note that it was an open case, then printed out the ballistics report and photos. Then he went to the microscope and pressed a button that automatically sent what he saw in the eyepiece to a printer where it came out in full color on gloss-coated paper for special clarity.

He took both sheets and put them face down on the glass top of a special scanner. A click of the comptuer mouse and the machine hummed and bits of light flashed out from around the lid.

The computer displayed the result of the comparison scan on its hi-def screen, and Marv Bent's eyes got as big as saucers.

"Damn!"

Chapter Three

Peter McDermott got to his office a little before eight-thirty. Rather than going for the coffee machine, as did most of the staffers of the *North Bay Times*, McDermott pulled the tab on a can of caffeine-free Diet Pepsi from the refrigerator in one corner of his office. He took a perfunctory sip as he walked to his desk and sat in the leather judge's chair behind, touching the mouse on his computer. The screen lit, and his Outlook Calendar came into view. But before he could peruse his morning schedule, a harrowed-looking Rod Pitcher burst into his office without fanfare or preamble.

"Mac, did you find out anything at the Probate office?"

McDermott smiled and picked up the sheaf of papers from his desk, tossing it obliquely to Pitcher, who missed.

"Not much there," he said. "Certainly nothing jumps off the page as to a cause or motive for murder. But it might give you a place to start."

Pitcher bent to pick up the pages that had come loose from the paper clip, and were strewn about the carpet."

"You're not going to teach me basic journalism again, are you Mac?"

McDermott's face clouded over and his smile dimmed.

"I realized I was doing that as soon as I said it," he replied. "Sorry."

Pitcher nodded once in silent forgiveness. He stood and shuffled the papers until the edges were even. "I'll check all this stuff out and see what I can come up with."

He turned to leave.

"Pitch," McDermott called after him. Pitcher turned.

"Don't waste a lot of time on all that," the editor said softly. "We have stories to finish and a paper to get out."

Pitcher clouded over for a moment, but recovered quickly. He nodded again and disappeared into the newsroom.

Back in his cubicle, the reporter looked over the list of heirs. The list was long, but not so long that he couldn't work the phones and try to find out something about the estate. He would do that, he thought, and if he didn't find another strand of the thread, he would consider the death of Albert Lowenstein and Reesa Lowe to be totally unrelated. Well, he

31

would satisfy himself, one way or the other, then he would return to his regularly assigned duties.

He looked at the list. The names were there, and their addresses, as they had been notified by the attorney in charge of the estate. He pulled a D.C. phone book from a shelf behind his chair and started looking up telephone numbers.

There were eleven names in all, and eight of them were listed in the book. He sighed and pulled his desk telephone to him, and began dialing.

Peter McDermott looked at the composite page of the *North Bay Times* on his computer screen. It was Page Three and there was a gaping hole under a headline, and the statement, "By Rodney Pitcher, NBT Staff Writer."

There was a big hole where Pitcher's words were supposed to go, and there was another hole next to the space with a frame around it that was to hold a graphic that would assist in the reader's understanding of Pitcher's glowing prose.

McDermott punched the speaker button on his phone and hit Pitcher's speed-dial numbers. He was rewarded with an instant switch to the reporter's voice mail. That meant Pitcher was on the phone in his cubicle. Well, the editor thought, at least he was there.

This was Wednesday. The weekly *North Bay Times* went to press on Thursday for distribution on Friday to the dozens of news stands that carried the title throughout Maryland, Washington D.C. and part of Virginia.

Normally, on Deadline Day, most of the battles McDermott would have to fight to complete the paper were with the Sales Department. Their absolutely predictable penchant for failing to turn in copy on time was the thing that raised McDermott's blood pressure as nothing else could. Add to that the fact that the sales people were the only ones in the building aside from the paper's owner whom McDermott could not fire, but brother, how he wanted to. At least once, during the weekly cycle of pulling all the elements of an 80-page newspaper together, he would wage a battle with a sales person who would much rather spend his or her time selling another ad – and padding his commission account – than making sure the client's copy was turned in to Composing so it could be placed among the paper's pages. More often than not, the obstreperous sales person would wait until the final moment – the time when McDermott's face was purple and steam was coming out of his ears – a time shortly after McDermott would present himself in the office of publisher Charlie Hume – who ran the sales department – demanding that this or that errant staffer be fired. Hume would listen patiently to the ragings of his editor, mainly because McDermott was usually right – but he never would fire the staffer involved. He knew that later, when tension was relieved and the editor had calmed down, it would be all right. McDermott never wanted to be the cause of someone being unemployed. It had happened to him all too many times in his career and he hated that feeling. To cause it, he often said, would be worse. Not that he couldn't do it when he had to. What made him a good manager was that he would go to any lengths to avoid it, but when an editorial staff member – over whom he had jurisdiction – wouldn't take the correction and change his ways, McDermott would raise the Irish in his bloodstream and escort the staffer to the door, and then cut him dead, banishing him completely from his memory.

On this day, though, his fight wasn't with a sales person. Almost all the copy for the ads was in, and had been placed in the paper by the Composing staff.   Those items that weren't already inserted were promised before the day's 4pm deadline, and those who had made the promises usually delivered. That was the amazing thing.

The frustrating thing was that on this deadline day, the hold-out was a feature article by Rod Pitcher, the reporter who never missed a deadline. Pitcher, in fact, was the only one in editorial who turned his work in early.

Not this week.

At issue was an article pitcher hadn't wanted to do in the first place; one whose subject didn't interest him. Pitcher was notorious for just skimming by on assignments that were outside his sphere of interests and skills, a penchant that led McDermott to refer to the reporter as "our prima donna division."

McDermott punched Pitcher's number into his phone again and was again greeting with instant voice mail. Pitcher was still on the phone.

Doubly frustrated, McDermott slammed the phone back into its cradle and tried to concentrate on proofreading another page of the paper.

Pitcher had called four of the eight numbers he'd found. Three were home and talked to him readily about Reesa. It seemed everyone he talked to knew her better than he did. Small wonder, but it made him uneasy about what he was now perceiving as a familial failure on his part – and one woman on the other end of the phone had had the effrontery to tell him so.

Other than his own discrepancies as a family member, Pitcher learned little. He hung up from his last phone call and stood.

The reporter had demanded a large cubicle, much larger than McDermott had planned to give him. The reporter knew himself well enough to know that once he was concentrating on a story, he thought best when he could pace. He saw to it that his work area was large enough to accommodate his aimless back-and-forth meandering while he lost himself in thought.

This was one of those times when that extra space came in very handy.

The problem before him nagged at him. He was probably dealing with two completely unrelated things, and he knew that, but something deep in his journalist's soul refused to give up on the notion that the two deaths were related. He sat down behind his desk again, and riffled through the papers McDermott had given him.

His phone rang and he ignored it, continuing his careful reading of the papers from the Probate Clerk's office.

On page eleven, he found a list of personal property that was to be distributed among the heirs. It was mostly small stuff, but it was inventoried in small print. He ran his finger down the list, looking for something, he didn't know what. His phone rang again, and he scooped it to his ear absently.

"Pitcher," he said.

"When can I expect your piece, Pitch?" McDermott's voice droned in his ear.

"OK," Pitch said, not having heard a word that was said. He hung up the phone and continued his pacing, this time taking the property inventory with him. A few moments later, McDermott appeared in the opening of the cubicle that led to the hallway. Pitcher didn't miss a step, didn't even notice his boss standing there. For his part, McDermott had seen this phenomenon in his top reporter before. He knew that at times like this Pitcher was entirely turned inward, much like a sleep walker. He would have to be brought out of his fugue state delicately. Soft and casual was the word.

McDermott raised a plastic cup filled with ice water and waited until Pitcher was walking toward him. When the reporter reached the apex of his stride and was about to turn his back again, McDermott unceremoniously threw the water in his face.

"Shit!" Pitcher screamed, slamming his psyche back into reality. "What the hell is wrong with you?"

So much for delicate, McDermott thought.

"Pitch," McDermott said, in mock-mechanical tones. "Newspaper. Article. Graphic. Deadline. NOW!"

Pitcher backed up a step and shook his head to clear it. He looked down at the droplets of water on the papers he was carrying, and started trying to dry them out with his sleeve.

"I found out something interesting," Pitcher said to the air to one side of him. "There are several items of costume jewelry in this estate that are being passed around from one heir to another. And Reesa was the first one to have two of them."

"Pitch…!" McDermott snapped.

The reporter finally looked his editor in the eye and what he saw there was disturbing. He caught himself in mid-sentence and shook his head again.

"The Waxman story, right?" Pitcher said sheepishly.

"McDermott nodded with an irritated smirk on his face.

"Have it for you in fifteen minutes," Pitcher promised.

"Make it ten," McDermott snapped, as he turned on his heel and returned to his own office.

Fred Mattingly parked his car in the middle of the street at the intersection of H Street South East and Kentucky Avenue. Before him lay the entrance to the Congressional Cemetery, and there, between the brick pillars at the gate, was the reason for his midday trek.

The man on the ground wore a business suit of the currently popular style and color. His shoes were expensive, not new, and highly shined. The pockets in his suit coat – breast, both insides, and both sides – were ripped open. The pockets in his pants were turned inside out. The man's wallet – which contained his money and all his credit cards – was on the ground next to him.

Robbery not a motive, Mattingly thought. But then no one kills for no reason, no one but a psychopath.

And the inside-out pockets were an interesting touch.

Mattingly looked closer. The victim's eyes were open, staring at the sky above through unseeing orbs that seemed to be trying to look at the blue hole in his forehead. The man had apparently been aware of his killer; he had a terrified mask on his face, and *rigor mortis* was profound. It would take a medical examiner to fix the time of death – and one was on the way.

Absently, Mattingly stooped and picked up the brown leather wallet beside the body. He looked at it. No blood stains, no indication it was

35

forcibly removed from the body. He flipped it open and felt for a driver license.

It was a Maryland license with the name Albert Lowe II, and an address in Upper Marlboro.

Lowe?

Too much of a coincidence.

Rod Pitcher ignored the jangling of his desk phone, and continued his two-finger pounding on the computer keyboard. Like most journalists of his generation, Pitcher had never taken the time to learn a touch-typing system, preferring instead to use the system he called "The Biblical method – seek and ye shall find." And after years and years of practice, his two-index-finger system was easily as fast as could be had with a QUERTY system.

For the last quarter-hour, Pitcher had been referring to his notes and pounding out the story he had promised McDermott. It would be finished in two more minutes – seven minutes later than the editor wanted it, but finished nonetheless. He had already completed the graphic work, using PhotoShop and building it with the aid of some clip-art. The graphics were already in Composing. All that was necessary was the last graph of his story – a quick proof-read, a quicker spell check, and he'd be effectively finished for the day.

But the clanging desk phone would not be ignored, and finally, the electronic bell crashed into his train of thought, derailing it. He pulled the receiver from its cradle and before it was all the way up to his ear he barked out his greeting.

"Pitcher. And this better be good"

He expected to hear the voice of Peter McDermott wondering where his story was, and that was why he answered the phone thus. But the voice that answered his greeting wasn't McDermott

"Mattingly," the voice said. "I need you at the DC Morgue. Right now."

"What?" Pitcher demanded.

But Mattingly had put the urgency of the call into the simple expedient of hanging up.

Pitcher pulled the phone away from his ear and stared at it for a long moment before finally hanging it up. He looked off into space for a few seconds, deciding what to do. Then, with a resolute look on his face, he returned to his keyboard, batting out his final paragraph. He did a speed-proof-read, then spellchecked, and then sent the prose to the

Composing room for fitting into the page McDermott was waiting for. His task done, he turned again to the phone, punching a three-digit extension.

"Pitch, Mac," he said when the line was answered. "The story and graphics are at Composing. I'll see you later."

He didn't wait for a reply. He merely grabbed his suit jacket and barreled out of the cubicle, through the office outer doors and down the stairs into the parking lot.

Chapter Four

"It's like someone is systematically trying to wipe out your family," Mattingly mused. He and Rod Pitcher were sitting in at the Chevy Chase Lounge a few blocks from the D.C. City Morgue. "I just think it's strange that two members are murdered within a week – and anything you can tell me might help me figure out who's doing this and why."

Pitcher took a sip from his glass of beer and shrugged.

"How do I know what to tell you, Fred?" he asked, exasperated. "That's a branch of the family I am not close with."

"What's the familial relationship?" Mattingly asked.

"Huh?" Pitcher replied, stupidly.

"How are you related to these people?" Mattingly retorted gruffly.

Pitcher paused a few moments, draining his beer and signaling for another while he organized his thoughts.

"They are from my mother's side of the family," Pitcher said slowly. "She was Jewish. Dad was Christian, and that's how I was raised, and Mom didn't practice her faith all that much. She died when I was about 14. The Lowes, as I recall, shortened their name from Lowenstein – at least some of them did. Others were kind of pissed-off at a branch of the family sort of de-Hebrewing their names, so they didn't talk to the Lowes for a lot of years – some of them still don't talk, or so I'm told. But a few of them show up for Thanksgiving and Hanukkah or Christmas or something."

"So what's the connection?" Mattingly asked. "What did these two members of the family have in common that would cause them to be murdered this close together?"

"I thought it was your job to find that out," Pitcher snapped.

Mattingly ignored the jab.

"It is. I just thought maybe you could shed some light on the matter."

Pitcher sighed heavily.

"Wish I could. I don't know but what I'll call my Aunt Louisa and see if she knows anything."

"Aunt Louisa?"

Pitcher nodded grimly.

"She's the only one who talks to the Gentile side of the family other than on holidays."

"It she a Lowe or a Lowenstein?" Mattingly wanted to know.

"Lowenstein," Pitcher said flatly.

Mattingly blew through his nose and drained his beer.

"Good luck!" he said, standing and clapping the reporter on the shoulder.

Pitcher left the lounge and decided to check into his Washington office before heading back to Baltimore. He called McDermott's office on his cell as he drove toward Capitol Hill, and was told that his story was in place, his work was done for this issue and he could have the day for his own pursuits. Finding no messages or assignments in his Washington office, he returned to his car and went home.

Marv Bent stacked evidence boxes neatly against one wall of the cavernous properties room deep underground at the Washington D.C. Police Building. The room was well-lit but the light from the huge overhead fluorescents barely pierced the darkness in the part of the room he was searching – far back in the stacks of cases unsolved yet long dead. Again he consulted a piece of paper with the flashlight in his hand, checking the case number he had memorized hours ago. He was nearing his destination. There were, perhaps, three more layers of cold case boxes to move before he found the one he wanted. Sighing, and in so doing, tasting the dust that permeated the air in this repository, he hauled out the next row of boxes, and then two more, and stacked them against the wall on top of the last ones he had moved. Plying the flashlight into the deep shelf he was rewarded by seeing the case number he wanted, crudely lettered in crayon on the side of the box.

There were supposed to be four boxes with the same case number, labeled A, B, C and D. Bent shined his light into the dark space in the shelf and his eyebrow raised – the boxes were stored out of sequence. He reached in and grabbed one of the boxes and pulled it free; it wasn't the one he wanted. Box A was discolored from age and trailed dust as it came free from the spot where it had sat for decades. He consulted the printout again and reached back into the darkness. This time Box B came out. He was surprised to note the difference. The first box was covered in enough dust to make a small even pile of dirt on the top. But Box B had only a thin layer of dust on its top; not even enough to raise a cloud when he lifted the top from the box. He rummaged around the

40

inside, and his forehead furrowed in deep concern. After a few moments, he carried the box under the powerful light and looked carefully at the contents.

What he sought was not there, though the computer printout, which inventoried the evidentiary items from a long cold case, said it should have been.

Frantically he returned that box to the shelf and pulled out the other two. They were covered with layer upon layer of dust, as had been the first one. He dragged all three boxes back to the light, dumped their tops over and rummaged inside.

He was supposed to fund a gun, a Beretta 7.62 pre-Korea model semiautomatic pistol, and the gun that had been used to kill a band member in front of an audience at the Blue Heron, adjacent to the Metropole Hotel, shortly after World War II.

The printout listed the notes, the clothing from the victim, the bullet taken from the victim's body, and a couple of dozen other items of evidence. Also the gun.

Bent searched all four boxes a second time.

The gun was gone.

"Damn!" he breathed.

Rod Pitcher was performing a time-honored bachelor function – eating his dinner over the kitchen sink in his Baltimore apartment.

Samantha Parker wasn't there when he returned home, but she had left a note indicating that she would be back late that evening, and hoped to find Pitcher in residence. Recently, their relationship had progressed to the point that they had exchanged house keys, so he knew she could have gotten in had he not been there. Right now, he anticipated her arrival.

He had occupied himself since arriving home at checking his emails and responding to a few, returning phone calls and generally tidying up his home. He sat in the second bedroom he used as an office and paid a few bills. By then it was dinnertime, and he wished Samantha Parker was there already; she was an excellent cook as well as being excellent in other, important ways. He had reheated some red beans and rice from the fridge and was using a spoon as he ate over the sink. He mused as he did so that some might interpret his actions – if they could see them – as a secret longing for matrimony. But like many others of his craft, Pitcher's career had left behind the wreckage of his personal life.

He'd married his college sweetheart shortly after taking his journalism degree. They struggled for the first several years, both working, as Rod toiled to help his career take hold. They consciously delayed having children until they felt they were well enough entrenched to afford it. But by then, Kimberly Niles Pitcher discovered what it was like to be a reporter's wife. She could never get used to his sudden comings and goings. She could never forgive the editors who would call her husband from their bed into the wilds of wherever, at times keeping him away from home for weeks at a time. She even braved staying alone in their home while Rod covered the first Gulf War, following his writings in the *New York Times*, the *Washington Post* and in his wartime blogs on the Internet, worrying every day that Pitcher would become one of the thirty-eight reporters killed in that war.

When Pitcher's writings overseas suddenly stopped, Kimberly Niles Pitcher feared the worst, and went into the hardest, most protracted depression of her life.

It was shortly after that episode that he abruptly returned, explaining that his lack of contact and lack of product in the newspapers was due to a news blackout while the Allies mounted a secret offensive.

Kimberly Niles Pitcher accepted her husband's explanation. What she could not accept was the fluid, unpredictable nature of the craft he loved. They had several rows about it. And later, while Rod was away on a press junket with several members of Congress, Kimberly Niles Pitcher calmly packed her belongings and left.

She didn't take Pitcher to the cleaners as well she could have. She merely forced the sale of their house and took half the proceeds.

That was the end of Kimberly Niles Pitcher. He lost track of her a few months later, and in time he got over her.

Samantha Parker showed all the signs of having the stuff to be the consort of a reporter, especially since Pitcher's overseas days were clearly behind him. Their time together had been abruptly interrupted several times, but she handled it well and was quick to forgive. She had even formed a friendship with Peter McDermott, who was the one who often interrupted their evenings and weekends.

The ringing of his doorbell disturbed Pitcher's reverie. He set his plate down and gulped the rest of his glass of milk. He glanced at his watch as he walked toward the door. Not time for Samantha to arrive -- and she had a key so he didn't understand why she would ring the bell.

If this was another Avon saleslady...

On the other side of the door was a scene from hell.

The apparition that stood on his front porch was more frightening than any movie he had ever seen, any nightmare he had ever experienced.

The man wore a tattered and dirty business suit. His white hair was mottled in blood and dirt; his face was raw as a beefsteak and streaked in blood and filth.

He was a shade over six feet, thin as a rail, his clothes were ill-fitting and loose, and appeared recently torn and rumpled as though he had been in a fight for his life.

Blood poured from gaping holes in the center of his chest and under his left armpit.

Pitcher recoiled in horror as the apparition stepped forward and held out a red-dripping hand. When Pitcher didn't hold out his own hand, the apparition took his other picked up Pitcher's arm and forced something into his hand.

"*Even*," he whispered almost silently, in a voice fraught with desperation and fear.

"*Even*," he said again, and fell forward onto his face, blood congealing about his prostrate body. Pitcher needed no further information to know that the man was dead.

"Mother!" he yelled aloud to no one, fighting down the bile that rose in his throat.

Peter McDermott dropped his car keys on the table just inside the front door of his condo and walked through the tiny foyer into his study near the back, guided by the glow of the fluorescent light over the kitchen sink to his right. He draped his sports jacket over a living room chair as he passed it, and was loosening his tie and opening his shirt collar as he entered the large, airy room on the marina side of his condo that he used as his study.

His desk lamp still glowed as he glided into the book-lined room and dropped unceremoniously into the recliner chair near the desk. He sat quietly for a moment catching his breath, sighing audibly in pleasure at the thought of another edition of *North Bay Times* completed for posterity. Even now, the night pre-press crew at Chesapeake Printing in Easton, Maryland, was opening his emailed files and turning them into aluminum printing plates that would be hung on the web press the following morning. The paper would be printed on Friday and distributed Friday evening and through the weekend to be available on newsstands by Monday morning.

Indeed the last of his deadline-day battles – this one with a recalcitrant sales manager, had been fought and won with a minimum of fuss, and the paper was "put to bed" on time.

The phone rang.

Irritated, McDermott hoisted his frame out of the recliner and rounded his desk.

"Hello," he barked into the phone, remaining standing near his chair.

No one spoke, but McDermott was aware that the connection was still open.

"Hello," he said again, letting the anger sneak into his tone.

Again, no answer. McDermott returned the phone to its cradle with a resounding bang. He stared for a moment at the offending instrument, and then dropped into the soft leather swivel chair behind his desk. He snapped on the TV with the remote he kept there and leaning back, elevating his feet on the desktop, neither knowing nor caring what was on the TV.

Again the phone rang. McDermott took his feet off the desk and looked at the caller ID. No Data, it said. Irritated anew, he snapped the handset to his ear.

"Hello?" he snarled.

And again there was no answer, but this time he could discern faint breathing sounds. He picked up the remote with his free hand and muted the TV. Now he could be sure that someone was on the other end of the phone, not deliberately breathing into it, a la' an obscene call, but breathing in such a manner as to betray uncertainty, nervousness, or even fear.

"Hello," he said again, this time in a much gentler voice.

There was an audible click in his ear and the line went dead.

Disgusted, McDermott hung up and stepped from his study into the kitchen where he buttered the outside of a large potato and stuck it in his oven. Then he went to his bedroom and took of his clothes, taking a steamy, leisurely shower. He stood for a long time under the water, allowing the heat and the pelting drops to chase away the tightness in his shoulders and torso, brought on by his high-stress job – the highest of which was always deadline day, and the battles he would always have to fight to get all the elements into the paper on time.

For this week that was over and the shower's massager-head was loosening his muscles and making it easier for him to relax.

Tomorrow was his day off. During the summer months he invariably took three-day weekends after he put the *Times* to bed. It was an indulgence that his publisher tolerated because of the long hours McDermott put in on the other four days of the week.

Tomorrow he would do one of the things that always made him smile. He would dress in cut-off denim shorts and his dirtiest, raggiest t-shirt and his awful-est sneakers and row his dinghy over to the Set and

Drift restaurant in the Eastport Marina. The boat owners in the community and guests who brought their yachts into the marina most often patronized the restaurant. They would be dressed in their boating finery and would present themselves in genteel, upscale manners. McDermott's appearance would be as welcome as a dose of the clap. It was a Friday morning ritual during boating season. The restaurant management tolerated it because they knew who McDermott was, they knew his company had a corporate membership in the yacht club, and they knew that McDermott appeared in the restaurant at other times in proper attire and with the proper attitude. And because the restaurant management knew it was a joke, and they played along by being properly indignant to McDermott's weekly disheveled appearance.

McDermott smiled at the thought as he dried his body and knotted the sash of the blue terrycloth robe before padding into the kitchen. He melted some margarine in a skillet, to which he added two pieces of cubed steak. He put the lid on the skillet and took flatware from a nearby drawer, which he clinked on his tiny kitchen table. Before getting a plate out of the cupboard, he liberally poured Worcestershire sauce into the skillet, and replaced the lid, then put the margarine and some sour cream on the table. He was beginning to salivate in anticipation.

He put his potato from the oven on the plate and broke it open with a table knife, then, using his fork, he loosened the meat of the potato inside the skin. He added margarine and sour cream and a touch of salt, then pulled the meat from the concoction in the skillet and slid the pieces onto the plate near the potato.

He placed a paper napkin on his lap as he sat down. He forked a bite of potato and raised it to his mouth, taking a moment to enjoy the aroma of his dinner. But as he opened his mouth to taste, an insistent, urgent knocking came to his door.

The potato bite stopped midway into his mouth, and the fork came back down toward the plate.

"This isn't happening," the editor thought.

But the knocking continued, demonstrating beyond doubt that it *was* happening. Disgusted, McDermott dropped the fork onto the plate, flung his napkin onto the table, and stomped to the foyer where he threw open the door and stared, mouth agape, in disbelief.

There, on his doorstep, a sheepish grin on her face was Eve Somers, the woman McDermott had been sure he would never see again.

Chapter Five

For the last hour, while McDermott's potato was cooking in the oven of the editor's Eastport condo, Rod Pitcher had been staring non-stop in unremitting horror at the apparition that now lay on the floor of his apartment's entryway. The body hadn't been moved, and the growing pool of blood was congealing before his eyes. He just couldn't take his eyes off it, even as he underwent a grilling from a detective of the Maryland State Police.

"And you're absolutely sure you've never seen this man before?" the detective asked Pitcher for the fourth time.

The officer was a thinly-built African American with close-cropped hair and a pencil-thin moustache. He was dressed in a brown business suit over a blue shirt and a tie that didn't match.

Pitcher merely shook his head.

"Two members of your family have been killed in less than a week," the detective pointed out. "Could this be another one?"

Pitcher shrugged.

"Anything's possible. My family tree spreads out in a lot of branches and twigs. I'm sure there are a bunch of them I don't know."

"But you're not sure if this was one of those?" the detective prodded.

Pitcher huffed.

"If I don't know all the members of the family, how would I know if this was one of those?" he asked, exasperated.

The detective smiled thinly, accepting the point.

"All right, Mr. Pitcher," the detective said, almost a sigh. "We'll try to find an ID on this guy – since you don't know him, you say – and since he had nothing on him, no wallet, no damned car keys – we'll let you know."

"Yeah, thanks," Pitcher said absently, watching in rapt fascination as the workers from the coroner's office scooped the remains into a rubber body bag. Pitcher finally tore his eyes away as the body was loaded onto a gurney and wheeled from the apartment to a waiting meat wagon.

"Someone from the coroner's office will help you clean up that blood," the detective said, as he, also, left the apartment.

47

Pitcher smiled his thanks and flipped open his cell phone, punching Peter McDermott's number in speed dial.

But McDermott didn't hear the cell phone ringing. He'd left the phone charging on his dresser as he showered. And as the musical chime began in his room, he still stood, mouth agape, swathed in his bathrobe, staring in disbelief at the woman on his front porch.

Aren't you going to ask me in?" Eve Somers asked, tentatively.

McDermott stood aside, and Eve slipped by him into the condo. McDermott closed the door and followed her into the living room where she sat on the couch. McDermott, recovering his composure, didn't notice, or didn't appear to notice the gesture she made with her head, a tacit invitation to come and sit next to her. McDermott plopped into an easy chair nearby and faced her, his face turning hard.

"You are the last person I ever thought I'd see again," he said, with a sharp edge to his voice.

She looked down at her feet.

"I know."

"Last I heard you were putting in permanently with Willie Sykes."

"Willie Sykes is dead," she said emphatically.

McDermott's mind raced.

Willie Sykes operated a slimy salvage company along with an even slimier partner named Leo Chack. Sykes got wind of treasure buried in the Chesapeake Bay watershed by a pirate named Theophilus Turner – information she got in her job at the Maryland Historical Authority, from which she was suddenly laid off.

Somers had been dating McDermott off and on since meeting him at an Eastport Yacht Club party, and she knew of his involvement – and that of his newspaper – in the hunt for the treasure. She took the information he gave her "on the pillow" and gave it to Willie Sykes.

Sykes was a great bear of a man, totally uncouth, living hand to mouth. Sykes kept the wolf away from the door, and diesel fuel in his fetid boat by occasionally running drugs ashore from ships that sailed to an off-shore location from South America. Sykes stole a clue to the treasure literally from McDermott's hands, and the race was on to solve the Code of Theophilus.

Eve Somers' duplicity, in playing Sykes and McDermott against one another nearly got McDermott killed – and did lead to Sykes's murder by a Russian assassin in the employ of the drug cartel.

"I'm surprised you didn't slam the door in my face," she said matter-of-factly.

McDermott smiled wryly

"I'm a little surprised myself."

Eve Somers sniffed the air, catching the aroma coming from the kitchen. Her face clouded.

"Were you having dinner?" she asked, a little sheepishly.

"Just sitting down."

"Please go ahead."

McDermott looked away.

"No, it's OK," he said, softly.

"I insist," she said, punctuating her statement by rising and walking toward the kitchen. Arriving, she took appreciative note of the fare on the table, and pulled out a chair so McDermott, who followed her, could sit.

"Cube steak sautéed in Worcestershire sauce," she commented. 'One of your best dishes."

She indicated with her head and hands that McDermott should sit at the table.

"I've always admired a man who could cook," she mused. "And you were always good at it."

McDermott stirred the margarine and sour cream in his potato, which was still steaming.

"Comes from not being good at marriage," he said, taking a bite and pointing to the meet with his fork.

"I have two pieces here," he said. "Won't you join me?"

She smiled broadly and shook her head.

"I'll just have some milk," she said, opening the correct kitchen cabinet for a glass, and pouring from the gallon jug in the fridge. She tasted the milk and sat across from McDermott who was cutting a piece of meat with his fork and steak knife.

"Why are you here?" he asked, chewing.

She sat back.

"Mainly because I owed you an apology and an explanation."

McDermott shook his head.

"You don't owe me anything."

She ignored him.

"I did you a great wrong," she said softly."

McDermott nodded deeply.

"More than one," he said.

Her eyes grew cloudy for a moment and she looked down toward her lap.

"Granted," she said, almost a whisper. "So why haven't you thrown me out of here?"

McDermott's eyes grew hard.

"I may yet. But I wanted to hear what you had to say. And I wanted to find out why you came to see me at all."

She paused a moment then shrugged.

"It was wrong of me to lead you on while I was diddling with Willie Sykes," she said. "I'm sorry."

"That's a match-up I will never figure out," McDermott said sharply. "Sykes was uneducated, uncouth, unwashed, undisciplined, virtually unemployable, and unprincipled."

Somers looked away.

"All true," she said.

"And certainly no match for you," McDermott continued through bites of potato and meat. "You are well educated, highly intelligent, and beautiful, poised, raised well, and until the Historical Authority laid you off, you were gainfully employed."

"Thank you," she breathed.

"Simple facts," he said, emphatically. "I'm completely mystified by your taking up with him."

"I am too," she said. "Willie had something... some kind of an animal magnetism that some women find irresistible. He was earthy and crude; he was all the things you said he was. And I couldn't get enough of him. I was with him and it was heating up and I never even knew it was happening, let alone why."

"Go on," McDermott prompted, after a few moments of silence.

"I know you were a much better match for me," she said, staring him in the eye.

McDermott made a face.

"But Willie was adventure, rebellion, excitement..."

"OK," McDermott interrupted, putting his fork down next to his plate, which now contained only the empty potato skin.

"He was wrong for me, I know that now," she said sadly. "I ruined what you and I could have had."

McDermott nodded at that. Somers stood and took his plate, scraping the skin in to the garbage disposal, which she ran. She rinsed the plate, utensils, and the pan he cooked the meat in, and placed them in the dishwasher, which she noted with satisfaction was empty of other dishes. She took a Diet Pepsi from the fridge, popped the top, and set it in front of McDermott.

50

"You disappeared right as Sykes was shot," McDermott said, accusingly. "Police thought for awhile you had something to do with his murder."

She nodded shallowly.

"I had been trying to find the courage to break away from him for some time, Mac," she said. "I knew it was wrong, I knew it could never work, and I knew I had done wrong by you…"

McDermott waved her off.

"Never mind that," he snarled. "Go on."

Somers' eyes misted.

"That's part of it, Mac," she said. "I was trying to break away, and when he started talking to the State Police, well, I knew he was going to go to prison – and I couldn't stay around and watch that happen, so I left our room at the Maryland Inn and…"

She choked and the tears flowed. McDermott handed her his napkin, and she daubed her eyes.

"Where did you go?" he asked. "Where have you been hiding all these weeks?"

"I stayed with an aunt and spent time just listening to her talk about family. She's not doing well and wanted to discuss family business. She's another one I tried to break away from, after a time, and couldn't."

"How did you finally get away from that one," he asked her, sipping the soda.

"She died five days ago. I buried her yesterday."

"Oh," McDermott said, softly.

There was a long pause, and then Somers stood and ambled over to McDermott's side of the table, resting a hand on his shoulder.

"I came to ask you to forgive me, Mac, and if you can find it in your heart to do that, perhaps you will consider giving me another chance." Somers spoke softly, but rapidly, as though she expected McDermott to interrupt her.

But Mac reached up and rested his own hand on hers.

"I'd love to," he said, turning to look up at her. "I'd really love to. But there's a trust matter involved here, Eve, one that isn't going to be easy to overcome, especially…"

"… especially when I nearly got you killed."

McDermott patted her hand and nodded, returning his own hand to the table.

"Me, along with Rod Pitcher and especially Charlie Hume," he said harshly.

She took his hand again and tugged slightly, indicating that he should stand and follow her. He allowed himself to be led.

"I don't know how I will be able to make that up to you, or to your friends, Mac," she said with conviction. "But I'd like to try."

Mac noticed that she was leading him back to his bedroom and he allowed himself a slight smile.

"And I'd like to begin the process right now."

They crossed the threshold into McDermott's bed chamber and she turned to face him, kissing him lightly on the lips. She took the hand she was holding and moved it to her breast, and began fiddling with the knot in the sash holding McDermott's robe closed. They were beginning to enjoy the encounter when the electronic summons of McDermott's cell phone broke the spell.

"Let it go, Mac," she breathed into his ear, nibbling on his lobe. "It can't be as important as this."

For a moment, Mac allowed himself the idyllic notion of making love to Eve Somers. But the harsh sound of the cell phone ringing would not let him surrender to the idea. Reluctantly, he disentangled himself from Eve Somers' arms and walked the two steps to his dresser which held the phone. A glance at the number in the window told him it was important.

"It's Pitcher," he announced, flipping the phone open. "McDermott," he barked.

"Mac, this is Samantha Parker. Pitch has been trying to get you for quite awhile. We need you here, at his apartment. Something's happened."

"Is Pitch OK, Sam?" he asked quickly.

"Physically, yes," she said. But we need you. Get going and call me back when you're on your way, and I will, explain everything."

"On my way," he snapped and closed the phone. In the same motion he pealed the robe off and stepped to his dresser, taking a pair of brief underpants from the top drawer. Stepping into them, he reached for his pants on the valet.

"Mac," Somers lamented in a disappointed voice. "Can't it wait?"

"Afraid not," he said, matter-of-factly. "We'll have to resume this another time."

He pulled a casual shirt out of his closet and buttoned it quickly, then pulled socks from another drawer and sat down on the bed with his tan boat shoes.

"Call me later tonight and we'll see where we are. Perhaps we can resume."

"Call you?" she asked.

"McDermott nodded. "My cell number is still the same.

"Well I thought I'd just wait here for you," she said, flustered.

"No, I don't think that's a good idea," he said tersely.

Her expression turned icy and she jammed her fists onto her hips.

"You act like you don't trust me," she said, angrily.

McDermott stood and took her by the shoulders, leading her to the front door which he opened.

"I don't," he said simply. "If you want to resume this charming tete 'a' tete, call me tomorrow. If you don't, I'll understand."

He shoved her onto the porch and closed the door behind her. Aware that she had once had the code to the intruder alarm in his condo, he went to the keypad and quickly changed the combination before picking up his keys and opening the door again. He noticed, as he stepped from the condo bound for the parking lot, that Eve Somers was gone.

Chapter Six

Rod Pitcher was seated on the couch in his living room when McDermott arrived, about 55 minutes later. The editor was instantly very concerned about his friend. Pitcher sat motionless, a blank stare on his face, and seemed oblivious to everything going on in the room.

And there was a lot going on.

There were uniformed and plain-clothes police all over the living room and kitchen. Paramedics were working on Pitcher, trying to get some kind of response out of him, but they weren't having much luck.

Samantha Parker was sitting on the arm of the couch stroking his head; she stood and crossed the floor as McDermott approached.

"Let's go outside," she suggested.

The air was cool and crisp. McDermott removed his black suede windbreaker and draped it across Parker's shoulders, since she wore only a t-shirt top and sweat pants. She pulled it tight around her shoulder and shivered.

"Pitch is in shock," she said simply. She took a deep breath and told McDermott the story of his opening his front door and finding a dying man on his porch covered in blood. This was the cadaver, McDermott perceived, that was being picked up by the coroner's team that was huddled on the floor just inside the apartment fussing with rubber blankets and a body bag.

"When I got here he just wrapped his arms around me and bawled," Samantha Parker said. "He just wouldn't let go for a long time, and then the detective came up to us and Pitch managed to tell him the story – then he just sat down on the couch and zoned out. And I can't bring him out of it. Neither can the paramedics. I think they want to take him to the hospital.

"That might be the best place for him right now."

"He said no to that, just no, nothing more. But you know what I think?"

"What?" McDermott asked.

"I think he won't go to hospital because he doesn't want to disappoint you."

The editor pursed his lips and pondered that statement for awhile. Finally he nodded.

"I'll talk to him," he decided, and turned, walking quietly into the room past the people who were at their jobs and paying no attention to him whatsoever. He walked to the couch and sat down gently, positioning himself so that he was looking at Pitcher – or at least looking at the side of his head.

"Pitch," he said softly. "It's Mac."

The reporter didn't move.

"Pitch, it's OK. You get yourself taken care of. The paper's been put to bed, it's gone to press, you're ok for a few days, take some time…"

"They're doing my family," Pitcher breathed, his voice hissing deeply and barely above a whisper.

"What?"

Pitcher's head turned slowly, his eyes still blank and dilated.

"They're doing my family, Mac. This is the third member of my family murdered in a week. Who is doing it? What do they want?"

McDermott sat back against the cushions and gave the questions a moment's thought. At length, he leaned back into his friend's ear.

"I don't know, Pitch, but we'll put the resources of the paper to finding out. That's a promise."

Pitcher nodded, and for the first time seemed to be aware of his surroundings. He looked down and saw the blood spattered on his shirt, and started to wipe it with his hands. His face took on expression for the first time that evening – bewilderment. The reporter opened his hand to reveal an object. He closed his hand around it and stood, walking toward the front door. McDermott thought Pitcher gestured to him to follow, so he did so.

Outside, Pitcher turned to McDermott and whispered.

"I'm going to be all right, Mac. You can send the paramedics home."

McDermott shook his head.

"I'm not so sure," he said gravely. "You looked terrible when I first got here."

"I've recovered," Pitcher said firmly. "And now we have something to go on."

"What?"

Pitcher opened his hand to reveal a small box, smaller than a jewelry ring box. It was metallic and silver in color, with mottled blood staining the exterior.

"What is that?" McDermott demanded.

Pitcher turned it over.

It was a watch. Pitcher and McDermott could see the face, with roman numerals, and the hands, stopped at 2:40. The case was tapered to bend with the contour of the wearer's wrist. The crystal was dirty but intact. There was no watch band.

"Our corpse touched me before he fell down," Pitcher said. "He stuck this in my hand before he died."

"What does it mean?" McDermott wanted to know.

Pitcher looked up at the sky.

"Damned if I know," he said plaintively. "But someone is killing members of my family over it."

"Are you sure that's what all the killing is about?"

Pitcher sat down on a concrete bench near his front door and studied the object in the light from his porch and the moon.

"Why else would someone who's all shot up come all the way to my place and hand it to me with his last breath? "

"That makes sense. Do you know who the latest cadaver is?"

"Yeah," Pitcher said, nodding. "It's Uncle Albert, Aunt Louisa's husband."

"Full name?"

"Albert Lowenstein the Third," pitcher said, huffing.

"OK. So do we turn that watch over the police inside?" McDermott asked. But he already knew what his best friend and top reporter would say.

"Hell no," Pitcher thundered. "I suppose we'll have to give it to them eventually, but we need to sit down someplace and try to figure out what it all means."

McDermott's smile was masked by the darkness surrounding him.

"OK here's what we do," the editor said softly. "Go back into your catatonic state. I'll tell Samantha that I'm taking you to Johns Hopkins to get checked out."

Pitcher grinned, he enjoyed intrigue, a fact well known to McDermott."

"Sounds cool," he said, his eyes twinkling again, but only for a moment. He pocketed the watch, and turned to face the house. At that moment, his face lost all expression, his eyes dilated, and his shoulders slumped. McDermott smiled big and winked at his friend, then turned. His own face suddenly became a mask of concern, and his eyes turned to tiny slits as he stuck his head in the front door.

"Samantha, will you step out here for a moment please?"

Parker was on the porch in moments, looking past McDermott at the stooped figure of Pitcher, sitting in the dark a few feet away.

"I want to take Pitch over to Johns Hopkins for a checkout," he said.

"The detectives want to talk to him before that," she said.

"Sam, the guy's a vegetable," McDermott pleaded. "Tell the detective that as soon as he snaps out of it, I'll have him call in and tell them everything he can remember."

She pursed her lips and stepped inside the apartment, returning a moment later.

"The detective says he objects, but there's not much he can do about it, just be sure Pitch calls in tomorrow or the next day."

McDermott nodded solemnly.

"Is he really a vegetable, Mac?"

Peter McDermott smiled shallowly and winked, placing his index finger over his lips. Samantha Parker grinned broadly, then turned her face back into a mask of sorrow and concern, turning to re-enter the apartment. McDermott watched until she was out of site, then turned back to his friend.

"Let's go," he said.

The two men walked briskly from the porch to the parking lot and McDermott's black Jeep.

The murderer of Albert Lowenstein III pulled a knotted bundle from behind a bush that sat before an Eastport condominium cluster, and added some rocks and other weights to the wad of cloth. A few steps later, the bundle was laid into the waters of Weems Creek, from the edge of a dock in Eastport Marina. The murderer watched it sink inexorably to the sandy creek bottom, confident that the bundle and its contents would forever be shrouded from human view.

The bundle contained the blood-spattered clothes worn by the killer in the act of killing, and represented the only objects that could tie the killer to the act.

Satisfied that the bundle had reached the creek bottom, the killer walked down the dock to the land end, and disappeared into the night.

The Jeep Unlimited was parked in McDermott's personalized space in the *North Bay Times* lot.

Upstairs, the lights blazed in McDermott's office, as the editor and Rod Pitcher sat around the small circular table just off McDermott's massive desk. In the center of the table was the object Pitcher had found in his shirt pocket. The two men were alternately turning it over on the table and staring at it from every angle. Both men frowned.

"We don't even know what we're looking for," Pitcher exclaimed, frustrated.

McDermott sat back in his chair and folded his arms across his chest.

"You're right, of course. What we need is an expert."

"And there are no experts that we can call at this time of night."

McDermott raised a single finger in front of Pitcher's face.

Au Contraire," he said. "I know one I can call just about any time."

Pitcher looked up with a degree of hope in his eyes.

"Who?"

"Julian Peebles."

"Who's he?" Pitcher demanded.

"An expert," McDermott replied.

"On what?"

"Just about everything."

"Swell," Pitcher spat.

"If it helps, he made a considerable fortune out of a talent for recognizing and marketing antique jewelry," McDermott said, looking at Pitcher through squinty eyes.

Pitcher looked perplexed. McDermott smiled.

"Julian is a PIHA," McDermott said, seriously.

"A what?" Pitcher asked, aghast.

"PIHA," McDermott explained. "P-I-H-A."

"And that stands for..."

"Pseudo-Intellectual Horse's Ass."

Pitcher chuckled.

"He's a heavy thinker, been with all the think tanks on the Eastern Seaboard. He's loaded, foppish and speaks with an exaggerated but highly affected English accent."

"He sounds like he's pretty crazy," Pitcher snorted.

"Of course not... No... No... A little bit," McDermott stammered.

Pitcher glanced at his watch.

"And we can get him this kind of night?

"Peebles is a night owl," McDermott said.

"And he's not crazy?"

"Of course not... No... No... A little bit."

"Oh God!"

"I'll give him a call and see when he can see us, Pitch. You'd better get out of those bloody clothes and clean up before we go."

59

Pitcher looked down as though seeing the blood that stained his shirt and pants for the first time.

"Not *de rigueur* for an audience with the bluebloods, hey?" Pitcher grinned, and walked out of the office, to his own cubical in the newsroom.

Like many reporters, Pitcher kept an extra set of clothes in a tote bag under his desk. He retrieved the bag and made his way to the large men's room on the Sales side of the building. It had a shower. Pitcher stripped to the skin, putting all his clothes into a plastic trash bag that he filched from an empty trash can. He showered and put on the clothes he had in the tote bag – fresh duds from the skin out – and hung the towel and wash cloth on the shower door. He put the plastic bag into his tote and set it on the top of his desk so he would remember later that it needed attention. Completing his mission, he sauntered back to Editorial and Peter McDermott's office. The editor was at the door with his car keys.

"Let's go," he said, simply. The two men left the office.

Julian Peebles lived in a large house located in a gated community in North Baltimore. The gates to his home were open and McDermott drove his Jeep into the long driveway that ended in a brick-paved circle before the well-lighted front door. The door opened before McDermott could ring the bell, and a tall, broad-shouldered man in a tailed tuxedo and an obviously aloof manner stood at something akin to attention waiting for them.

"Mister McDermott, Mister Pitcher," the man droned in a heavily British monotone. The *mawstah* will see you shortly. Will you be good enough to wait in the Library?"

McDermott started to reply, but the gargoyle in the suit merely turned his back.

"If you could walk this way," he said, stepping from the knees without moving his upper torso at all. Pitcher looked at McDermott and winked.

"If I could walk that way I'd need a lot of talc," he said flatly."

McDermott chucked, as both men followed the butler down a wide corridor done in impeccable woods and carpet, dotted here and there by obviously old, obviously good quality furnishings. The butler turned left out of the corridor, leading the newsmen into a high-ceilinged, softly-lit room, lined on all walls from floor to ceiling with books of all sizes, subjects and degrees of wear. In the center of the room was a large, heavy wood library table with four wooden, un-cushioned chairs. In one corner was a plush recliner and foot stool with a dark wood table on each side, and a reading lamp above. The butler indicated the chairs around the wooden table, and he watched steely-eyed as they sat.

"The *mawstah* will be with you shortly" he said in a meaty, basso, heavily accented voice. "May I bring you a refreshment?"

"With two straws?" Pitcher asked, flippantly.

"Coffee will be good for both of us," McDermott said, trying not to laugh. "Cream and Sweet and Low in both."

"Veddy good, Sir," he fog-horned, bowing as he backed out of the room, closing the double doors.

"So," Pitcher said, as the doors latched with a barely audible sound. "Based on this butler fellow, are you still sure Peebles isn't crazy?"

McDermott seemed to shrink into his chair.

"Of course not... No... No... A little bit.

The butler returned and noiselessly slid a tray containing a silver coffee service onto the library table. He withdrew without a word. McDermott and Pitcher poured and treated coffee in china cups complete with matching saucers and silver mini-spoons.

At length, Julian Pebbles came in – well, not so much 'came in,' as he made an entrance. He wore soft gray slacks with a razor crease under a blue silk robe cinched with a matching wrap with tassels. On top, he wore a silk, cream-colored Burberry shirt and an ascot of the same material, in gold.

Julian Peebles approached the table, stopped five paces away and bowed graciously from the waist.

"Peter McDermott. I bid you greeting and felicitations," he said with an exaggerated waving of his hands above his head. "And what is it that your humble servant can do for you?"

"Is he kidding?" Pitcher asked *sotto voce*.

McDermott slapped the reporter's knee under the table.

"We need to determine the significance of a piece of jewelry," McDermott said in what he hoped was significantly formal English.

"Quite so?" Peebles said with a flourish. "Then thank God you sent for me. So tell me, Old Boy, where is the bauble in question?"

McDermott handed Peebles the watch. Peebles pulled a loupe from his robe pocket and made a big show of inserting it in his right eye, with which he scanned the watch on all sides.

"Hmmm," he said knowingly. "Ziess-Baden. Made in Munich from 1921 to 1945 when the factory was bombed out by the Allies during the last throes of the Second World War."

He pulled the loupe from his eye and walked across the room to a bookshelf, searching for a title. He found a book and flipped it open, looking for a page.

"It was a small company, but they made functional jewelry for the masses in Nazi Germany. They made everything from gold and white-gold movement watches for the Nazi hierarchy, to steel-cased Swiss jewel movement watches for the masses.

"So this one is probably one for the elite," Pitcher said. "What is it under that silver coating, 14 carat gold?"

Pebbles turned to face McDermott.

"More like 14 carat cheap," he said. "This is one of the watches made for the average German factory worker. The Swiss jewel movement made the watch work on a zircon or perhaps a slab of quartz. These watches were heavy, fairly well made, and manufactured to wear out in three to five years.

"So this one is worn out?" McDermott inquired.

"Well I don't know, Old Boy, there is no winder to tighten the main spring and see. Or didn't you notice that?"

McDermott reddened.

"No actually I didn't," he said quietly.

"I did," Pitcher piped up. Peebles and McDermott stared at him.

"Well, not so much," Pitcher continued sheepishly.

"It appears you've got a bit of a sticky wicket, Old Boy. Is there anything else I can do for you, then?"

"Just one thing," McDermott said sternly. "Never, never say 'sticky wicket' to me again."

Peebles clouded over, but recovered quickly. He turned the watch onto its side and returned the loupe to his eye.

"The serial number of the watch is on the long end under where the band would normally go. Tell you what I'll do. I'll research this number and get back to you whatever I find."

McDermott turned to Pitcher.

"Think we can trust him"

Pitcher shrugged.

"He's your friend."

Mac pondered a minute, then turned and with an exaggerated swagger, offered his hand to Peebles.

"OK, it's a deal," he said, expansively. "But don't let it happen again."

Peebles took the hand with a puzzled look on his face.

"Yes, of course," he said, "Thank you for giving me another chance."

McDermott took the watch out of Peebles' fingers and nodded to Pitcher, who fell into step with him.

"Never mind calling Lurch," Pitcher said over his shoulder. "We'll find our own way out."

Chapter Seven

The killer lay in wait across the parking lot, lightly concealed by some low bushes. The gun-wielding villain hadn't been in that position long, just long enough to have parked the car only a few steps away and find a vantage point that virtually guaranteed success.

The gun was in hand, a small, reliable gun that had proven its worth on more than one occasion in more than one setting. It fit the hand that held it, and despite the silencer screwed into the end of the barrel, it was balanced and comfortable.

In front of the killer was a small parking lot; beyond that was the brick and mortar of the Utt Funeral Chapel on Massachusetts Avenue in northwestern Washington D.C.

The service was just letting out; the killer had timed the matter perfectly and was prepared for the intended victim to walk unwittingly into the crosshairs.

It wouldn't be long.

Rod Pitcher fingered the knot in his tie for the fifth time in a single minute. It was uncomfortable because a tie was one garment he rarely wore. How smart do you have to be, he said often, to begin the day by putting a noose around your neck? He noted wryly that only men seemed to perform this silly ritual each morning; women didn't, but then they wore shoes that put them on perpetual tip-toe. Unconsciously he ran his finger around his neck inside his collar to loosen it a tiny bit. He was starting to sweat in the early-spring warmth, made stickier by soot and carbon monoxide, as he made his way to his car.

Pitcher was attending the funeral of Reesa Lowe.

It took him several minutes to find his car. It already had a "funeral" flag stuck on the roof with a suction cup, for the drive to the cemetery in nearby Virginia.

He was the flick of an eyelash from going there himself – to be a permanent resident.

The hunter spotted the hunted and assumed a comfortable position from which the shot could be fired. The gun was steadied on a knee, an eye squinted shut as the other looked down the barrel. A finger tightened on the trigger as the wrist adjusted for the movement of the target. The finger exerted five-point-five foot pounds of pressure on the trigger, and it snapped back against the guard. Inside the weapon, a hammer fell, a firing pin made contact with a center-fire cartridge, the powder in the casing exploded. The projectile, a jacketed hollow-point leaped from the end of the barrel as the recoil pushed the slide back against its spring. The mechanical arm pushed up ejecting the spent shell. As the slide's spring pressed the mechanism forward, the next shell in the magazine slid free and chambered.

Smoke wisped from the end of the barrel.

Rod Pitcher's penchant to be fumble-fingered saved his life.

Less than a heartbeat before the bullet left the barrel, Pitcher, in the act of unlocking his car, dropped his keys. As he bent to retrieve them, the bullet passed harmlessly above his head and shattered the window in his car.

No sound was heard from the shot, but the crack of the impact against the tempered auto glass. Shards flew in every direction, raining down on the reporter who hit the deck at the sound of the impact.

Pitcher thought someone had thrown a rock or something and shattered his car window; it didn't occur to him that someone might actually take a shot at him. He hadn't seen the wisp of smoke from the gun barrel a hundred feet away, but others, including the motorcycle cop who was to lead the funeral procession, had. Pitcher, from his prone position next to his car, saw the blue-clad officer snap his kickstand down and draw his weapon as he dismounted.

Pitcher ripped the necktie from his neck and threw it away, as he rolled under his car.

"Shit!"

The killer should not have missed, but the bullet had not found its mark, and attention was called to this position. The killer crawled to the far side of the hedge line, dropped the gun into a pocket, and rose, walking casually down the street to a nondescript, older model sedan. In seconds the engine clanked to life and the car shot away from the curb into the Friday morning Washington traffic.

Peter McDermott didn't follow his usual Friday morning warm-weather ritual. He would normally dress in absolutely the worst, dirtiest, greasiest clothes he had and row his dinghy to the Set and Drift restaurant in the marina, which was part of Eastport Yacht Club. McDermott's pilgrimage was a personal joke, one that he played routinely on the operators of the restaurant, who normally entertain boaters of a more genteel attitude than the disheveled editor would present. The restaurant went along with the joke because McDermott did patronize the restaurant at many other times in the appropriate attire, and his company did have a corporate membership in the Yacht Club.

Instead, McDermott returned to his office, much to the astonishment of publisher Charlie Hume, who walked by what he expected to be a dark McDermott office, finding the editor at his desk staring at a computer screen.

"What are you doing here?" the publisher asked. "I had hoped not to have to look at your ugly face until Monday."

McDermott's expression didn't change. Nor did he look up from his computer screen.

The publisher vanished down the hallway and across the building to his own office.

But he was back ten minutes later, and this time he walked into McDermott's office and stood there, stone-still, his face white, his lips marked from his biting them. McDermott continued for a moment, working at his computer on the one side of his brain while waiting for Hume to state his business with the other. When the publisher didn't speak up, McDermott's mind reacted, sending an alarm bell. The editor looked up and saw his boss's expression and his own face, turned to a question mark.

"What?"

"I got a call," he began slowly and evenly. "From the D.C. Police. Pitcher was attending the funeral of the cousin of his who was found in that old night club."

He paused.

"Yes?" McDermott prompted him, urgency creeping into his voice.

"Someone took a shot at him."

McDermott came out of his seat like a jack-in-the-box.

"Is he hurt?" McDermott demanded.

Some of the color returned to Hume's face.

"No, he wasn't hit," Hume said, with relief in his own voice. "He's being checked out at Sibly Hospital and the police want to debrief him, but he's OK."

"Did they catch whoever fired the shot?" McDermott wanted to know.

Hume shook his head.

"No, but the police are pretty sure Pitcher was targeted." He lowered his voice and dropped into a chair in front of the desk.

"Do you have any idea of what it's all about, Mac?"

"Kinda-sorta," he said. "I don't know that what Pitch has been going through and working on has to do with what's just happened, but I think it could be."

"I'm listening," Hume said sternly.

McDermott sat back in his swivel chair.

"But it's a good guess," Hume suggested.

"Damned good, if you ask me."

McDermott's cell phone chirped, and he scooped it out of his belt holster and flipped it open.

"McDermott," he snapped.

"Mr. McDermott, my name is Marv Bent. I am a ballistics expert with the Washington Police Department. I'm calling about the shot that was taken at one of your people today."

"You know Pitcher?" McDermott inquired.

"Yes, I just spoke to him and he asked me to call you. He's going to be with the doctors for awhile longer, and he says there's something you should see."

"Can you tell me what it is, Mr. Bent?" McDermott pushed

"Detective Bent," the caller corrected. "I think you should see this for yourself. I'm at the Washington Police Crime Lab. It's..."

"I know where it is," McDermott snarled. "Shall we say an hour and a half?"

"Let's say an hour," Bent said, and hung up.

An hour and ten minutes later, wearing Guest badges from the Washington P.D., Hume and McDermott shook hands with Marv Bent in the detective's cluttered ballistics laboratory.

"I know you guys are busy," he began. "So am I, so I'm going to cut right to the chase."

Bent made a few passes over the keyboard of his computer, and a picture of four bullets appeared on the screen.

"We have an interesting situation here," Bent began without further preamble. "What you see here are four bullets. Each is a 130 grain 7.65 of German manufacture."

He picked up a pencil from his filthy desk and began pointing at the bullets in turn, beginning on the left.

"This first bullet is the one taken from the body of Reesa Low. The second came from the remains found outside the Congressional Cemetery, and the third was from the body of the man who came to Mr. Pitcher's apartment last night."

"And the fourth?" Hume prompted.

"The fourth came from the door panel in Mr. Pitcher's car," Bent said, seriously. "I have had a chance to compare all four of them. In fact, I've compared them several times, with identical results."

"Well if you're showing them to us all at the same time like this, Detective, they must have something in common," McDermott said.

"That, and more, Mr. McDermott."

He touched a couple of keys on his keyboard and the picture of the bullet was replaced with a picture of a semi-automatic pistol."

"This is a Beretta M-1935. It's manufactured in Germany and was used extensively by the Italian army in World War II. The bullets I showed you are 7.65 millimeter slugs fired from a gun just like this one."

"All from the same gun?"

"Very perceptive, Mr. McDermott. Yes, all from the same gun, one very much like the one."

"So whoever took the shot at Pitch was using the same gun that killed these three other people," McDermott asserted.

"That is correct,"

"You said, 'that and more,' Detective Bent," Hume interjected. "What's the 'more'?"

Bent dropped into his desk chair and looked, first at one of his visitors and then at the other, taking a good minute before speaking.

"This is off the record until further notice, is that understood?" he demanded.

"Reporters don't like to work off the record," McDermott snapped. "It causes too many problems, both for the reporter and for the person he promised an off-the-record interview."

"We can't deal off the record until we know what we're agreeing to," Hume chimed in.

Bent took another look, this time staring for a long moment at both men at the same time.

"I'm going to trust your integrity," he said at last. "I'll give you what I've got and trust that you two will do the right thing."

"Thank you," Hume said softly.

"Back in 1946, there was a nightclub in South Washington that was doing pretty well – even though the hotel next door wasn't. It was called..."

"The Blue Heron," McDermott interrupted. Bent stared daggers at him. "Pitcher told me about it," McDermott finished.

"Do go on," Hume prompted.

"Anyway, there was a guy who joined the orchestra at the Heron, a trumpet player named Chance Caine. It probably wasn't his real name, but that's the name he gave to the club orchestra leader when he auditioned and no one ever questioned it.

"Anyway, Caine had been at the club for a couple of weeks, and one night, during a show, and in front of a full audience, he was shot and killed."

"Right on the stage?" Hume asked.

Bent nodded.

"The D.C. police determined that the shot came from a ringside table just to the stage left of center, and it appears the shot was fired by a woman in a red evening gown."

"Oh God," McDermott groaned. "We've got our own Lady in Red!"

Bent ignored the outburst.

"The woman apparently dropped her gun on the way out of the club, during the pandemonium surrounding the witnessing of a cold-blooded murder during a show on the stage."

"Who was she?" Hume wanted to know.

Bent shook his head.

"We never found out, but we did learn the identity of her companion that night."

Bent went back to his keyboard and called up a mug shot, in black and white.

"His name was Wicht. Armande Wicht. He was an agent of the Nazi *Abwer*, or spy network, working in the United States throughout the war. He kept a low profile and was never positively identified as taking any overt or covert action against the U.S. Probably he was a mole, a plant to be called up when needed. We don't know why he was in the club that night, and we don't know what the woman wanted."

"She just shot him and left?" Hume asked, incredulous.

"Some of the witnesses told police that she ran to the body and seemed to be searching it or checking for a pulse before she ran out of the club. Wicht disappeared in the bedlam and it's not known if she and he hooked up after that."

"What happened to the two of them?" McDermott asked.

Bent shrugged.

"They melted into Washington society and disappeared. There is no mention of either one of them again, and we never found out who the woman was."

"This is a nice fairy story," Hume barked. "But how does a 60 year old mystery figure into three murders and one attempt in the here and now?"

Bent reached into his desk lap drawer and came out with a manila folder. From it he took several black and white 8X10 photos which he laid on the desk in front of McDermott and Hume.

"These are ballistics photos of the bullet taken from Chance Caine's body, and a test bullet fired from the gun found in the gutter outside the club. They matched. And that's not all."

Hume and McDermott looked at Bent with inquiring eyes.

"These bullets also match the bullets from the three murders – and one attempt – that have taken place in the last few days!"

McDermott and Hume looked at him dumfounded and open-mouthed.

"We're dealing with a 60 year old mystery that has come out of the woodwork, then?" Hume asked.

"*We* do, not you,"Bent said firmly.

McDermott had been staring at the ceiling for a moment. At length, he held up his hand and his eyes burned into Bent.

"Wait a minute here," McDermott said. "You said the gun used in the '46 murder was recovered."

"That's right," Bent confirmed.

"And yet, you're now telling me that bullets from that self-same gun were used in three murders and an attempt just recently."

"Right again," Bent said lamely, knowing where McDermott was headed.

"So you don't have the gun."

"Nope."

"Who does?"

Bent cringed.

"Whoever took a shot at your friend has the gun," Bent said. "And we're moving heaven and earth to find whoever that is."

"You and your friendly neighborhood *North Bay Times* team," Hume said hotly.

"This is a police matter, Mr. Hume," Bent snapped.

"In your ear, Bent," Hume thundered, coming out of his chair. "Someone took a shot at one of my reporters. They don't get to do that. I am putting the entire spate of resources of my newspaper and our allies into the investigation. We'll cooperate with you in terms of finding the person who did this, but I have to tell you, Bent, it's probably going to be a good thing if you get to whoever it is before I do."

"In that case," Bent said with a huge smile, "you're going to need this."

He handed a CD to McDermott, who took it with a quizzical look.

"Everything we have on the investigation is on there," Bent said. "I'm counting on you to keep your promise and make sure we're in the loop on anything you find out."

"We'll do that," Hume said, turning for the door. McDermott followed him.

As the door closed behind them, McDermott turned to his boss and friend.

"You didn't tell him about the watch," he said.

Hume grinned.

"No, it didn't seem to come up in the conversation, did it?" Hume said, airily.

"That doesn't seem like cooperating with the police investigation to me, Charlie."

Hume turned to McDermott without breaking stride, but grinning from ear to ear.

"I lied," he said.

Chapter Eight

Peter McDermott gave up on the idea of going back to work after being dropped off in the *Times* parking lot. He said his good-byes to Charlie Hume, and drove back to his Eastport condominium.

McDermott had lived on the Eastport Marina for several years, and the only boat he owned was a 12-foot rowboat. It was his running joke with Charlie Hume that he, McDermott, really did have both oars in the water most of the time.

For a long time, McDermott had planned to buy a small cabin cruiser, and to make the time in his hectic schedule to enjoy it. He had often looked with envy at the weekend boaters kicking back and relaxing in the marina, and he had a not-so-secret yearning to join them. Thanks to the paper's corporate membership in the Eastport Yacht Club, and his frequent dinners at the Set and Drift, he knew many of the boaters, and had, in fact, been out on their boats on occasions. He had also taken and passed a Coast Guard safe boating class.

Today, since he had nothing else planned, he thought he would walk the piers at the marina looking for something he could afford.

He parked in the lot near his condo after the 35 minute drive from Baltimore and walked directly to the marina gate. He knew the touch-pad combination, and he went right in, beginning his walk on the pier farthest from his home.

This being Friday, many of McDermott's boater friends were in residence in the marina, and he stopped to talk with several of them. One, a tree surgeon named Phil Myers, wanted to know what brought the editor to the marina.

"You just want a boat ride this weekend or are you seriously thinking of joining the mariner's ranks?" Myers asked, smiling broadly.

"I think I am about ready to take the plunge," McDermott told him. "I am looking for a boat I can afford that's fairly low maintenance."

Myers snickered.

"Low maintenance? Hell, Mac, B-O-A-T stands for 'Bring On Another Thousand.' You don't know what you're getting into."

McDermott smiled and nodded.

"There is something, though, over on B-Dock. It's a nice little boat, about 25 feet, just right for the learner who might want to trade up in a few years, it's single-engine with an outdrive. My neighbor owns it. I have the key."

McDermott stepped to one side to allow Myers to come off his boat and onto the pier.

"Lead on."

The boat was backed into the slip, showing itself stern-first as McDermott stood admiring. She was blue and white with the traditional right-hand-drive of the motorboat. She was trim, with an L-shaped lounge on the main deck, and a cabin tapering downward toward the bow, an attempt at aerodynamic ground-effect.

"Go on aboard," Myers suggested, handing McDermott a key with a floating fob.

McDermott keyed open the Plexiglas door leading to the cabin and eased his frame down the narrow companionway. He looked around admiringly. To starboard was the door to the head, a ship's bathroom. He pulled it open to find a marine toilet, a vanity and small sink with two spigots. There was a shower head on a flex hose hanging above the vanity. Coming back into the main cabin, McDermott noted the two burner stove atop the galley pedestal. Under that, toward the center line, was the refrigerator. The boat also had a microwave oven and a TV set with a small DVD player located forward of the v-bunk in the forecastle. Moving aft, McDermott saw the crawl-in cabin under the main deck and couldn't resist the urge to go in and try it out.

Two hours later, Myers expertly backed the boat into the slip, and McDermott secured the lines and connected the shore power cord.

"OK," Mac said, invigorated by the cruise into the Chesapeake Bay. "Get hold of your friend and get me the best price he'll give me. And do you have the name of a marine mechanic I might hire to look her over before we close the deal?"

"Yes, I'll. Write down the name of my mechanic and you can call his company." He went into the cabin of the small boat and found a scrap of paper and a pencil from the navigation table, scratching down a note, which he handed to McDermott. The editor thanked his friend, exchanged a bit more small talk, and accepted an invitation to a cook-out aboard Myers' Marinette on Sunday night.

McDermott walked back toward his condo feeling better than he had in a long time. He had wanted to own a nice boat for quite a long time but had despaired of being able to afford it. The 25-foot Bayliner he had just test-driven was the perfect size and had a price tag he could

74

afford. He decided to stop by the marina office, which he would pass on his way home.

It was all of an hour later when McDermott turned onto the walk leading to his front door. The editor wore a huge smile. The harbormaster of Eastport Marina made him a great deal, enabling him to move the boat – once he bought it – to a slip nearer to his condo. And the new slip was several dollars less expensive than the one the boat was in now. And the marine mechanic had called his cell to say there had been a schedule cancellation, and the mechanic could check out the boat that day.

McDermott was looking forward to a sterling weekend.

But as he approached his condo, his smile faded.

Eve Somers sat on a tiny wrought iron bench just to the left of his front door.

Under different circumstances, before her liaisons with pirate Willie Sykes, he might have been glad to see her. But too many of her actions during her time with Sykes were, to say the least, questionable – to say the most, felonious.

She wore flat, open sandals and a mid-thigh blue skirt, topped with a peach strapped top. Her hair was loose and flowing, something that he had always found attractive.

She still drew him to her; he could feel the pull, the tug on his heart strings, to say nothing of his baser instincts. But his reporter's sixth-sense also warned him that she could be major trouble if he surrendered entirely to her.

He made a snap decision to keep her at arm's length, but to allow an association with her of sorts, purely for reportorial curiosity's sake.

Right.

Eve Somers kept her seat, with a weak, tentative smile on her face as the editor approached. McDermott waited until he ascended the porch's two steps before speaking.

"I thought you would call," he said flatly.

She shrugged, trying to smile bigger, but wound up making a pathetic face.

"I was going to, but I guess I just gave into a girlish desire to surprise you," she said, lightly.

McDermott keyed open his door and walked in ahead of her, dropping his keys on the table in the foyer. Without preamble or further comment, he walked into his study and took up residence in the leather chair near the reading lamp. Somers followed, a step or two behind, and found a seat in a straight-back chair near the bookshelves. McDermott looked at her inquiringly. She hesitated a moment, collecting her thoughts.

"Have you thought about it?" she asked, tentatively.

"About what?" McDermott came back, brusquely.

His answer seemed to fluster her.

"You... me... us... we?"

"No," McDermott said, sharply, and then he softened. "Maybe a little."

He tried to smile but Somers could see the hardness in his eyes.

"I don't blame you for not trusting me, Mac."

McDermott abandoned all pretext.

"Well that's good news, Eve," Mac snapped, leaning forward ominously in his chair. "I was losing sleep at night wondering if you blamed me for not trusting you!"

Somers seemed to shrink back in to her seat.

"You don't have to be so unpleasant," she said, recoiling.

McDermott leaped up from his chair and paced the floor near the sliding doors on the marina side.

"Don't I?" he nearly shouted. "Seems to me that the key for this whole thing with us is for someone to get unpleasant."

"Well if that's true," she snapped, "there's no one more qualified than you."

McDermott stopped dead in his tracks, staring at her with fire in his eyes. After a moment, though, his expression relaxed, and his shoulders drooped a bit. Somers picked up on the signs immediately, and softened her stance also.

"I know I hurt you really bad, Mac, and you need time. I can give you time if you want..."

"Time?" McDermott asked with a voice dripping in irony, as he walked over to her. "Time is what you think I need? Don't you understand what a bad case of you I had? I was nuts about you, but I couldn't keep you out of Willie Sykes' bed." He stopped and paced a lap or two before the open-draped sliding glass doors, then resumed his seat in the leather reading chair.

"And if it were all to start again I'd always wonder, 'is she comparing me to Sykes?' I'm not sure I want to be on the before or after side of your poster, Eve. I'm not sure I could forget being thrown over for a greasy pirate."

Somers momentarily flared at the insult of Sykes, but it cooled almost instantly and she walked to Mac's chair and perched on the arm.

"If it's comparing you're worried about, Mac, you should know that you would win hands down."

"In what way?" he inquired, without expression.

She stood, waving her arms in the air.

"In every way!" She paced the floor in front of him, looking away. "Willie Sykes was an anomaly, an affectation, an adventure. It was forbidden fruit, something out of character and exciting for a time. But when it came right down to it..."

"... you'd have come back to me?" McDermott snapped. "Is that what you're saying?"

She nodded seriously.

"Of course, Mac, who wouldn't?"

"I can think of a few," he replied, trying to smile.

"Mac, you're educated, successful, ambitious, and not bad looking..."

"I'm not fishing for compliments, Eve..." he began, but she cut him off.

"And I'm only answering your question. Willie was an adventure, but when it got dull --as it was beginning to do – I certainly would have returned to you."

"So you say," McDermott said in a hurt tone.

"So I say," she replied firmly.

McDermott sighed, and his harsh tone relaxed a bit.

"What is it you want of me, Eve?"

Somers stopped her pacing and resumed her seat on the arm of his chair, allowing her arm to brush his shoulder. She was happy to note he didn't recoil from the contact.

"I want you to at least make an attempt to recapture what we once had, what we were building together."

"And that would be..." McDermott asked, softly.

Eve Somers hesitated, just a moment, no more, then reached down and pulled the peach tank top over her head, dropping it on the floor. She wore nothing underneath. She looked at McDermott, whose eyes betrayed momentary shock as she slid off the chair arm onto his lap, encircling his neck with her right arm. She bent down and kissed him, tentatively, on the lips, and she wasn't sure, but she thought he responded. Just a little. She smiled and was rewarded with an answering smile, so she took his hand and placed it on her breast before leaning forward to kiss him again. His response was more tangible this time, so she was bold enough to pull his t-shirt over his head and drop it on the floor next to her top. She kissed him a third time and then paused to look deep into his eyes, not certain what she was seeing there.

77

"Oh what the hell," McDermott breathed, and kissed her again.

Peter McDermott slid carefully out of his bed, trying hard not to disturb the sleeping Eve Somers. He stepped into a pair of brief undershorts and his flip-flops, and pulled a t-shirt over his head. His brow was furrowed and his lips set in a thin line as he padded from the bedroom into his study, dropping into the chair behind his desk, purposely avoiding the reading chair and Eve's top, still resting on the floor nearby.

Eve's reappearance --- and his seemingly all-too-willingness to start getting involved with her – was stirring some unexpected reactions in him. It wasn't the warmth and the passion that had permeated their relationship before – before he became aware of her affair with Willie Sykes.

He had finally been able to shrug off the incongruity of that relationship. He was acutely aware that women – and many men – forged unlikely relationships with people to whom they were a total mismatch. Adventure? Passion? A way of making someone jealous? A weird fling? It could be any one or all of those things. Eve had tried to explain her affiliation with the hapless salvage boat operator and sometime drug runner. Willie had been shot to death in broad daylight on Statehouse Circle in downtown Annapolis by a Russian expatriate assassin with an especially silent pistol. Sykes was a loose end for the Colombian drug cartel for which he had made occasional drug-cargo landings from cartel ships anchored offshore. He was expendable, disposable.

Eve, at least in Mac's determination, was not.

Passion and warmth – two things he always felt being with her. But last night neither of those things mustered through their flailing lovemaking. Instead, through the entire romp in his bed, he'd had a feeling of anxiousness, and the hair was standing up on the back of his neck – like it was doing now.

One of the things that makes a good reporter is an indefinable sixth sense, that feeling that leads a journalist to play a hunch – or warns him that something is amiss. For McDermott, the telltale sign was the hair on the back of his neck standing up and tingling. While he admitted that his feelings were right only about fifty percent of the time, experience had taught him never to ignore them.

It was the hair-standing-up message that he was getting now, that he had been getting from the moment Eve Somers had removed her top in this room the night before.

And despite the feelings he had been developing for Eve Somers – and despite his anger about her having dashed them with her dalliance with Willie Sykes -- he wasn't going to ignore the warning this time either.

Best he keep her at arm's length until he either found out what the problem was, or he learned that his feeling was unfounded.

Yes, he thought, that's the ticket.

He heard some stirrings from the living room and looked out the door of his study. Eve Somers was walking toward the room, dressed in a t-shirt of his that she had taken from the pile in the bathroom laundry basket, and her very brief panties.

"Good morning," she said, in a husky voice, stopping under the door frame.

"Hi," he said lamely.

"You in the mood for some breakfast?" she smiled at him.

Mac hesitated.

"No, I don't think so," he said. "I think I'll skip breakfast today."

Her eyes narrowed and her face showed genuine concern.

"You do that often," she said.

He nodded absently.

"Mainly on Saturdays."

She appeared to hesitate herself for a long moment, then stepped into the room and seated herself on the love seat under the shelves that held his stereo and CD collection.

"I need to talk to you, Mac."

McDermott smiled.

"I think my life might be in danger," she said, simply.

There it was, he thought.

"Oh?" was all he could muster.

"I think the people who killed Willie are after me now."

"Why do you think so?" he asked. "Have there been any attempts on your life?"

She shook her head.

"Not overt ones," she said, her voice thinning. "But I think I've been shadowed for the last few weeks."

"Did you go to the police?"

She screwed up her face.

"After all that happened with the cartel and all that, you can ask me that question?"

McDermott merely stared at her.

"Can you protect me, Mac?" she asked with a pleading look in her eyes. It was a look McDermott made note of with the thought that it didn't appear entirely sincere to him.

"I'm a newspaper editor," he said evenly. "Not a bodyguard."

"You seemed to be pretty good with my body last night," she said with a faint smile.

"But guarding it wasn't what I was interested in," he returned.

"It could be like that more often if you can help me, Mac."

"Depends on how much Vitamin C I can get my hands on," he muttered.

"What?"

McDermott took a deep breath and launched himself out of his chair, rounding his desk. But before he could say anything to her, his desk phone jangled. He gave her a withering look, re-rounded the desk and answered.

"That sounds wonderful," he said at length. He glanced at his watch. "Why don't you meet me at the Eastport branch of the Bank of Annapolis and we'll complete the deal. Say one hour?" Great. Until then..."

He hung up and walked around, sitting next to Somers on the love seat – an irony not lost on him.

"I have to run an errand," he said. "Completing a personal business deal." He paused and thought a moment. "In for a penny, in for a pound," he said to himself. To her, he said, "You go over to the Set and Drift and get yourself some breakfast. I'll meet you there in two hours."

"I could wait here," she said, tentatively.

McDermott shook his head vigorously.

"I don't think that's such a good idea," he said. "Get dressed."

McDermott stepped into the shower in the large bathroom in the hallway, leaving the one in his bedroom for her. When he came back to his room, toweling his hair, she was pulling on her shoes. She waited while he dressed and filled his pockets with the items he usually kept with him; wallet, checkbook, pen and pencil set, change, and the computer jump drives he usually carried. Wordlessly, he led her to the front door of his condo and made a big show of setting the intruder alarm, making sure she saw him do that.

"You've changed the pass code on the alarm system, I take it," she said lamely.

"Yes," he said, pressing the Enter button.

"Set and Drift?" she asked.

He nodded.

"Two hours," he said, and closed the door behind them.

Chapter Nine

McDermott was all smiles as he drove his Jeep back toward his condo complex. On the seat beside him was the title and keys to a used Bayliner cabin cruiser. Mac was already mentally planning his three-day weekends out on Chesapeake Bay, anchoring out in the many coves he knew of in the area. He could see visiting all the other marinas in the Annapolis area – and they were legion – and making all kinds of new friends. He thought it might be time to retire his Friday morning grubbies joke at the Set and Drift and start leading the life of a respectable boater. His company had a corporate membership in the Eastport Yacht Club, but he was already thinking of someone to sponsor him for a personal membership. In a couple of years he could be on the Board of Directors or the Nominating Committee. Why not?

A glance at the digital clock in the Jeep's dashboard told him he was right on time for his appointment with Eve Somers. That took some of the starch out of his smile. His reporter's sixth sense told him she was up to something. That she was using him was a foregone conclusion. But he was curious to know why she was using him – what she wanted. He was sure she was involved in something nefarious, or dangerous, or both, and perhaps she wanted to use him and his position and reputation as a shield.

Could she be telling the whole truth, he asked himself? Could he possibly just believe her and take what she said as the gospel?

Not for a minute.

But while his reporter's sixth warned him of her apparently off-the-west-wall intentions, his reporter's curiosity wouldn't let him alone until he ferreted out her game. He was pretty sure she'd let it slip when she was ready. Not at the meeting he was about to arrive at, but later.

He remembered a famous quote of Abraham Lincoln. "Keep your friends close, and your enemies closer," said his favorite president.

And he had an idea about that.

The chirping of his cell phone brought him out of his reverie. A glance and the number brought a smile as he flipped open.

"McDermott."

"This is Julian Peebles, Dear Boy," came the affected accent of the pseudo-British fop.

"Julian!" he exclaimed. "To what do I owe the pleasure of your conversation?"

Peebles drank in Mac's attempt at sophistication.

"I've been doing some research since I last saw you, Old Boy," Peebles began. "It seems that watch you showed me has a deeper significance than first thought."

"Oh?" Mac inquired, his interest suddenly peaking.

"Yes, I found a reference to it in a book on the Resistance within German-held territory in the second world war. I rang a friend of mine and got him out of bed to get the rest of the information, and I think it will be helpful to you, Old Boy."

"So go ahead, Julian, fill me in."

"Not so fast, my friend. This will take some time," Julian Peebles said, amusement obvious in his voice.

"OK," Mac said, frustration creeping into his.

"Why don't you drop by the old shack, soon as you like, I'll be here all day. And I'll have everything you need to know about Ziess-Baden and what its significance is. Is it a pact?"

McDermott knew it was pointless to argue with a determined Julian Peebles.

"See you there," he said at last, and clicked off.

He eased the Jeep into a parking space at the Set and Drift Restaurant.

Mac walked in, dressed in crisp black jeans, deck shoes and a white North Bay Times polo shirt. He smiled at Polly, his favorite waitress, whose jaw dropped.

"May I help you, Sir?" she asked, a smile playing on her lips as she approached him.

McDermott raised an eyebrow. Polly feigned shock and slapped her cheek with the flat of her hand.

"My God, Mac, I didn't recognize you dressed like a human being," she said in mock seriousness. "You look almost human this morning."

McDermott grinned widely.

"Someone should be here waiting for me," he said.

Polly jerked her thumb over her shoulder.

"Your usual table," she said with a smile.

McDermott looked past her and his eyes fell on the table he usually occupied on his Friday morning invasions.

She was there already, leaning over the table with a morose expression, worrying a coffee cup. Her expression brightened somewhat as McDermott approached and scraped back a chair.

"Been waiting long?" he asked, seating himself and gesturing for Polly's attention. She lifted an eyebrow and he nodded. With no further urging, Polly brought a Diet Pepsi, which she set before the editor, and she refilled Eve's cup, dropping a couple of cream packages on the table and removing the empties.

"About forty minutes," she said impatiently.

McDermott glanced at his watch.

"I'm right on time.

"I know," she said. "I just had nowhere else to go, so I took a walk then came here."

"Couldn't you just go home?" he asked.

She looked at him sternly.

"It costs money to have a home, Mac. I lost my job, remember?"

"There are other jobs."

"Like on your paper?" she asked hopefully.

McDermott sipped his drink, looking at her over the rim of the glass.

"That wouldn't' be... appropriate," he said softly.

She looked away.

"I know," she said at last. "I have some money saved, I'll find a place and a new job soon."

She looked up pleadingly at him.

"I can't go to a hotel because I know someone is following me and I am in danger. Can I stay with you for a few days, just so I can find a place and get settled?" She asked her question quickly.

McDermott drained his drink and signaled for another, giving him a few moments to think. He waited until Polly slopped another glass in front of him and scooped up his empty. She indicated Eve's cup, and Eve shook her head. Polly retreated. McDermott leaned back in his chair and crossed his legs at the ankles.

"First of all, Eve, if someone is following you, I think you're pretty safe. If whoever it might be wanted to kill you, you'd be dead already. Second, Willie Sykes had to have left something you can use to raise cash, and third, I'm not running a hotel."

She clouded over.

"I don't mean to be blunt," he said, soothingly, "but I don't think having you stay with me would be wise."

She answered rapidly

"But I could cook and..."

McDermott cut her off by raising a hand to her.

"It's not in the cards, Eve. We just don't have that trust we once had, and I'm not comfortable cohabitating until we do."

She looked down at the table and rubbed her eyes, and McDermott could see her back spasming.

Oh God, he thought to himself, it's come to that. There is no way on God's green earth that any man can deal successfully with a crying female.

He grinded his teeth for a moment, then sighed heavily.

"Here's another idea," he said lamely. "I just bought a boat. I am moving it to a slip near my condo this afternoon. It has a galley – kitchen – and a bathroom with a shower. There's a stove and a microwave, and TV with DVD. You can stay there for a few days, until you find out what's happening and start to get on your feet."

She looked up, her eyes a little red, but not much, and the downturned lips had been replaced with a weak smile.

"No more than a month, Mac, I promise."

McDermott had control, now. He shook his head.

"A week. Tops."

"I'll get my things and meet you at..."

"Six o'clock in front of the condo," he finished. "Sorry I can't do it now but I have a message to follow up on."

"That's the deal?" she asked.

"That's the deal," he affirmed.

"Sold," she said, and left the restaurant with her check laying on the table.

McDermott called Pitcher. The reporter was excited to hear that Peebles had new information about the Ziess Baden watch, and wanted the editor to pick him up for the sojourn to Peeble's home. Pitcher was in Annapolis, as it happened, and he asked McDermott to pick him up. They arranged a meeting place and Mac closed his cell phone.

Twenty minutes later, Mac and Pitcher were in the editor's Jeep heading for what Pitcher sarcastically called Stately Peebles Manor.

"Did he give you any kind of a hint as to what he's found out?" Pitcher asked.

McDermott shook his head.

"No he went all mysterious on me, and said he had some special information, but he didn't elaborate.   But he did say that it was something of significance."

Pitcher nodded, his lips pursed.   McDermott knew that the events of the last few days were weighing heavier and heavier on his friend – and that Pitcher was being tugged in two different directions. First, there was the familial connection.   It was, after all, members of Pitcher's family who were being killed.   For that reason he wanted answers.   It was important for him to know – and through him, other family members – why these killings were taking place.   On the other side, there was his professional persona, Pitcher the ace reporter. Murders were happening, and thus far there appeared to be no rime nor reason for them.   His nose for news smelled a big story, far bigger than the pieces that had been revealed thus far by the bodies that had been turning up – and the bullet that had been meant for him.

That made it personal, and clouded the line between his personal and professional thinking.   McDermott was worried that when the time came for everything to gel, when all the pieces came together, Pitcher's objectivity might be compromised.   He didn't for a moment doubt Pitch's professionalism, but the man was only human, after all.

McDermott turned into the gated estate of Julian Peebles and parked in front of the massive front door.   It swung open as the two men approached, and the massive form of the butler stood back-lit from the interior of the house.   As they ascended the steps, the butler bowed formally.

"Good evening, Gentlemen," he said, in his deep, muted basso voice. "The *mahstah* wonders if you will meet him in the library."

Pitcher matched the butler's formal bow, but came up with a cheesy grin on his face, a grin McDermott knew well.

"Thanks, Lurch," Pitcher said grandly.   "Please tell the *mahstah* that we would be delighted to meet him in the library."

The butler seemed not the least perturbed by Pitcher's mocking condescension.   He merely turned and walked into the wood-lined corridor to the open door of the library.   He stood aside and beckoned for Mac and Pitch to enter before closing the double doors.

The room was lit as before, and was comfortable in atmosphere and furnishing.   Julian Peebles was standing before the bookshelf against the far wall, appearing to be absorbed in something he was reading.   He looked up as the doors latched behind Pitch and Mac, and broke into a grin as he removed his reading glasses.

"Ah, there you are," Peebles said, expansively. "Do have a seat, can we get you anything? Mac I know you favor Diet Pepsi, I had my man lay in a supply, would you care for one?"

McDermott nodded with a smile, and Peebles turned to Pitcher.

"And what for you, old boy?"

"Beer is fine," Pitcher said.

Peebles walked to a cord hanging from the ceiling opposite his library table and gave it a tug. Nothing happened immediately, but within seconds, the double doors swung open and the butler sauntered into the room.

"You rang?" he asked flatly.

"Is he kidding?" Pitcher whispered to McDermott, who shushed him.

"A Diet Pepsi, a beer and a cognac, please," Peebles said to the massive man in the tuxedo, who bowed again.

"Veddy good, Sir," he rumbled, backing out of the room and re-closing the doors.

Pitcher started to say something, but McDermott clapped his hand over the reporter's mouth, just in time. Peebles watched the exchange with a look of puzzlement.

"Something wrong?" Peebles asked.

McDermott shook his head.

"No it's fine," he said quickly. "Pitch just needs to be adjusted now and then, you can see that, right?"

Peebles nodded but it was clear he didn't see.

"Do have a seat, Gentlemen," he said after a pause. "The drinks will be here shortly and we can have a sip, and then I'll give you... what is that quaint expression... the lowdown?"

"That'll work," Pitcher asserted.

The library doors swung open on well-oiled hinges and the butler lumbered into the room carrying a tray, which he sat down on the library table. He poured Diet Pepsi from an open can into a crystal glass with ice, then poured beer from a bottle into the perfect glass for it. The third item on the tray was a small heavy glass with a half-inch of brown liquid, which the butler handed to Peebles.

"Will that be all, Sir?" the butler asked. Peebles nodded and the servant withdrew, re-closing the doors. Peebles took a tentative sip from his glass.

"Ah!" he exclaimed. "Excellent cognac."

He raised the glass in their direction.

"Sure you wouldn't like a splash? Ripping good stuff!"

"No thank you, Julian," Mac said, sipping his Diet Pepsi.

"Just the lowdown, if you please, Old Boy," Pitcher said, making a pathetic attempt to imitate Peebles' accent.

Peebles look askance at Pitcher, but settled himself into a leather armchair without comment. He still had the book he had been perusing in his hand and he referred to it from time to time. He took another sip of the cognac and placed the glass on a coaster on the table next to his chair, crossed his legs and flipped the book open.

"I emailed a friend of mine in Europe after our last talk," he began. "I remembered reading something about those watches somewhere so I contacted Nigel Pompey, who reminded me of it."

"Who's Pompey?" McDermott wanted to know.

"Sterling old chap, Pompey," Peebles said. "English fellow whose family emigrated to Germany before the war. He was a member of the Resistance fighting within Germany against the Nazis."

"My God," Pitcher exclaimed. "He'd have to be past 90 years old!"

"Ninety-four two weeks ago," Peebles smiled. "I sent him a digital photo of your watch and he wrote me back all excited. Seems he hadn't seen one of those in decades but he knew them well."

"So it's something expensive after all, then?" McDermott asked. "I thought you said it was the cheap version."

Peebles waved him off.

"You're missing the point, Old Boy," he said sharply. "It is a cheap version of the Ziess Baden watch. But that's not why it's significant."

"Well then why?" Pitcher demanded.

Peebles smiled. It was as close as he could get to a snarl.

"If you'll shut the old cake hole, Mr. Pitcher, I will be glad to fill you in," he said through gritted teeth.

Pitcher seemed to shrink into his chair. To cover the way he felt, he took a deep drink of his beer.

Peebles went on.

"These watches were made rather large, as you know. Very cumbersome to wear. It occurred to members of the German resistance that the bulk of the watch case could be put to good use.

"The Resistance did business with tissue-roll technology. They could reduce an entire document to a tiny image of itself and put it on a tiny roll of paper no larger than a thumbnail. That was how they moved delicate information from Resistance cell to another."

"And the watch...?" McDermott began.

Peebles nodded.

"Exactly, Old Boy," he said in triumph. "The watch was the vessel that carried the documents. It was a trick the Resistance used for some time, until the Germans got wise."

"What tipped them off?" Pitcher wondered.

"Simple, Old Boy," Peebles said. "Resistance couriers wore the courier watch on their right wrists. On their left..."

"...They wore a real time piece," McDermott finished.

"Exactly!" Peebles exclaimed. "Your watch, the one you showed me, has no internal works because it contains – or once did contain – photographically reduced documents of great importance. Where is that watch now?"

Pitcher spoke up. "It's at my apartment in Baltimore."

"Then," Peebles began, solemnly, "I would like to suggest that you go immediately and get it and make certain it's in a very safe place."

Pitcher looked confused.

"Why do you say that?"

Peebles threw up his hands in exasperation.

"Dear Boy, three people have been killed – and the third one used his dying breath to get that watch to you – and since then there's been an attempt on your life."

"So you think there's something in the watch," McDermott observed.

"Don't you?"

McDermott drained his glass and moved to stand.

"We'll get the watch and open it up right away," he declared. But Peebles held up a restraining hand.

"There's something you ought to know before you do that," Peebles said. "Pompey told me that once the Germans started getting wise to the courier watches, Resistance cells started booby-trapping some of them. If you open the back of one of those, there's a tiny vial of acid that will be released destroying anything that's inside."

McDermott looked worried.

"So how do we find out?" he wondered.

"Pompey sent me instructions on how to open the watch safely," Peebles said. "There's a special tool I am trying to locate. In the meantime, keep that watch in a safe place."

"It's been sixty years," Pitcher said. "How can you be sure the right tool exists?"

Peebles stood.

"It exists," he said, draining his cognac glass. "And I will find one and get it here quickly. You, for your part, need to hide that watch in a very safe place. And you need to do it right now."

Ten minutes later, Pitcher and McDermott emerged from the Peebles mansion and headed toward McDermott's Jeep. As they got into the vehicle, a motor revved to life outside the gate, and a nondescript tan colored car shot away from the curb.

A moment later, the Jeep left the Peebles driveway and turned in the same direction.

Chapter Ten

It was beginning to get dark when McDermott and Pitcher stopped for dinner at a restaurant in south Baltimore. Both ordered steaks and potatoes with salads, and Pitcher asked for a side order of mixed vegetables. They spoke very little as they waited for the food to come. But a few bites of a well-cooked steak loosened their tongues and they started going over all they had learned.

"There's something I haven't told you yet – about that attempt on you," McDermott said quietly.

Pitcher raised an eyebrow.

"About the gun that was used to take a shot at you…"

"They didn't find the gun as far as I know," Pitcher asserted.

"But they did find the bullet," McDermott said, seriously. "In your car."

"And so," Pitcher prompted

"And so the bullet that was meant for you came from the same gun as the one that killed three of your relatives this week."

"No foolin'?" Pitcher asked, trying to appear nonchalant.

"No foolin', McDermott returned. "And there's more."

Pitcher waved his hands

"Oh please," he pleaded. "I've had all the fun I can stand already tonight."

"Be serious, Pitch."

"OK."

"We talked to a ballistics guy by the name of Bent," McDermott began.

"Yeah, Marv Bent, I know him," Pitcher said.

"Good. Well, anyway, Bent told Charlie and me that the same gun was used in a 60 year old unsolved murder."

"What?" Pitcher exclaimed. "What murder?"

"A trumpet player at the Blue Heron night club back in 1947. He was killed while he was performing on stage in front of an audience. Shot from a table in the audience."

"With the same gun that took a potshot at me?"

Mac nodded.

"And the same gun that's being used to wipe out my family?"

Mac nodded again.

Rod Pitcher's face hardened to the consistency of granite.

"This is the straight dope?" he asked.

"That's it," McDermott said firmly.

"That makes a big difference," Pitch retorted.

It was Mac's turn to raise an eyebrow.

"Now it's personal," he stated with determination.

"Pitch you can't let your personal feelings interfere with your professional duties.

Pitcher's eyes glowed with fire and hate.

"Professionalism be damned," he spat. "This is personal. Someone is trying to kill my family and someone tried to kill me. You handle the story. I'm going to find out who is doing this – and why!"

"*We* are going to find that out, Pitch. Come on. We'll talk to Charlie and see…"

"Come on, Mac," he said, pulling some bills from his pocket, more than enough to pay their dinner bill. He threw the bills on the table and headed for the door with McDermott in hot pursuit.

Mac literally chased Pitcher into the parking lot, pulling his Jeep keys from his pocket as he ran.

"Pitch, calm down, will ya?" the editor yelled after him.

"Come on, Mac," Pitcher yelled, stopping for a moment beside a plumber's van to catch his breath. "We're going to get some answers."

McDermott caught up with him panting, acutely aware of his age for a few moments.

"Pitch," he began.

But his thought was interrupted by a sharp crack from the darkness beyond the restaurant.

The sound in no way sounded like a car backfire. McDermott recognized it immediately as a gunshot. There was a pause, just a blink in time, followed by a faint whizzing sound in McDermott's right ear, and then, instantly, a metallic thud, and a hole, a bit smaller than a dime, opened in the side of the van just off McDermott's right shoulder, farthest away from Pitcher. Another pause, no longer than the first, and

92

both men instinctively hit the ground, Pitcher rolling under the van and McDermott following in concerted suit.

They waited for perhaps thirty seconds for their heart rates to return to normal. It didn't happen. They lay for long moments under the van facing in the direction from which the projectile had come. They lay in fearful silence with cold sweats breaking out on their foreheads, erupting in brown stains on their shirts. There was no second shot, and no movement in the darkness to give away the shooter's position.

"Why don't you crawl out of here and see if it's safe?" McDermott hissed.

"Why don't you?" Pitcher retorted in a grimaced whisper.

A pause.

"Who do you think they were shooting at this time?" Pitcher asked, a little louder.

"Well they missed you last time," McDermott returned.

"The bullet was on your side," Pitcher reminded him.

"So what?"

"So maybe this time it was someone you pissed off," Pitcher whispered.

"I don't think I've pissed anybody off that much," McDermott said aloud.

"You haven't heard the scuttlebutt at the water cooler lately," Pitcher answered.

McDermott looked daggers at Pitcher for a moment, then his expression changed. Pitcher got the impression that Mac had made a decision. A moment later, the editor started to drag himself out from under the van. Pitcher grabbed him by a handful of shirt-back.

"Hey, I was kidding about the water cooler talk," he said anxiously.

McDermott stared back at him, a determined look on his face, and hauled himself the rest of the way from their cover. As he stood, Pitcher snuck out from under the van also, and got to his feet.

"You didn't have to come out here," McDermott told him.

"Didn't want you to think you're the only one with balls around here," Pitcher said, chucking the editor on the shoulder.

For a moment both men stared intently into the darkness before then. There was no shot and no movement beyond. In the distance they could hear a siren approaching.

"I think he's gone," Pitcher said, more a question than a statement.

"Brilliant!" McDermott rejoined.

93

The shooter was driving away, not fast, but keeping up with the flow of traffic so as not to arouse suspicion. The shooter cursed and pounded the steering wheel – two shots, two misses, the mark was still alive. With a great sigh, the shooter dismissed the incident; there would be another time, another chance, and the item being sought would be found and used as it was intended.

In the meantime, nothing had been forgotten. The empty brass now nestled in the shooter's pants pocket. Nothing had been left to chance.

The shooter stopped for a traffic light, and deftly slipped the handgun under the front seat out of sight.

The light turned green and the car moved off, melting into the night.

Charlie Hume was beside himself. He had raced to the restaurant from his home in response to McDermott's call, and had listened to the police report of what had happened.

Someone else in the parking lot had heard the shot and had seen the muzzle flash; someone who knew and understood guns and had no doubt that a shot had been fired in anger. That person had called 911 on a cell phone to report the shot, and had hung around to report his findings to investigating officers.

McDermott and Pitcher demonstrated for the officers the exact way they had been standing when they heard the shot and what they had done immediately thereafter – and they had to do it again for Hume.

The three newspapermen and the police were also dealing with the irate owner of the van.

"How come you had to be standing here," the owner said, angrily, in a thick Brooklyn accent. "How come you couldn't be standing in front of your own car when people started shooting at you?"

"What, you think we planned to get shot at?" Pitcher fumed.

"Yeah, right, what's it to you my insurance rates are going up?" the driver screamed. "You gonna pay for the damage?"

"I think you are going to have to take that up with whoever fired the shot," Hume interjected. "These men are not responsible for it and they've been through enough."

"The hell they have," the owner shouted, moving toward McDermott who was in the beginning stages of losing his temper.

A Baltimore police officer stepped in front of McDermott, offering a card to the owner.

"This is my card," the officer told the owner. "It has my phone number and a case number for your insurance company. If you run into any problems – or if the company does – call me. Right now, back up and cool off."

The driver glared, first at McDermott and then at the officer. He took the proffered card, and without another word, sat down on the curb and folded his arms, cursing fluently under his breath. The officer looked unruffled by the obvious gesture of defiance.

"He'll calm down," the officer said. "And if he doesn't, I've got colleagues all over this side of town, they'll cool him off." He grinned. "You guys have had a night," he said. "Go on home and get some rest. We'll call you if we find anything."

Hume turned to McDermott.

"I want the two of you in my office as soon as you can safely get there," Hume thundered. Without waiting for a reply he turned, got into his Lexus and drove into the Baltimore traffic. McDermott and Pitcher looked at one another and shrugged simultaneously.

Marv Bent arrived a few moments after Mac and Pitch drove away. He was there on special invitation from the Baltimore Police, considering he had dealt with an earlier attempt on a *North Bay Times* staffer before. BPD was hoping that the DC ballistics expert might be able to shed some light on who might have fired the shot.

Bent and the CSI from Baltimore entered the back of the plumber's van and found it filled with metal and plastic pipe, along with tool boxes and various cans of compounds peculiar to the plumbing industry. The two men, who knew each other slightly, were down on their knees looking by the glow of their flashlights, and as one, they sighed hopelessly.

"We're going to have to unload it," the CSI said to Bent, who nodded helplessly.

"Piece by piece," Bent whined.

They sighed again and began removing each object from the back of the van, carefully inspecting the area it came from.

The bullet had not penetrated the other side of the van, so it was reasonable to assume that the slug was somewhere inside.

A few moments into their task, the van owner came up to them and began assisting them in unloading the vehicle.

"I figure I'll get home a lot sooner if I shut my mouth and help you," he explained simply.

"Good thinking," Bent said flatly.

95

Charlie Hume flipped on the light in his office and turned on his computer as he rounded his desk. The laptop came up quickly and Hume sat, calling up his "contacts" page. He took a sip of rancid coffee, left on his desk that afternoon, not tasking the cold, thick liquid as it coursed down his throat. He found a telephone number and scratched it down on a small pad next to his phone. He was about to dial the number when McDermott and Pitcher ambled into his office and took seats without being asked.

"Gentlemen, the time has come for action," Hume said firmly and sternly. "There have now been two attempts on the lives of two of my key staffers on this newspaper."

"I'm not interested in having a damned bodyguard," Pitcher rasped.

"Me neither," Pitcher chimed in. "If we're going to find out who's doing this, we are going to need freedom of movement."

Hume sat back and smiled thinly.

The two men in front of him were the best in the business. It had taken Hume quite awhile to sell McDermott on the idea of coming over and running Editorial for the *North Bay Times.* At that time the paper was a flat-broke nothing, rescued from obscurity in a tax sale by Charlie Hume, who intended to make it a news voice to reckon with along the Eastern Seaboard. Hume had been impressed with McDermott's work in broadcasting, with his writing skills, with his ability to separate the chaff from the wheat on any news story and put together something hard-hitting, accurate and interesting. Hume had had to promise McDermott editorial autonomy – which he rarely violated – and a lot of money, which, in retrospect, had been a bargain after the five years Mac had been at it.

He'd also had to promise McDermott that he could do the hiring of reporters and newsroom staff – and the newly appointed managing editor didn't miss a trick. His first hire – another expensive one – had been to lure Rod Pitcher away from the traditional dailies.

Pitcher already had one Pulitzer Prize under his belt when he came to the *Times.* The reporter had always wanted to research, gather, and write stories in much more detail, with more explanations of how facts related to the reader, than he was able to accomplish making a daily deadline. McDermott promised him the best positions in the paper and the opportunities to do the kinds of stories he wanted to do – but that he would also have to do some of the stories he *didn't* want to do, just to keep things balanced. Pitcher and McDermott, as it turned out, developed a strong friendship and a professional relationship so tight that they often passed thoughts between one another in a non-verbal way – and when they did talk they finished each other's sentences. That bonding between them made for a team that ferreted out stories no one else had, on a regular basis. And the two had managed to infect the rest of the editorial staff – seven other reporters, two researchers and two copyists – with their own zeal for the tough stories. It didn't take long for the *North Bay Times* to develop a reputation for clarity and truth that was the envy of virtually every other paper.

Advertising revenue had been tough to come by at first. Hume spent the money to hire a sales staff every bit as productive as the Editorial side of the building, and his investment paid off. As the paper's quality improved, so did sales. Nine months after renaming his paper, Hume was able to show a profit, and it had been onward and upward from there.

So yes, the two men sitting before him were the best in the business, and he was going to be double-damned if some two-but hood with a gun was going to rob him of that.

But he also knew that McDermott had been right; a bodyguard wasn't the answer. In fact, employing bodyguards for the two would definitely call attention to them. And they did need the freedom of movement to pursue their own investigation of this matter – freedom that a bodyguard – or two – would compromise.

That the two journalists would conduct their own investigation, Hume had no doubt. Even if Hume told them No – hell, *especially* if Hume told them no, they would proceed anyway and would use whatever newspaper resources they could slip out from under the publisher's nose to do it. Better that he sanction their activities – and even join them. Hume, an old reporter himself who came into his own in the newsroom of the *Detroit Free Press*, could almost feel the elation of being back in the trenches again, and were the stakes not so high, the elation would have been verbalized.

Yet he wasn't going to sit idly by and do nothing. He had made up his mind that the *Times* staff did need professional help, and he had just the fellow in mind to provide it – if he could convince the man to come to Baltimore from California.

"All right," Hume said at last. "No bodyguards."

Pitcher and McDermott stared at Hume open-mouthed. Rarely did Hume give in so easily.

"But that doesn't mean I'm going to let you knuckleheads plough forward without expert help. I'm putting in a call right now."

Hume pressed a button and a dial tone came through the speaker on his desk phone. He dialed the number written on his scratch pad and waited as the connection was made and the line began ringing.

There was a click.

"Casio Investigations," a female voice droned. "May I help you?"

"Sy Casio, please, Charlie Hume calling."

"One moment please," she said.

McDermott came out of his chair.

"Casio's in California!" he said sharply. "Aren't there private detectives in Baltimore we can use?"

"None that I trust like I do this guy," Hume said. "If I can get him, I will." He raised a hand as he saw McDermott open his mouth to protest. "No arguments on this, Mac. I've met you half way. And I'll go one step further and say if Casio doesn't take the case, you're off the hook. But if he does, he's on the team."

"Charlie!" came an effusive voice on the phone. "It's been too long."

"Yes it has," Hume agreed. "Sy we need your help back here. We need someone we can trust so I called you first."

"I'm flattered," the detective said. "What can I do for you?"

In a few sentences, Hume outlined all that had happened in the last few days, leaving nothing out.

"What I need, Sy, is for someone to ramrod the *Times'* portion of the investigation, working with Peter McDermott and Rod Pitcher to try to run this thing to earth."

"Hmmm," Casio mused on the other end of the phone. "All this and a 60 year old murder mystery thrown in as a tantalizer, huh?"

"That's it," Hume said flatly. "You interested?"

There was the briefest of pauses.

"I'll call you later and let you know what time my plane gets into BWI," he said.

Hume smiled and said his thanks, and hung up.

"There you have it," he said to the two in front of him. "We're a team, now, all of us."

"Hooray for us!" McDermott said in a voice full of sarcasm.

"Yay for us," Pitcher finished. "The Four Muscatels."

Chapter Eleven

Eve Somers was waiting on the stoop again when McDermott arrived back at his Condo. From the look of her, she had been sitting there quite awhile. She had a suitcase, a duffle and a tote at her feet, and she was reading by a penlight. But her smile at McDermott's approach was genuine and she seemed not at all perturbed by his tardiness.

She stood and picked up the suitcase.

"I'm ready, Mac," she said with a touch of anxiousness in her voice.

McDermott tapped his pocket, satisfying himself that both sets of boat keys were there, and took her suitcase and duffle. She fell into step next to him as he turned right at the end of his sidewalk and headed into Eastport Marina proper.

"Rough day?" she asked casually.

"Rougher than most," he replied simply.

They took a few steps, then she looked at him hard without breaking stride.

"I hear someone took a shot at Pitch."

McDermott turned quickly to her.

"Where did you hear that?"

"Radio news," she said.

"Yeah," he answered in a stony voice. "Someone took a shot at him."

"He's OK, right?"

"He's a little shaken up but otherwise healthy," McDermott said, looking away and stepping over a hole in the concrete.

"That's good," she said flatly, keeping in step with McDermott.

They turned left and departed the concrete. Beneath their feet was the traditional gapped planking of the Chesapeake Bay piling docks.

Eastport Marina was made up of 26 main piers designated A through Z. These jutted off the main pier and out toward the open water of Spa Creek, which led into the Severn River and thence to Chesapeake Bay.

From each of the alphabetized piers there grew twelve secondary, or "finger" piers, much closer together and held in place by pilings.

These piers formed the "slips" in which boats were tied. Slips rented by the linear foot of the boat that would reside in it. Almost every one of the slips in the marina was rented.

D-Dock was the closest main pier to McDermott's condo; indeed, he could see the fingers from D-Dock from the glass doors in his study and from the deck immediately outside those doors.

McDermott and Eve Somers turned onto D-Dock and walked about a third of the way down to the finger pier marked D-6. There, the blue-and-white Bayliner rocked on the gentle creek swells. McDermott smiled, mentally thanking the harbor master who promised to have the boat towed to this slip, which was cheaper and would be visible from his condo. He stepped aboard and keyed open the door to the cabin, stepping down and out of sight inside. A moment later a light glowed from within, and McDermott appeared, back lit, and gestured Somers aboard. She complied.

McDermott backed up as Eve descended the two-step companionway to the lower deck of the small boat. McDermott tossed her luggage on the leg of the V-bunk on the port side and faced her, with his back to the bow.

"This is it," he said. "Your home for the next few days." He slapped the galley pedestal on the port side. "There is a two-burner stove on top and a microwave behind me in the forecastle." He indicated and she nodded. "There's a small fridge on the center line face of the galley." He indicated this by opening the door. The fridge was, of course, empty. He reached past her and opened a door on the starboard side at the base of the companionway. "Here's the head – bathroom."

"I know what 'head' means," she said hotly.

He smiled and indicated the shower head, held in a fork-like holder on the bulkhead.

"Pump toilet, and here's the shower."

He examined a breaker panel on the galley pedestal and moved a red switch.

"The water heater is on now," he said. "Nine gallons. You go in and wet down, turn it off, lather up, rinse, turn it off and wash your hair and rinse again. Navy shower."

She curled her lip.

"Not exactly a four-star hotel, Mac."

He shrugged.

"Best I can do for a few days," he said.

She smiled fetchingly.

"I can always just stay with you," she said, hopefully.

McDermott shook his head firmly.

"Not in the cards."

She looked toward the deck for a moment then back at him.

"How about giving me the gate combination? I'll need to go out and get some groceries."

Access to the marina was one of two ways – through fenced-in condo yard, or by a steel gate protected by a four-digit electronic lock. McDermott wrote the combination on one of his business cards and handed it to her.

"Call me if you need anything," he said, and turned to the companionway.

"Even if I need some lovin'?" she asked?

McDermott turned, one foot on the first step up.

"Yeah," he said.

Marv Bent found the bullet. The plumber's van was almost empty and the slug still hadn't turned up/. But as Bent himself always observed, nothing is ever found until it wants to be found. In this case, the bullet wanted to be found but wasn't going to make it easy.

Bent, the CSI from BPD and the owner of the van had unloaded most of the pipe and five of the seven tool boxes. That exposed the spare tire area.

"Bullets have a habit of hiding behind the spare tire," the BPD technician said with a smirk. Bent smiled also and shrugged his shoulders.

"Why not?"

He probed his flashlight around the spare tire on the right side read of the cargo compartment. Nothing was immediately apparent; no telltale scratches or gouges in the metal of either the side of the decking. He held the flashlight in his mouth and shined it around the tire, probing above and behind with both hands. He dropped the light, and didn't have to look to know it would be useless. He heard the bulb shatter. He was about to swear, but the fingers on his right hand, which was still behind the spare tire, felt a small mass just out of sight behind the leaning wheel. It was just far enough away that he had to reach, press his shoulder against the tire to get two fingers on the metallic object, and pull it back to where he could get a whole hand on it.

"Got it," he said, triumphantly.

Bent opened his hand and the BPD technician shined his light on it.

101

The bullet was flattened a bit at the tip, but had not pancaked or shattered. Bent recognized it immediately.

"7.62," he said. "I've seen a lot of these lately."

"We can run this back to my shop and put it through the meat grinder," said the CSI.

Bent nodded and dropped the slug into a small manila envelope which he handed to the CSI.

"Lead the way," he said with enthusiasm.

Thirty minutes later, McDermott swiped his press card and the front door to the *North Bay Times* offices unlocked with an audible Click. He ascended the small stairway to the sales-editorial suites (the lower floor was Composing and Circulation), and keyed the glass door near the reception area. Down a short hallway was his own corner office. On the way there he saw the glow of a table lamp from the largest of the cubicles in the newsroom, and he knew that Pitcher was already there, having driven himself to the office after McDermott dropped him at his car.

"Pitch!" he called as he passed, and he heard the shuffle of a wheeled chair as he continued to his office. The reporter walked through the door while McDermott was still turning on the lights and gaining a spot behind his desk.

"Charlie wanted us here ASAP," Pitcher mused, dropping into the comfortable chair in a corner of McDermott's large office. "You'd think he'd be here."

"He is," came a booming voice from the door.

Charlie Hume beckoned with both hands, a clear message that Pitch and Mac should follow him over to the sales side of the second floor, a corner office only a fraction larger than McDermott's

Hume seated himself behind his desk – which he was fond of pointing out, was quite a bit larger than McDermott's – by about a third, he always beamed when he talked

This time, though, Hume looked across his massive desk with a scowl.

"Who's trying to kill my key staff, Gentlemen?" he asked without preamble.

"Charlie I don't know what to tell you about that," Pitcher said, defensively. "I know someone is trying to knock off members of my family, but..."

"That doesn't explain why someone shot at Mac tonight," Hume interrupted.

"I'm not all that sure someone did," McDermott interjected. "How do we know the bullet wasn't meant for Pitch?"

"Oh, thank you, Mac," Pitcher whined. "I feel *so* much better now!"

"Any time," McDermott smiled back at him.

"This isn't anything to laugh at," Hume thundered.

McDermott leaned forward.

"Charlie, if we can't laugh at this, we're in serious trouble."

"Considering that someone tried to kill you tonight, Mac, I think we are in serious trouble."

"Oh yeah," McDermott said, shrinking into his chair. "Now that you mention it..."

"Do you have any thoughts of who could be doing this?" Hume asked.

"I've been thinking," McDermott began.

"Now that's funny," Hume smirked.

"Could it be the Colombian Drug Cartel that we mixed it up with recently?" McDermott pondered aloud.

"It's certainly their style," Hume mused, which McDermott found interesting since Hume was unconscious when the cartel's transport ship, *Bohemian*, crossed swords with McDermott and his friends toward the end of the search for pirate treasure.

"My opinion, for what it's worth, is that all the shooting is over that watch," Pitcher said, seriously. "One of the victims – a relative of mine, I might add – used his last breath to put that watch into my hands, and now we know it comes from Germany during World War II and was used by the Resistance..."

"Bent says the same gun used in the killings was used in another murder sixty years ago," McDermott ventured. "Could that be the tie-in?"

"That's a thought," Pitcher answered, picking up on the thread. "But how do we investigate something that ancient?"

McDermott's face illuminated as though the 'idea' light bulb had just gone on above his head.

"I may have just the thing," he exclaimed, and dashed out of Hume's office.

Bent was bent. While that might seem on the surface to be an incredibly bad joke, it was nevertheless his current posture. The ballistics expert was bent over the comparison microscope in the Baltimore Police Department's Crime Lab, staring intently at the bullet recovered from the plumber's van. For long moments, Bent didn't move, didn't twitch, he seemed not even to be breathing. The Baltimore CSI who was standing next to him started to worry.

"Are you OK?" the CSI asked, tentatively.

Bent didn't answer verbally, but waved him off, continuing without pause to stare into the microscope eyepiece.

Finally, long and silent minutes later, he straightened.

"May I use your computer?" he asked, not turning toward the CSI

"Of course," the other man said.

The set-up was similar to the one Bent had in his own lab in Washington. Bent touched a switch on the microscope and turned the desktop computer monitor to face him. Slowly, a line that started at the top of the screen moved downward, resolving in a picture of the bullet as seen through the scope. Bent pulled a flash drive from his pants pocket, popped off the top and slipped the USB plug into the slot on the computer tower. The picture on the screen was replaced with a menu of the contents of the flash drive. Bent selected a file and touched "Enter," as yet another picture appeared, strikingly similar to the one from the microscope. Bent split the screen and brought up the original picture, then sat on a low stool and stated for long moments at the two slugs on the computer monitor. At length, he got a white-knuckle grip on the computer mouse and moved it to a button labeled "Compare."

"I already know what it's going to say," he mused aloud. "But I have to see it."

The Baltimore CSI said nothing, but unconsciously backed away from Bent, thinking the ballistics expert was on the very edge of a nervous breakdown.

Bent left-clicked the mouse and waited. The computer hummed, and a red banner appeared across the bottom of the screen.

"*Match*," it declared.

Shit!" Bent breathed. "Not again!"

Bent touched "Save" and directed the computer to dump the photo and the comparison to his flash drive. He pulled the device from the computer, capped and pocketed it, and reached for his cell phone.

McDermott returned to Hume's office waving a square envelope containing a compact disk.

"Marv Bent gave me this," he said. "Bent says everything concerning the bullets and the gun is on here."

Hume took the disk from Mac's outstretched hand and set it in the carriage on his computer. Several file folders appeared on the screen. Hume double-clicked on the one marked "1946."

There were seven photos in the folder, and Hume maneuvered the computer to show them in thumbnail. Mac and pitch hitched their chairs closer to Hume's desk to look at the pictures as the publisher called them up.

The first was a wide shot of the stage area of what was obviously a post-war era night club. There were people milling about a form on the stage floor.

The next picture showed the same seen, but from a different angle. The body was clearly visible, a man lying on his back, a red stain ruining the front of his starched shirt. McDermott consulted his notes.

"According to Bent, this guy is Chance Caine. He was a trumpet player with the house band at a place called the Blue Herron."

"Isn't that the club adjacent to the Metropole Hotel where the first body…" Hume stopped and turned a sad face to Pitcher.

"I'm sorry, Rod, bad choice of words."

Pitcher nodded in silent forgiveness.

"…where Pitcher's cousin was found?"

"I have thought since that night that there is some significance to finding Reesa there," Pitcher said. "I couldn't imagine her being in a place like that at the best of times, let alone where and how she was found."

"Who was Chance Caine?" Hume asked aloud, but more to himself than to anyone else.

"That's one of the questions we're going to have to answer," McDermott said.

Pitcher was staring at the photo. He didn't join in, or even appear to listen to the talk between Hume and McDermott, and when they noticed his deep concentration, they stopped and stared at him, and then past him onto the screen trying to see what he obviously saw.

"Pitch?" Hume prompted.

Pitcher pointed.

"There," he said. "There's the one thing that pulls all this together."

The two men tried to see what he saw, but the significance escaped them.

Pitcher seized the mouse and made a few passes. The picture changed, as Pitcher zoomed in on the corpse's arm.

"There," he said. "Don't you see it?"

McDermott and Hume screwed up their faces, still missing pitcher's point. He sighed and zoomed in tighter.

105

"There," he exclaimed, pointing, and now McDermott saw it – or thought he saw it.

They were looking at Chance Caine's right wrist. The zoomed-in picture was grainy and blurred by the processing it took to bring in that one part of the image, but what Pitcher was driving at. The arm was mostly concealed by the starched sleeve of his tuxedo shirt. But when Caine fall, he landed with his right arm above his head, and the sleeve had hiked up slightly, revealing his wrist. There were small dark marks that seemed to surround the wrist. They were diagonal and evenly spaced. McDermott looked once, twice, and then again, before looking up at Hume.

The publisher indicated his own wrist – his left one – and the watch with the expansion band he wore. He nodded to McDermott and slipped a finger under the band, lifting. Under his band, Hume sported marks very similar to those the men were looking at on the right wrist of Chance Caine.

"Wow!" McDermott breathed. "Do you believe this?"

"But people wear their watches on the *left* wrist," Pitcher whined.

"But what if..." McDermott started.

He snatched the mouse from Pitcher and moved the image, zooming in on the dead man's other arm. Most of it was concealed by the sleeve of his formal shirt, but McDermott could still see what he was looking for.

"There's your answer," He said.

The two men looked.

There, on Chance Caine's left wrist, plain as day, was a wrist watch. It had a brown leather bracelet, and a white or silver face – and despite the distortion from the zoom-in, McDermott could make out the stem on the hand-side of the round face.

Pitcher's jaw dropped.

"Then that means Caine was wearing one of the Resistance courier watches the night he was killed," he said with awe. "That's why he has band marks on his right wrist."

McDermott nodded, getting into the conversation.

"So we can postulate that whoever killed him took that courier watch, the Ziess Baden watch as Peebles describes it."

"Right," Hume said.

"The police report from the time – there's a Photostat, as they used to call them, on this CD. The report says that witnesses indicated a woman in a red gown approached the body immediately after the shooting and appeared to be searching for a pulse," McDermott said, talking fast and full of enthusiasm.

"What she must have been doing was removing and palming the watch," Hume speculated. "The one from the right wrist, obviously."

"Pitch, where is that watch?" McDermott demanded.

"It's locked in a floor safe in my townhouse," he said. "It's safe there."

"OK, for the moment we'll assume it's safe," McDermott stated, beginning to organize his thoughts for the work that lay ahead. He turned to Hume.

"How do you want to proceed, Charlie?" McDermott asked.

"I think we need to think about it some more over the next couple of days," Hume began. "But my first impression is to run the pictures from that CD and ask our readers if anyone knows anything about Caine or whoever killed him," Hume said, scratching his chin. McDermott pulled the ever-present reporter's notebook out of his hip pocket and his silver Cross mechanical pencil danced across a page.

"Do we write about the three killings?" Pitcher wanted to know.

Hume nodded again.

"I want Mac to write about the three murders, since he's not directly involved." He turned to McDermott. "Sorry, Mac, I'm stepping on your editorial toes."

McDermott smiled.

"That's just the way I was going to handle it, Charlie, so you're fine. In addition, I'd like you to write about the two attempts, the one on Pitch and the one that may have been aimed at me, since of the three of us you're the most detached."

"I'll need the police report," Hume said, rubbing his hands together.

"I'll see to it," Pitcher volunteered.

McDermott was about to speak again when the cell phone at his hip chirped.

Chapter Twelve

"McDermott," the editor barked into his phone.

"This is Detective Bent, D.C.P.D.," the voice in the phone said.

"What can I do for you, Detective?" Mac inquired, with looks at Hume and pitch.

"You won't believe it, Mr. McDermott, you just won't believe it," Bent hissed.

"Try me," McDermott prompted.

"Guess," Bent prompted back.

"Oh come on!"

"Come on nothing," Bent said, his voice serious, but on the edge of mirth. "Guess!"

McDermott huffed into the phone and stopped a moment to clear his head and concentrate.

"OK," Mac said, tiredly, into the phone. "I'll guess. You found a bullet in the van."

"And..." Bent pushed.

McDermott touched a button turning on the speaker phone on his blackberry, and set the instrument on Hume's desk.

"And... what?"

The three men in the office could hear Bent sigh on the other end of the connection.

"We found a bullet in the plumber's van. I was permitted to run the ballistics on it..."

"And it's the same gun that all the fuss has been about?" McDermott finished.

"You guessed!"

The three men in the office seemed to shrink into their chairs.

"So what now?"

"Who is that?" Bent asked.

"Charlie Hume."

"Oh, of course, Mr. Hume. Well the D.C. Police and the Baltimore P.D. are working on every angle we can come up with," Bent said. "I have to say we're no closer than we were when I saw you last, but something will break."

"Do you have any more on that fellow who was killed with that same gun back in the 40's" Pitch asked.

"Everything we had on him, you have on that CD," Bent said decisively.

"It isn't much," Pitcher observed."

"Nope, it isn't," Bent agreed.

"I guess we'll have to run our own investigation," Hume mused.

There was an uncomfortable pause.

"I assume, then, that you and your team will share with the appropriate police agencies whatever you happen to come up with?" Bent asked tersely.

"We might," Hume responded, equally terse. "Thanks for the heads up, Detective Bent. Good night."

Hume extended his right index finger and made a swiping gesture under his chin. A grinning McDermott broke the connection and returned the Blackberry to his belt.

Hume leaned back in his chair and clasped his hands over his head, looking at the two men before him.

Hume marveled again at the competence of the two. They were the best in the business.

"Thoughts?" he asked.

McDermott stood and paced the office floor.

"My thought is that the police will concentrate on the here and now."

"Whaddaya mean?" Pitcher asked, watching McDermott pace with disproportionate interest.

"I think they will concentrate on the three murders and the two attempts on you, Pitch. I'm still not convinced that I was the target of the most recent attempt..."

"Yeah, yeah," Hume waved him off.

McDermott nodded at Hume.

"Anyway, I agree with Charlie. Let's run the pictures from the old murder in the paper next week and do a detailed story with sidebars on what's happened in the present so far."

"And..." Hume prompted.

McDermott smiled.

"Another angle is we delve into this Chance Caine character. He had to have come from somewhere. I have a few ideas."

"OK," Hume said. "I'll write the stories of the attempts on you and Pitch. Pitcher can do the stories on the murders of his relatives, without mentioning that he is related to them... and a sidebar on the gun that was used in all the killings. Get Art to help you with graphics on all of this, Pitch."

The reporter nodded vigorously.

"Mac you'll obviously have the rest of your staff write on their own beats and flesh out the daily stories from the week as you always do. But let's put the three of us on this story and use all the resources at our command and solve this before someone else really gets hurt."

McDermott rose and faced his boss with an admiring smile on his face.

"You know what Charlie? That Knute Rockne speech of yours makes me want to go out and stop a freight train with my bare chest."

The killer gently closed the door and brushed away the evidence of having picked the lock. Soundlessly, the killer turned and stepped off the sidewalk and into the shadows, moving away from the building toward a waiting car. The engine was warm; the killer hadn't been gone long. In moments, the engine was running again. The killer shifted into Drive and the car disappeared into the night.

Rod Pitcher ambled into Peter McDermott's office to find the editor pecking away at his computer keyboard. He had left his cubicle moments before and started to turn left, for the exit door to the newsroom, but he'd seen light coming from McDermott's door. Thinking the editor had left the building without turning out his lights – something he rarely did – Pitcher went to the office to check.

"What are you still doing here?" Pitcher demanded.

McDermott kept typing and didn't look up.

"I want to get a jump on things. I'm filing a request under the Freedom of Information Act."

"For what?"

"It's going to Teddy Burnside over at the Department Of Defense," Mac said. "Chance Caine was murdered not quite two years after the end of World war II. At the time of his killing he was apparently wearing a watch casing used by German resistance fighters. I want to begin by finding out if he has a military record."

Pitcher nodded, stroking his chin.

"Not bad. But you and Burnside have been friends for years. Why the FOIA filing? Just ask him, he'll give it to you."

111

"Privacy act. We don't need any problems from that. The FOIA filing will give him a way out of any problems he might get when he gives me the information. And he will."

Pitcher pondered that a moment.

"Yeah, he will. Well Mac I am going to try and get some sleep. Tomorrow is Sunday. See you on Monday?"

McDermott finally stopped typing, and looked at Pitch with a mask of concern.

"Pitch, please be careful going home. Call me and let me know you got there OK."

Pitcher started to protest, then caught himself and nodded.

"Yes, I will," he said. "Good night.

"Night, Pitch," McDermott said. The editor watched Pitcher as he walked out of the office, turned right and headed down the darkened corridor into the newsroom, toward the exit. He resumed his typing for a few minutes. His work finished, he opened his email and typed an introduction, then attached the FOIA request, addressed it to Teddy Burnside, and pressed SEND.

That completed, McDermott snapped off his desk lamp, leaving lonely a small night light burning in a corner of his office. The light came from a ceramic lighthouse once given to him by someone who meant a very great deal to him – before Eve Somers. He always looked at it as he left his office. This time he lingered a moment, looking and remembering. Coming out of his reverie, he picked up his coat, snapped the lock on his office door and closed it behind him. He stepped across to the other side of the building, and noticed that Charlie Hume's office was dark. He shrugged, and realized that he hadn't eaten since lunch.

Well, he thought, there's a Denny's a couple of blocks from the Inner Harbor. He reached into his right-hand pants pocket and pulled out some crumpled bills. He had two twenties, a ten a five and a couple of singles. More than enough for a Slam breakfast. Smiling at the thought he let himself out of the building and climbed wearily into his Jeep.

The engine fired on the first crank, and Mac dropped it into first gear, turning toward the exit.

He had accomplished the first part of his plan to run down Chance Caine. He was going to get any military information the man might have. He would also check on Monday and see if the musician's unions in Washington, Maryland or Virginia had anything on him. 1946 was not that long after the labor movement had gained acceptance in the United States, and most night clubs were union shops. So in order to play trumpet in the Blue Heron band, Caine had to belong to a union. If he did there would be records, and McDermott would find a way to unearth them.

He would also send his researcher to the Halls of records for Washington, Maryland and Virginia and see if there was any information on him – birth certificate, marriage license, record of divorce – anything.

Then there were the Bureaus of Motor Vehicles. Did Caine ever apply for a driver's license? He might even be able to track down any hospital records he might have.

McDermott parked the Jeep in front of the restaurant and walked in head still spinning, making mental notes of things he would need to check on Monday morning. He was escorted to a booth in the back dining room. He debated whether to order coffee. When he got home, perhaps an hour and a half from now, he wanted to sleep and he was concerned that the caffeine would block that.

No, he thought, the caffeine wouldn't do it, but his racing mind would. So the coffee wouldn't make any difference and he nodded when the waitress got his attention from across the room and held up a pot.

She walked over and splashed coffee into his cup, dropping two creamers on the table. McDermott ordered eggs and Taylor Ham along with wheat toast and scrapple.

Scrapple is a mush of pork scraps combined with cornmeal and flour and fried. Marylanders like their scrapple spiced with cayenne and black peppers and a good bit of salt.

Taylor Ham is the colloquial term for John Taylor's Pork Roll, an east coast breakfast delicacy. It's sold commercially in chub rolls or in eight-slice packages, and is a unique flavor never duplicated anywhere else. It's made in New Jersey and is available along the Atlantic coastline as far south as North Carolina.

Taylor Ham was a particular favorite of McDermott's. His grandmother often served it to him in his grandparents' Washington D.C. apartment when he visited, and he always savored the taste.

Only a few restaurants served it, and McDermott had been delighted to find this Denny's did.

Mac stirred Sweet and Low and some cream into his coffee, taking a preliminary sip absently. He was right. His racing mind showed no signs of slowing down. He continued to think of Chance Caine, wracking his brain in the hopes of coming up with another way to get information on the victim of a sixty-year old murder mystery, a mystery that visited not only his time, but his circle of friends.

Rod Pitcher was McDermott's reporter, and also his close friend. Three members of Pitcher's family had been murdered, and someone had made an attempt on Pitcher. And then there was that other shot, the most recent one. McDermott was still not convinced that he was the target, even though the bullet came closest to him – it still could have been a second attempt on Pitcher. But since it was unclear – and after all, it could have been aimed at him, well, that made it personal.

The waitress slid an oval-shaped platter under Mac's nose and refilled his coffee cup, two actions that snapped the editor back into the world his body was in. McDermott pondered the meal – the eggs, cooked the way he liked them, and the meat, plus the black-and-brown square of scrapple served up on a small, separate plate. Idly, he salted his eggs, cut off a piece with the edge of his fork and tasted. It was good. He chewed idly, contemplated the rest of is meal with fervor, looking forward to enjoying it. But his cell phone's insistent ringing interrupted his good thoughts. Disgusted, he dropped his fork onto the plate with a loud clang and unlimbered the offending instrument.

"McDermott," he barked.

"Mac," came the panicky voice of Rod Pitcher. "Come quick, my apartment's been broken into."

"Are you OK Pitch?" he asked first, but then brushed aside his own question. Pitcher was all right, albeit a bit panicky. "What happened?"

"I came home and opened my front door and everything in my place has been riffled through and dumped."

McDermott found himself panicking now.

"The watch, Pitch, is the watch still there?"

A pause.

"To tell you the truth, Mac, I haven't checked. I was so upset when I saw my place I just ran out and slammed the door shut and called you."

"Stay right there," McDermott ordered. "I'm on my way!"

He snapped the phone closed and holstered it, looking regretfully at his plate. Quickly he made a sandwich out of two pieces of Taylor Ham and some toast, dropped a sheaf of bills on the table, and headed out of the restaurant.

McDermott raced up north to Pitcher's apartment complex and parked against the curb behind a sheriff's department car. He trotted up the walk to find Pitcher standing on his porch along with Samantha Parker, who had arrived just before he did. He nodded at the woman and took an appraising look at Pitch under the porch lamp. Deciding that his friend was all right, he looked past him into the room.

114

"Go on in," Pitcher invited. "The cops are just looking around."

McDermott stepped over the threshold into the apartment and his jaw dropped.

The apartment living room and vestibule were in shambles. The furniture was overturned, much of it broken. Carpet was torn up. Lamps were on the floor, a couple were broken, and there were scrape marks on the walls where framed pictures and art had been taken off and slammed to the floor.

McDermott penetrated the apartment, looking in the kitchen, the two bedrooms and the bathroom. The scene was the same. Shaking his head he returned to the entranceway where the sheriff's deputy was just finishing penciling in his report. The deputy asked for McDermott's identification. McDermott supplied it, and the information was written into the report. The deputy handed Pitcher a carbon copy and left.

"The watch, Pitch," McDermott said desperately. "Was the watch taken?"

"I was waiting for the cops to leave before I checked," he said. He and Samantha headed for the second bedroom that Pitcher used as an office, with McDermott right at their heels. Pitcher stopped at the door, and Samantha Parker bumped into his back. McDermott, in turn, bumped into her.

It took a moment for them to reorient themselves. Pitcher, moving slowly into the room, stared at a large book case against one wall. All the books had been pulled from the shelves and to the floor haphazardly. Pitcher walked to the book case and reached his right arm down the side the cabinet. It slid aside as though ion a hinge, revealing a section of wooden floor beneath. Pitcher and Samantha Parker walked in and looked amazed at the section of wood, an island in a sea of ugly apartment carpet. Pitcher bent down and touched a section of the wood nearest where the front of the bookcase had been. A small wire handle popped up, and Pitcher grasped it. Tugging, the section of wood came up on a hinge, opening toward the book case. McDermott and Parker craned their necks to see what was underneath.

It was a safe.

Pitcher twirled the dial and grasped the handle, jerking it sharply toward him. The door to the safe opened upward at his touch.

Pitcher stared into the hole with a vacant look on his face.

Chapter Thirteen

Pitcher stared into the floor safe for only a moment letting his mind breathe. He reached down, finally, and came up with a small cardboard box, perhaps the size of a computer mouse. He flipped it open to reveal the Ziess-Baden watch handed him by a relative, moments before his death across the threshold of this very apartment.

Pitcher held up the box with the exposed watch as though it were a magic talisman. McDermott reached out and plucked it reverently from the reporter's hand, staring intently at it.

"I wish we could pry this thing open," he said in a hushed tone. "But Peebles said they put fail-safe's inside to keep people from doing that without destroying the message stored there."

"We have to wait until Peebles comes up with that special tool he was talking about," Pitcher said.

"In the meantime, what do we do with this?" McDermott demanded.

Pitcher sat back on his haunches with a playful grin on his face.

"What we have here," he said with a strong dose of irony, "is a game of hide and seek."

McDermott grinned and nodded.

"My guess is that whoever is after this watch won't come back here because he did a pretty thorough search and didn't find it."

"Logical," McDermott agreed.

"They didn't find the safe this time, so the bauble should be OK in it now," Samantha Parker chimed in.

Pitcher took the watch back from McDermott and gingerly lowered it into the safe. Then he turned to the inside of the safe door and punched several tiny DIP switches.

"What's that?" Samantha Parker asked.

"Twenty-first century safe technology," Pitcher explained, closing the door and twirling the combination knob. "If the safe is opened, and the switch positions aren't reversed in the correct order within twelve seconds, the safe signs onto the internet and sends a silent alarm to the police department – and it also alerts my cell phone so I know what's going on."

"Get serious," McDermott scoffed.

Pitcher grinned from ear to ear.

"Dead serious."

"So why didn't you have it set before?" Samantha asked.

Pitcher's grin turned sheepish.

"Because I'd forget about the DIP switches and the alarm would go off – it's silent, so I wouldn't know till my cell rang and by then the police would be on their way. It's embarrassing. More than that, they fine me a hundred bucks for every false alarm over two."

"How many have you had?" Samantha wanted to know.

"Two," Pitcher said, simply.

"But this time it'll be worth it," McDermott declared.

"That's the way I see it," Pitcher said.

He closed the trap door over the safe and stood. McDermott and Parker also rose, and Pitcher slid the dresser back in its place over the wood section of floor. McDermott looked closely and noted with amazement that there were no drag marks in the carpet where the dresser had moved.

"Maybe you'd better not stay here, tonight, Pitch." McDermott suggested.

"I was just thinking the same thing," Pitcher replied, winking at Samantha.

She smiled broadly.

"You just want to get me in a hotel room," she said, returning his wink.

Pitcher looked at McDermott.

"Nothing gets past her, does it?" he said, placing an arm around her and heading for the front door.

McDermott followed, said his good nights and got into his Jeep for the drive back to Annapolis.

Eve Somers returned to the Bayliner carrying three bags of groceries from a nearby Safeway. She had walked by McDermott's condo on her way into the marina and had noted the place was dark. She then walked a few steps out of her way to check the parking lot, noting that his Jeep wasn't there. She was disappointed, because she would have liked the company, and perhaps intimacy, but for now it was enough that she had an out of the way place to stay.

She put a foot gingerly on the dive platform and waited for the boat to react to her weight. It listed to starboard a bit as she put a second foot on the platform, and then rocked as she stepped over the gangway coaming and onto the aft deck. She walked forward, negotiating the tiny up-step that led to the main deck, with its L-shaped lounge to port, and the driver's station to starboard. The Plexiglas doorway wasn't locked, so she folded it back and carefully descended the three steps into the cabin. It was long past dark, and she hadn't left a light on in the cabin. She set the bags on the starboard V-bunk and snapped on the light over the galley by feel. It took her only a few more moments to put her things away. She sat down on the port V-bunk and used the remote to snap on the television set.

There was obviously no cable; the signal was brought in on a set of ancient rabbit-ear antenna which would bring in only local stations. WMAL-TV Washington and WJZ Baltimore were the two that came in the clearest. But neither had anything on she wanted to watch. She went through the DVD collection she was already accumulating, but again found nothing. Disgusted, she stashed her purse close by for easy reach, turned on the radio to an oldies station and stretched out on the bunk, head near the galley.

For a moment she thought of making some popcorn in the microwave oven near her feet. But she wasn't hungry, and at the moment didn't feel much like moving. She lay for a few more moments before drifting off into a fitful sleep.

It was nearly midnight when the black Jeep glided into a parking space in front of McDermott's condo. McDermott parked, locked the vehicle and keyed his way into his home, starting the process of undressing while he made his way through his darkened rooms.

He was beyond tired. Every fiber of his body ached for sleep. His shirt went on the back of an overstuffed chair in his living room near the hall. One shoe wound up in the kitchen door. The other in the middle of the hall. He made it to his bedroom where the rest of his clothes found their way into a heap on the floor. With only one eye open, McDermott turned on the hot water in the glass-enclosed shower in the bathroom off his bed chamber, and stepped in, not realizing he was still wearing his shorts. Embarrassed for not good reason, he shucked out of them, wrung them out, and hung them across the top of a glass panel.

After soaping up and putting shampoo in his hair, he turned off the water and completed his wash-up – a habit he developed during his service on the *U.S.S. Enterprise*. It was what was called a Navy shower,

119

and was meant to conserve water on a ship. Once soaped completely, he turned on the water and rinsed, then reached for a towel just outside the door, blinded for a moment by the shampoo running out of his hair. He stepped out of the shower and started drying off while letting his eyes focus again. That's when he saw her.

Eve Somers stood in the bathroom door wearing a blue flannel bathrobe Mac recognized as his. On her feet she wore black rubber flip-flops, also his. He stopped to stare at her.

"You really should lock your front door," she said.

McDermott forced a smile.

"What brings you here?" he asked, weakly.

"I just thought you might want some company and perhaps a bit more after your hard day," she said with a smile.

McDermott's shoulders drooped.

"Eve, I gotta tell you, I'm so tired I couldn't do anything if I tried."

The robe fell to the floor. She wore nothing underneath.

"There's always the morning," she said wistfully, turning toward the bed.

Fred Mattingly gestured to the bartender for this third whiskey sour. The first two had failed in their task of dulling the ache in the back of his head, caused by the recent rash of familial killings.

It's not like he needed an excuse to come here. Mattingly seemed to have a permanent reservation on this self-same bar stool, and there were few nights he wasn't thus perched, listening to the clinking of the ice in the glass. He took another sip and shook the glass to hear that lovely sound again.

Like many veteran officers, Mattingly had seen too much. He was a first-hand witness to the horrors of which human beings were capable. He had seen death in all its manifestations and all its methods.

When he had first gone into the Homicide squad of the Detective Division, eight years before, he had been excited. For many officers who make Detective, Homicide is the plumb, the excitement, the chance to do some real police investigating, bringing the bad guy triumphantly to justice. Like others he had seen only the glory that comes from watching too many episodes of "Kojak." He never considered the misery that surrounds someone's violent, untimely death, the elusiveness of the perps, who didn't follow the rules and weren't subject to the cleverness of the TV detectives. He never considered the pressure brought about by the higher-ups in the department to get results, to solve the cases.

Real investigation has little to do with the derring-do of the fictional heroes. True detective work is long hours of drudgery and research. There is little of the bare-bulb interrogation where the bad guy trips himself up with his own testimony. Mostly, the crooks didn't cooperate with the cleverness and skill of the detective and managed to stay hidden behind their "I didn't do nothin'" declarations.

And digging up evidence wasn't anything like "CSI" or any of those shows. It was slogging through dumpsters, executing search warrants and finding lots of illegal things but nothing like what he was looking for, long nights on stake-outs.

Add to that the unbelievable stress that the job puts on a man or woman – stress that is absolutely impossible to leave behind at the station when the day and night of work are done. Too many homicide detectives find themselves married to a job, to the extent that their human spouses become secondary, and often, those spouses wind up being the whipping children for the stresses that the detectives can't vent on the job against suspects, victims or families of victims – so much would they like to.

The result is an exceedingly high divorce rate among detectives, particularly and especially homicide detectives.

It was when those realizations finally hit a homicide detective that he started hating what he did – and by then there was no going back. Requests for transfer to bunko, auto theft, vice, or even back to uniform patrol were universally laughed out of the office. The higher-ups knew; once you get someone into Homicide, you leave him there because no one – no one – with any experience, wanted to go there. The newbies coming up through the ranks barely were enough to replace the veteran detectives who drank themselves into oblivion or ate their guns.

Every homicide detective gets one case that defines him, that details his entire career. He usually gets it after he's been beaten to a pulp by man's inhumanity to man, when his level of experience matches the level of disgust at his profession.

Fred Mattingly suspected strongly that the Lowenstein case was his waterloo.

He thought that because the case was proving particularly difficult to run down. Clues were sparse, there was nothing, really, but the bullets found around and in the victims. That was really about all. There were few threads for him to grasp.

Mattingly was aware that the shots were being fired from a gun used in a very public 1947 murder, a gun stolen from the police evidence room. But without the nun itself and a serial number to go on there wasn't much he could do. He had put out feelers from among the many snitches he had cultivated around Washington. Not a peep. That led Mattingly to believe that the killer wasn't one of the wackos who go around shooting people to gain attention. That would make the killings almost routine, with a perp that would be caught when he wanted to be caught badly enough – or when Mattingly got lucky.

For a few minutes the detective tried to watch the basketball game that was on the color TV hanging over the bar, but the whiskey was starting to take hold, and he couldn't concentrate. He considered going home, but he really had no home to go to. His house in suburban Virginia was home to his wife and their two teenage children, all of whom he rarely saw. Home for him was a walk-up room with a bath on P-Street Northwest, toward the center of Washington.

He pondered ordering another whiskey sour, but thought better of it. He was tipsy enough already, so much so that he didn't even consider driving back to his room. He'd left his brown police-issue Crown Victoria at the station, nine blocks away. Through increasingly bleary eyes he watched his hands come out of his pockets with crumpled bills. He counted out some money and set it on the bar.

"Call me a cab, will you Sam?" he asked.

"OK," said the bartender, snickering. "You're a cab."

Mattingly scowled at him, and the bartender chuckled as he picked up the phone next to the cash register.

"I'll wait outside," Mattingly told the bartender as he eased his way off the stool. Waving at Sam, he turned to the door, walking on wobbly legs.

"The Captain has turned on the 'fasten seat belts' sign as we are now on final approach to Baltimore-Washington International Airport," the stewardess said over the cabin loudspeaker. *"Please turn off all electronic devices, and make sure your tables are stowed and your seats in their upright positions, and thank you for flying American Airlines."*

Sy Casio stirred in his seat. He had slept for most of the second leg of his trip from Los Angeles. He had taken a Northwest flight from LAX to Detroit, then boarded an American Airlines flight to BWI.

On the tiny table in front of him were the papers he'd assembled before he left his office in Hollywood. It was his research on the people and places he was likely to encounter. It was something he had done since he had gone into business with a partner, so many decades ago, after a long stint on the Los Angeles Police Department. The Internet had made much of his dogged research absurdly simple. There was, however, some data he couldn't find on the World Wide Web – and that required the degree of intrepidity and boldness that he had used before the advent of the information superhighway.

Casio stuffed the papers into his battered brown leather briefcase and shook it to pack the papers down before he buckled the two straps. He tapped it to make sure his laptop computer – one of his few concessions to the 21st century – was securely in its place in the briefcase before his straightened his chair back and amused himself buy looking out the window at the Maryland countryside.

Sy Casio could have stepped out of the pages of a Dashiel Hammett novel. He was broad shouldered and barrel-chested with thick, muscular arms and large, steady legs. He normally wore a three-piece suit that was two fashion seasons out of style, brown or gray, topped by a battered brown Fedora, usually tilted at a jaunty angle.

His face might have been handsome once, but today it was lined and puffy, the ravages of age, too many close calls and too much Scotch. His hair was graying, beginning at the temples, but, by now, the gray penetrated deep into the full head of hair on top. Casio made no attempt to hide it or disguise it.

He normally carried his gun, a nine-millimeter Browning with a 16-shot magazine, with much of the bluing worn away. He kept it nestled loosely in an ancient leather shoulder holster under his left armpit, thought right now, even though he had a permit to carry it, he had removed the weapon and stowed it in his checked bag, out of deference to the air security regulations.

Casio felt the bump as the plane's wheels kissed the runway, and immediately he heard the sound of the engines rise to a crescendo as the pilot reversed the thrust and stood on the brakes. The MD-80 leaned into the braking thrust and slowed appreciably from the two-hundred-mile-per-hour landing speed. He waited a moment, until he felt the pilot ease off the breaks, then unsnapped his seatbelt and pulled his briefcase onto his lap.

"Ladies and gentlemen, this is Captain Silvers, welcoming you to Baltimore-Washington International Airport where the local temperature is 61 degrees, and the local time is 1:10AM. We have a clear path for taxiing to the terminal, so please hold your seats till we get there and the engines have stopped. When I turn off the Seat Belt sign, you can deplane as you wish. And again, thank you for flying American Airlines."

The captain had been right, it didn't take long. The plane was at the terminal in less than ten minutes, and had no sooner snubbed its nose into place then the whining of the engines died to nothing, and the jet way was quickly rolled into place on the portside forward door. Casio stood. As a frequent traveler, he knew how to exit a plane – he elbowed his way into the narrow aisle in front of an obviously impatient businessman who jostled him in return. Casio only grinned.

He waved goodbye to the stewardess at the door, sailed through the jet way and into the terminal, taking the escalator down to the street level. The wait for his suitcases was mercifully short. He shouldered his briefcase and headed for the cabstand right outside the terminal door.

"Pier Five," he said, simply, to the driver, who nodded and started the meter. In seconds Casio was on his way to the Pier Five hotel, a luxury suite inn located at Baltimore's Inner Harbor – just a few short blocks from the *North Bay Times* offices. Casio reasoned that, first, since he would be using the hotel as a combination sleeping room and office, he should have a three-room suite in which to live and work, and second, since he was accustomed to the best hotels wherever he went (except when the rigors of his work demanded that he stay in less-than-stellar establishments), and since Charlie Hume and the *Times* was picking up the tab, he could afford to stay in the $225-a-day hotel.

Casio sat back in the cab and closed his eyes for a moment.

"The Four Muscatels," he whispered aloud, referencing Hume's latest email quoting Pitcher's offhand remark. "I like that."

Chapter Fourteen

Eve Somers stared down at the sleeping figure of Peter McDermott with a mixture of affection and rage. Their lovemaking had been adventurous and lengthy, taking up most of the night, and it had seemed to invigorate the tired-out editor. It was the wee hours of the morning when they finally collapsed, spent, into deep sleep. Eve, a lifelong early riser, stood at the foot of the bed trying to sort out her feelings.

Since their first meeting at an Eastport Yacht Club mixer two years before, they had enjoyed an on-again-off-again romance, and both had reveled in its casual manner. They met for lunch or dinner as often as possible – when neither one was otherwise involved – and they talked on the phone often. Such was their relationship that they could even talk about other lovers to one another. They had sex when they felt like it, and it never failed to burst into blazing passion, an all-consuming, steamy encounter that took their whole beings to the brink of Nirvana, and wrung from each of them every morsel of their collective souls.

They never discussed any form of commitment aloud, though each, in his and her time, had considered such a thing privately, not daring to give it voice, not wishing to interrupt the blinding passion that enveloped them.

More and more, Somers found herself comparing her other lovers to McDermott – and the others came up short. It angered her that no one else had ever ignited her as Mac always did; no one ever touched her and instantly found the buttons that snapped her to flame. She thought a moment, bringing to mind all the men she had had in her life – not that there were many. She sighed. They all felt the same inside her, but where most were a moment of tingling sensation, good for what they were, McDermott did many of the same things and turned her into a wanton, ravenous beast anxious to drain every drop from Mac and to give to him totally and unabashed. He also did other things, endearing things that would always bring thoughts of him to mind, especially at the worst possible times.

125

She softened her gaze at the sleeping newspaperman, longing for the commitment they had never voiced, wishing that there could be something permanent between them. Certainly they had exchanged something – the fact that they kept falling back into one another's arms was proof that something existed there. But neither had developed the courage nor the linguistic legerdemain to define it.

Finally, she tore her eyes from the slumbering lump of covers on the bed and padded, naked, into the kitchen, finding eggs and link sausage in the refrigerator. Absently, forcing her mind into neutral, she began the rote task of making breakfast.

Presently, the tantalizing aroma of sausage and coffee wafted through the house, and the lump of blankets stirred in the master bedroom, shook itself out of a fog, and began to dress itself, accompanied by assorted male early morning noises and tactile rituals. From this reverie, Peter McDermott struggled into a pair of colored briefs and his ragged blue flannel bathrobe and padded off to his bathroom.

By and bye, he lumbered into the kitchenette of his condo and stood at the door, looking at Eve Somers who was wearing an apron and nothing else.

"I usually don't eat breakfast," he informed her, softly.

She turned to him and smiled.

"Most important meal of the day," she said.

"Baloney," he scoffed.

"No, sausage," she retorted with a bigger grin.

McDermott surrendered and pulled out a chair, sitting at the tiny table as Somers scooped eggs from the skillet onto a plate, and used a pair of tongs to add sausage. She set the plate, and cup of coffee in front of the editor, then fixed a plate for herself, sitting across from him.

McDermott still looked groggy to Eve as he added Sweet N Low and powdered creamer to his coffee. He was bleary-eyed and absently yawned without attempting to stifle it.

"So what are your plans for today?" she asked, trying to make conversation.

"What day is this?" he asked, with his eyes closed.

"Sunday," she said. "All day."

He took a sip of his coffee, and it seemed to give him a jolt. Instantly he was more awake and more aware, He looked for a moment at his plate, as though he was surprised to see it there, then looked at Eve, winked, and picked up his fork.

"I thought perhaps we might try out the boat," he said, spearing a piece of sausage and guiding it to him mouth."

"You mean go out into the river?" she asked, a little frightened.

He nodded.

"Do you know how to do that?"

He nodded again, more absently this time, cutting his egg with his fork and taking bites as he went.

"Done it many times on other people's boats," he said. "I think it'll be a kick to do it on my own."

She sighed, resigned.

"OK," she said, tentatively.

McDermott seemed to warm to the idea. His pace increased as he enjoyed the breakfast she prepared. When they were finished, Eve stacked the dishes in the dishwasher and the two headed for the bedroom to dress.

Sy Casio did skip breakfast, even though the Pier five offered one. Instead, he made some contacts with the weekend people at the D.C. Police Department.

Mainly, it was a legal thing. He had to inform the police that he, a private detective from another jurisdiction, was operating in the District – and that he had a permit to carry a gun – which he was doing. He informed the police sergeant on the desk at police headquarters of the make and caliber of his weapon, and its serial number. He then asked for, and received, an introduction to the officer in charge of the evidence room on this Sunday morning.

From that officer, Casio managed to sweet talk a look at the evidence boxes on the 1946 murder at the Blue Heron. That look included the crime scene photos that McDermott already had on a CD – although Casio didn't know that McDermott had them.

Fortunately, the officer in charge of the room hadn't had breakfast yet. Casio gave him ten dollars and told him to go – that he, Casio, would sit at the desk and read through the crime scene reports and files and would watch the store for the custodian. The officer grinned his thanks and scampered out of the building. Casio bought a cup of muddy water that was labeled as coffee from the basement floor vending machine, leaned back in the officer's chair, put his feet on the desk, and began to read.

Fifteen minutes later he burrowed through the assorted clutter on the desk until he found a telephone directory. He looked up a number, dialed 9, and called it.

Every major city has one. The Andrew Johnson Library is Washington's repository of local history, a place where periodical articles, photos and other archival items are cataloged and stored.

Casio gave his name to the woman at the library desk and was escorted to a musty, badly-lit cavern on the building's fourth floor – the level that the elevator didn't even go to. Casio and his escort rode up to the third floor, then took a rickety flight of stairs to the fourth-floor stacks. The woman handed Casio a role of paper towels and showed him to a library table near the center of the room.

"The towels are to dust off the table and chair," she explained simply." Out janitorial service doesn't come up here."

"Wonder why?" he asked casually.

She grinned sheepishly at him.

"Well they used to," she began, slowly. "But they stopped because this part of the library is haunted."

"Oh go on!" Casio scoffed.

She seemed to recoil as though he had struck her, but recovered quickly.

"Seriously," she said. "When we're working on the nights we're open late, we can hear the chairs scraping on the floor and when we come up to look, they've been moved."

Casio jumped out of his chair as though it had suddenly become hot. She motioned him back down.

"Don't worry," she counseled. "It rarely happens during normal business hours."

She smiled at the detective and disappeared into a metal jungle of box-filled shelves. Casio busied himself brushing a couple of layers of dust off the table in front of him, using several of the paper towels on the roll.

The librarian returned in less than four minutes carrying two bankers' boxes that were obviously quite full and very heavy. Casio leaped up and went to her aid, but a look on her face brought him up short.

"Don't worry about it, Mr. Casio," she said. "I'm quite used to this. My doctor wants me to exercise."

"But you don't need to be inhaling all that dust," he noted, eyeing the layers on the top box, quite a bit more than was on the table he had just wiped clean.

"I'm used to that, too," she declared, plunking the boxes down on the table.

She straightened up, and gestured toward the boxes.

"This is everything archived on a business called The Blue Heron Night Club located adjacent to the Metropole Hotel on the other side of Washington. The inventory sheet we have on file indicates that it has the lease agreements, band information, attendance figures, and a large file of photos. I don't know what the photos are, nor why there are so many."

Casio raised his left eyebrow.

"How many photos?" he asked

"More than five hundred, according to the inventory."

"Why so many?" the detective wondered.

She shrugged.

"I guess you'll find out when you go through them," she said. "Anything else I can get you?"

He nodded.

"I am going to be here quite awhile," he said. "I will want to send for lunch after a while. Is it possible to have something delivered up here?"

"Certainly," she said. "There's a deli that delivers a block behind the library. I'll send up the number, you can order from them and I'll have them bring it up here."

Casio smiled broadly.

"Thank you… what is your name?"

"Ruth," she replied.

"Thank you, Ruth." He pulled the lid off the top box. "I'd better get to work."

Ruth recognized that as her dismissal. She smiled back at the craggy man in the out-of-style suit and walked back to the stairs with an exaggerated wiggle.

Rod Pitcher took a sip of a take-out coffee brought to him by Samantha Parker, while sitting on what was once a rather expensive living room chair – and was now a twisted, broken frame of metal and wood with a tatter of material here and there. Samantha Parker looked forlornly at what had been a tastefully apportioned apartment, which, in many places, bore her touch.

The apartment was a total loss. There wasn't a chair, wasn't a table, wasn't a picture from the wall that hadn't been smashed into matchwood and left on the floor, along with a wall-to-wall carpet ruined by ink from all the Sharpies Pitch kept in his desk.

Pitcher swept his hand around in a circle and turned to Parker.

"For once I could kiss a sales person," he mused.

Parker looked at him speculatively.

"Oh?"

"Yeah," Pitcher rejoined. "That lady who badgered me over and over about buying renter's insurance. I wound up doing it just to shut her up – which I guess in retrospect was her plan all along. Anyway, I paid an annual premium and had planned to cancel it when that ran out."

"Has it run out yet?" she asked.

Pitcher smiled for the first time that Sunday morning.

"Nope," he gloated. "Four months to go.

Samantha Parker matched his grin.

"When you going to call her?"

Pitcher set his coffee down and rummaged around in a pile of rubbish that had once been the contents of his desk, which was a pile of splinters halfway across the room. He found what he was looking for, a business card, and reached for his cell phone.

"No time like the present," he said with an even wider grin.

Only Linda Hume knew what her husband did to unwind. And Charlie Hume made her swear under pain of death that she would never tell anyone, especially anyone at the newspaper.

Hume painted.

Most often he spent his Sundays ensconced in an attic room of his suburban Baltimore home, standing before a tall easel. He wore a pair of brown pants from a long-forgotten suit, stained over every discernable inch with various shades of oil paint – and a ragged, holey sweat shirt stained with every color of oil paint his pants had missed. On his feet were sneakers that were so differently paint-stained that they looked like shoes from two different pairs – as indeed, they could have been.

His paintings ranged from superficial still life's to absolutely brilliant conceptual landscapes, painted from his mind's eye, or copied from photographs he often took on weekend trips he and Linda would take for that purpose.

A number of his paintings hung in his home, and two of them were in his office at the newspaper. To conceal the origin of the works, he signed his paintings "Henry St. Vincent."

One of those conceptual landscapes was on the easel now, roughed out in pencil, as his technique dictated. He was working with an extremely fine brush, painstakingly filling in detail when his cell phone buzzed.

He grimaced in annoyance. Normally he didn't bring the offending instrument into his attic studio. But this day he'd had it in his pocket and had forgotten to leave it on his dresser on the home's second floor, as he usually did. He tried to ignore it. He knew that after seven rings it would jump automatically to voice mail – and he was reasonably sure that whatever message wound up there, it would wait until he tired of his art and listened to it.

He also knew that McDermott was planning on taking his new boat out that morning, so he was pretty sure his editor wasn't going to call him.

The buzzing stopped. Hume grinned at his canvas.

"That's that," he whispered aloud. "If it's important, they'll call back."

As if in answer, the cell phone chirped again. Hume slammed his brush down on the ledge at the base of the canvas and pulled the offending instrument from his pocket, holding it out and away from him as though it was alive. Finally be controlled his anger sufficiently to flip the phone open and hold it to his ear.

"Charlie Hume," he barked.

"Charlie, this is Sy Casio. I need to see you right away. I've got something."

Hume waited but Casio didn't take the hint to elaborate.

"What do you have, Sy?"

"I can tell you, but I'd rather show you. Where can we meet?"

Hume moved his left sleeve and glanced at his watch.

"Starbucks, around the corner from the office. Noon."

Casio paused a moment.

"You might consider calling Peter McDermott and Rod Pitcher and asking them to tag along," Casio suggested.

Hume thought a moment, about how his Sunday of rest was being interrupted, and considered the prospect of ruining someone else's Sunday of recreation and rest. He smiled in what can only be described as a 'shit eatin' grin,' and leered at the phone.

"They'll be there," he promised, ringing off and punching McDermott's number in speed dial.

Chapter Fifteen

Sy Casio found it in a thick sheaf of photographs wrapped in newspaper in the second box.

During his visit to the Washington D.C. police station, he read the crime scene report,
and the narrative on the subsequent investigation into the 1946 murder at the Blue Heron. He already knew some sparse facts about it. He had done some Internet research before leaving Los Angeles, so he knew the basics.

His reasoning had been that a night club like the Blue Heron would have had a house photographer. His hope was that somewhere, the photos taken by that photographer had been preserved, and perhaps there was an off-chance that one of those pictures might be revealing. But first he had to know what he was looking for. The reports he read at the cop-shop gave him that information. Then three and a half hours in the musty-dusty archives of the Andrew Johnson Library did the rest.

For a moment, Casio allowed himself a respite to think, to smile at the notion that detective work was all Sam Spade adventure, dealing with shady characters and exhibiting the derring-do that makes for a good book or a pyrotechnic-filled movie. The truth is that most detective work is like what Casio had been doing – reading reports and sitting in musty libraries looking for a button to sew a vest on.

Even though he dressed like something out of The Maltese Falcon, a personal eccentricity, Casio actually enjoyed what he perceived to be the drudgery of investigative work. And he was doubly enthusiastic about it when the drudgery paid off, as he believed it just had.

He opened his battered leather briefcase and slid three pictures into a folder between pages of the police report he'd read at the D.C. station. He took another half hour and looked at the remaining black-and-white glossies in the package, and rummaged through the rest of the box. Satisfied that he had glommed all the relevant information he could, he capped the box and ambled down the stairs, avoiding the elevator, and let himself out through a side door. Then and only then did he unlimber his cell phone and call Charlie Hume.

He had a very big piece of the puzzle.

Peter McDermott loved the feel of the wind through his hair, the sensation of speed and the motion of Chesapeake Bay transmitted through the hull of the Bayliner to his feet. He stood at the pilot station of the blue-and-white boat with the throttle pushed forward to its stop and let the boat dance over the low chop and occasional capped waves just outside the Severn River.

He'd offered Eve Somers a chance to share his first ride in his new toy, and she appeared to be enthusiastic about the idea. She stood on the dock as McDermott sat on the main deck lounge stripping the plastic off two new life jackets. He set one aside, and extended the other to her, noting with trepidation her hesitation to accept it.

"Come on, Eve, it's just precautionary to have a life jacket – not to mention it's the law. Come on aboard, let's try her out."

Eve Somers crossed the transom onto the aft deck, but made no move to accept the life jacket.

"I'm not sure about this, Mac," she said, tentatively.

"Ah come on," he prompted, extending the orange-and-yellow life jacket again. "The boat's fully equipped and safe."

She hesitated, and then shook her head.

"You know," she began, "I think I will just stay ashore, maybe do some shopping. Maybe I'll find a hotel where I can feel safe."

McDermott pursed his lips.

"Why a hotel? What's the matter with staying here?"

She sat next to him on the main deck lounge.

"You don't' want me staying at your condo," she said, quietly. He gave a barely perceptible nod. "And while I appreciate your letting me stay in your boat, I think I'd be more comfortable in a hotel."

"What about your fear that someone is after you?"

She took in a quick breath but recovered in a blink.

"I'll be careful. Having the time to relax on your boat has made me a little calmer. If it's OK, I will just go below now and get my things."

She stood and backed down the companionway into the main cabin. McDermott looked at the two life jackets sitting on the deck in front of him.

"I'll come back tonight, if you like, and make you dinner," she yelled from the cabin. "What would you like?"

"Surprise me," he said.

134

"I can certainly do that," she returned, matter-of-factly.

A moment later she reappeared, carrying two tote bags and a larger, cloth duffle. McDermott helped her take them ashore, but she declined help in taking them to her car. She waved to him as she walked up the pier past his condo and into the parking lot.

McDermott stared after her for a long moment, not thinking, but noticing that something about that conversation bothered him. After a time, he brushed it off, considering it nothing more than what women describe as a repressed desire for matrimony. He snapped the rocker-switch that started the engine compartment blower, a device meant to purge the enclosed space of any gasoline fumes before starting the engine.

After a few minutes he hit the key. The OMC six-cylinder motor cranked three times and caught, belching blue smoke for a few moments before settling down to a slow, throbbing roar. McDermott let it warm up while he disconnected the shore power cord, and took in three of the four mooring lines. Stepping back to the conning station he checked the boat's instruments. Satisfied that all was as it should be, he slapped a Greek fisherman's cap onto his head and let go the last line. Easing the boat out of the slip, he turned left – to port – and let the boat creep out of the marina through the "no wake" zone.

Shortly, the boat was in the Severn River, and McDermott was picking up speed, gauging the way the boat handled, much as he had when he was giving it a test-hop before buying it. By the time he reached the mouth of the river, he had the boat's number. He entered the normal chop of Chesapeake Bay with confidence in his ability to maintain control of the boat.

An hour later, he was orbiting the Thomas Point lighthouse at greatly reduced speed.

McDermott had been to the lighthouse many times on excursion boats out of the Annapolis City Docks, but being there, in control of his own vessel, was a new and exhilarating feeling.

The lighthouse wasn't accessible by land – it was two miles off shore and marked a shoal in the bay that was a menace to navigation. The light was automated; no keeper lived aboard. For several years, the historic light, oldest one in the bay, was owned by the City of Annapolis.

McDermott was making his fourth orbit of the red-and-white hexagonal structure known as a "screw-pile" lighthouse, when his cell phone rang insistently. Annoyed, he pulled it from the leather holster on his belt and looked at the caller ID. Hume. Resigned, he flipped it open.

"McDermott," he sighed.

"Where the hell are you?" Hume demanded.

"Thomas Point," McDermott replied, his irritation beginning to show. "Trying out the boat. It's a blast! Wish you were here."

"Wish you could stay there," Hume said, smoothly.

McDermott's heart sank.

"What's up? He asked, not really wanting to know.

"Starbucks, around the corner from the office. Noon. Be there."

The phone went dead.

Sy Casio chose a long table in a back corner of the two-room coffee house, away from the counter and the general proletariat that came through for a jolt of caffeine in all manner of exotic flavors and degrees of potency.

As Hume entered, Casio was standing with his back to the wall, laying the 8-by-10 pictures he had filched from the Andrew Johnson Library in a row along the length of the table so that Hume could see them. Hume nodded to Casio and ordered an espresso at the counter before coming to the table.

Pitcher came in a moment later and ordered a crème de menthe latte before ambling over to the table with an annoyed look on his face.

Finally, about ten past twelve, McDermott arrived, and ordered a simple cup of Folgers with creamer and Sweet N Low. He walked purposefully to the table and took a seat next to Pitch, but across the table from Casio, who assumed a lecturer's stance.

"Well now that we're all here," Hume began with a strong note of sarcasm, "let us begin."

Casio pushed his Homburg back on his head and regarded the three men with a toothy grin.

"I suppose you're wondering why I asked you all here," he began, dramatically.

Pitcher rolled his eyes.

"You're going to name the murderer?" Hume asked, drolly, trying not to laugh.

Casio shook his head lightly.

"Not name, unfortunately, but certainly to point out."

McDermott arched his left eyebrow and took a sip of his coffee. Casio noted the gesture, and exaggerated his lecturer's stance.

"It seems to me that the key to this whole affair is the public murder at the Blue Heron," he said. "Solve that, and we should be able to work forward and solve the killings that are happening today."

136

"Police have been trying to solve that killing for sixty years," McDermott pointed out.

Casio clapped his hands together and studied the ceiling.

"Then thank God you sent for me," he retorted with mock seriousness.

Pitcher rolled his eyes again, and Hume took a sip of his espresso, frowned at the cup and looked back at the detective. Casio resumed his lecturer's pose.

"All anyone knows up to now is that a woman in a red gown shot a trumpet player named Caine. We don't know who she was or why she did it. We just know that she used a Beretta, and that the same gun is killing members of Mr. Pitcher's family in the sweet here and now.

"I know from reading the reports that the D.C. police are ignoring the old murder and are working to solve the recent ones. I think they'll get it done, but not before someone else gets hurt. My thinking is that we solve the old one and the new ones should unravel."

"Only problem with that," drawled Hume, "is that the principals and any witnesses to the old murder are probably all dead."

"I didn't say it was going to be easy," Casio retorted.

"Easy?" exclaimed Pitcher. "Let's try something easy, like going over to the Navy Yard and shagging shells!"

Casio extended a calming hand.

"Nothing good ever comes easy," he admonished. "But we have a start."

He indicated the pictures on the table and the three men studied them.

"In those days, most quality night clubs had a house photographer. It was usually a well-dressed woman who went through the crowd taking pictures of people at random. She would offer copies of the pictures to the people involved – and sometimes even use them for blackmail."

"Like if someone was there with someone other than their spouse?"

Casio nodded.

"Exactly. Sometimes the photographers would print the pictures as contact sheets – laying the negatives on photo paper and exposing them – and sometimes they'd just go ahead and use an enlarger and print them, as you see here, thinking they might sell them later."

"And so..." McDermott prompted, indicating the photo.

"We're looking for a woman in a red evening gown. She is the one that the police report from that time says fired the shot that killed Chance Caine." Casio indicated a figure on the left photo. "Here is a

137

woman seated at a ringside table, just on the edge of the dance floor opposite the band stand. She is sitting with an older, impeccably dressed gentleman."

"But you can't tell if the gown is red," McDermott complained. "The picture is black and white."

Casio nodded appreciably at the point.

"You've got me there," he said. "But we can infer it from the shading in the picture."

"Kinda like watching the old Superman TV episodes in black and white," Pitcher said, smiling. "You know the colors of his uniform, but they're still just gray shades."

"Right," Casio said. "I see this woman's gown as red in the same way."

A siren pierces the lunch-time air, close by and increasingly loud.

"You know we could take that picture over to the University of Maryland's science wing in College Park," Hume muses.

"I know where you're headed, Charlie," McDermott said brightly, warming to the point. "We did the story on that spectroscopic analyzer..."

McDermott has to raise his voice because the siren is much closer now, and is joined by at least two more.

"Can we get to that on Sunday? Pitcher asked?"

McDermott nodded.

"We can if I make a phone call," McDermott said, reaching for his cell.

"You can't make the call with all that noise," Casio said, gathering the pictures and stuffing them into his briefcase. "Do it in the car."

The sirens are quite close now, and through the picture window at the front of the store, the four can see the red trucks of the Baltimore fire department screaming into the parking lot. The three men from the *North Bay Times* look at one another, and Pitcher scampered out the door ahead of them. By the time the other three are at the door of Starbucks, Pitcher is headed back to them, his face grim.

"What is it, Pitch?" McDermott asks.

"Car fire," he says simply.

"Oh?" Hume returned. "Which car?"

Pitcher exhaled noisily.

"Mine."

Chapter Sixteen

Rodney Pitcher stated forlornly at the burned-out hulk that had once been his car. Peter McDermott stood next to him, pinching his arm to keep him from going to pieces. The editor could see that his friend and ace reporter was on the verge of tears.

A fire department captain sidled up to the four men carrying something in a gloved hand.

"Whose car is this?" he asked, in a kind voice.

Pitcher raised his hand timidly. The fire captain held out the item he was holding. It was the bottom half of a wine bottle, with part of the label still attached, though charred and almost illegible.

"Did you have a wine bottle like this in your car, Sir?" the fireman asked.

Pitcher's face hardened.

"Certainly not!"

"Then I believe I can safely say your car was torched, Sir. What you are seeing is the base of that I think is a Molotov Cocktail – and the side window on the passenger side was smashed. At first I thought we did it to fight the fire, but it turns out it was already out when the crew arrived."

"So what do I do now?"

The fire captain tried to look sympathetic, and just barely missed.

"If I can see your drivers license, Sir," he began.

Pitcher supplied it, and the fire captain jotted down the name and address.

"Before you leave, I'll have the paperwork for you on the fire run, for your insurance company," the captain said. "I'm sorry we couldn't save your car."

"I know you did your best," Pitcher said, his voice beginning to crack.

The fire captain tipped his white helmet, smiled thinly, and walked away.

McDermott could hear Pitcher grinding his teeth.

"I – Am—So—Tired—Of—Being—*Targeted*!" he hissed through tightly clenched teeth. McDermott could feel every muscle in the reporter's body tense. He felt sorry for his friend, and now he was more convinced than ever that the bullet that had whizzed by his right ear was actually meant for Pitch. But he was starting to wonder – why were things like the car fire and the destruction of his home happening? Why wasn't Pitch an assassin's target again? Not that he was complaining. Certainly not that Pitch was complaining.

"Let's go back inside," Hume suggested, putting a sympathetic hand on Pitcher's shoulder. Casio nodded and led the way at a slow gait. Hume followed Casio. McDermott walked beside Pitch. The four men resumed the same table they'd had before and Hume went to get the drinks. Pitcher leaned back in his chair and covered his eyes with the fingers of his left hand.

"Someone is getting nervous," Casio observed, seriously.

"Meaning...?"

"This was a warning. Whoever is doing all of this is telling us to back off – or else."

"Maybe we should abandon trying to solve the old murder and concentrate our efforts on today's happenings – before someone gets hurt," Hume suggested.

Casio thought about this a moment.

"I'm still convinced that the Blue Heron killing is the key," he said. "The D.C and Baltimore police are working on today's crimes. Why try to duplicate their efforts, especially since they have resources we don't have?"

Pitcher dropped his hand and stared with a granite expression at the anachronistic detective.

"I don't know why, Mr. Casio, I really don't, but my gut tells me you're right. I believe the 1946 shooting in Washington is the key. I don't know why I believe that – but believe it I do. So if my vote means anything here, let's do it your way. But please, let's do it quickly."

Casio nodded, satisfied.

"Then let's be off to the University of Maryland's Science Building," he said, draining his cup, not really knowing what he was drinking.

"You can call your insurance company on the way," Hume said to Pitcher.

Pitch rolled his eyes.

"They're going to love me!"

The killer drove from East Baltimore, where a well placed wine bottle half-full of kerosene and stuffed closed with an oil-soaked rag had done in Rod Pitcher's car, crossing into Washington via the East-West Highway. The car turned left out of Montgomery County onto Chevy Chase Circle, and then onto Connecticut Avenue. The killer obeyed the traffic laws, but no more or less than any other driver on the downhill avenue, not wanting to attract any undue attention. But the drive had purpose, and the killer maneuvered the vehicle through the Federal triangle and into the Southeast portion of the city.

Spotting the biggest landmark, the decaying RFK stadium, the killer turned again and entered the darker, seedier portion of the city. Here, deteriorating row houses and decrepit walk-up apartment buildings reached to the sky like bony, malformed fingers. The black of the car's body easily matched the hearts of the denizens of this cloudy place, who walked with eyes over their shoulders, giving furtive looks to everyone who passed by. Many of them melted into the shadows of the filthy buildings at the approach of a strange car – resurfacing in the killer's rear view mirror as the dark car passed.

The killer parked and got out of the car, staring up at a brick edifice that took up space at the intersections of three streets. The Metropole Hotel was as it had been for decades before. It was cold, dark, uninviting and foreboding.

"The Spectroscopic Analyzer isn't a new idea, but computers have made it a lot more accurate," said Doctor Keith Mulreedy. He was standing in front of a device that resembled an old-style photographic enlarger connected by USB cable to a laptop computer on the table next to it. "Mainly it's used to colorize old black-and-white movies, frame by frame. This device is able to determine the original colors of objects, clothing, backgrounds and so on – and it's more accurate than the other methods that basically involve using electronic paints to color frames.

"So your device can analyze this black-and-white photo and determine the colors of everything in it, including the color of the clothing on the people?" Casio asked.

Mulreedy nodded and reached for the picture, which Casio handed him. Mulreedy placed the picture on the easel under the enlarger-like object, centered it in a square of light, and turned on the device. A shaft of light began on the left side of the picture and moved slowly to the right, scanning the picture.

On the computer screen, the picture began to reconstitute itself, but this time in full color. It wasn't the brilliant, glaring color of a treated monochrome movie, but the natural shades and nuances of a modern, digital color photo.

There could be no doubt of it. The woman in the photo taken by the Blue Heron's house shutterbug, was indeed the elusive "Lady In Red,"

"Hard to believe," Hume said, with a degree of awe, as he stared at the 60 year old picture.

"Lady in Red," Casio breathed. "Could it possibly be more cliché? Right out of a pulp novel."

"Dashiell Hammet?" Pitcher asked with a half-smile.

"Damn right," Casio snapped back.

"What do we do now?" Hume asked, straightening up from looking at the picture.

"We find this woman," Casio said. "And it's going to be a major challenge."

"Oh?" McDermott asked

Casio folded his arms across his chest.

"First and foremost, this picture was taken 60 years ago so the woman is probably dead. Secondly, the chances are everybody who was in the club that night is probably dead too."

"So what the hell do we do?" Hume demanded, exasperated. "Go out to the graveyard and dig them up?"

Casio smiled, which just made Hume madder. He turned to Doctor Mulreedy.
"Can you give us print-outs of the picture?" he asked?

In answer, Mulreedy passed his hand over the laptop keyboard, and a printer on the floor across the room whirred to life. The doctor also slid a 512mb jump drive into the computer's USB port and moved the mouse. A light on the jump drive blinked a few times, and then everything stopped. Mulreedy walked to the printer and pulled out four pictures on plain paper, and handed them and the jump drive to Casio.

"How about starting by running the picture in your newspaper, Charlie," Casio suggested, extending the jump drive to the publisher. "Maybe one of your readers knows who she is ... was."

"I think we can do that," Hume declared, turning toward his editor, and extending the jump drive. "Mac?"

McDermott accepted the drive and pocketed it.

"No problem," he said. "Page one."

"Really?" Hume asked, lifting an eyebrow. "Why page one?"

McDermott shrugged but there was a twinkle in his eye.

142

"All the world loves a good mystery" McDermott grinned.

Hume matched the smile.

"That they do," he answered and clapped the editor on his back. "Get back to the office and get after it. I'll take Pitch to the car-rental agency and the paper will pick up the tab for the rental until his insurance company pays off."

That last declaration stopped both McDermott and Pitcher in their tracks. Such a display of corporate generosity was totally out of character for Charlie Hume, whom, many thought, could be a relative of Ebeneezer Scrooge. Or Jack Benny. But Pitcher knew Hume felt bad about the reporter's car, being destroyed, as it was, in the line of duty.

The lobby of the Metropole Hotel looked like the skeleton of a huge animal. There was no ceiling – the pipes and wires and conduit were clearly visible above, the plaster of the walls was bare and crumbly, and there was no prettifying of the load-bearing columns that had once been decoratively gracing an ornate lobby. There was no rotting furniture, as there would be had this been a newly discovered sunken ship – but it couldn't be more like a sunken wreck. The floors and the remainders of the walls were blank, unadorned, and covered with three or four layers of dust. It was dark – just a few rays of sun pushing their way through filthy windows near the tops of the walls toward the registration desk – a dilapidated construct decaying at one end of the massive room.

The killer could almost see the desk clerk as he must have been so many eons ago, smiling an insincere greeting as someone approached the desk – the clerk would emit an audible sniff as he turned the registration card holder to face the potential guest, and as the clerk read the name upside down he would try to decide whether to tell the guest the hotel was all full – whether it was or not – or quickly produce a heavy steel key on a wooden fob with a room number burned into it. In that event, the clerk would slap the top of a bell with the flat of a hand and yell "Front!" And a bellboy in a red uniform and a smart, pillbox hat would snap to attention before the guest, take the bags and lead the guest into an elevator and to the correct floor where doors would be opened, curtains would be pushed back and bathroom supplies would be quickly checked. Finally the prep would be finished and the bellboy would withdraw, hopefully with a generous tip -- a ritual that would be repeated often during the stay – or so hoped the bellboy.

The killer passed the desk and walked with a purpose to the bank of elevators against the far wall. A gloved finger stabbed a call button. In an instant, the eerie silence of a dead hotel lobby was pierced by the sound of machinery activating far below, and after a three-count, the doors of the ancient elevator parted, and the killer stepped inside, pressing "3."

The third floor of the Metropole Hotel was nothing like the first. The elevator doors opened on a brightly lit hallway, immaculately clean, carpeted and painted, with inexpensive prints every so often hanging along the corridor. The windows at each end of the corridor were boarded shut – lest light rays become visible at the street. But otherwise, the hotel floor was well kept and habitable.

The killer walked about halfway down the corridor and opened – without a key – a door on the right. Snapping a switch, the killer ambled unhurriedly into a nicely-apportioned, well lit room with soft-colored furniture and a large, well-made bed. There was a television set in the room, but the killer didn't bother with that. Instead, the killer produced a number of news clippings – all having to do with murders and attempted murders – and fixed them with thumb tacks to a bulletin board that sat on the desk and leaned precariously against a wall, partially obscuring a typical hotel mirror.

The bathroom worked, and the killer made use of it before laying down on the bed, trying to sleep, but instead allowed thoughts to go on, planning and rejecting a next move, a move calculated to get rid of a person who was now a major threat – a threat because a failed attempt had rallied his resolve and that of his friends.

There could be no more failures. Rod Pitcher had to die.

Peter McDermott consulted his notes from the 1946 murder and resumed his frantic typing as Sy Casio looked over his shoulder. McDermott was an incredibly fast, four-finger typist. Not accurate. Just fast. He made up for his frequent misspellings with generous utterances of guttural obscenities, which amused Casio no end, and used his spell-checker liberally. The article on Page One of what would become the next edition of the *North Bay Times* was taking shape, and was wrapping around a two-column cut photo of the "Lady In Red," and extending down the column. McDermott would "jump" the article to an inside page when he had used up the available space.

Under the headline, **"Do You Know This Woman?"** the front page disgorged all that was known about the subject of the photograph, and the circumstances surrounding the taking of the picture – and the death of Chance Caine.

144

Casio suggested a change or two here and there, some of which McDermott used, some of which he rejected in favor of his own ideas on the prose. In a short time, the entire first page was filled, dominated by the picture of the woman in the red gown, with a smaller picture of the Blue Heron as it appeared in modern times, and graphics he had developed quickly in Photo Shop.

Hume came in and joined Casio, looking over McDermott's other shoulder, but neither standing man said anything. They watched in rapt fascination as the story took shape right before their eyes.

McDermott wrote directly into the page template, rather than scribing his story in a word processor and transferring it.

The editor was totally focused on what he was doing; he ignored the two men standing behind him and concentrated on the screen before him.   Hume was used to McDermott's unconscious displays of journalistic professionalism, but Casio watched him with a look akin to awe. The detective watched, enraptured, as McDermott snipped out a word here, added a phrase there, switched a punctuation in another place. The effect was an article cobbled together in a smooth, cohesive, easy-to-read manner, needing little or no revision.

"How do you do that?" Casio asked in a whisper."

"Do what?" McDermott asked, not turning to him, but continuing to concentrate on the screen.

"Just wave your hands over the keyboard like that and wind up with an article that's as well written as that one is?"

Hume cluck-clucked.

"The same way you ferret out clues, the same way you instinctively know who's lying to you or what someone's reaction to something will be. Mac knows his job and he's exceptionally good at it. He and Pitcher are examples of a dying breed – true journalists who know their craft and do it well."

"That explains who the *North Bay Times* is as popular as it is," Casio said definitively.

"Damn right," McDermott chimed in, finishing his article and touching SEND on his keyboard, transmitting his page to Composing where it would be finalized for pre-press. Hume smiled broadly and slammed McDermott on the back before heading back to his own office. McDermott finished his duties and closed the program on his computer. He was about to turn and talk to Casio and Pitch when his desk phone rang. He scooped it to his ear.

"McDermott," he barked.

A moment later he touched the SPEAKER button and hung up the phone so all and sundry in the office could hear.

"Would you start again, please, there are other people here in the office who need to hear what you have to say."

"I said..." came a foppish, effected-English voice, "... that this is Julian Peebles and I have the tool that will open the watch. If I might be so bold, I'd like to suggest that you go and retrieve the bloody thing and bring it by my shack sometime today and we will open it together and see what all the ruddy fuss is about."

McDermott looked up at Pitcher who was reaching for his keys to the rental car Hume had provided.

"I'll get it," Pitcher declared. "And I'll meet you back here in..." he glanced at his watch, ..."say 90 minutes?"

McDermott checked his own watch and nodded.

"Mind if I tag along Pitch?" Casio asked, casually.

"Not at all," Pitcher returned in a friendly voice. "Any particular reason?"

"Someone is going to a great deal of trouble to get your attention. And the next time they do I want to be in a position to get *their* attention."

He pulled open his suit coat and showed the men in the room the butt of a Browning Hi Power Mark III 9-millimeter in well-cared-for working order, nestling under his left armpit in a Boosey Hawks self-gripping shoulder holster.

Pitcher grinned and beckoned. He and Casio left the room and headed down the hall to the building exit.

"Now we're getting somewhere," Casio said with a grin.

"Like where?" Pitcher wanted to know.

"When we find out what's in that watch, perhaps we'll find out what's important enough to take three lives."

"What if there's nothing in the watch?" Pitcher speculated.

Casio stopped and stared for a moment at the reporter, then the two resumed their stride, a little quicker.

"I don't know," Casio said, considerably mollified. "I just don't know."

Chapter Seventeen

Five men gathered in the library of Julian Peebles' palatial home. The butler that Pitcher called Lurch had served coffee and soft drinks and had withdrawn, leaving Pitcher, Hume, McDermott, and Sy Casio sitting around a table erected in the center of the room. In the middle of the table was the Ziess-Baden watch Pitcher had brought with him, and two other items.

One was an unusual tool. It had a handle perhaps three inches long that terminated in what was apparently a sharp point. At the other end were two points curved inward like a falcon's talon, with a button on the upper shank at the handle's level. That made the tool about five inches long overall. Underneath the tool was a one-sheet document.

Julian Peebles leaned back in the leather-covered chair at the table and sipped from a stemmed glass containing a splash of white wine. Peebles had been introduced to Sy Casio and the two seemed to develop a quick rapport, hardly surprising, since Peebles considered himself a kind of intellectual detective, among his other self-illusions.

"The moment of truth, Gentlemen," Peebles said in a conspiratorial tone, laced with his affected English accent. "There before you on the table is the tool that can safely open the watch. But what you have to understand is that one error, one wrong move, and the vial of acid inside the watch will break and the document in there will be destroyed in seconds. Then all this is for nothing."

He leaned forward and put his elbows on the table, tenting his fingers in front of him, as he looked at each man on the other side of the table, one at a time.

"Who's got a steady hand?"

There was a pause, then Hume raised his hand.

"I'll do it."

Peebles smiled.

"Bravo, Charles, you're running the controls. Now we're going to need someone to read the instructions out loud while Charles turns the screws, as it were."

"Mac will do it," Hume said with certainty. "He was a broadcaster all those years he can read out loud and make himself understood."

Peebles turned to McDermott.

"Peter, do you concur?"

McDermott blanched at being called by his given name. He preferred "Mac." Finally, he shrugged.

"All right by me," he said.

Peebles smiled and moved his eyes side to side several times, taking in each man at the table.

"Very well, then," he said, reached for the watch.

"You're sure that this is a courier watch?" Pitcher asked.

"Quite," Peebles said, definitely.

"And you're sure there's a vial of acid inside?" Pitcher continued.

"All the Ziess-Baden watches used as courier devices had acid vials in them to guard against the information being carried falling into the wrong hands," Peebles said with conviction. "That means if there's something in there, and this watch isn't opened properly, the acid vial will break and the liquid will dissolve the document."

"Can the acid have survived intact this long without breaking down?" Casio wanted to know.

Peebles shrugged his shoulders.

"Who knows," he said. "Do you want to take that chance?"

"I don't," Pitcher declared. "Let's do it by the book."

"Quite so," Peebles exclaimed, picking up the tool and handing it to Hume. McDermott pulled the single page document to him and scanned it.

"Fit the two wrench points into the notches on the round bevel on the back of the watch," McDermott read. Hume eased the wrench into position and nodded to McDermott.

"With a free finger, press the button on the end of the wrench to lock the wrench in place," the editor continued.

Hume reached up with the index finger of his other hand and pressed the tiny button on the front of the wrench. There was a tiny but audible click as the teeth of the wrench clicked into place on the notches cut into the round bevel cap in the watch back. Hume looked up at McDermott expectantly. The editor returned his eyes to the printed page before him.

"Turn the wrench and the back bevel one-eighth turn counter-clockwise," he read.

Hume exerted pressure on the wrench and on the watch held in his left hand. The watch was old and had been sealed a long time, so it wasn't inclined to break loose easily. Hume paused a moment and gathered his strength, then applied even pressure with both hands. The bevel gave a fraction of an inch, but it was enough to bring out a smile on Hume's lips. He twisted again, a bit harder this time, and the bevel turned yet more.

"One eighth turn," McDermott reminded him, "until the bevel pops up."

Hume nodded, his face showing the effort, but it was rewarded as the bevel was turning more freely now. At length it seemed to rise under the wrench. Hume sighed heavily and turned back to McDermott.

"Now, turn the bevel one-quarter turn clockwise, and remove it," McDermott said, reading from the form.

Hume took a moment to let his pounding heart return to a normal beat pattern, then looked down at the watch in his left hand, and the wrench in his right. He made an effort and the bevel turned to the right easily. Reaching a quarter turn, it became obviously loose, and Hume raised the wrench, taking the beveled disk back with it, and put them aside. He set the watch back on the table, face down, and all five of the men leaned forward to peer inside.

They could see a tiny glass vial, clear, with a yellowish-tinged liquid still inside. Next to it was a tiny roll of paper, perhaps a half-inch high, a thin, gossamer-like paper that appeared brittle and delicate.

"We need tweezers," Casio said softly.

Peebles turned away and shouted at the closed door.

"James!"

Pitcher looked up at him.

"Who's James?" he asked.

"The butler," Peebles said, returning his gaze to the opened watch.

"I thought his name was Lurch," Pitcher retorted.

Peebles just glared at him for a moment, eliciting a big smile from Pitcher. After a moment, the door opened and the huge, expressionless man ambled into the room.

"Tweezers and some jeweler tools please," Peebles requested.

The giant man bowed from the waist and withdrew, walking backwards, closing the doors as he went. Inside the room, no one moved, no eye came off the back of the watch and what it revealed, unseen by human eyes in more than 60 years.

"What do you suppose is on that paper that is worth three human lives?" Pitcher whispered.

"I don't know," McDermott breathed.

"But we will know, lads," Peebles said, softly. "Almost any moment now."

The butler returned to the room as noiselessly as before and placed a pair of tweezers and a small black plastic box on the table next to Peebles' elbow. Peebles dismissed the butler with a wave of his hand, and the man bowed again and backed from the room as before.

Peebles picked up the tweezers and looked at McDermott, who returned his eyes to the paper.

"Remove the paper first," he read. "Do not up-end the watch to do so or the acid vial will break."

Peebles nodded as though what McDermott read confirmed something he thought he knew. With the tweezers, he gingerly took hold of the tiny paper roll and lifted. The paper came away easily and cleared the back of the watch with no fuss at all.

"Anything else?" Peebles asked.

McDermott laid the sheet down on the table.

"*C'est tout, fini,*" he said.

"What?" Casio demanded.

McDermott smiled sheepishly.

"That's all," he translated.

Hume ignored his editor and picked up the watch, setting it far aside, well away from the tiny roll of paper. If anything happened to break the acid vial, he didn't want it even close to the item they had come so far to find.

As he did so, Peebles opened the plastic box and removed a small surgical clamp. He used the forceps nose of the instrument to find and hold the end of the roll, setting the clamp down on the table. Using two fingers, he gently began unrolling the paper. The rest of the men at the table watched intensely, as the paper slowly opened. One inch, two, Peebles went about his task in a deliberate, unhurried manner. Finally, the paper was laying flat on the table, a discolored, yellowed ribbon. Gingerly, Peebles used the clamp to turn it around, and he set another clamp on the other end to hold it open. The five men stared at the faded writing on the tiny parchment strip.

"Numbers," Casio said softly.

"Numbers," Peebles echoed.

"Well what did we expect, the answer to the meaning of life?" inquired Pitcher. "Numbers are better than nothing; at least we have something to go on now."

"What?" Hume demanded. "What do we have to go on? Numbers! What do they mean?"

"Pitch is right," McDermott interjected." We might not know what they mean right now, but they have a meaning, one that we will have to dig up. I'd suggest that we all write the numbers down and each of us try to figure out what they mean independently. Tomorrow we'll meet at the *Times* and compare notes."

The tension in the room noticeably lessened.

"Peter is right," Peebles said firmly.

"Yes he is," Hume chimed in. "Let's do just that."

Peebles walked to the library table where he opened a drawer. From it he took a note pad and a handful of sharp pencils, which he passed around.

"Peter, if you will dictate the numbers," Peebles said as he resumed his seat.

McDermott leaned over the paper, concentrating on the faded marks.

"38," McDermott read aloud, and the pencils scratched on the papers around the table. "then a dot, then 8-8-1. Then there's a long space, then a dash, and then 76, another dot, and 9-7-9."

"That it?" Casio asked.

"McDermott looked for a long moment at the paper.

"That's it," he declared.

Peebles took the paper and carefully rolled it back up.

"If there are no objections," he began in a soft English drawl, "I will take this bit of paper and lock it up in my personal vault in the basement of my little row house, here."

McDermott looked around at his colleagues and saw only stony faces. He nodded back at Peebles.

"Very well, then," the foppish man said. "Let's adjourn for the night and try to figure these numbers out."

He ended the meeting by simply walking out of the room. Hume and McDermott stared at the doors as they closed, and a moment later they opened again, and the butler filled the frame.

"May I show you out, Gentlemen?" he rumbled with no expression at all in his voice.

Hume looked at Pitcher.

"I think we've been dismissed."

"If you'll walk this way, Gentlemen," the giant butler drawled, and turned to head toward the front door, moving only his legs not his upper body at all.

"Gawd," Pitcher said, winking at McDermott." If I could walk like that I'd hurt myself!"

Outside, Hume and Casio got into the publisher's Lexus, but McDermott and Pitcher stood between the editor's Jeep and Pitcher's rental car.

"Numbers," Pitcher said, disgusted.

"I thought you were OK with that," McDermott said, puzzled.

"I was trying to put on a positive face."

McDermott snorted.

"Stick to poker," he drawled.

"So what do we do now?"

McDermott sighed heavily.

"We carry on," he said, simply. "We go and try to figure out what these numbers mean."

He pulled the note paper from his shirt pocket and looked at the numbers again, hoping that a light bulb would go on above his head. It didn't.

"Let's get some dinner and meet in two hours at the office," Pitcher suggested.

McDermott tapped Pitcher's chest with his finger.

"It's a date," he said, swinging into his Jeep.

The two cars drove out of the Peebles estate driveway and turned right into the gathering evening traffic. And as they did so, a nondescript Ford, whose principal color was Bondo pulled away from the curb, obviously following the two men. When the two lead cars separated at a stoplight, the driver of the old wreck hesitated a moment, then opted to follow the black Jeep.

McDermott stopped at the Bobalu Grill near the Inner Harbor. He ordered a Tom Collins, an uncharacteristic drink for the near-teetotaler, and asked the waiter for some mozzarella sticks and marinara sauce. While he waited, he thumbed through the entrée menu and spread the note paper out on the table in front of him. His appetizer and drink came. He munched without tasting and drank without noticing as he let his mind wander over the numbers, trying to figure out what the sequence was all about. It didn't console him when a thought forced its way past his consciousness, a thought that told him Pitcher was probably doing exactly the same thing in another restaurant.

Finally, he shook himself out of his funk and regarded the empty plate, from which he remembered not one single bite.

The waiter came, and McDermott ordered a medium-well Rib-Eye steak with a baked potato and a glass of cold milk.

Again, while he waited for his food, he contemplated the sequence of numbers. They had to mean something.

At length his food came, and he folded the paper back into his shirt pocket, trying to redirect his thoughts as he enjoyed his dinner as he had failed to enjoy his appetizer. But the numbers wouldn't leave him, and his mind wandered again, forcing him to pull the note paper from his pocket and stare again even as he cut his steak into bite-sized pieces.

McDermott was a classic example of the obsessive-compulsive personality. Most journalists fall into that category – never able to leave a puzzle alone. McDermott knew he would never feel right until he – or another of his coterie – solved the mystery on the page in front of him.

38.881 -76.979

Chapter Eighteen

The next edition of the *North Bay Times* hit the stands that Saturday with the picture of the Lady in Red splashed across the front page. By Monday morning the receptionist operator was threatening to quit over the volume of phone calls, most demanding to know who the woman was. It didn't matter that there was a 72-point headline asking "Do You Know This Woman," most of the callers probably thought it was some kind of a contest.

But those weren't the calls that interested McDermott, Pitcher and Hume. They were waiting for one particular call. And about 1:30 on that Monday afternoon, it came.

McDermott came sauntering into Hume's office a few minutes after that, entering the inner sanctum-sanctorum without knocking, and dropping into a soft armchair near Hume's massive, oaken desk.

Hume looked up from his work and stared at McDermott as though he had just heard an ass bray in his office. People didn't come into his office unannounced and without invitation, and certainly not without passing through the woman in his outer office. Not even McDermott, who was the paper's second-in-command and a friend of long-standing. Hume was a great one to stand on protocol in the office.

"Something on your mind, Mr. McDermott?" Hume purred, venom apparent in his voice.

The editor started to open his mouth, but Hume held up a restraining hand.

"I'll be interested in it once you've gotten your ass out of here and have come back in the proper manner."

He pointed.

"You know where the door is."

McDermott grinned, stood and made a show of trying to find it, then opened it, and turned back to his boss.

"Actually," he said, in a conspiratorial tone, "I only had a moment. Sy Casio and I are meeting someone about the Lady in Red in Washington an hour from now."

Hume, who had returned his attention to the papers on his desk, merely grunted and waved his dismissal at the editor, who then closed the door. It was two full minutes before the light bulb went on above his head. He bolted from his chair and ran to the door, flinging it open, and passing through his outer office on the dead run. He slammed open the hallway door and looked both ways.

"He's already gone," said Nancy, his executive assistant.

Hume turned to her trying to look innocent.

"Who is?"

"Mac is," she said, hoping Hume didn't notice that she was trying not to laugh.

"Mac is what?" Hume demanded

"Gone," she said firmly.

"Gone?"

She nodded.

"Gone."

"Gone where?"

She shrugged.

"Dunno"

"Washington?"

"Guess so."

She made a big show of filing her nails with an emery board. Hume just stared at her with steam coming out of his ears. After a moment the publisher turned and stormed out into the corridor. A half-second after the door slammed, Nancy collapsed in uncontrolled peals of laughter.

Bon Jovi was playing on the speakers as McDermott and Sy Casio ambled into the Madhatter Lounge on M Street Northwest. It was 3:30 in the afternoon, and only a few of the tables at the front of the place were occupied. Toward the back, two women, obviously stoned, were dancing close together, out of time with the music – which, though loud, wasn't overpowering.

Casio nudged McDermott and indicated with a shake of his head. Mac looked in the indicated direction and saw a lone man seated at a postage-stamp table in the corner. He was perhaps eighty, white stringy hair peeking out from underneath an old-style hat remarkably like the one Casio was wearing. He wore a gray pinstripe suit with gaudy padding, obviously from one of the cheaper shops along Broadway in New York. There was a bottle of beer on the table, sitting on a tiny napkin. Next to it was an unused glass, and a small pile of crumpled bills.

McDermott noticed that the man's hands trembled. His face was lined with age and abuse, and the thick glasses he wore were from a bygone era.

"Maybe we shouldn't double-team the old geezer," Casio whispered. "Why don't you go over and see if you can strike up a conversation. I'll sit at the bar and back you up."

McDermott nodded and sauntered across the semi-dark room to the table. Casio picked a stool near the center of the bar, ordered a beer from an obliging barmaid, and turned to watch. McDermott spoke to the old man for a moment, then sat. No handshakes were exchanged. But Casio didn't expect friendliness. The old man obviously wanted something from McDermott, just as McDermott wanted information from him. Casio sipped his beer and appeared to be totally disinterested in the proceedings, when, in fact, he was taking in every nuance of what was happening in the entire room.

Casio was pretty sure the old man didn't have a back-up, someone doing for the old man what Casio was doing for McDermott. If he had, Casio hadn't made him yet. He leaned back on the bar stool, putting his elbows on the bar, holding his beer in his left hand, and watched every movement in the room, paying particular attention to the animated discussion going on at a corner table farthest away from the dance floor.

McDermott studied the man across the table from him, and knew he was being studied in return. He had confirmed that this was Harry Oglesby. At least that's the name he had given McDermott on the phone when this meeting had been set up.

McDermott waved the waitress away when she came to get an order from him.

"You know the woman in the picture?" McDermott got right down to cases.

"Who's asking?" the man countered.

McDermott dropped his business card on the table. Oglesby looked at it carefully without touching it, then turned back to McDermott with piercing sky blue eyes whose intensity had not been in the least dimmed by the ravages of age.

"So you're the guy from the newspaper," he said trying to sound like a Chicago gangster, but the effort was more comical than intimidating.

"I'm the guy," McDermott declared, suppressing a smile.

157

"You look like too smooth a guy to be messing around in something like this," Oglesby said, taking a pull on his beer bottle.

"Obviously not."

"They call you Pete?"

"I'd prefer to be called Mac," McDermott said, a little testily. "What do I call you?"

"Mr. Oglesby," Oglesby replied with a straight face.

"You know who the woman in the picture is?"

"Yeah, I know who she is," Oglesby said, his voice turning hard.

"So give," McDermott prompted.

"What's in it for me?"

"What do you want?"

Oglesby scratched his chin.

"A piece of the action."

McDermott draped an arm over the back of his chair.

"You don't even know what the action will be," he grinned, stretching his body across the table.

"Oh I think I do," Oglesby said with assurance. "In fact I think it will be a pretty healthy percentage."

"Percentage of..." McDermott prompted.

"Whatever you realize in your search," Oglesby said.

"What if all I'm looking for is a name?"

Oglesby leaned across the table, right into McDermott's face.

"Do you take me for an idiot, Sir? Do you think I'd be here if I didn't know you were after something more than just the name of a long-dead broad?"

"OK," McDermott said angrily, not moving. "What do you want?"

"One-twentieth of the take," Oglesby hissed, moving even closer to McDermott's face. The editor crinkled his nose.

"Done," McDermott affirmed.

"And done," Oglesby said, clasping the editor's hand, though neither man surrendered his position.

"One thing, though," McDermott said, looking Oglesby right in the eye.

"What?"

McDermott let his face become an impassive mask.

"Your mouthwash ain't makin' it."

The killer stood just inside the door of the Madhatter taking in the situation. McDermott was at a table to the left of the killer's position, sitting with an older man, and the two seemed to be locked in intense

158

discussion. The killer knew who the older man was. And then there was the other man, the one McDermott had entered the club with. The killer knew that this newcomer had joined the party recently – probably in response to the killer's bungling of attempts to take out the *North Bay Times* team.

Too dangerous and too public to take care of business in here. But the time would be right soon.

The killer stood still long enough to know that none of the participants had paid attention to the darkness-swathed figure in the door before turning and stepping back into the teeming city.

Rod Pitcher ripped a piece of paper from his reporter's notebook, balled it up and threw it at a wastebasket near the entrance to his cubicle. He missed. Disgusted, he picked up his pencil and recopied the numbers from the watch onto a clean page and worried over them.

He had tried adding them, he tried dividing and subtracting, and he tried a couple of crypto patterns for decoding that he found on the internet. Putting his pencil down, he returned to his computer and Googled 'World War II codes.' None of the few examples, including those of the famous Enigma code, fit the pattern of the numbers before him.

Further disgusted, he entered the number into the search field. His computer seemed to hiccup, and his hard drive became audibly sclerotic. A message appeared on the screen: "Search in Progress. Estimated Time... 4 Hours.

Pitcher ground his teeth and glanced at the clock on his desk near his printer. Nearly 5PM. Perhaps dinner, and a few more phone calls to car lots, now that he had his insurance check – and a threat of cancellation from the company that had his car and his apartment insurance. Pitcher knew he had given them a workout and had depleted their reserve funds more than a single client should. They had paid, not cheerfully, but they had paid. And they were still paying every day Pitcher had the rental car. Already, someone from his insurance company had called and encouraged him to go car shopping. So with four hours before the computer would come up with an answer – if there was an answer to be had – he would have the time. He pulled on his jacket, picked up his keys, and left the office.

On the other side of the office, Charlie Hume was coming to many of the same conclusions as Pitcher, having done many of the same things the reporter did, and a few inventions of his own. But the results had been much the same.

159

Hume had pointedly ignored Nancy for much of the afternoon, not because he was mad at her – he was, for a few moments, but later he appreciated the humor. He ignored her because he knew it would drive her nuts. And it did. She had left the office at 4:30 with her nose in the air and the high heels of her shoes beating a rapid *Thwack Thwack* rhythm on the parquet floor of the hallway.

Hume paced his office, mumbling to himself as he looked for the umpteenth time at the piece of note paper in his hand. The numbers meant nothing – and yet they had to mean something. Three people – no, make that four, if you count Chance Caine – had died for the contents of that watch.

Not for the first time, he wondered if the numbers perpetrated a fraud. What if, over the course of decades, someone else had taken what had been in the watch and replaced it with a roll of numbers that represented gibberish? But he dismissed the notion. The very delicacy of the opening of the watch convinced him that the brittle roll of paper they had found was genuine, and would certainly have been destroyed by the vial of acid had anyone not in the know tried to open it. And then there was the difficulty that Julian Peebles had in getting the tool, and finding someone who knew enough to warn him not to try to crack the watch without the right procedure.

He forced the matter from his mind – no easy task – and called Linda's cell number, intending to suggest dinner in town. Her voice mail answered. Hanging up he sighed, put on his suit coat and flipped off the lights as he closed the door to his office.

Sy Casio suppressed a smile as he sipped his beer and watched the two men at the table across the room. He couldn't hear a word of what was being said; the two men were talking close together and in whispers. It wasn't easy for a man with a booming broadcaster's voice like Peter McDermott to be quiet – he would have to be conscious of his voice every moment which would make him uneasy. Casio could see the editor fidgeting in the uncomfortable wooden chair. But the chair's comfort didn't seem to bother the old man across the table. He remained casual, comfortable, and seemingly in control.

For a few moments, Casio considered sauntering over to the table and intervening. But he dismissed it. McDermott was a big boy and seemed to be carrying himself well even in a situation with which he was unfamiliar – a situation Casio had been in all too often and knew how to handle.

160

And Casio had finally put the make on the old man's back-up. One of the young women dancing on the tiny wooden section of floor was keeping an eye on the table. While seeming to be stoned, the woman was carefully taking in all that was happening at the table in particular and the room in general. In his periphery, Casio had noticed her checking him out several times, taking in his bulk, his clothing, his own attention to the table across the room, and depending on how professional she was, she may have noticed that his suit was specially tailored to conceal the Browning under his left armpit.

The woman was dancing with another woman who apparently *was* actually stoned. That convinced Casio that he was dealing with someone who knew what she was doing. The backup had managed to find a way to blend in with the atmosphere and patronage of the bar, to the extent that only a highly trained operative – which Casio was – would spot her. He was nearly sure she was armed, but hadn't yet decided where she might keep her weapon.

No matter. Casio preferred things to be out in the open. She had made him, and now he had a make on her.

Casio drank off his beer and ordered a second. He was enjoying the foam head on the glass when McDermott reached his hand behind him at the chair seat level and made a circle out of his thumb and index finger.

Good. McDermott had talked his way past the verbal fencing the two men had obviously been doing, and was now about to get information. Casio turned himself on the stool to where he could pay more attention to the two dancing women than to the men at the table, and did something that only highly trained, well seasoned detectives seemed to be able to do well.

He waited.

Chapter Nineteen

"OK," McDermott finally conceded. "One twentieth of the take, whatever it might be."

Oglesby sat back, satisfied, with a grin.

"Great," he grinned. "Now let's see if that barmaid can find us a sip of quality whiskey to take the taste of sedition out of my mouth whilst I give you the low-down."

He signaled for the waitress, who came swishing back to the table. Oglesby ordered a double Glenfiddich scotch for himself and one for McDermott, who didn't protest.

"I'm going to have to tell you a story," Oglesby said softly as he waited, almost salivating, for his drink.

"Can you start with the name of that woman?" McDermott demanded.

Oglesby waved him off.

"You have to take things in their proper order, Mr. McDermott. You'll get the name. All in good time."

He paused while the waitress served the drinks. From across the room, Casio noticed that McDermott paid for them, and nodded in satisfaction. His job now was to keep his eye on the woman he had pegged as Oglesby's backup.

"American companies did business with the German underground during the war," Oglesby began. "That sounds pretty straightforward, but you have to understand that for political reasons, the U.S. couldn't do business directly with splinter groups, not if they expected to be able to effect a prisoner exchange as the war came to an end."

"So they worked under the table?"

"Way, way, *way* under the table," Oglesby replied, sipping his scotch.

"You're telling me that American companies were profiteering with German resistance fighters during the war?"

Oglesby got a "d'uh" look on his face."

"Mac this may come as a shock to you, but even today, companies with defense contracts are rarely run by Shirley Temple."

"OK, so a few companies did business under the table?"

"More than a few, a lot of companies did business with the undergrounds in France, Belgium and Sweden, to name a few, and that doesn't even include what we're talking about – the German resistance."

"How does that fit in with what we're talking about."

Oglesby drained his scotch and signaled for another. McDermott sipped his, and pulled some bills out of his wallet which he laid on the table.

"Ever hear of Roag Arms?"

McDermott looked off into space for a few moments, then shook his head.

"They were one of two companies that manufactured the Taurus submachine gun – the U.S. version of the German Schmeiser. A simple weapon, easy to field-strip, few moving parts, light weight and easy to maintain."

"How do you know so much about this weapon?" McDermott inquired.

Oglesby smiled.

"It's not necessary for you to know that,"

McDermott elected not to pursue the matter for now.

"Go on."

"The Taurus was almost the exclusive submachine gun weapon used by the German resistance against their own government. Roag also made a useful handgun used almost exclusively by the Resistance.

"So..." McDermott prompted.

"What's important here is how the Resistance got the weapons that were made in Pennsylvania."

"I have to admit, I'm curious as to how they did that," McDermott said. "It's a long way to Germany and there was a war on."

"Yes there was," Oglesby smiled. "It was in all the papers."

McDermott frowned.

"And so...?"

"Like I said, it couldn't be done in the open. In war there's a lot of back-channel politics mixed in with all that killing and mayhem. No American company could do open business with foreign resistance movements, but the U.S. officials turned a blind eye to the clandestine activities. They knew about it, they had to, but no one ever said anything."

"Was the U.S. the only country selling arms to the resistance?"

Oglesby nodded.

"The English couldn't make it happen and besides, they were buying most of their weapons from us, the Sten gun being the one exception. The French were in German hands and the Swedes couldn't create a network that the German Gestapo was unable to penetrate. Thus, the Resistance turned to this one American company that was willing to sell as long as it was all done under the table."

"So how did they do it?" McDermott prompted again.

Oglesby smiled widely.

"That's the interesting part."

"I'm all agog," McDermott said sarcastically, taking another tentative sip of his scotch.

"The German Resistance had agents in this country, sympathetic citizens who were not otherwise serving in the war, and who could be relied on to carry out instructions with discretion. This was real cloak-and-dagger stuff, with all the furtive sneaking about, and all the benefits of being a spy-type – and this was twenty years before James Bond."

"What did these swashbuckling agents do?" McDermott inquired, openly becoming impatient.

"OK," Oglesby responded, "I'll give you the executive summary – but I think later you're going to want the whole story."

McDermott sipped again and nodded. Oglesby motioned for another drink, and the waitress waved acknowledgement.

"The agent would deal with Roag directly, and see to the shipment of the guns to a safe port, a little-used pier in Hamburg. It was the agent's job to pick up the payment when it was smuggled into this country, convert it to cash, pay Roag, and supervise the loading of the weapons onto a tramp steamer, usually one of Liberian registry. The agent would take a cut of the payment to Roag as his or her fee. Simple, yes?"

"You said convert the payment to cash," McDermott interjected. "From what?"

The waitress brought Oglesby's scotch and picked up a couple of the bills McDermott had left on the table, giving him his change and quietly withdrawing.

"Again, not a simple answer," Oglesby said. "The agent I'm talking about – the one who arranged to deliver payment and load the guns, was one of a network of people involved in moving the merchandise. You have to understand that the Resistance wasn't the only one that had agents working in this country. The Nazi regime did too, and they knew

165

about the clandestine sales of guns and would move heaven and earth to stop it."

"And that's where the cloak-and-dagger stuff came in?" McDermott inquired.

Oglesby sipped and nodded.

"Well, after all, it was war, and it's kind of natural that the two factions would try to one-up each other in the spy business," McDermott mused.

"You don't know the half of it," Oglesby returned.

"Oh?"

"I said it was long before James Bond, but I have to tell you, James Bond couldn't measure up," Oglesby snapped, raising his voice slightly. He realized he was talking loud enough to be heard away from the table, so he moved back across the table and continued in an angry stage whisper.

"These people were the real deal, they understood clandestine operations, they understood that they could get killed. They didn't do a double-back-flip, rub out the bad guy, and then make a wise crack and order a martini while they fondled a balloon-chested babe in some den of iniquity. They kept to the dark corners, they dealt with shady people who had no scruples whatsoever, and if they did get into bed with some woman they had to make sure she didn't put a hole in him right in the middle of the festivities. It happened. This was serious business, McDermott. That's the first thing you have to understand. I won't sit here and listen to you make light of it. Even if you're not making light of it, don't make light of it. You got that?"

McDermott drained his own scotch glass and gestured for another. Oglesby held up two fingers. The waitress waved.

"All right, Mr. Oglesby, I won't make light of it," McDermott back-pedaled. "I didn't think I was."

Oglesby backed away slightly.

"Well just don't, that's all," he returned, as the waitress brought to more scotches and took the money from McDermott's dwindling pile of bills.

McDermott nodded and made strong eye contact with the older man.

"An agent would bring the converted funds into the country and hide them in a safe place. That agent would rendezvous with another agent, and pass on a trinket that contained the location of the money. The second agent would then retrieve the payment and deliver it to a trusted person inside the Roag Arms company. Then that second agent would arrange to transport the guns by train to a secure pier in Baltimore where they were taken by blacked-out ship to Hamburg. There, the resistance took the guns and ammunition and distributed them as needed. Get it?"

"Sounds like a good working system," McDermott remarked, taking another swallow of his drink.

"It was when it worked – and it worked many, many times. But there were other times when the opposition won."

"Tell me about the opposition."

Oglesby drained his glass in a single gulp and wiped his mouth on his sleeve, gesturing for yet another drink.

"They were good. They had to be. They were agents of the Gestapo and the German *Abwehr*, their answer to the OSS, or Office of Strategic Services."

"That later became the CIA," McDermott filled in.

Oglesby continued as though McDermott had not spoken.

"Their goal was to disrupt the smooth operation of moving the guns. And the best way to do that was to intercept the agent who was carrying the trinket containing the location of the payment – then go get the payment. They'd get a cut for their trouble, and the rest would be transferred by another system of agents into the Nazi funds deposited in U.S. banks. That would be used to buy information and in some cases buy politicians."

"Bribery too?" McDermott exclaimed.

Oglesby shrugged.

"It was war," he said simply.

"And people can get killed," McDermott finished.

"People did," Oglesby said as the waitress served his new drink and withdrew. "Like when the Nazi agent would intercept the Resistance agent? The Nazi agent would kill the opposing agent and take the trinket from his or her warm body."

"They used women?" McDermott asked, incredulously.

"Both sides did. They had the ridiculous idea that a woman wouldn't draw such a drastic response. That didn't work for either side."

"Sounds rough."

"Rough isn't the word for it," Oglesby said firmly. "It was brutal. It was instant death if you made a mistake, if your cover was blown, of a Nazi agent got wind of who you were, you were dead. It was that simple."

"You mentioned a trinket," McDermott said. "Can you tell me more about that?"

Oglesby eyed him speculatively.

"Why?"

McDermott shrugged.

"Call it reporter's curiosity."

That seemed to satisfy the older man, who sat back and seemed to relax a few moments before he continued.

"The location of the payment was carried inside a watch. It was a watch with its works removed so there was room inside."

McDermott could have shouted out loud, but he had a useful poker face, and he kept his expression impassive.

"Sounds like easy pickings for the enemy agents," he mused.

"It was," Oglesby agreed. "At least until the resistance worked out a failsafe system. They installed a small vial of acid inside the watch. If it wasn't opened properly, the acid vial would break and destroy the contents. There was a special tool that would open the watch safely, and it absolutely could not be done without it."

"Did the enemy ever figure a way to overcome that?" McDermott wanted to know.

Oglesby shook his head definitely.

"No. Even if the Nazis intercepted an agent carrying the payment location, the acid always seemed to do its job," he said.

"You certainly seem to know a lot about this system," McDermott said. "How do I know you're not just making all this up?"

Oglesby exhaled noisily.

"Listen, McDermott," he snapped. "If you don't find what you're looking for, I get nothing. It's not to my advantage to lie to you at this point. I need you as much as you need me."

"Agreed," McDermott nodded. "So give, Oglesby. How do you know so much about all this?"

Oglesby grinned widely. "Simple," he said. "I was one of the couriers."

"Baloney!" McDermott scoffed. "You're not old enough to have been into that!"

Oglesby drank off his scotch and swirled the liquid around in his mouth before swallowing.

"How old do you think I am, young fellow?" he asked, casually.

"I figure you for about 70, perhaps 72 or 73, but no older than that.

Oglesby laughed aloud with genuine mirth.

"Ninety-one in December," he said with a huge grin.

McDermott echoed his grin.

"You sure could have fooled me," the editor said.

Oglesby nodded again and signaled for yet another round.

"Drink up, youngster, and I'll tell you everything else you've asked about – and a few things you didn't."

McDermott held up his glass. Half his scotch was still there.

"I'm good," he said.

"Bullshit," the old man cackled. "If I don't teach you one more thing today, I'm going to show you that the spy business must at all times be liberally laced with good booze."

The waitress set new glasses in front of both men, and McDermott paid again from the money on the table before him.

"How much money was involved in the purchase of the guns?" McDermott asked casually.

"Each delivery was for two million dollars American," Oglesby said. "There were twenty successful deliveries during the war."

"How many unsuccessful?" McDermott asked, sensing a payoff.

"Completely unsuccessful – meaning the money was never delivered and the guns were never transferred?"

"Uh huh."

"Just one."

McDermott stole a furtive look toward Casio and was bold enough to wink. Casio returned it.

"And the money," McDermott interjected. "What did they convert it into?"

"Diamonds, my boy," Oglesby smirked, licking his lips. "Diamonds."

Chapter Twenty

The killer sat in the Bondo car outside the Madhatter keeping a close eye on the canopied entrance to the club. Several people came in, and several others left. The killer knew that impatience was an often fatal disease under these circumstances, but time was passing and too little was happening. Impatient, the killer opened the door of the nondescript car. Fingers touched cold steel and ascertained that the weapon was there, ready to do the work it was made for. The killer pulled a collar tight against the evening's coolness and headed back for the entrance to the lounge.

Rod Pitcher stared dumbly at the computer screen, which displayed white numerals on a blue screen, the numbers changing once every three-tenths of a second. The reporter tried to concentrate, but the numbers changed far too fast, and meant far too little.

Charlie Hume looked over his shoulder, equally nonplussed, staring almost cross-eyed as the numbers disgorged onto the screen, blinked, and disappeared, only to be replaced in the blink of an eye with another set of numbers.

It was at Charlie's suggestion that Pitcher typed in the numbers from the watch to a Google search field. The result was a cascade of numerical combinations that was hypnotic, but basically meaningless.

"How are we going to know when we see what we're looking for?" Hume asked.

Pitcher's eyes didn't' move from the screen.

"I haven't the faintest idea," he said, in a monotone.

"Then why are we doing this?" Hume asked in roughly the same type of voice.

"I haven't the faintest idea," Pitcher returned in exactly the same voice.

"Then shut the son of a bitch off," Hume demanded, tearing his eyes away from the screen and turning away.

Pitcher sighed in relief and hit the ESC key on his keyboard. The numbers mercifully stopped. He "X'ed" out of the field and leaned back in his chair with his eyes closed, trying to purge the sight of the rapidly changing numbers from his numbed brain. At length he forced himself to stand and push his chair under his desk. He walked from his cubicle in the newsroom, still staggering a bit from the numbing numbers, and passed through the empty anteroom into Hume's inner office. The publisher was just settling onto the small couch that sat against the wall to Pitcher's left. Pitcher turned the overstuffed chair in front of Hume's desk and sat.

"Any more bright ideas, Charlie?"

Hume scratched his head and propped up his feet on a tiny coffee table.

"Not at the moment. But we have to come up with one, those numbers are the key to something that's important enough for people to get killed."

Pitcher stared at the ceiling.

"Tell me about it."

"Where's Mac?"

Pitcher returned his gaze to the publisher.

"I assume he's still over in Washington trying to get information out of that guy who called about the Lady in Red's picture."

"Let me know when he gets back."

"OK," Pitcher said, making no effort to move.

"As soon as he gets back," Hume prompted.

"OK," Pitcher said, stifling a yawn.

"Go away," Hume snapped.

"OK," Pitcher said, launching himself out of the chair.

Pitcher recrossed the sales and executive wing of the newspaper offices and passed through the double glass doors that led to the newsroom. He stopped by McDermott's corner office on the off-chance that the editor might have returned, but no, his door was locked and the blinds were drawn in his picture window that allowed him a full view of the desks and cubicles of his editorial staff. No light shown around the blinds. So Pitcher was positive that McDermott had not returned. He turned left and walked down a corridor of cubicles until he reached his own, oversized work space. He snapped on the desk lamp and sat down, contemplating the dark overhead fluorescent fixtures above. Pitcher hated the garish light of the overhead, and when he was forced to endure it, he invariably went home with a headache. Instead he preferred the soft light of the three incandescent lamps he placed strategically around his little room.

He contemplated firing up his computer and running the numbers again, but that was one headache he didn't want right now. He was hungry and thirsty and tired felt himself becoming cranky. At times like these he would have enjoyed talking to McDermott. Their traded repartee never ceased to rejuvenate him. Not much chance of that, with McDermott over in D.C. talking to some guy who might know something that could unlock this whole mystery. In the meantime, he had what he had to work with.

Numbers.

A sequence of numbers that has to mean something, but not even his computer's internet access, with all the knowledge available there, the sum total of man's knowledge, Pitcher believed, and still the numbers remained an enigma.

Pitcher tried his best to push the puzzle from his mind, tried not to think about how those numbers that came from the courier watch somehow tied in with the killings of members of his family. He was sure that when the answer was supposed to present itself, it would. It always had. He was simply hopeful that he lived to see it, and that no one else got killed in the meantime.

Pitcher's rumbling stomach finally overcame the pain behind his eyes that he got when he over-contemplated the numbers. He rose from his chair, picked up his keys and let himself out of the newspaper offices in Baltimore's Inner Harbor. He got into his rental car and pulled out into the night.

Pitcher did not see the beauty of the harbor area, the result of years of political wrangling and millions of dollars in investment that turned the grimy seaport into an upscale residential and commercial area and mammoth tourist attraction. He didn't notice the historic submarine and Coast Guard cutter moored in the piers a half-block from his office. He turned left and drove aimlessly.

He took the Baltimore-Washington Highway until it crossed Suitland, and got off. Without knowing exactly why, Pitcher found himself driving toward Southeast Washington. He seemed to be little more than automaton behind the wheel of a relatively unfamiliar car. He knew where he was headed; he just didn't know the purpose of it.

He would return to where it began.

Forty minutes after he left Baltimore, he stopped the car in front of a grimy Rexall drug store that he knew had a lunch counter. He locked the car with his key fob and found a place to sit on a cracked and decaying swivel stool at the counter. The menu was clipped on the edge of the counter across from him. He ordered a cheeseburger and onion rings, and a Pepsi, and ate them absently, not noticing, nor making a mental note to make jokes about the large amount of grease that seemed to slather all over his food. He nibbled and sipped until everything on his plate was gone, stifled the urge to hurl, paid and left.

Outside, night was falling, and Pitcher turned and looked down the darkened avenue. Street lights didn't last long in this God-forsaken area of the capital city. Its denizens preferred the cover of darkness, preferred to cloak their movements in the shadows, and they would scatter like cockroaches when light invaded their shield.

A half-block away, Pitcher could see the shadowy profile of the Metropole Hotel. He knew, just to the right of the hotel edifice, there was the boarded-up Blue Heron night club. He also knew that his life had been a whole lot simpler before he was summoned here, less than a week before. He walked toward the hotel, heedless of the danger from the night's predators. Humanity gives of an aura of its feelings, particularly when danger threatens. No mugger, no stick-up artist, not even a half-crazed crack-head would have dared challenge Pitcher tonight, so obvious and vibrant was the aura he gave off. He was an absolutely determined man as he strode with a purpose toward the long-dead hotel and its bandaged appendage.

Pitcher was drawn inexorably to the source of the mystery, the moldy darker-than-dark building where his cousin was found dead, where he had been called, routed from his blankets and the company of Samantha Parker, into a mystery that crossed time and space, a mystery that had proven fatal to three members of his family and had tried to prove so to himself and, he thought, Peter McDermott as well. And McDermott was more than his boss. The editor was Pitcher's best friend. And on a level just below that, his apartment had been ransacked and his car destroyed.

Pitcher stopped at the intersection of three streets, a phenomenon quite common in Washington D.C., where numbered streets and lettered streets intercepted named streets with alarming regularity. He stood at the intersection of Potomac and 19th and C Streets, SE, swathed in a cloak of darkness and looked before him at two buildings that were darker still.

For a moment, Pitcher tried to force his body to turn and walk back up the street to his car, which he would drive back to Baltimore and home to Samantha. But he could feel the pull of the buildings, particularly the one to his right, where it all had started. Without knowing how or why, he found himself walking toward the boarded-up Blue Heron night club. He stepped under the peeling marquis, his shoes kicking up a generation of dust and disturbing various pieces of trash, debris and unspeakable things left behind by human flotsam that sought shelter or seclusion here.

He tried the front door and found it locked. It was the same door he had entered not so long ago at the behest of Detective Fred Mattingly, when the body of Reesa Lowenstein had been found on the stage, stretched out in death amid the dust of ages.

Involuntarily, he shivered.

Pitcher tried another door under the marquis and found it equally impenetrable, so he walked toward the side of the building farthest away from the Metropole, following the dirty brick wall until he came to what he believed to be the stage door. He grasped the knob and his hand came away covered in dust – but before it did, the door gave a little. Just a little. Brushing his hands on the legs of his suit pants, he grasped the filthy knob again and pressed with his arms and his right hip. He reared back and hit the door with his shoulder and hip and was surprised to find it opened before him. He pulled a small pencil flashlight from his inside jacket pocket and played its beam across the threshold.

Cautiously he followed the beam into the building and pushed the door closed behind him. Shining the light around him to get his bearings, he saw the remains of the stage rigging – ropes and counter-weight systems, belaying bars and light clamps, all dusty and cobwebbed. He pushed himself forward and up a small flight of cement stairs which took him into the stage-left wing. One whole wall was taken up by an ancient Altman lighting control console, with its oversized lever-like dimmers. Pitcher noted that all the levers were in the fully down – or off – position.

His eyes were becoming accustomed to the darkness, and he could see more in the beam of the tiny light. He tiptoed his way across the bridge wing past the rotting draperies – the tormentors and legs that helped divide the entranceways to the bandstand that still, after decades of disuse, contained several music stands and wooden folding chairs. He stopped and closed his eyes for a moment and he could almost hear the musicians tuning up and preparing to play for the customers with Arnie Bigalow at the baton and Chance Caine on trumpet. His place would have been right above Pitcher's head at the top of the riser, stage-left.

Pitcher opened his eyes and continued down-stage until he found the stairs that would take him to the orchestra section of the audience, where tables and chairs once held the Washington elite who mingled in the club with the famous, and the infamous, all the way to the notorious.

Pitcher could see the disturbances in the dust from the body of his cousin, and the footprints of the police officers and detectives who investigated the strange death. He knew that these phenomena would be short lived – that in weeks, perhaps a little longer, they would disappear beneath new dust from who-knows-where, and they would remain thus buried until the building itself was torn down – or fell down – around them.

Pitcher scanned ahead of him with his light and moved toward the center-stage apron and then beyond, focusing on the opposite wall of the club. The dust was unbelievable, stinging his eyes and gunking up his lungs, making it hard to see and hard to breathe.

He turned left at the wall and moved toward the front of the club, away from the stage. About halfway up the wall he found a door. Even through layers of dust he could see it had an arrow and the words, "to hotel." It was open. He went through it and passed through a short corridor, emerging into an equally dusty, but much smaller room that appeared, at one time, to have been a hotel lobby. But there was something different here, something he couldn't put his finger on right away. But it was different enough to send a tingle down his spine that he recognized as his internal warning system. He could also feel the hair on the back of his neck standing up. These are sensations that are designed to trigger the human's 'fight or flight' instinct, and Pitcher's first impulse was flight, to turn and run back through the darkened corridor and night club and to the door he forced open to get in here. He hoped he could still find it.

But to a reporter there is a stronger instinct, there is the need to know, an innate curiosity that won't abate until all questions have been answered. Pitcher took a deep breath, coughed some of the dust out of his system, and moved deeper into the hotel.

Then he had it.

There was a power hum coming from a darkened fluorescent light fixture nearby. Pitcher followed the sound, walking cautiously, until he found himself facing a bank of elevators. Idly, he pressed the UP button, then jumped, startled, as he heard the sound of machinery powering up, and engaging. A moment later, the elevator door in front of him slid open, revealing a brightly-lit car. Pitcher stared for a long moment, mouth agape, before he snapped off his pencil flash and stepped into the car. The doors closed automatically. Pitcher turned to face the doors, replacing the pencil flash in his shirt pocket, and waited.

The lit figure on the floor indicator showed "3" when the car stopped and the doors parted, and again, Pitcher stood agape.

Far from mimicking the dust and disuse of the first floor, this part of the hotel was softly lit, immaculately clean and well appointed. He could hear the hum of air conditioners somewhere nearby, and felt a wisp of cool air cross the skin of his arms and neck as he stepped from the elevator car onto the carpeted floor. He stepped gingerly, not knowing quite what to expect, and reeling from the stark contrast of the lobby versus the third floor.

He passed several room doors that were tightly closed, and he paid them scant attention, beyond noticing that they were clean, dust-free and obviously locked.

But the second-to-last door to the end of the cream-colored corridor was ajar; using his fingertips he pushed the door open and found himself in a well-furnished, comfortable hotel room. Just inside and to the right was the door to the bathroom. Across from that, to his left, were sliding doors – obviously a closet. He stepped inside to find a small refrigerator, a desk with a cord that was obviously internet access, a television set, one of the new High Definition flat-screen sets, and a large bed covered with an immaculate comforter. There were also night stands and a table and chairs a grade better than the usual hotel furnishings.

Pitcher tiptoed into the room and looked around. There was a manila folder on the desk. He took his mechanical pencil from his pocket and used its point to flip the folder open, and his blood ran cold.

There, on top of a small stack of photos, was a color picture of Reesa Lowenstein. His mouth agape yet another time, Pitcher used the pencil to flip the photo over. He saw an address and a phone number that he assumed was Reesa's, and a penciled date below that – the day before Pitcher was called to identify her body in the night club next door.

Pitcher stepped into the bathroom and pulled two tissues from a box built into the vanity and returned to the desk. Using the tissues over his hands, he spread out the contents of the folder. Photos of the two Albert Lowensteins, both of whom met their deaths in mysterious ways and both of whom were related to him stared up from the desk and burned themselves into his memory. He pulled his cell phone and took a picture of the photos on the desk, before restacking them as they were and replacing them in the folder. Quickly and furtively he looked around. There were pieces of costume jewelry and a suitcase full of female clothes, but a terse examination showed no identification in the suitcase, nor in a tote bag that contained a calculator, a Blackberry cell phone and two boxes of 7.62 ammunition.

177

He was scared to death of being discovered. By whom, he had no idea. He knew he would have to leave quickly. So he did his best to return the things in the room as he found them. He took pictures of the room from several angles with his cell phone camera. That done, he pocketed the tissues he'd been using and tiptoed out of the room, returning the door as he found it.

Pitcher didn't summon the elevator as he returned to the end of the hall, but looked for and found the stairs. He needed his pencil flash again, because the stairwells were unlighted and as dusty as the rest of the building had been – the dust shocked him for a moment after the experience of the clean and orderly third floor. He used the tissues again, to keep the dust from dirtying his hands on the steel banister as he eased his way down the stairs, leaving footprints in his wake.

To his horror, his pencil flash dimmed noticeably as he completed his downward climb, and he was worried that he wouldn't be able to find his way out before it went out completely, leaving him to grope in the dark in a forgotten building.

He could make out his footprints made on the way in, but they were already beginning to fill with dust. Carefully he picked his way back the way he came. The light dimmed even more in the dank corridor between the hotel and the night club, and he quickened his pace back into the other building, and to the stage. He was walking up the stage-left stairs when his light died completely. Frustrated he jammed it into his pants pocket and groped his way through the pitch-black backstage area to the outside door. Finally, his fingers grasped the knob and he yanked the door open and stepped out into the night.

Even the night air of southeast Washington smelled good to his soot-invaded nose. The gasses and hydrocarbons that seemed to permeate the air more so in this part of the city than even the downtown Federal Triangle seemed sweet and delicious. He leaned against the wall for a few seconds, savoring the sensation and purging his lungs and sinuses of the dust and grit from the inside. At length, his strength renewed, he made his way up a half block to the Rexall drug store where he treated himself to another Pepsi to take the taste of the dust out of his mouth.

Pitcher couldn't get over what he had seen in the musty old building. He knew he would need at least the night to sort out the images in his mind. After that he would talk about them to McDermott. Not before.

He pulled out his cell phone and called up the pictures he took in the hotel. He emailed them to his personal address, with the thought of printing them out at home. They would be important when he accosted the editor in the office tomorrow morning.

With that matter resolved, Pitcher drank off his Pepsi, paid, and left.

Chapter Twenty-One

"This was a real game of cat-and-mouse," Oglesby says, wiping his mouth on his sleeve which contained an unsteady hand. With the other, equally unsteady hand, he gestured to the waitress yet again. She nodded and headed for the bar, and McDermott pulled another handful of bills from his wallet.

"And James Bond couldn't measure up?" McDermott asked, sarcastically.

Oglesby shook his head definitively.

"Not in a million years," he said.

"I assume we're talking about the gun transfer that didn't work right," McDermott prompted.

The old man searched his memory, rolling his eyes as he did so, trying to remain cohesive under the debilitating effects of the alcohol. After a moment, he seemed to have it.

"Yyyyyes," he said hesitantly. "This was the one that didn't go down properly."

He stopped talking and his eyes seemed to go vacant for a time.

"So what happened?" McDermott prompted after a moment.

The waitress put a fresh drink in front of Oglesby, took a few bills from McDermott's stack, and removed Oglesby's empty glass from the table. Oglesby leered after her, then shook his head in an effort to clear his thoughts. McDermott looked at Casio, across the room, and surreptitiously waved his hand. Casio nodded and whispered to the barmaid.

"The old man's had enough," he said.

"Says who?" the barmaid snapped.

"Says Andrew Jackson," said Casio, sliding a twenty dollar bill across the bar. The barmaid picked it up, folded it, and stuck it in her bra.

"I hear ya, Mr. Jackson."

Across the room, Oglesby appeared to be looking inside his forehead for the right words. He finally found them, and returned his gaze to McDermott.

"OK," he said, breathing heavily. McDermott winced at the strong odor of used scotch.

"It was the last year of the war," he said, clear for the moment. He picked up his glass to sip, but McDermott placed a hand on his wrist and the drink went back onto the table untasted. "The final transfer of guns to the German resistance never took place because the payment never reached the manufacturer. The payment was converted to stones and was in the United States, but the Resistance agent in D.C. was unable to affect the transfer to the back-channel agent representing Roag Arms.

"I won't bore you with the gory details other than to say that three agents – one for the Resistance and two for the Germans, were killed during that last year in an effect to recover the location of the stones."

"Never found?" McDermott inquired, straight faced.

Oglesby shook his head. He continued, sipping as he talked.

"The information on the whereabouts of the payment was carried in a hollow watch. It was brought in from Germany on the wrist of a crew member aboard a tramp steamer and transferred, in a harbor tavern, I guess, to the wrist of another agent who carried it to the representative of the arms company, who then took it, made certain the payment location was inside, then arranged to have the guns trucked back to that same tramp steamer that would take them to Hamburg."

"I've got all that," McDermott said

"Do you know that there was a vial of acid in the watch that would break and destroy the contents if the watch wasn't opened properly?"

McDermott's face remained an impassive mask.

"Interesting," was all he said. "It worked through the whole war."

"It worked until 1945," Oglesby said. "By that time the Nazi agents had their number."

He gestured to the waitress for another round, but the barmaid gave a high sign and she suddenly busied herself polishing a tabletop.

"In 1945, the swap from the tramp steamer to the agent for the resistance in this country went as planned, and the agent got to Washington D.C. as planned. After that it unspooled."

"Unspooled?" McDermott asked."

"Unspooled," Oglesby repeated, eying McDermott's unfinished second drink.

182

"Someone cold-cocked the Resistance agent and took the watch. It was traced to a Nazi agent, whom someone also cold-cocked and took the watch, where it was later found back in Resistance hands. This time the Resistance agent was murdered and again the watch disappeared."

"Quite a little game of 'who's got it now,'" McDermott commented, irritably.

Oglesby hesitated, holding up a restraining hand.

"Hang on a minute, let me think," Oglesby slurred, starring at the ceiling. He appeared to be gathering strength; he closed his eyes and balled his fists, then reached across the table and picked up McDermott's drink, which he downed in a single gulp. For some reason, that seemed to help.

"Quite a game indeed, Mr. McDermott. It went on for nearly six months, switching back and forth – but that wasn't all. It seemed that no matter which side had the watch, the other side had the tool that would open it safely."

"There was only one tool?" McDermott asked, his voice beginning to drip venom. The editor was a mild social drinker and he had little patience with drunks.

"There were half a dozen tools, but they were closely guarded. The tools made the rounds the same as the watch did – and there were even a few bogus watches slipped into the mix, just to add to the intrigue."

"For six months?" McDermott snapped, no longer disguising his irritation.

"Yes, for six months," Oglesby snapped back. "And their frustration was not unlike yours, now. So much so that for the last exchange of the watch, things got nasty."

"What do you mean 'nasty,'" McDermott demanded.

"Maybe you'd better hear about the players, Mr. McDermott. They are the ones you came here to pump me about. I'll save you the trouble."

"Good," said McDermott, rapping his knuckles on the table. "Start with..."

Oglesby waved him off

"I'll start with whom I wish to start with, if you don't mind, Mr. McDermott."

The editor leaned back in his chair, nodding. Oglesby got a self-satisfied look on his face and leaned across the table.

"The man you know as Chance Caine was really a fellow named Karl Elmendorf. He was an operative with the Resistance faction in the United States. He was born in Utah, and recruited by the Resistance out of the University of Illinois. He was 4-F so he couldn't serve in the military – being a courier for the Resistance was his way of fighting the Nazis.

"So Chance Caine was a spy..." McDermott mused aloud.

Oglesby smiled widely.

"He was a good one, and his cover as a trumpet player in that night club was nearly perfect. But somehow, no one knows exactly how, sometime in early 1946, his cover was blown. We think someone in his own organization sold him off, but since they only knew one or two of our colleagues – for safety's sake – we may never know how it happened and who sold him out.

"He was taken out live, on stage, at the Blue Heron night club by a Nazi femme-fatale named Ursula Spiedel. Just as Caine stood up to play his solo, she took a gun from under the table and shot him as he performed. During the pandemonium that followed the bold, public shooting, she ran forward and took the courier watch off his wrist, and disappeared from the room. She was with a guy named Enoch Chambers, which I think was an alias for a particularly nasty Gestapo agent named Armand Wicht. After they left the nightclub in Southeast Washington, they met up with a third agent she believed to be a Nazi sympathizer, next door in the old Metropole Hotel. There they were to make their escape and find someone with a watch key, recover the stones, and escape back to Germany with the payment."

"Wait a minute, wait a minute," McDermott shouted, standing up. "You spin a good yarn, old man, but you couldn't possibly know all this."

Oglesby tented his fingers on the table.

"Oh, but I can," he said, enigmatically.

McDermott folded his arms over his chest.

"Oh? Pray, tell, how?"

Oglesby grinned wider.

"I was there," he said simply.

The killer stood in the shadow of the short vestibule just inside the Madhatter doorway and kept a sharp eye on the table across the room. The discussion there was low and intense, that was obvious. But the killer couldn't hear. Instead, the black-clad figure paid particular attention to the number of times the waitress visited the table with new drinks. The killer noted that usually only one drink would be delivered, and the older man in the business suit would take the glass. It wouldn't be long now, the opportunity would present itself. The killer waited until all the attention in the room was directed elsewhere, then sauntered across the floor.

The killer passed Casio with a normal step that was specifically aimed at not attracting the detective's attention. The killer was gratified when Casio didn't give the walking figure a second glance. The killer pushed open a door and stepped inside, letting it close on its own.

"I was there," Oglesby said again. "Chambers and Speidel and the third man met on the third floor of the Metropole Hotel. They saw the writing on the wall, they knew the war was nearly over. Their thought was to hide there until the heat was off. Then someone would find out how to open the watch safely, and they, the three of them, would find the stones, hidden somewhere in Washington D.C. After that they would get on a ship that would take them to Argentina where some of the ex-Nazis were trying to set up a puppet government that would take over in Germany at the right time."

"You were there," McDermott scoffed.

"I was the third man," Oglesby affirmed, unconcerned about McDermott's skepticism. "When we got onto the third floor of the Metropole, I left to use a rest room and Chambers and Spiedel tussled. I came back to see them locked in combat and I intervened. I won't bore you with the details of the fight, but as it ended up, Spiedel was shot and killed and Chambers was wounded and escaped. And when he escaped, he took the watch with him.

"But remember what I said about this being a game of cat and mouse? Chambers got less than a block before he had his head stove in, and the watch was taken yet again. This time it was a Jewish agent who recognized Chambers as a Nazi agent.. He beat Chambers to death, took the watch and disappeared."

"Do we know who he was?" McDermott asked, enraptured.

Oglesby nodded.

"He was a young man named Albert Lowenstein."

"Lowenstein!" McDermott exclaimed involuntarily.

Oglesby nodded.

"We were told he had passed the watch on. That was what was supposed to happen, so no one bothered him after the new Nazi state collapsed before it even got off the ground. He went on to live a long life, and he died just recently – and we have now discovered that he had the watch all the time. He kept it in a wall safe in his home"

"How did you find out that he had the watch?"

Oglesby studied the floor.

"Mr. McDermott, some questions are better off unanswered. That is one of them."

"So who exactly are you?"

Oglesby sighed heavily.

"I can't tell you everything," he said softly. "Suffice it to say I was working for two masters, the anti-Nazi Resistance in Germany, and the United States Government. I posed as a Nazi sympathizer, quite effectively as you can see. Both of them paid me quite a hefty salary to keep an eye on the Nazi spies – all of whom I thought I knew. But Speidel was a new one on me. Ballsy bitch, she was, snuffing that guy in front of an audience. That shows a certain panache, don't you agree?"

McDermott shook his head and Oglesby's smile faded.

Who killed Ursula Speidel?" McDermott asked softly.

"I did," Oglesby said with devastating simplicity.

There was a pause as McDermott adjusted to the idea. Oglesby picked up the conversation thread.

"OK. Anyway, Lowenstein's daughter married a man named Wallace Pitcher. Their son is your reporter, Rod Pitcher."

"And that's why Pitcher's family is being targeted?"

Oglesby nodded. Throughout his talk he had slurred his words a little, but appeared to have remained fairly coherent. Now, as the whiskey came back for its boomerang effect, he was having problems concentrating.

"Someone thought the heirs to Lowenstein's estate got the watch. My guess, and it's only that, is that your killer or killers were tracking the watch as it passed from heir to heir, and each of them was killed for it – but apparently the heirs were one step ahead of the killer."

"Apparently," McDermott agreed. "And now they think Rod Pitcher has the watch?"

Oglesby shrugged unevenly as the whiskey began to weigh him down.

"If they do, your friend is in terrible danger."

"Mr. Oglesby, do you have any idea who the killer might be?"

"Again, it's a guess, but I'd say they were the descendents of Elmendorf, trying to get the watch back. And it doesn't look like they're saying Pretty Please."

"Specifics, Mr. Oglesby, do you know who the killer is?"

Oglesby adopted another blank stare, apparently trying to get his mind to focus. It took several moments for the lights to come back on in his eyes.

"Yes, I think I might have the answer for you," he said, scraping back his chair. "But first, that scotch is doing a number on me, and I gotta pee."

He pulled himself to his feet and staggered unsteadily toward a blank wall. The waitress intercepted him and carefully guided him to the door of the men's room.

"You on your own, now, Hun," she said as Oglesby pushed the door open and reeled inside.

Casio had watched Oglesby's odyssey to the rest room with faint amusement. When the door closed behind him, Casio let his eyes sweep the room.

The woman in the miniskirt that he had pegged as Oglesby's second was pretty much where she had been before, bopping up and down out of time from the juke box music, and placed in a position where she could take in the entire room. Casio nodded, satisfied, to himself.

A moment later, a dark figure, face obscured by a slouch hat, emerged from the restroom and strode to the outside door with a quick gait. Red flags rose in Casio's mind, and he stared after the stygian figure for a moment, then eased off the bar stool he had occupied for the better part of the last two hours.

"Mac," he called, *sotto voce*.

The editor got up from the table and stepped quickly to the detective's side.

"Check on him will you?" Casio said, urgently. "I think I might have missed something."

McDermott nodded and stepped into the men's room.

At first he saw no one. He looked around and noticed that the room was eerily quiet.

"Mr. Oglesby?" he called aloud.

No answer.

There were two wooden toilet stalls against the far wall. McDermott pushed open the door of the first one and saw nothing. The second was locked.

In the bar room, Casio saw a change in the demeanor of the mini-skirted second. She was staring intently at the restroom door. Moments passed. When the door didn't open, she stepped toward it and pushed it open with an audible bang, stepping inside after the *North Bay Times* editor. She got into the room just as McDermott's heel crashed against the stall door, shattering the wood and knocking it off its hinges. Inside the stall, McDermott could see the sprawled figure of Harry Oglesby, lying supine in a spreading pool of blood that was oozing from two holes in the center of his chest.

The woman hiked up the front of her mini-skirt revealing a tiny holster in the inside of her left thigh. From it she pulled a Fie Guardian 25 caliber pistol, snapping off the safety as she drew. But before she could get the gun level, she head four telltale clicks from very close behind her. Turning quickly, she found herself looking into the bore of a Browning 9mm automatic, held in a rock steady hand belonging to Sy Casio. Without a word, Casio held out his empty left hand. Mollified, the woman slapped her weapon into the hand and turned to face the wall near the sink. McDermott was on the floor next to Oglesby.

"He's alive," McDermott said to no one in particular.

Casio pulled open the door, and without taking his eyes off the woman, shouted to the barmaid.

"We need an ambulance and the police here right now," he said, letting the door close on its hydraulic device. Casio could see Oglesby moving his lips. McDermott put his ear next to the man's mouth and listened. Casio watched as Oglesby's face turned a deathly white and his lips stopped moving. McDermott straightened and pressed two fingers against Oglesby's neck just below the right ear. He turned to Casio and shook his head.

"You can forget the ambulance," he said.

Casio nodded and let himself take a moment to think. Things were happening fast.

"Get out of here, Mac. Go and warn Pitcher. He's in some serious danger, probably Hume also. Go and warn them."

McDermott nodded and rose from his position on the bloody floor. He stopped only long enough to make sure he had no blood on his clothes, blood that would attract attention to him, then he tried to slide past Casio to the door.

"Wait a minute, Mac," Casio said. "What'd he say?"

McDermott raised his left eyebrow.

"He said 'End Seize.'"

"'End Seize?'"

"That's what it sounded like," McDermott affirmed. It was all raspy and bubbly but that's what I think he said."

Casio's lips pursed, and he beckoned toward the door with his head.

"Get out of here before the police come," he said.

McDermott locked eyes with the detective for a moment, then yanked the door open and he was gone.

Chapter Twenty-Two

Sy Casio's hands were already in the air when the uniformed D.C. police officer drew down on him. The detective had the muzzle of his Nine pointed skyward and his finger away from the trigger.

"Put the gun down, Mister," the cop commanded.

Gingerly, Casio set the weapon on the tiled floor and stood again, hands still elevated.

"My ID and my gun permit are in the left-hand inside jacket pocket. You'll also find paperwork on my visit to D.C. police headquarters before I began working as an operative.

The officer that had given the order holstered his weapon as his partner provided cover. The uniformed officer reached into Casio's pocket and pulled out a leather wallet. Opening it, he saw Casio's investigator's license, a folded paper from the D.C. police, and his gun permit. He spent several second perusing them, having stepped back out of Casio's arm's length, and his partner kept the Glock 9 millimeter trained unerringly on Casio's chest. At length, the first cop handed Casio back the wallet and motioned to his partner, who lowered his weapon.

"Thank you, Mr. Casio," the cop said. "What do we have here?"

Casio pointed to the toilet stall.

"There's a dead man in there," he said. "Apparently shot twice." Casio indicated the woman who was still facing against the wall near the men's room sink.

"This is his back-up," he said, reaching into his suit coat outside left-hand pocket. "Here's her gun."

He dropped the Fie Guardian 25 caliber semiautomatic into the surprised officer's outstretched hand. He looked at the weapon and then at the woman in the corner.

"Did she kill him?"

Casio shook his head.

"Not from the look of those holes. And I think you'll find her gun hasn't been fired."

The uniformed officer smelled the barrel of the small weapon and handed it to his partner. He also sniffed the barrel of Casio's weapon, which he then returned. Casio replaced his weapon in the holster under his left armpit, butt up and facing forward. His coat dropped back into place perfectly concealing the weapon.

"Besides, Casio said, "I watched her come into the room and to the best of my knowledge, the man in the stall had already been shot. I saw her draw the weapon and I took it away from her."

"So who iced this guy?" the second officer asked, confused.

"Did anyone else go into or come out of this room?" the first cop asked.

Casio nodded.

"There was a small person, dressed in black with a wide-brimmed hat that went into the room. I didn't think anything of it at the time because the people I was watching were out in the bar room at a table. The small black figure walked into the room a few seconds before the victim did, and came out perhaps thirty to forty-five seconds after that. The small person went directly to the front door and left the building."

The first officer had begun taking notes in a leather-bound memo book he pulled from his flapped shirt pocket. As he did so, investigators began arriving, and the uniformed police, the mini-skirted woman and Casio were gently ushered to a table in the bar room nearest the men's room door.

"You notice anything particular about the person who went into the room?" the second cop asked.

Casio shook his head with gritted teeth.

"No, I noticed the person going into the bathroom but no details since it didn't seem to concern my business here."

"And what was that business, Mr. Casio?"

"I was backing up a client who had come here to meet someone who possessed some information my client was interested in obtaining."

"That was the victim?"

Casio nodded.

"Who was he?"

Casio shrugged his shoulders.

"I was never introduced. So I can't know for certain who he was."

"Who's the client?"

Casio shook his head.

"I'm sorry, I can't tell you that."

The uniformed officer stood, nodding.

"OK, Mr. Casio, he said with authority. "The detectives will want to talk to you. Don't leave the building."

"I'm not going anywhere," he said, gesturing to the barmaid for another beer.

Peter McDermott dialed Pitcher's cell phone number the moment he was outside the nightclub. It rang seven times and went to voice mail. McDermott clicked off and dialed Pitcher's home number. It rang five times and went to the answering machine. Frustrated, he checked his pocket, handwritten "panic list," and dialed Samantha Parker's cell phone. She answered on the second ring.

"Samantha, this is Mac. Have you seen Pitch?"

"I'm at his apartment," she said, calmly. "And he just walked in the door. You want to talk to him?

McDermott ground his teeth.

"Please."

There was a pause of perhaps three or four seconds, and then Pitcher came on the line.

"Sorry, Mac, I left my cell phone on the front seat."

"Get it," McDermott ordered. "And listen to me while you do it."

"OK."

McDermott told Pitcher what had transpired over the last couple of hours in the Washington night club, including the violent death of Harry Oglesby.

"Crap, he was shot right before he was going to tell you who he thought the killer was," Pitcher exclaimed. "What do we do now?"

"Lock your door," McDermott ordered. "Turn out the lights and lock your place up tight, and stay there until I call you back. Don't let anyone in and don't take any calls from anyone other than me. Use the time to pack a small bag. I'll call you back within five minutes."

"OK, Mac."

McDermott pushed END on his cell phone, then punched Charlie Hume's cell number in speed dial.

Charlie Hume was one of those like McDermott who was never without his cell phone, even when he was at home, and its occasional rings would make Linda Hume want to scream. So Mac was pretty sure his boss would answer. And he did.

"Hume," he barked.

"McDermott," the editor answered, and repeated the story of the night's adventures for his publisher. Hume wasted no time on commentary.

191

"What do you need?"

"Do we still have the corporate suite at the Paramount Hotel?" he asked.

"Yes, it's available," Hume said. "You need it?"

"I want to send Pitcher there right away and button him up tight."

"That's fine, Mac, all he needs to do is show his press card to the desk clerk. I'll call them and tell them Pitcher is on the way."

"Thanks Charlie. One thing more. I think you and Linda should get out of town for a few days as well, just until we get a handle on this thing."

There was a pause of perhaps fifteen seconds. McDermott heard Hume put his hand over the phone's transmitter and mumble. Then he came back on.

"OK we're going to go to Linda's brother's house on Long Island. But we still have to keep the paper going, Mac."

McDermott sighed.

"I know. I'll be the point man for that. Casio's still here, he can watch my back."

Another pause.

"OK, Mac, we're leaving in a few minutes. Get Pitch to that hotel suite and get underground yourself. This is getting too serious for my digestion."

"Yours and mine both," McDermott affirmed and clicked off. He redialed Samantha Parker's number, and Pitcher answered the phone.

"We're ready, Mac, we're packed and I have my laptop so I can continue doing work for the paper."

"Good thinking, and thanks, Pitch. Now, you and Samantha call a cab. Don't use your own cars, I don't want them spotted by accident in a parking lot somewhere. Take the cab to the Inner Harbor, but stay as far away from the office as you can. Switch cabs once you get there, and go to the Paramount. The desk clerk knows you're coming."

"OK, gotcha, Mac, but what about you? You're on the line also!"

McDermott breathed heavily for a moment. The thought had occurred to him.

"I'm in Washington and I came with Casio and he is being detained by the police right now, so I'm waiting for him – surrounded by police, so I should be all right."

"I think you probably need to stay away from the office, Mac," Pitcher admonished.

"Yeah you're probably right."

"And your condo," he continued.

192

"I think I might take my boat over to one of the other marinas and work online for a few days. And Hume is going to his brother-in-law's house. Let's stay in touch, Pitch. You or Samantha call me every four hours."

"OK, Mac, will do."

"I'm serious, Pitch. Set the alarm on your watch and call me every four hours. If I don't hear from you at four hours and one minute I am calling the police, the FBI, the White House, and anyone else I can think of."

"Every four hours. Gotcha. Sam is calling a cab. I'll call you when we're settled in and then you can start the clock."

"Fair enough," McDermott said, relieved, as he broke the connection and dialed Hume back.

"We're on our way to the airport, Mac," Hume said. "We got a flight out within the hour so we'll be OK."

"I've got Pitch calling me every four hours," McDermott said. "I'd like you to do the same."

"I was about to suggest that," Hume said. "I need to know that *you* are ok. Let's make it simple. You call me right after Pitch calls you."

"Done," McDermott said, and rang off.

McDermott slid his cell phone back into its leather holster on the right side of his belt and walked back into the Madhatter.

The killer slipped the Bondo-mobile into gear and drove into traffic the moment McDermott disappeared back into the club. The killer allowed for a slight smile as the nondescript car blended into Washington traffic heading past the Federal Triangle and turned north onto the Baltimore-Washington Highway.

Private detectives are required to disclose any information concerning the commission of a crime to the police, and Casio, as a visiting detective from another jurisdiction, knew he would be particularly scrutinized by the D.C. Metro Police department. Their questions to him were pointed and left no room to equivocate. The only thing they couldn't require him to disclose was the name of his client. Casio considered his client to be the *North Bay Times*, and as such, its senior staff members were confidential insofar as the D.C. Police were concerned. So Casio didn't tell them that he had shooed McDermott out of the place moments before their arrival. He didn't mention McDermott's name at all, and implied by his answers – without saying so directly – that he didn't know whom Oglesby had been talking to.

McDermott took a table well away from the one where Casio was talking to plain-clothes detectives, and ordered a Diet Pepsi, high-signing the detective to let him know McDermott was aware of the situation and would wait discreetly.

It took well over an hour. McDermott ordered one of those cardboard pizzas they always seem to serve in bars, and later supplemented that with a basket of pretzels and a squirt-bottle of mustard – a combination McDermott had learned to enjoy in his youth on the beaches of Edgewater.

At length, the detectives finished their third degree of Casio and waved him out the door. Casio winked at McDermott and ambled out the front entrance. McDermott, an old campaigner, remained at his table for several minutes, casually finishing his pretzels and Diet Pepsi before he, too, walked nonchalantly out the front door. He turned right and walked a half-block, where he found Casio's rented car at the curb with the motor running, and the detective behind the wheel. McDermott jerked open the door and got in. The car set to motion before the door closed.

"Rough time?" McDermott inquired.

"Rough enough," Casio replied. "These D.C. cops are good. They're thorough and unyielding, and they don't take kindly to the 'sanctity of my client' crap."

"You didn't..." McDermott began, but Casio held up a restraining hand.

"No I didn't rat you out, Mac, but they're going to find out who you are after a time."

"Hopefully we'll have some more answers by then."

The editor described his phone calls outside the Madhatter, and his insistence that Hume and Pitcher seek shelter. Casio nodded appreciatively.

"That's one worry we don't have. We can work all this out without having to watch their backs."

"They're both pretty good at watching their own," McDermott commented.

Casio nodded and concentrated on his driving, headed for the Beltway, and Anne Arundel County. They rode in silence for several moments, each considering what their next move might be.

"I have to say," Casio began, breaking the uneasy silence, "that this is probably the most unusual case I've seen."

"I'm sorry," McDermott said flatly.

"No, not at all," Casio said, hurriedly. "That's what makes it interesting. I like cases that are departures from the norm."

"Seems like you find one of those every time you associate with us," McDermott said.

"Amen to that," Casio said.

They rolled into Annapolis in the wee hours of the next morning, and Casio dropped McDermott at his condo. The two shook hands before Casio drove off. McDermott walked from the entranceway of his condo onto the marina piers. He checked his boat and found all in order. The lights were out in the cabin so he figured Eve Somers had either made other arrangements for the night or was asleep below. He retraced his steps, walking to his condo's front door. There, he found the woman, seated on the white wrought-iron bench on the top step. She smiled sheepishly at his approach.

"I thought you'd never get home," she said tentatively.

"Been waiting long?" he inquired,

She shrugged.

"Only forever," she said with a toothy smile.

McDermott stepped past her and keyed open the door of his home. He stepped aside and beckoned her to enter, then followed her inside and closed the door.

No sooner had the latch clicked into place, she turned and threw her arms around his neck and kissed him deep and long. McDermott resisted at first, but then allowed himself to relax and melt into the kiss, snaking his arms around her waist. At long last the kiss broke, and Somers looked deep into McDermott's eyes for a long time.

"You don't want to be alone tonight, do you McDermott?"

She kissed him again and stared deep into his blue-gray eyes.

"Neither do I," she breathed.

Sy Casio had driven perhaps five miles before his conscience started to bother him. He turned his rental car onto I-97 North, headed back into Baltimore and his hotel suite, when he suddenly had a thought. He had not gone with McDermott to his condo to make sure all was well. He was aware that there was reason to believe a bullet with McDermott's name on it had been fired in anger.

His car was actually on the ramp headed onto the interstate, but the instinct to turn around was very strong. He checked his mirror. Damn. Traffic behind him, so he couldn't stop and back down the ramp back to where he had begun. He would have to go all the way to the Severna Park exit before he could get turned back around.

Determined, he merged into traffic at the top of the ramp and pushed the accelerator to the floor.

"Forgive me, I need to get out of these clothes and get comfortable," McDermott whispered as he broke their tenth kiss. They had become longer, deeper, and much more passionate as they stood inside the door of his condo. McDermott removed his hands from her waist and walked tiredly into his bedroom, with Eve Somers right behind.

"You could have stopped after you said you were getting out of your clothes," she said playfully, pulling her shirt over her head. She wore a filmy white bra that left little to the imagination. She dropped the shirt to the floor as she walked, following McDermott into his bedroom.

He sat on the end of his bed and removed his shoes and socks, tossing them toward a shoe-rack outside his closet. He missed, and she walked over and corrected it. Standing, he pulled off his suit jacket and draped it over the valet against one wall. He wore a wilted dress shirt and no tie, his collar button open. He emptied his pockets, putting his wallet, checkbook, pen and pencil set and computer jump-drive on his dresser, then turned to Eve, noticing for the first time that she was nearly naked above the waist. He smiled.

She smiled back, and stepped to him, kissing him again and shaking her long brown hair in a seductive way.

"Rough day?" she asked.

His arms encircled her waist again and he gave her a peck on the forehead.

"The roughest," he said, sighing heavily.

"Want to talk about it?" she asked, tilting her head for another kiss, which she got, after which she resisted the impulse to scratch here his Van Dyke beard tickled her.

"Not really," he said softly. "What I really want is a shower."

She smiled, a big, evil grin.

"Want some company?"

He smiled and slid his hands up her back, unhooking her bra and letting it fall.

"Thought you'd never ask," he said.

Chapter Twenty-Three

Rod Pitcher stuck the magnetic card-key into the slot on his third floor room. Nothing happened. He pulled it out and re-stuck it. Still nothing. Sighing tiredly, he sat his case down on the floor and tried a third time. No green light. Frustrated, Samantha Parker took the key from his hand and slowly inserted it into the slot. The red light turned to green, and she pressed the lever. The door swung open at her touch.

"You've got to put it in right," she said with a sly smile.

Pitcher's smile matched hers exactly.

"Give me a few minutes," he said, "and you can show me how."

They went into the room and set their suitcases down, looking around the newspaper's reserved suite. It had a sitting room with a desk, TV, and a couple of armchairs, and a gray cloth couch. Another door led to the bedroom, which was spacious, despite having a queen bed centered against the far wall. In this room there was another TV and armchair, and a wooden armoire. In the wall to the right was a door that led to a roomy bathroom with a large vanity and a tub-shower combination that had Jacuzzi jets inside.

"Not bad," Pitcher commented after touring the room. He turned to Samantha Parker and put his arms around her waist. "Now about that lesson in accuracy..." he grinned.

She stayed inside his arms, but put a finger on his lips.

"You need to call Mac first," she reminded him.

Pitcher's face clouded over and he snapped his fingers.

"I forgot," he said, reaching for his cell phone.

"I don't blame you," she said, disentangling herself from his embrace.

She went about unpacking what they would need as Pitcher thumbed the number in speed dial. It took McDermott six rings to answer.

197

Peter McDermott disengaged himself from a passionate kiss from Eve Somers and rolled over in the bed to his night stand where he had placed his cell phone. He flipped it open and pulled it to his ear as Somers propped herself up on one arm.

"McDermott," he said softly.

"We're here, Mac," Pitcher said. "Nice place."

"OK, Pitch," McDermott said, ignoring the urgings of Eve Somers that he drop the phone and return to what he was doing. "Double-lock the door and don't go out. Order meals from room service. We'll see if the police and Sy Casio can sort all this out in a few days, and things can get back to normal."

"OK. Please be careful, Mac."

McDermott raised an eyebrow.

"Thanks for your concern, Pitch," he said.

"It isn't that," Pitcher declared. "I just hate breaking in a new man."

"You bum!" McDermott laughed, and snapped the phone closed, returning it to the night stand. He rolled back over to face Somers, who lay pouting with her hair spread out on the pillow, her face haloed in the flickering light of the candles she had lit in strategic spots in the room.

"One call down, and one to go," he told her.

She kissed him, just for a moment, but it was one that was urging and unmistakable.

"Put your hands on me, Mac," she breathed, and she sighed in unmitigated pleasure when he did.

Sy Casio parked his rental car next to Peter McDermott's Jeep Wrangler Unlimited and walked carefully up to the front door of the editor's condo. He noticed as he ascended the steps that no lights showing through the windows at the front. He pecked on the door and got no answer. Shrugging, he turned and walked down the two steps to the main sidewalk level. Thinking McDermott might be on his new boat, Casio walked to the pier where the editor told him the boat was kept. Again, no lights inside the cabin, and there was no response to his rap on the hull. Shrugging yet again, Casio walked back to McDermott's condo. As he passed the Jeep he placed a hand on the hood. Dead cold. The Jeep had not been moved for at least eight hours.

Casio pursed his lips and stepped back onto the porch. He had dropped McDermott off here not an hour ago, and he didn't appear tired enough to have gone straight to bed – and it wasn't that late, he noted, glancing at his watch.

He knocked on the door, harder this time, and his knock was returned with a hollow ring. He waited a respectful three minutes.

Casio tried the front door knob and found it locked. He reached into his inside suit jacket pocket and pulled out a small leather case. Unzipping it, he pulled out a long thin rod that looked a little like a straightened-out paper clip with a small plastic handle on one end. He also took out a shorter, slightly thicker rod with a small hook on one end. He inserted the longer rod into the lock on the doorknob and turned it slightly, then inserted the hook below it and moved it slowly in and out. After a moment he heard a tine 'click,' and he withdrew both rods, putting them back into the case and zipping it closed. Again he tried the door. It swung open at his touch.

The detective stepped into the tiny foyer and closed the door behind him. To his left was a small table on which he noted McDermott's car keys. A step or two forward, and to his right was an opening into the living room which was completely dark. Casio navigated from the glow of a single light whose origin he could not determine, never having been in McDermott's home. He inched forward and finally noticed that the light he was steering by was a fluorescent over the sink in the kitchen.

At about that same moment he heard a loud moan off to his left. Drawing his gun, he moved furtively toward the sound. As he walked he noted articles of clothing several steps apart on the floor. He smiled. Just like bread crumbs, he thought.

His travel took him to what her perceived to be McDermott's bedroom. The door was open. He stepped into the doorframe and looked into the room.

He saw the figure of a woman, kneeling upright on the bed, very active and very naked. It was just a wild guess, Casio mused, but he thought she just might be the one who moaned. He watched for perhaps fifteen seconds as she undulated her hips, and suddenly arched her back, pulling her bare breasts tight across her chest. She trembled, her alabaster skin shining from a layer of sweat. He heard another moan, this one decidedly more masculine, and in a voice he recognized. Grinning widely, Casio carefully retraced his steps to the front door. He turned the lock, eased the door closed, and walked back to his car with a smile that showed all of his teeth.

Fred Mattingly followed the gurney out of the operating room at the Washington City Morgue on Loughboro Road. On the wheeled table was the body of Harry Oglesby, covered with a stained sheet. Doctor Hidashi Itsoku met him at the swinging door in equally stained scrubs and handed the detective a small brown envelope. The medical examiner had a wan smile on his face, almost a grim mask built around his Oriental features. Mattingly smiled his thanks, regarded the envelope in his hand and turned away.

He drove more or less automatically to the police building and parked in the fenced-in lot behind the building. From the lot, he was able to go down an exterior staircase into the lower level of the police building. He walked past the locker rooms, the fitness center and the roll-call room and entered the Ballistics lab. Marv Bent was pounding away at his computer keyboard as Mattingly dropped into the chair across the desk without being invited.

"What's up, Freddy-boy," Bent inquired without looking up from his screen.

Without a word, Mattingly dropped the envelope on the cluttered desk. Bent didn't even look at it.

"What kind of case?" he asked, without a pause in his keyboard-assault.

"Shooting in the Madhatter," Mattingly said, simply.

Bent stopped typing and looked up, surprised.

"I know that place. Not the kind of drinkery I'd expect to see a shooting in."

"True," Mattingly said.

"Who's the stiff?" Bent asked.

"Some old geezer. The private detective who witnessed it says he used to be a spy in the Second World War. The detective says he was sitting at a table with some guy named Peter McDermott when he got up to go wee-wee, and that's when he was iced.

Bent's jaw dropped.

"Whom did you say?" he demanded.

"Peter McDermott," Mattingly said, casually. "He's the editor of that weekly newspaper up in Baltimore..."

Bent waved him off.

"I know who he is," Bent snapped. "You got any hardware from the autopsy?"

Mattingly pointed to the brown envelope on the desk. Bent ripped it open and a bullet dropped into his hand. Rising, he walked to his workbench and fitted the bullet into his comparison microscope. For long moments he peered, nearly motionless, into the eyepiece, only the rasp of his breathing betraying the life still in him.

At length he rose from his lab stool and walked to a file cabinet. Jerking open the top drawer he rummaged for a moment and came up with a small white envelope, which he opened. Inside there were other bullets in tiny plastic bags that had labels on them. He selected one, removed the bullet from the plastic, and set it up under the microscope.

He spoke not a word to Mattingly as he balanced his ample butt on the edge of the worn wooden stool and resumed his unmoving study at the eyepiece of the microscope.

After several long minutes, during which Bent moved not a single muscle, he stood, stretched and belched loudly. Pouring a cup of viscous coffee from a dirty glass pot on his bench, he leaned against the edge of his desk and raised his cup to Mattingly.

"Coffee?" he offered.

Mattingly looked at the motor-oil-like substance rolling sluggishly in Bent's clear glass mug and quickly shook his head. Bent leaned over his desk and tapped a few keys on his computer keyboard, then turned the flat-screen monitor toward them. The report he had been writing dissolved, and a very sharp, very clear color picture from the microscope shimmered into existence on the screen. Bent picked up a pencil and pointed as he talked.

"The bullet on the left is the one you just gave me," he said. "The one on the right is the one taken from the body of the woman on the stage in that old nightclub. Note the lands, grooves and striations." He pointed at those items on the bullet surfaces with the pencil. Involuntarily, Mattingly leaned forward to take a closer look, then straightened.

"They look identical to me," he said flatly.

Bent nodded.

"Bingo."

He removed the left bullet – the latest one – and fitted another from the envelope taken from the file drawer. In a moment, the microscope auto-focus brought it into sharp, crystal clear resolution.

"Now look at this one against the bullet taken from the nightclub corpse," he said, his voice getting harder.

Mattingly took a close look, leaning over the desk, then sat back down with a quizzical look on his face.

"Those look identical also."

Bent nodded, his lips a thin line.

"They are."

He went again to the white envelope from his file drawer and took out yet another bullet, which he put on the microscope in place of the bullet from the nightclub.

"How about these?" he asked, when the picture congealed.

Mattingly leaned over the desk and looked carefully at the two bullets in the picture, but he knew what he would see before he saw it.

"Which bullet is this?" he asked.

"This is the one that was fired at Peter McDermott, which I pulled from the back of a plumber's van," he said.

"Also identical," Mattingly stated. "All these bullets – including tonight – were fired from the same gun."

"Yes they were," Bent said. "And unfortunately, it's your job to figure out why."

"Don't remind me,' Mattingly drawled, staring without blinking at the computer screen.

Peter McDermott awoke with a start and rolled over to find the space in the bed next to him empty. Turning back, he noted no light emanating from under the door of the bathroom, and the red LED numerals on his clock read 3:45AM. Puzzled, he sat up.

"Eve?" he called tentatively.

No response.

He threw the covers aside and walked from his room, looking around, but not turning on any lights. The only lights already on were the one over the sink in the kitchen, which showed no one, and the one he always left on in his office. He turned left and walked unerringly in that direction.

From the door he could See Eve Somers, standing naked behind his desk and riffling through the papers stacked in the middle of the blotter. That raised an eyebrow on the editor's face.

He had made no noise as he walked across the carpeted floor of his home, so he didn't attract the woman's attention as he approached. Deftly, he stepped into the shadow to one side of his office door to where he could still see inside the room, but seeing him from in there would be more difficult.

"What in the world could she be looking for?" he thought, his eyes riveted on her as she riffled through the papers on his desk, then rounded it and walked to his reading table. There were assorted papers there, as well, and she looked through them, being careful to return them as she found them, and, apparently not finding what she wanted, she turned to his file cabinets, recessed into one wall. He noted that she opened the bottom drawer first, giving it a perfunctory glance before opening each one above it in ascending order. Each got a riffle-through and a quick glance. Carefully, she closed the four drawers in reverse order. She stood there for a moment, apparently in thought, bathed in the ethereal glow of the single desk lamp always left on in the office. McDermott sensed she would leave that room soon, so he turned and silently made his way back into the living room. He had ducked successfully into the bedroom before she stepped out of the office, and had made it into his bathroom, closed the door and turned on the light before she arrived there. McDermott could hear her sliding back into the bed. He waited a respectful minute or two, then flushed the toilet and turned off the light before moving back into the bedroom. She was laying, covered up in the bed, on the side nearest the bathroom, smiling at him in the darkness.

"Oh, hi," he said softly, trying to smile, but she couldn't see his unsuccessful effort. "Where did you go?"

"Leg cramp," she said. "I got up to walk it off and I didn't want to disturb you."

"Considerate of you," he said, grinding his teeth.

She reached behind her with her left hand and patted his side of the bed.

"Care to join me?" she invited.

He hesitated.

"I think I need a cold drink," he said, turning and walking toward the door.

"Hurry back." She said seductively.

He nodded with a grin she could almost see as he shuffled out of the bedroom and into his kitchen.

McDermott sat in a chair across from the sink and tented his fingers in front of him. He was having another one of his hunches. Eve Somers' actions didn't make sense. Why was she rifling his desk papers in the middle of the night? If she wanted something from him she could have asked for it. Normally she did.

Unless...

McDermott had a fleeting thought. He tried to dismiss it, but it nagged him, landing at the very front of his brain and staying there. For a moment he considered a lobotomy for what he was thinking.

He sat there for what seemed to him to be a very long time, but in reality it was no more than three minutes. Finally, he stood, pulled a chilled can of ginger ale from the fridge and headed back to his room, popping the top and sipping from the can as he did so.

She was lying on the bed as before, covers pushed to the foot, reclining seductively with her head propped up on her crooked arm, a come-on smile on her face.

"This is just a diversionary tactic," McDermott thought to himself as he stopped to look at her in the eerie glow of light through the curtained window.

"And a damned effective one," he thought again as he drained the can and slid into the bed next to her.

Chapter Twenty-Four

Rod Pitcher sat at the hotel desk in his underwear, staring at the screen of his laptop computer, as it spat out various combinations of numbers and letters. He had accessed some ancient, declassified encryption codes cast off by the U.S. and British military for no other reason than he wanted to see if they would recognize the number from the watch. So far, the computer was spitting out gibberish from all the known codes.

38.881 -76.979

After all you went through, those numbers have to mean something," Samantha Parker said. She sat in an uncomfortable hotel chair dressed in a sheer nylon eggshell-white nightie that hugged her knees and continued from there to her neck.

"To say nothing of what the original people who carried the watch and information went through," he said grimly. "It was war."

She nodded and said nothing as Pitcher tried another encryption protocol and typed in the numbers, checking them to be sure they were right before starting the computer on its quest.

"Have you talked to Mac?" Samantha inquired.

Pitcher shook his head.

"There's been so much going on the last day or so we haven't had a chance to sit down and compare notes."

"So you haven't told him about the third floor of that old hotel?"

Pitcher turned in his seat to face her.

"No I haven't and that has been digging at me," he said. "It's like finding a jet plane in King Tut's tomb, it's just so out of place it's unbelievable."

He glanced for a moment at the computer as it started spewing out random numbers that meant as much to Pitcher as Egyptian hieroglyphics.

"There are so many pieces of this puzzle that just don't fit. We have much of the border pieces assembled, but there are still some things on the outside that haven't found the groove yet. And I think it's important that we all trade what we've found out."

He reached for his cell phone and flipped it open.

"I'm calling him," he declared. But Samantha parker held up her watch so he could see it and pointed to its hands. They showed 4:05AM.

"He was awake when I called awhile ago," he defended.

"He was expecting your call then," she said. "And besides, you said you thought he had company."

Pitcher considered this, then minimized the encryption code and called up his email account. The laptop automatically connected to the hotel's wireless Internet, and Pitcher opened a new email, typing in McDermott's address.

"Call me as soon as possible, important. Pitch." He wrote, and touched SEND with the mouse pointer. A wheel appeared to spin on the screen for no more than a moment, before being replaced by the legend, MESSAGE SENT.

"I'll make sure we find time to exchange information tomorrow," he said, maximizing the encryption device and watching as more meaningless numbers spewed out. He worked the mouse and stopped the process.

"The hell with this," he said, frustrated. He clicked on "Shut Down" in his Start menu and watched as the computer went through its termination protocol. When the screen went dark he closed the laptop and turned to Samantha Parker.

"You know you don't have to be here," he said. "You're not involved in all this and you haven't been threatened, there's no reason to put your neck on the line with me here."

Their eyes locked for a moment, and tacit communication passed between them. Finally, he nodded knowingly.

"Nuff said," he declared.

"You mean 'nuff *un*said,'" she said with a smile.

"Let's get some sleep," he said, standing and walking toward the queen sized bed that dominated the next room in the suite.

"All in good time," she said softly, pulling the nightie over her head.

Morning broke over Chesapeake Bay, turning the green, rolling surface of the brackish waters into a kaleidoscope if rainbow colors, changing every second with the movement of the low waves. Light pushed the darkness out of the way as it began the new day, the sun warming the chill left behind by the stygian hues of night.

The light snuck through the window under the curtains of a ground-floor, single story condominium in Eastport, stabbing into the eyes of a woman who slept with her face toward the window. Eve Somers' eyes popped open, then squinted against the invading brightness. In a moment she rolled onto her back and turned to look at the man in the bed next to her. McDermott was facing the other way, his hair tousled, his mouth agape as he snored through his moustache. Eve laughingly thought that when he snored outward, he looked like a party favor.

She pushed the endearing thought out of her mind. Flipping the covers off her, she stood, stretched, and stepped into a pair of sheer bikini briefs. She was pulling on her bra as she stepped from the bedroom, careful not to awaken the sleeping man whose bluster continued apace and aloud. She walked noiselessly to the living room, hooking her bra deftly in the back, and stepped into the tiny foyer near the street-side door. She smiled again at the realization that Mac referred to the street-side door as the "back door," and the glass portals that led to the deck as his "front door." She was aware that most Bay dwellers thought of their homes that way, but for some reason it was doubly cute coming from McDermott.

Again she pushed the fond thought of him from her mind and resumed her search, which now took her into his office toward the "front" of the house. She found what she was looking for on the floor, leaning against his desk. It was McDermott's battered leather briefcase. She picked it up and set it on the desk, holding it, lest it topple over on its side. With one hand she unfastened the two leather straps with belt-buckle closures, and opened the curved top.

Inside she found a list of advertisers with ad sizes for the new edition he would start on the next work-day, a report from the paper's Web Master on some changes that needed to be made to the paper's web site, on which he had scratched some notes in what she recognized as his Cross mechanical pencil. There were several file folders containing completed stories, notes on stories, a penciled rough draft of the editorial calendar, and dozens of CD-ROMs that had various cryptic labels on them, doubtless newspaper things he was concerned with – perhaps art or pictures for the next edition.

There were side pockets in the briefcase and she checked them all, finding a sheaf of press releases that were loosely shoved into the cubby. In another she found some apparently blank CDs and a single jump drive.

She sat in Mac's high-backed leather chair and clicked the mouse on his computer, hoping against hope that he hadn't shut it off. He hadn't.

The flat-screen monitor came alive in seconds. She bent down to the computer tower and jacked the jump-drive into a handy USB port. The screen flickered and opened a menu block. She highlighted the prompt that said, "Open and display files" and clicked. A light flickered through the plastic skin of the jump drive, and the screen shifted, showing a list of the files on the drive. She perused the list carefully, but as quickly as possible.

McDermott was suddenly awakened by his own snoring, and as consciousness turned on the motor to his brain, he realized that he was alone – and shouldn't be. There was still the feminine scent of Eve Somers in the bed with him, mingled with the aroma of passion they had shared – and he had the sense that though she wasn't in the bed, and didn't appear to be in the bedroom nor its adjacent bathroom, that she was still somewhere in the condo. He forced himself into a sitting position and snaked his shorts off the floor, pulling them up to his waist. He considered getting out a t-shirt from his dresser, but it was warm in the condo so he dismissed the notion and carefully edged his way out of the bedroom. The bedroom door led to a short hall that became his foyer on one end, and emptied next to his kitchen on the other. He turned left and peeked around the end-wall into the kitchen. Seeing no one, he stepped into his living room, which was also empty. But it was there that he noticed that the light coming from his office wasn't quite right. Carefully, he tiptoed to the double-door entrance to that room and peeked around the jamb. There sat Eve Somers, her back to him, obscured by the back of his desk chair as she manipulated the computer. McDermott noted his briefcase sitting on the desk, with the strap closures unfastened. He distinctly remembered closing them at the office, and remembered leaving the briefcase on the floor next to his desk – its accustomed place.

McDermott raised his left eyebrow as he watched. What in the world could she be looking for? And why the clandestine search, why did she not simply ask for what she wanted?

Somers was making motions like she was finishing up what she was doing. McDermott took the hint and sprinted back to his bedroom on the balls of his bare feet, dropping his shorts where they were and sliding back under the covers.

Eve carefully extracted the jump drive from the computer tower and returned it to the correct pocket in Mac's briefcase. She closed the straps and carefully returned the briefcase to the same spot where she found it.

For a moment she sat in the chair, studying the contents of Mac's desk. There was nothing out of the ordinary there. Just things that made him who he was, and things that related to his work. The only thing she had not seen before was the title slip and bill of sale for his boat. Under that, as she turned the papers over, she found a receipt for six months of slip charges from the marina, making note of a hefty discount since Mac was a condo community member, and an Eastport Yacht Club corporate member. She returned the papers as she found them, and leaned back for a moment, studying the ceiling. After a moment she sighed and bare-footed it back to the bedroom.

She stood again at the foot of the bed and regarded the sleeping man. He wasn't snoring, but his mouth was still slightly open, and his breathing was deep and regular. For a moment, a hard glint came into her eyes as she stared at him, but she recovered in a moment and stepped to the window wall and yanked the drapes open.

"Rise and shine, Sleepy Head," she enjoined, stripping the covers from the bed and leaving Mac to shiver, naked, as he drew up into the fetal position.

McDermott had been aware of her from the moment she had stepped back into the room. One eye was open, just a slit, as she looked down at him, he could see the hardness that came across her just for a couple of heart-beats. He made a show of trying to pull the covers back on, allowing Somers to yank them off him again. At length, he sat up and made a big show of stretching and reaching for his shorts on the floor. He stepped into them and ambled into the bathroom where he threw some water on his face, and returned to the bedroom. Eve was sitting on the foot of the bed and he sat next to her.

"You're going to be late for the office," she observed.

McDermott shook his head.

"I think I'm going to work from home today," he said.

"Oh?" she said in surprise. "You don't do that very much."

"I will today, though, not many people will be in the office."

"Where's Pitch?" she asked, casually.

"He's at the papers corp... " he saw that hard look come back into her eyes. "He's on assignment."

"Where?" she asked, a note of something a little stronger than casual interest creeping into her voice.

McDermott smiled at her.

"Hither and yon," he said, noncommittally.

Somers decided not to push her luck.

209

"Coffee?" she prompted.

He nodded, running his fingers through his hair.

"Get a shower," she said. "I'll make it."

McDermott walked into the bathroom without any more prompting and made a quick job of washing up and shaving. He left the water running and came out of the shower, running a towel over his body as he tiptoed out of the bedroom in search of Somers. She was in the kitchen, deep in the motions of making a pot of coffee and laying out mugs, sugar for her, sweetener for him, and powdered creamer for them both.

Satisfied, McDermott ambled back to his bedroom where he pulled on shorts, tattered jeans, and a yellow t-shirt he'd bought the year before in a restaurant on the North Carolina Outer Banks.

It was while he was fastening the strap of his sandal that he noted the hair on the back of his neck was standing straight up. He paused in mid-buckle and stared off into space, a thought coursing through his mind that was so incredulous, so ridiculous that he hesitated to give it credence. He thought for a long moment of the two times he had seen Eve rummaging about in his office. His suspicions had been aroused at that time, certainly, convinced as he was that there was more than feminine curiosity motivating her actions.

Yet the thought that now found a root in his brain was so off-the-wall, so "out there," that he could scarcely believe he'd had the nerve to think it, let alone to entertain it.

There was one single question that prevented him from dismissing the thought, one single impulse that stopped him from forgetting, out of hand, what he considered a cockamamie proposition.

What if he was right?

Sy Casio's phone rousted him from a deep sleep in his suite at the Pier Five.

He had spent the evening – too much of it, in fact, alternately paying attention to his laptop computer, and to the bottle of Scotch he'd picked up on his way into the building. He hadn't gotten blotto-drunk, just enough to be happy as he stared at his computer screen as it disgorged many of the same numbers that had vexed Rod Pitcher and Charlie Hume. He'd hoped to find something the other two men had missed, but as the evening progressed, and the Scotch bottle emptied, those hopes diminished.

Late that night he'd put through a call to Madalyn, his secretary and confidante in his Los Angeles office. He asked her to run Harry Oglesby through their computer program, the one that did Internet searches through genealogical data bases. The system didn't work all the time, in fact it only sometimes gave them answers they could use. He had given Madalyn the names of everyone involved except McDermott and Hume, and asked her to put the names through a meat grinder. He wanted a call first thing in the morning, he had said, win, lose or draw.

Bleary-eyed, he stared at the red display on the digital alarm clock next to his bed. 7:22. Way too early for a man with a hang-over.

"Yeah," he hissed, trying to make his cashmere tongue work.

"You think you got it bad, it's three-thirty in the morning here, asshole."

Madalyn got away with talking to her boss like that because of her years of dedicated, unselfish service to her employer.

Casio cut through the woman's obvious discomfiture.

"What do you have, Madalyn?"

"I just emailed you the results of the genealogical search on all the involved names."

"You find much?"

A slight pause on the other end of the phone.

"Not much at all, Sy. I hope you find something in there that you can use."

"It's a long shot anyway," he said, tasting his tongue and wincing. "You been up all night?"

"Most of it," she said.

"Go home and get some sleep," Casio said, swinging into a sitting position.

"I'll do just that," she said in a heavy, deep voice. The phone went dead in his hands.

Casio stumbled to the bathroom and threw some water on his face. He looked at the room's coffee maker and picked up the foil envelope of ground coffee that came with it. He made a face at it, put it down, and ambled back into the bedroom where he lifted the phone and dialed room service. He ordered some sausage and eggs, and took McDermott's suggestion and asked for some Taylor ham as well. While he waited, he stepped into the shower.

He was toweling himself off when a knock came on his door. He pulled on a light cloth robe and let the bellman in. The messenger placed a tray on the desk near the TV stand, accepted a tip, and bowed out of the room. Casio took the cover off the dish and nodded approvingly.

The detective turned on his computer, and while he waited for it to boot up he salted his eggs and took a couple of bites, then started cutting up his sausage and Taylor ham with the edge of his fork.

The computer booted, and Casio hit the hotel's wireless hot spot and called up his email account. There was Bridget's note. He opened it, and nibbled on his breakfast as he started to read. He was perhaps two minutes into the note when his left eyebrow raised. He reread the passage, then went to the closet where his suit was hanging. From the inside pocket he pulled a spiral notebook, which he flipped open. He scanned through the pages until he found a phone number he needed. He picked up the hotel phone and dialed.

"Ms. Parker," he said, when the phone was answered. "May I speak to Rod please? It's Sy Casio."

There was a pause of perhaps fifteen seconds before a sleepy voice came on the line.

"Yeah, Sy, what's up?" Pitcher asked.

"I've got something I want you to see," Casio said casually. "I'd like to drop by your hotel."

"I can come to yours," Pitcher said,

"No," Casio said firmly. "I'd rather not expose you and Samantha to anyone who might be on your tail.

"You had breakfast?" Pitcher asked.

"Having it now."

"Then let's say lunch time, OK?"

Casio smiled. He had a feeling Pitcher and Samantha Parker were going to have a morning repast of their own.

"OK, lunch," he said. "And call McDermott and get him there if you can. And have McDermott call Charlie."

"Charlie's in New York," Pitcher said. "Mac can fill him in – and I'm due to call him in a few minutes for our usual check-in anyway."

Casio nodded,

"Tell him to take a cab, that Jeep of his sticks out like a sore thumb. And have him change cabs several times to shake off anyone who might be tailing him."

There was a short pause, and Casio could almost feel Pitcher smiling.

"Mac will enjoy that. He likes this kind of intrigue."

Casio grinned. So many people think of crime-fighting and crime detection as lots of fun and intrigue like that – few know how boring it is – or that it is frequently a deadly proposition, especially in this day and age when no one respected anything or anyone.

"See you both at your place for lunch. I think I will have something very interesting to show you."

"See you then," Pitcher said, airily, and clicked off.

Casio stared at his computer screen for a long moment. "Very interesting indeed," he said aloud to himself.

Chapter Twenty-Five

McDermott leaned back in the high-backed swivel chair behind the desk in his Annapolis condo office, sipping the coffee Eve Somers had brought to him. He accepted the cup and saucer without comment, confident that the coffee would have been sweetened and creamed to his taste. It was. He turned his back on the desk and stared out through the glass doors at the marina, and past it, to Weems Creek, which led to the Severn River and thence to Chesapeake Bay. Yet he did not see the beauty and splendor of the area he so loved. Instead he was inwardly turned.

He had had some strange thoughts lately concerning Eve Somers, and not just being repulsed by her not-so-subtle hints at matrimony. These feelings created a collection of butterflies in his gut, and made him look at her for the first time with suspicion. But suspicion of what? All he had was anomalous behavior on her part, the two times he had seen her going through his office, using his computer to snoop on his doings. He didn't have the foggiest notion of what he was looking for. At least he thought he didn't.

A delicate hand reached around his chair and took his cup, refilling it, and returning it a moment later, doctored to suite.

Eve Somers was dressed in crisp new jeans and a spaghetti strap plum top and leather open sandals. She moved to a spot on the other side of the desk and regarded him, knowing better than to disturb his reverie. When he wanted to talk he would do so. It would not go well for her to interrupt his train of thought at this juncture. She had done it once before and had felt his wrath. Mac, she knew, was a deep thinker and when he was lost in thought like this he was hard to reach – and succeeding in reaching him was done at one's own peril.

For long moments she looked at him, much as she had in the bedroom while he slept, but now she was seeing another part of him. It as a part she had seen before, and knew she could never join with. After

215

a moment she returned to the kitchen and spent a few moments sprucing it up. McDermott was a fair housekeeper; there were only a couple of dishes in the sink, and those in the dishwasher were clean. The stovetop needed a wipe-down, and a swish with a brush in the sink took care of that matter. She wiped off the drain board and hung the dish towel on a hook near the fridge. As an afterthought, she checked the refrigerator to see if he needed anything, and was mildly surprised to note that it was fully stocked with food and beverage. Eve retrieved the morning paper from the step outside, and sat down in the living room to read it, secure in the knowledge that Mac would return to her – mentally – when he was ready.

Back in the office, McDermott had not moved. The coffee, in the cup that rested on the saucer, and then on his knee was slowly getting cold, and he probably wasn't even aware that the cup had been replenished. So lost in thought was he that he didn't even notice the land-line phone on his desk was ringing.

In the living room, Eve heard the phone ring twice, three times, four times. Aware that McDermott was out in la-la land somewhere, she strode to the kitchen and lifted the wall phone.

"McDermott's residence," she sang into the phone.

There was a pause.

"Who is this, please?" the voice asked.

"This is Eve Somers," she replied. "Your turn."

"Eve, this is Rod Pitcher," he said, elated. "Is Mac around?"

"He's in his office, lost in thought," she said casually. "You want me to interrupt him?"

Another pause.

"No not right now, but soon, if you can. Sy Casio wants us to meet over hear for some new information on this thing we're working on."

"Over here?" she prompted. "Where's Over Here?"

"The company suite at the Paramount," Pitcher said, swallowing the bait. "I'll need Mac over here as soon as possible."

"I'll tell him right away, Rod," she promised.

"Thanks, Eve, and tell him I called for our regular check-in and he should call Charlie as soon as he gets the message."

"Will do. See you Rod."

"Thanks, Eve."

She hung up. For a long moment she leaned against the wall next to the phone, lost in thought, but with a curt smile on her face. Suddenly her eyes went hard. She walked back through the living room, picking up her purse as she passed, and stepped out the front door, closing it behind her.

The jangling of the phone on his desk had penetrated McDermott's closed mind, but only just. It took him several minutes to shake off the fugue-like state and come back into the world of reality.

By then he knew he had missed taking the call. He sat the cup and saucer on the desk and checked the caller ID on the phone. He didn't recognize the number, so he lifted the phone and dialed. As it rang he took a sample sip of the ice-cold coffee, winced and forced himself to swallow it, and looked around for something to take the taste out of his mouth, when the phone was answered.

"Paramount Hotel, Vincent speaking, how may I direct your call?"

McDermott was momentarily taken aback, but he recovered quickly.

"*North Bay Times* suite, please, Mr. Pitcher."

"One moment, sir, I'll ring."

The phone rang three times and went to voice mail. McDermott hung up, highlighted the caller ID and copied the number into his cell phone. He walked from his office into the living room looking around. He didn't see Eve, so he walked toward the bedroom passing the kitchen on his way. Still no Eve. He arrived in the bedroom to see the bed still unmade – unusual for one of her visits – and nothing of hers left in the room. He sauntered back into the living room, his mind racing, and looked in the chair where she habitually dropped her purse. It was empty.

It suddenly dawned on him what must have happened – the call had not gone unanswered; she had taken it. And if his random thoughts of what was going on were correct, he had committed an unpardonable blunder by allowing himself to retreat inwardly so deep.

"Oh, shit!" he breathed.

He raced to the foyer, grabbed his car keys and dashed out the door, punching numbers into his cell phone as he went.

Sy Casio was frustrated by the street system in Baltimore. He knew the area fairly well but still managed to get himself lost on occasion. His rental car had GPS built into the dashboard, but he was loathe to use it. Fearing he would finally have to, he pulled into a gas station parking lot and started fiddling with the GPS controls.

He finally got the screen to come up and was punching in the destination information when his cell phone purred in his pocket. Wincing in irritation, he yanked it out and flipped it open.

217

"Casio."

"Sy this is Peter McDermott. I've done something incredibly stupid."

"I find that hard to believe," he said sincerely.

"I just tried to call Pitcher at the hotel for the second time and I'm not getting any answer, and there could be trouble – not right now, but damned soon."

"Why do you say that?"

McDermott explained to the detective what had happened in his condo, and Casio was becoming more and more concerned with each word McDermott spoke.

"Where are you now?" Casio asked.

"Just out of Annapolis getting onto I-95," McDermott said, shouting now. "You've got to get to the hotel fast, Sy."

"Say no more, I'm on it," Casio snapped, and flipped the phone closed. He dropped it on the car seat, punched in the address of the Paramount from his pocket notebook, and studied the map that showed up on the screen. A voice came through the car radio giving him driving directions. He dropped the car into gear and screamed back into traffic, making several other cars slam on their brakes.

McDermott shifted the Jeep Wrangler down from fifth gear into third, let out the clutch and slammed his right foot and the accelerator to the floor. Unconsciously, he leaned forward against his seat belt, urging the black vehicle to greater speed. By the time he passed the next mile marker, he was going nearly 75 miles an hour in a 65 speed limit section of Interstate 95. He was at first concerned that a state trooper or county mountie might stop him – then he hoped one would. Then he could explain the situation and get some official help. He thought for a moment about calling the Baltimore City Police on his cell phone, but going this fast he didn't want to take the chance of diverting his attention. He watched his tachometer as it edged toward the red zone, then clutched and pulled the six-speed transmission to fourth gear. Again, he mashed the gas pedal as far as it would go, and the Jeep shot ahead, eating up the miles. He power-clutched through the next two gears until he got into cruising mode, moving along the concrete strip at nearly 90 miles an hour, daring a police car to catch him.

While he concentrated on his driving, carefully passing slower traffic, he allowed his mind to work. He was more convinced than ever that the random thoughts, the terrible thoughts, he had been having about Eve Somers were right. It pained him because he knew he had some feelings for her, some feelings he had been keeping under wraps.

He understood that now. That's why he didn't slam the door in her face the first time she showed up on his porch. That's why he let her back into his condo every time she showed up, why he allowed her to live for a time on his new boat even though he had just acquired it.

And yet he had not permitted her to remain in his place when he was away. That was new. In their past relationship, before Willie Sykes, she had come and gone from his home at will and even, for a time, had possessed a key to the back door, the "streetside" door. She had left it at the condo the last time she went there, right before she disappeared. – and even at that, he had changed the locks on his place after she went away.

The gaggle of butterflies that had been flying about in his stomach grew to the size of bats and increased their avian speed.

If he was right, Eve Somers would be driving right now toward Baltimore, and this road was the fastest and most direct route. He hoped to overtake her car, and pass her before she got there, and he was keeping a sharp eye out for her vehicle. And yet even as his Jeep ate up the miles, her car did not come into view. That gave him the fleeting hope that all he was thinking was wrong. Yet there was no explanation for her searching his office, and none either, for her sudden disappearance from his home.

There were too many pieces, far too many pieces, that didn't fit together. And until they did, his first priority was to warn Pitcher. Chancing it, he pulled his cell phone from its holster and punched in Pitcher's number on speed dial, and touched the Speaker button. He heard the rings add up, but no answer. He rang off and called Samantha Parker's cell number. Same result. Checking the phone's log, he called up the hotel number and pressed Send, asking for the corporate suite when it was answered, and again, his summons elicited no response.

McDermott gritted his teeth and slammed the cell phone against his thigh.

The tachometer on his dashboard aimed at six-thousand rpm's, and the speedometer crowded 100 miles per hour.

McDermott sighed and punched the speed-dial number for Charlie Hume.

Sy Casio's car screeched into the Paramount Hotel's parking lot and came to a sudden halt in the sally port near the front door. Casio leaped out of the vehicle, tossed the key to the valet parking attendant and raced into the building. He moved quickly, without preamble, to the elevator bank, and a beefy finger stabbed the UP button. Without realizing he was doing it, he paced in a small circle until the elevator doors opened. He stepped inside and hit the button for the third floor. The ascent seemed to take an eternity, though the car didn't stop on any other floor. As the doors open, Casio shot from the car and turned left, looking at the arrowed direction plaque on the wall at the end of the elevator alcove. He turned right from there and sprinted to a room near the end of the hall where he banged unceremoniously on the door. No one answered. He banged again with the ball of his fist, the raps reverberating down the hall. If anyone was in that room they'd have to be deaf or...

With a stony look on his face, he stepped back from the door. He drew his Browning, stepped forward and hit the door with the heel of his right shoe, hard, right at the spot where the lock was. The wood splintered and the door swung open. He leveled his gun and ran into the room.

In the suite's living room he saw no one. It was obvious that the suite was occupied but there was no evidence of a struggle.

Keeping to the shadows, he inched his way into the bedroom. The bedclothes were askew and there were items of clothing strewn haphazardly about. He could hear sound coming from what appeared to be the bathroom. He stepped inside to confront a closed shower curtain and running water. He leveled his gun, not knowing what he would find, and reached out with his left hand and swept the curtain open.

Standing in the tub, facing one another, their bodies mashed together, were Rod Pitcher and Samantha Parker, both very wet and very naked.

Pitcher's jaw dropped to the floor.

Samantha Parker stifled a scream.

"What the hell are you doing?" Pitcher screamed when he found his voice.

He kept Samantha Parker pressed against him so as little of her as possible would be visible to the detective.

Casio lowered his gun and sat on the stool, trying hard not to laugh.

"I don't see what's so damned funny," Pitcher exclaimed indignantly as he reached down gingerly to turn off the water.

Casio, without looking, plucked a large towel from the rack over his head and passed it to the reporter before turning his back, no longer making the effort to stifle his chuckle. Pitcher took the towel and handed it to Samantha Parker who wrapped it around herself above her breasts, and stepped from the shower tub, passed the guffawing Casio and into the bedroom. Pitcher grabbed another towel which he wrapped around his middle. He stepped to the bathroom floor and stood before the detective with his hands on his hips.

"You want to explain all this?"

Casio overcame his laughter with an effort.

"Something's happened, Rod, and we needed to contact you. Mac's been trying to call you for half an hour; he's on his way here."

"Well Samantha took the bedroom phone off the hook when we came in here, and obviously we couldn't hear the living room phone…"

Casio gave Pitcher an appraising look.

"And you obviously didn't have your cell phone on you…"

Pitcher grinned in spite of himself.

"Well, you know…"

"Rod?"

Samantha's voice came from the living room with a note of desperation in it. Pitcher grinned at the detective and headed that way with Casio a step behind. Parker stood at the hallway door, dressed in shorts and a tank top, looking at the shattered wood. She cast an angry look at the detective. Casio smiled back sheepishly.

"Well you didn't answer my knock," he said softly.

"D'uh!" Samantha spat. "What do we do now?"

"Well, I'd call the desk and have them send building maintenance up here right away," Casio mused with mock seriousness.

"D'uh is right," said Pitcher, slapping his forehead in mock seriousness as he went to make the call. He was back in a moment beckoning to Samantha and Casio to take seats in the front room.

"You said something happened, Sy," Pitcher began.

Casio nodded and explained the telephone call and McDermott's concern.

"Gee," Pitcher said, scratching his head. "I didn't think twice about telling Eve where I was, she and Peter have been an item – off and on – for a long time…"

Casio waved him off.

"It's OK, Pitch," he said, using the diminutive of pitcher's name that had become his sobriquet. "Mac's on his way, and he'll know what to do. In the meantime…" he pointed to Pitcher's towel, "perhaps something in a pair of pants would be appropriate."

"Not for me," spoke up Samantha Parker. She winked at Pitcher who blushed.

Casio checked his watch.

"Mac should be right along," he said. "We'll talk about what we need to do."

221

"Not without eating," Pitcher declared, moving back to the phone. He lifted it and called room service.

Chapter Twenty-Six

Eve Somers walked past the Paramount Hotel's desk with a purposeful gait, knowing no one would challenge her if she looked like she knew where she was going. She remembered something McDermott had once told her. He said, "You can get in anywhere. All you have to do is carry a clip board and look worried." She didn't have a clip board, but her manner and air were calculated to convince anyone paying her more than an appraising stare that she belonged where she was.

She had seen McDermott's black Jeep pass her at breakneck speed on I-95. But she was fairly sure the editor hadn't spotted her. She wasn't driving her own car, but instead headed toward Baltimore in the Bondo car. "Bondo... James Bondo," she had chuckled to herself at the time.

Somers was fairly sure McDermott would be looking for her as he streaked to be by his friend's side – little good would it do him. So she had driven the nondescript car rather than her regular car, the one McDermott knew about.

So she knew that McDermott was already in the hotel when she parked the car on the street a half-block from the entrance.

Now, inside, she walked behind the main desk and searched furtively until she found the laundry. She pushed open the door and found no one inside. She entered and locked the door behind her.

Against one wall was a hanging rack filled with freshly pressed employee uniforms. Taking her time, she checked the size tags until she found a shirt and pants that would fit her without being too tight or too baggy, which would call undue attention to her. She shucked out of her black pin-striped dress pants and silk long-sleeved dress shirt, but left on the undershirt she wore beneath. In their place she dressed in the off-white slacks and red jacket of the hotel wait-staff. Fortunately, she had noticed as she entered the building that other staff members wore white sneaker-like shoes, and that was what she had on, so she was safe. She carried her purse over her shoulder.

Leaving the laundry, she wandered a bit until she found the employee lounge. Inside there was a long picnic table down the center of the room, and some other chairs along the outer walls. In one corner was a computer station with a large flat-screen monitor. Eve took a chair near the computer and watched several employees use it.

The computer had several screens. One showed new room service orders that came in. There was a tab labeled "hotel guests," and one labeled "Rms To Clean," and a couple of others that meant nothing to her. She watched casually for quite awhile as other employees used the computer. She followed one staffer who was told by the computer to pick up a room service order, so she knew where to go. When she returned, no one was at the terminal, so she stepped up to it.

Fortunately there was no log-on needed for new users, so she flipped through the pages with impunity. Her first stop was the "Hotel Guests" page. She flipped through the list until she found a notation titles "*North Bay Times* Corporate Suite." She opened that link and found that the room was currently occupied by one Rodney Pitcher, and by one Samantha Parker.

Perfect!

As she smiled, an indicator lit on the computer's task bar, and she clicked on it. It was a Room Service order for the *Times* suite. Her smile even broader, now, she acknowledged the summons as the screen showed her, and as she had seen other employees do. Quickly wiping the keyboard with a napkin to eliminate any fingerprints on the keys and mouse, she walked down the hall to the room service wait station.

"Order for the *Times* suite," she said deliberately to the swarthy man on the other side of the counter. He nodded and slid an enormous tray across the Formica toward her. She noted that it contained four covered sandwich plates, four glasses and four drinks. There were two Coca Colas, a Sierra Mist and one Diet Pepsi, a dead giveaway to her that McDermott was on the scene.

She braced herself and spent a few minutes balancing the tray on her left hand, which was placed near the center of the unwieldy thing. Steady at last, she carefully picked her way down the fall until she found the employees' elevator. Stabbing the button with her free hand, she steadied the try yet again as she waited for the doors to open.

Upstairs in the corporate suite, Pitcher and McDermott were exchanging information. McDermott was finally telling the reporter and Samantha about the conversation with Harry Oglesby and the horror of his sudden murder in a night club men's room. Sy Casio was in the living room also, nodding in agreement with McDermott's description and including his observations, and his declarations to the police. Pitcher was listening in rapt fascination.

"Wow!" Pitcher exclaimed at length. "We're really making progress."

"Not enough," Casio retorted. "Harry Oglesby didn't live long enough to tell us who the killer was."

"Or who he suspected it was," McDermott corrected.

Casio nodded at the point.

"What about Charlie," Pitcher wanted to know.

"He's on his way down," McDermott said. "I called him and he said he's returning but he's leaving Linda with her relatives on Long Island."

"Wise," Casio asserted. "And now that we're dealing more out in the open with this thing it might be wiser still to get Samantha out of danger as well."

"The hell with that!" came a strong, assertive voice.

Samantha Parker clung to Pitcher's arm and looked at the detective with fire in his eyes.

"Whatever happens, I'm staying," she declared firmly. "You can't make me go and I'm not going."

Pitcher reached over and covered her hand with his. McDermott noticed the automatic gesture and smiled thinly.

"All right," he said. "There's no point in wasting time arguing that point. If Samantha wants to put her neck on the line with ours, I guess that's her privilege. Now we need to make some plans. Sy?"

Casio worried his hands and turned to McDermott.

"The first thing we need to do is get the police into this thing. This investigation of ours has gone just about as far as it can go without their involvement."

"Maybe," Pitcher said, tentatively. "But what do we tell them?"

Casio threw up his hands.

"Everything. We give them what we've got, and we tell them what our suspicions are. We can get the guys at the DC police to back up what we've said."

McDermott drew his lips into a thin line, pondering.

"Yeah but this whole thing is so bizarre," Pitcher said softly.

"It's not your usual murder case, that's for sure," Casio acknowledged. "And I don't mean for a minute that we give the cops what we got and call off our investigation. I mean we give them what we've got and we continue with what we're doing and try not to duplicate efforts."

McDermott stood and paced a short path.

"It's that duplication of efforts that I'm concerned about," he said. "How are we going to know that the police are working on so we don't try the same things they are, with less resources than they have?"

"Right," Pitcher returned. "And besides I still think we're on the right track in solving the 1946 murder..."

"We've all but done that," Casio said. "We know who killed Chance Caine, and we know who killed his killer, at least if Harry Oglesby was to be believed.

"Who's to say he wasn't just an old man trying to go out as a big shot?" Samantha Parker interjected. "What about that guy a long time ago that tried to convince everybody that he was Jesse James? He didn't even get to die under his own name. What's to say this Oglesby guy was just dealing out the bullshit to get attention?

The rest of the people in the room looked agape at Samantha Parker's longest speech ever.

"The thing about that," McDermott said, after a few moments, "is that he seemed to know everything about the Resistance and their courier system, and the watch. I'll admit there are some inconsistencies in his story, but it was a long time ago and he was no spring chicken..."

"But from what you've told me, it hangs true," Pitcher commented.

"I think so too," McDermott agreed.

"And let's remember, he was probably murdered for what he knew."

"It certainly appears to have been anything but a random killing," Samantha Parker interjected. "And he did know about the watch."

"Yes he did, didn't he?" Casio mused. "Do you think his death was calculated to occur before he revealed the name of the person he thought might be doing the killings?"

McDermott shrugged his shoulders.

"The killer couldn't have known how much he told me before he went to the rest room."

"True," Casio said. "But I'm pretty sure the killer knew Oglesby had been drinking a lot – and planned the assault in the men's room."

"But that would mean the killer was inside the club well before he went to the bathroom," McDermott said.

Casio only fixed the editor with a hard stare.

"That's true, and it makes me crazy," he said.

McDermott raised his eyebrow in an unspoken question. Casio's face clouded over.

"I was in there to watch your back and I didn't see the killer, whoever he was. That was my job and I didn't see him.

McDermott frowned.

"Don't beat yourself up over it, Sy. You were watching my back and you did a fine job of that. You pegged Oglesby's back-up."

Casio visibly brightened. The idea of his having missed the killer had been a blow to his professional integrity – at least in his own eyes, and he was happy to be forgiven by the man he was to protect.

McDermott knew that Casio had actually succeeded in his main task – watching his back as he talked to Oglesby. Had McDermott not come in with a back-up – which he made sure everyone on the Madhatter knew – who knew what Oglesby and *his* back-up would have done. So Casio had succeeded, and McDermott wouldn't let the detective beat himself up over the murder of the old operative.

"So what do we do now?" Samantha Parker asked.

"You mean besides call the police?" Pitcher asked.

She nodded.

"We need to know more about Harry Oglesby," McDermott began.

"That's a for sure," Casio returned, firmly. "I'll have my office run him through the FBI files and Interpol and some others, including the World War II Black Ops archives..."

"You have access to all those things? McDermott demanded.

Casio looked at McDermott as though what he said was a given.

"How do you get into those?" the editor demanded

Casio sighed.

"Mac, you don't spend thirty years in the investigation business and not run across some valuable tools you're really not supposed to have. I know I look like something out of Mickey Spillane, but I do use computers – quite effectively – and I know where to look for information."

"So you'll do the leg work on Oglesby?" McDermott inquired, dismissing Casio's assertion without further comment.

The detective nodded and reached for his cell phone, walking into the bedroom to complete his call in private.

McDermott turned to Pitcher.

"Charlie should be here this evening, Pitch," he said. "And as much as I know you're reeling from all this, he's going to ask about the rest of the stuff for the paper."

"Hell of a time to worry about that," Pitcher said, irritation clearly showing in his voice.

McDermott studied the floor.

"I know, but..."

227

"You know my time in this suite has been used for a lot more than enjoying Samantha," Pitcher said in the same tone.

"Amen to that!" Parker agreed.

Pitcher pointed at the room desk, on which his laptop computer and camera rested.

"I finished my work this afternoon and have already emailed it to Composing. So you and Charlie can just stop getting your panties in a bunch and give me a little credit for loyalty to my paper."

Pitcher's voice was rising in crescendo as he spoke, irritation giving way to anger. McDermott accepted the anger. He kept his eyes averted.

"I'm sorry, Pitch, I should have known."

"Yes, you should have," Pitch retorted, his voice softening as he forgave his editor and friend.

"I don't know how you do it," McDermott said, his voice developing an aura of admiration. "All the attacks on your family, and particularly on you, your home wrecked, your car burned, being sent to a hotel, and you still are able to complete your weekly assignments. You're professionalism is amazing, and I think you're the best."

Pitcher beamed, and Samantha Parker glared at McDermott seeing through what he was trying to do. She pulled her watch off her wrist and held it over her head. McDermott looked at her quizzically.

"It's getting deep in here," she said. "And I don't have a shit-proof watch."

McDermott's jaw dropped, and Pitcher bit his lip so hard the skin blanched.

There was a knock on the doorjamb, and a uniformed stewardess came into the room, her face partially hidden by the large tray she balanced on her left hand.

"Room service," she said in a muffled voice as she penetrated the living room of the suite, past the seated men who paid her very little attention.

But as she passed, something made McDermott take a second look, something he noticed but didn't notice, but there was enough there to cause him to take a second look. By that time the stewardess's back was to him, but he was still convinced that he had detected a moment of recognition.

Then he had it.

As she walked past them McDermott picked up a scent, a perfume he knew very well.

"Pitch!" he said, urgently, pointing.

The stewardess set the tray down and turned. Pitcher reached for his wallet on the desk to give her a tip, but in the same instant that McDermott pointed at her, he suddenly became conscious that it wasn't a tip she wanted.

The three people in the room were suddenly confronted with Eve Somers in hotel livery. The look on her face was hard as nails. Her lips were set in an ugly scowl, her eyes were impenetrable. She stood, feet spread wide apart, her neck thrust slightly forward.

And the Beretta 7.62 semiautomatic pistol was rock-steady in her right hand.

Chapter Twenty-Seven

"Eve?"

Peter McDermott's voice was incredulous as he stared, mouth agape, at his girlfriend and the silencer-equipped gun in her hand.

"Surprised, Lover?" she asked with a sneer.

"You have an unparalleled talent for understatement," McDermott managed to blurt out.

"Don't be. I think you had it pegged back in your condo."

"I was hoping I was wrong," he said weakly.

"You're too good of a reporter for that," she said.

McDermott stole a quick glance at Pitcher, whose jaw dropped also.

"I don't suppose it was me you were coming to see," McDermott said.

She shook her head.

"But it makes no difference that you're here.

"Why?"

She shrugged.

"Just as easy to kill three people as it is to kill one," she said almost casually.

"You can't mean that," McDermott asserted.

"Oh, yes, she can," Pitcher mumbled, his eyes fixed on the muzzle of the gun.

"Mr. Pitcher, you have something that is very important to me, and I want it. Now."

Pitcher and McDermott looked at one another, then back at Eve.

"Like what?" Pitcher demanded, fear creeping into his voice.

McDermott chanced a mild kick to Pitcher's shin to steady him.

"You came into possession of a strange-looking watch, I believe," Somers said, threateningly. "I want it."

Pitcher made a gesture of patting his pockets, not that he had any to pat.

231

"No watch here, Eve."

"But you have it, you know where it is."

It was more of a statement than a question.

"I didn't say so."

Eve Somers shifted her position slightly, but the gun never wavered nor did her hard stare that took in all three people in the room.

"Mr. Pitcher, if you don't tell me what I want to know I will surely put a hole in you – and that will force me to put holes in Mac and your pretty little girlfriend, here," Somers said seriously. "Excuse me, Sweetie, I don't think we've been introduced. I'm Eve Somers."

"Samantha Parker."

"Charmed, I'm sure."

"Eve," McDermott said again, almost pleadingly.

"I expect more of you, Mac. Tell me about the watch. Which one of you has it? I know damned well one of you does so don't try to bullshit me?"

"Would you mind telling me what this is all about?" McDermott demanded.

Somers smiled and nodded.

"All in due time, Lover. First things first. The watch."

McDermott and Pitcher glanced at one another again, just for a moment, and McDermott nodded imperceptivity.

"One thing," Pitcher began.

"Yes? Somers answered, venom dripping from her voice.

"Samantha goes free. I'll tell you what you want to know, but you let Samantha go. Deal?"

Somers took a tiny step forward.

"Mr. Pitcher you are in no position to make any deals."

Pitcher said nothing. Finally, Somers shrugged.

"But why not. OK, Pitch, you've got a deal. Samantha's neck for the watch. You have it with you?"

Pitcher shook his head. The glance that he and McDermott had exchanged moments ago had spoken volumes. The two were such lose friends that they had developed a strong non-verbal communications network, and it was working perfectly. Pitcher knew that McDermott wanted him to stall, to give Sy Casio an opportunity to call the play.

"I don't have the watch with me here," Pitcher declared firmly. "It's back in my apartment."

Eve Somers shook her head.

"Won't wash," she said. "I tossed your apartment, and if I do say so myself, I was thorough."

232

"I'll say!" Pitcher retorted.

"What?"

"Eve, you wrecked the place. There wasn't a stick of furniture salvageable in the whole dump."

She smiled as she nodded.

"So you see, I did quite the thorough search of your place, Mr. Pitcher, and there was no watch there, at least not the one I was looking for."

"It was there," McDermott said, declaratively.

"No way," Somers retorted.

"Floor safe," Pitcher said quietly. "Did you find the floor safe?"

Somers was startled.

"A floor safe in an apartment?"

Pitcher nodded.

"There's a floor safe in the master bedroom. That's where the watch is. I can tell you how to find it and give you the combination."

"And if you're lying to me?" Somers challenged.

Pitcher grinned.

"Well, that's one good reason to keep us all alive until you actually have the watch in your hand, isn't it?"

"Oh," Somers leered. "I can do far worse than kill you."

"Pitch is right, though, Eve," McDermott chimed in. "The trick here is to give you enough information to make you want to check it out, but not enough to make you want to bump us off until you have the goods. It's bad for business to snuff the only people who can tell you what you need to know."

"Maybe there's another way," Somers considered. "Was the watch opened?"

She turned her gaze, and the muzzle of the Beretta to McDermott.

"Don't try to lie to me, Mac, I know you too well."

McDermott paused a moment in thought, and stole another glance at Pitcher who now returned Mac's tiny nod of before.

"Yes," McDermott said softly. "The watch was opened. A friend of mine found the right tool to open it safely."

"And what was in it?" Somers demanded.

"What was in it?" McDermott repeated.

"Yeah, what was in it?" she growled again, raising the gun.

"Numbers," Pitcher said, simply.

"Numbers?"

"Yes," McDermott reiterated. "Numbers."

"What numbers?"

233

"What numbers?"

"Quit playing with me, Mac. What were the numbers?" She raised the gun again, more menacingly this time.

"I honestly wish we knew," McDermott said. "We haven't been able to figure them out."

"You expect me to believe that?"

"We wouldn't be here if we had," Pitcher said. "We'd be out looking for whatever the numbers led us to."

Somers pondered that for a moment. And a moment later, her gaze shifted, as though another thought had suddenly occurred to her. She took a glance, half-a-second, no more, at the tray she had brought to the room.

"One moment, Mac. There are four glasses and four plates on this tray. And there are only three of you in the room. Where's the other person?"

McDermott made a show of looking around.

"Other person?"

Somers nodded.

"Other person."

"There's no one else here," Samantha Parker piped in.

Somers stepped forward, her teeth gritted and her eyes even harder than before. The aim of her gun shifted, drawing a bead right between Samantha Parker's eyes.

"Maybe you two guys wouldn't be quite so funny if I put a hole in her pretty little head."

"You promised to let her go if we cooperated, Eve," McDermott said gruffly. "We're cooperating."

"I lied," Somers said through gnashing teeth as she visibly applied pressure to the trigger.

The hotel carpenter couldn't possibly have picked a better moment to appear in the door frame and knock.

"Hey there, looks like you've got a problem here!"

The voice from the door took Eve Somers' attention for only a moment, just the bat of an eyelash, but it was enough. Sy Casio burst into the room, gun drawn and cocked, and strode directly to Eve Somers. He grabbed her gun hand with his left, and screwed the business end of his Browning into her ear.

"Drop it, Eve," he growled fiercely. "Do it now."

The Beretta clattered to the carpeted floor, and McDermott scooped it up. He pointed the muzzle to the floor and waited for Casio to make

234

the move. The detective got Somers in a retaining hold and turned slightly to address Pitcher.

"Call the cops, Pitch," he said.

"Right," Pitcher replied and stepped quickly to the desk phone.

Somers worked her way to one side in Casio's hold and head-butted him on the bridge of his nose. The suddenness of the movement, and the stabbing pain from the contact broke Casio's attention for a heartbeat, but it was heartbeat enough. Somers yanked herself out of the detective's grip and batted his gun away from her head. With a lunge, she launched herself forward, executing a perfect, training-camp body block against McDermott, who was directly in her path. Both went down in a heap, McDermott losing the gun from the impact. Somers barrel-rolled and came to her feet with the gun back in her own hand, but by this time Casio had recovered and was aiming his own weapon.

Somers squeezed off a shot and missed, the bullet embedding itself in the plaster wall just to the left of the living room window.

"Oh my God," the hotel carpenter yelled, and turned and ran down the hall emitting a shrill, effeminate scream.

Casio returned fire with a single shot and also missed, the bullet finding a place to the right of the door frame, missing Somers' head by perhaps three inches, and slamming into the wall in almost the exact spot the carpenter had been standing seconds before.

McDermott was still on the floor. Quick as lightning, Somers lunged forward and grabbed Samantha Parker around the neck and pulled her toward the door, keeping her body between Somers and Casio's gun. She reached around the panicking Parker and aimed her gun at the two other men in the room to hold them at bay as she inched her way, dragging Parker's resisting form with her. Parker gurgled and repressed a scream.

Eve Somers had gained the room door. She yanked Parker into the hallway, and jammed the muzzle of her Beretta into the pliant flesh of the woman's cheek.

"Move, Bitch," she hissed, and turned right, walking backward at a fast clip toward the elevators and utility rooms, past the other guest rooms with Parker still used as a shield. Casio followed, gun at the ready looking for a clear shot, but he knew he couldn't chance it unless something changed radically.

Somers was about halfway down the hall when she broke stride, and snapped off another shot. There was a soft chuff from the silenced Beretta, and Casio stopped in his tracks and stepped aside, avoiding the bullet that took out the window at the other end of the hall.

Almost before the sound of her gun died away, Somers tightened her grip on Samantha Parker and resumed her flight, with Casio inching closer, Browning two-handed in front of him. But Somers had the advantage. Her perusal of the hotel computer system had given her information that she used to plan her escape in case her assault in the room went awry, and she was prepared now. All she had to do was make it to the second-to-last door on the left side of the corridor, and she was thirty feet away.

But Casio was getting close – too close. Somers could also hear additional footfalls, and without looking, she realized that McDermott and Pitcher had joined the chase.

She made it to the door and reached for the knob, praying silently that it wasn't locked. The door swung open and she dashed inside, slamming it behind her. She didn't bother looking for a lock, she just forced Parker inside and followed her, shoving the hapless girl across the room and pulling open a metal shoot built into the far wall.

This was the hotel laundry sorting room for the sixth floor. It was where the maids brought rolling baskets of sheets, towels, washcloths, and other washables, and dumped them, one type at a time, into the hopper, which then rotated into the wall and dumped the laundry into a shoot which led to the laundry room far below in the hotel basement.

Casio burst into the room just in time to see Somers pull open the hatchway in the wall, her weapon still in contact with Parker's head. The hatch opened like a mail-box slot, and had a hollow void inside that would empty into the shoot when the hatch was closed. She stuck the gun into the waistband of the hotel slacks she was wearing, shoved Parker hard toward Casio, blocking his body and his gun from her for just a fleeting moment. As she did so, she hoisted herself up into the hatch.

Casio carefully moved Parker aside, and into Rod Pitcher's arms, and leveled his gun, shielding the three unarmed men behind him.

"Give it up, Eve, game over."

She chuckled aloud."

"Don't think so, Detective," she said, grinning. She pushed herself completely into the hatchway and gave Casio a knowing leer. The detective tried to cross the distance from the hallway door to the hatch. He was about halfway there when Somers blew him a kiss and gave him a triumphant grin, and pulled the hatch closed.

There was a metallic sound inside the wall that seemed to head downward, and then silence. Casio made it to the other side of the room, still on the dead run. He yanked open the hatch and raised his gun, but he was staring at an empty clothes hopper.

Eve Somers was on her way to the hotel laundry, four floors below.

Chapter Twenty-Eight

Somers found herself in a rectangular shoot with smooth metal sides just wide enough for her to remain in a sitting position as she plunged in free-fall downward from the third floor. She managed to drag her rubber-soled shoes against one wall of the shoot, which, in turn, pressed her back against the opposite wall. By exerting pressure with her feet she managed to slow her descent, but it was painful, and she wouldn't be able to maintain it long.

At the same time, she was hopeful that there was a pile of laundry under the end of the shoot, something soft for her to land on, or all the effort and pain of slowing down her plunge would be for naught.

She was falling too fast, she thought, so she pressed her back tighter against the wall behind her, and stretched out her legs to make firmer contact with her shoes against the opposite wall. By this time, the fall had produced enough energy that she could feel the heat of the friction through the thick soles of her shoes, and she was certain that if she survived, she would have third degree burns on her back.

The pain of braking her fall was turning to abject agony, but she persisted, knowing that if she didn't – and especially if there was nothing below for her to land on – she would arrive in the hotel basement with a funny noise that would take her to the final nothingness. She pressed harder with her feet and back and tried hard to ignore the pain.

Just when she thought she couldn't take the pain or the burning sensation from the wall friction against her back, she came to an abrupt stop. Emitting an audible "oof," she lay supine in a wheeled laundry basket that was filled with dirty sheets.

Four floors up, Sy Casio yanked the hatchway to the laundry shoot back open and looked into the hopper, half hoping to find Eve Somers inside, balled up after failing to fit down the metal tube. But the hatchway opened to easily and as he had feared, its attached hopper was empty. Frustrated, he slammed the hatchway closed and turned to McDermott, who had been looking over his shoulders.

"Call the police," he snapped.

"Already done," McDermott said, holding up his cell phone.

The two men stepped from the laundry sorting room into the hallway where Rod Pitcher was calming a crying Samantha Parker. Casio noted with some admiration, that Parker wasn't hysterical, as she understandably could have been, but was merely reacting to having been frightened out of her wits. They looked at Pitcher who nodded, his own admiration for Parker increasing exponentially. Silently, the four walked back to the *Times* suite to await the arrival of detectives.

By the time they arrived at the room, Samantha Parker was largely put back together, but she indicated that she didn't want to talk about her ordeal as a "human shield for a crazy woman."

McDermott and Casio took seats in the living room, and Rod pitcher took Parker into the bedroom to let her lie down. He was back in a moment and he seated himself on the short couch next to McDermott.

"Well we certainly blew that, didn't we?" Casio asked rhetorically.

Eve Somers lay for long moments in the laundry basket with the wind knocked out of her, trying to muster the strength to move. Tentatively, she flexed her leg and arm muscles then her back and neck, and determined that everything on the inside appeared to be working. Carefully, she moved her right arm, then her left. They were stiff and sore, but none of the dull ache she would experience if there was a break. She bent her knees, and found her legs cramped and sore, but serviceable, so she reached up and found the rim of the basket, pulling herself into a near-sitting position.

Somers didn't know if Casio and McDermott would be legging it down to the basement to catch up with her – she guessed they would not. But one thing she knew for certain is that one of the people upstairs would be calling the police as early as possible, and the penalty for the crime she was guilty of – today it was "assault with a deadly weapon" – could be on the stiff side in Maryland.

Best course of action would be to get very lost, very fast, and very quietly.

Carefully, she pulled her achy body out of the laundry cart and looked around the dimly lit room. Against two walls were side-by-side washers and dryers. In the center of the room was a huge table on which sheets and other things were folded. Near that was a rack of newly-laundered employee uniforms. Against another wall there was a series of boxes, like mail boxes, but much bigger, stretching from floor to ceiling and from corner to corner. Many were filled with folded sheets, some fitted, some top sheets. Others were crammed full of pillow slips, towels, washcloths and cloth table napkins.

Between the columns of boxes was a door.

She hauled herself to the floor with an effort and walked gingerly to the clothing rack. She could almost tell that the back of the hotel jacket she wore had been destroyed in her descent, so she shucked out of it, dropping it to the floor. The undershirt followed, and she stood on the concrete floor dressed in the hotel pants and her bra. She skirted the hangers on the rack until she found a polo shirt with the hotel logo on it that she thought would fit her. She pulled it over her head, finding it a little snug but otherwise acceptable. Looking down at the pile of discards on the floor, she saw that she was right; the backs of the hotel jacket and undershirt were charred and holed. Satisfied, she went to the door, trying the knob. It was unlocked, so she let herself out into a short concrete block hallway. To her left was another door, and to her right was an elevator. She opted for the up-and-down conveyance, and stabbed the UP button. The doors opened instantly and she stepped in, pressing the button for the ground floor.

She discovered, during the short ride up, that she was in a freight elevator, a fact given away by the moving blankets hanging on the car walls. That meant, she hoped, that she wouldn't have to pass through the lobby. The doors parted, and she was confronted with another door, almost directly in front of her. The sign on the door said "Exit," and a sign over the top of the door said "Service." She crossed the short expanse and pressed on the swinging bar across the door. It opened, and she stepped out of the building and into an alley emptying onto a cross-street to the one on which the hotel entrance was located.

It was early spring, and the sun was taking its time about setting – twilight had fallen but there was still plenty of light to navigate by. She followed the alley to the street, keeping close to the hotel's brick outer wall. She furtively peeked around the corner from the alley into the street, then took a deep breath and walked boldly into the waning sunlight.

The first thing that greeted her eyes as she stepped into the open was a blue-and-white Baltimore Police car. Eve Somers didn't know how soon the police had been called by the people remaining on the third floor – but she knew they would be called. And she didn't know how much time had elapsed as she lay in the clothes basket with the wind knocked out of her – to be sure, she was still having problems drawing a breath. And she had no desire to be picked up so soon, not this quickly. She tried to walk, nonchalantly, down the sidewalk, but in her periphery, she saw the police car that was now behind her speed up.

"Seven-Mike-Seventy-Seven, assist traffic unit, possible fatal accident, 800 block of West Lombard Street, handle Code One. Seven-Mike-Eighty-One, assist also, second unit, same code."

The two officers in the police car just north of the north-south marker of Howard Street looked at one another. Code One on their radio meant no lights, no siren, and no hurry. Small wonder. Victims of fatal accidents seldom needed fast service. The officer in the right seat squeezed the button on his throat microphone, which was attached by a long wire to the portable radio on his belt.

"Seven-M-Seventy-Seven, roger on the call," he intoned.

"Seven-M-Eighty One, Roger," the other unit acknowledged over the radio.

The two officers sighed as one, and the one in the left seat pressed the accelerator down just a bit, gaining speed to eat up the twelve blocks as quickly as possible without causing a disturbance.

Four blocks directly behind them, the second police car was doing precisely the same thing.

But Eve Somers only saw a police car speeding up and heading in her direction. She had no way of knowing that the police officers inside the car knew nothing about her, and were, in fact, heading to assist a traffic unit.

Somers panicked.

Convinced that the speeding-up police unit had spotted her, she looked frantically for a means of quick escape. At that moment, the traffic light on the Howard Street side of the intersection with Fairlawn Street turned red. A silver Chevy Impala sidled up to a stop at the white line on the street. Eve Somers watched the car as it glided to a stop, and a thin smile formed on her lips.

She launched herself forward and stepped into the street at the light, ostensibly to cross – but as she rounded the car, she turned left and jerked open the driver's side door and shoved her gun into the driver's face."

"Out!" she yelled at the top of her lungs.

The driver needed no urging. The thin man in the glasses and business suit leaped out of the seat, and Eve Somers slipped in, all before the car, which was still in drive, could move more than a couple of feet.

The driver yelled aloud for help, flailing his arms as he gained the curb and raced toward the police car a half-block back, becoming bogged down in traffic.

Eve Somers hesitated not one second. She gunned the engine and released the brake. The car shot into the intersection, still against the red light. Oncoming cars from the left and the right swerved to get out of the way, and the two cars behind them slammed into their rear-ends, causing minor injuries, and would shortly close the intersection so the wrecks could be cleared away.

Back in Seven-Mike-Seventy-Seven, the two officers looked at one another. The driver turned out of his lane of traffic into the oncoming one, hit his blue lights and tromped on the gas. The right-hand officer keyed his radio mic.

"Seven M-Seventy-Seven, possible carjacking in progress, North Howard at Fairlawn. Victim is in front of the Paramount hotel, have another unit pick him up. We are pursuing the suspect now."

"All units," Central Dispatch began over the radio. "All units converge on the area of Howard and Fairlawn, possible hijacking in progress, description to follow."

The white police car with the blue lettering jumped the median into the oncoming lane and squealed sixty feet of BPD rubber on the pavement and started closing the distance. Behind them, another police car came into the pursuit, while a third, coming around the curve from another street, looked for and found the victim of the car-jacking.

"Seven-M-Seventy-Seven, car-jacking suspect is driving a gold-colored Chevy Impala, Maryland license 5-9-7-Adam David Quincy, now headed south on Howard at high speed."

Central Dispatch acknowledged the signal and passed the information on to all other units. Seven-M-Seventy-Seven sped up to close on the Impala. But the chase car seemed to leap ahead as Eve Somers pressed the accelerator to the floor and fish-tailed before gaining control of the unfamiliar vehicle.

Somers was still unaware that the police car behind her had been en route to something entirely unrelated to her and her crimes. She was unaware that her panic alone had put her in the situation she was in, a situation which, without coherent thought and a lot of luck, she might not get out of with her freedom – or alive.

The Chevy had an optional engine under the hood, a large one that could propel the car as fast, or faster than any police package on the street – and Eve Somers was a top-notch driver. She swung the car through traffic, passing, and even jumping the curb in her efforts to stay ahead of the police cruiser. The sirens, just coming on from the police cruisers behind her, were mean to unnerve her. She turned up the radio and with her free hand, punched the station buttons until she found some music she liked. She leaned over the steering wheel and urged the car to speed.

"No one's down there," said Detective Armando Santos of the Baltimore Police Department. "We saw evidence that someone was in a laundry basked under the shoot, and there's some clothing missing from the room, so there was definitely someone there. I don't understand why you didn't chase her down to that room."

Casio stared hard at the younger man. Detective Santos had only received his gold shield six months before. He was thirty-ish, tall, with chiseled features and a ramrod straight back upholstered in a new suit a cut above that usually worn by police officers of low rank. He was Hispanic and confident in his abilities.

"Look at me, Detective," Casio snapped. "Can you see me, or either of these guys, running down five flights of stairs and being alive at the bottom, let alone trying to subdue a criminal suspect?"

Santos looked the three men up and down, and at length, shallowly shook his head.

"OK, you got me there," he said, without a hint of an accent. "Why didn't you call us sooner?"

"By the time we knew what she was about, she had a gun on us," McDermott said. "I called you the moment she went down that shoot."

Santos nodded, satisfied with that explanation as well, and he scribbled a note in a leather-bound notebook he kept in an inside jacket pocket. Casio's eyes gleamed, he had the exact same notebook and kept it in exactly the same pocket.

"Well we've got an APB out on your girlfriend, McDermott. We should have her before long."

"Don't bet on it," McDermott said under his breath.

"What's that?"

"Nothing."

"And you say all this ties in with several other murders, and a couple of attempts, plus some property damage incidents, all in Baltimore and D.C.?" Santos asked, consulting his notes.

"You have the name of the D.C. detective that's been handling it, plus the ballistics officer who assisted in the attempt on Pitcher's life here in Baltimore," Casio told him.

244

"Riiiight," Santos said, apparently oblivious to Casio's words as he flipped page after page in his notes. His cell phone jangled and he lifted it to his ear.

"Santos."

The three men in the room with him could hear some jabbering on the other end, before Santos pressed the END button and replaced the phone in his coat pocket.

"There was a car-jacking a few seconds ago right outside the hotel. The perp is a woman with dark hair. A couple of our units are chasing her now."

"Dark hair, huh? Right outside the hotel?" Pitcher mused.

"You think it's this Eve Somers broad?" Santos asked.

"Unless female car-jackers are common in this part of town, I'd say it probably is," McDermott said, softly.

"The uniform guys will have her in a few minutes," Santos asserted.

McDermott grinned and pulled a bill from his wallet.

"I've got twenty bucks that says she gets away," he said, slapping the bill on the desk next to Pitcher's computer.

"You're covered," Casio said, slapping down another bill.

"I'm in," Pitcher said, adding his.

Santos looked at the three newspapermen as though they'd lost their minds.

Night was at last falling, Even Somers had to turn the stolen car's lights on to safely navigate around and through traffic. The evening rush hour was thinning out and she was able to bend on more speed and put more real estate under her wheels, opening the distance between her and the pursuing police cars. She noticed, in her most recent break-neck turn, that other police vehicles had joined the case, including, she thought, a Maryland State Police cruiser. She kept making random turns and circling blocks to keep them off balance and not allow them to get a cruiser ahead of her, but she knew that was a losing battle; sooner or later they'd have the whole area cordoned off and she'd be boxed in. She had to do something, and she had to do it now.

She mashed the gas pedal down the floor, pressing hard, trying to coax a little more speed out of the Impala. The gap opened to something over half a block. Not much, but maybe enough. In circling one block she had noticed a used car lot. If she could get there before they got her into line-of-sight...

Desperately she urged more speed out of the powerful Chevrolet engine, and it seemed to respond to her mental urges. She could see the gap widening between her and her pursuers, but she also knew time was ticking away fast.

Without signaling, or slowing down much, she made an abrupt left turn, then another into an alley about halfway up the block. From the alley, she turned onto the lot of a used car dealership she had noticed on one of her orbits, in an effort to shake off cruisers trying to get in front of her. The dealership had a row of cars facing the main street, that stretched the entire length of the lot, except for a single gap a bit more than halfway down, where one car had apparently been removed from the line, sold, driven home, or on a demo, she didn't care. She shut off her car lights and bounced the Impala into the space, grinding it to a quick stop. She slammed the gear shift into park and shut off the engine, ducking down under the dashboard.

Holding her breath, she listened for the sirens and they weren't long in coming. Tensely, she waited. The police cars ignored the entrance to the alley – telling her they had not seen her turn that way – and roared to the intersection to her right before turning against the light and barreling up the street. She let out her breath slowly as she heard the sirens recede.

She had fooled them for the moment, but she was not so naïve as to think she could fool them for long. When they didn't pick her up in a block or two, they would retrace their steps and find the Impala. The trick was for her to not be in it when they did.

She let herself out of the car and kept to the shadows while she made a cursory inspection of the dealership office, a tiny shack at the back of the lot. The face of the building facing the car lot had a retail store-like door and a large picture window through which she could see a desk, presumably belonging to the owner. She walked to the side of the building and found nothing, no windows or doors.

But at the back, facing the alley she had used to access the lot, she found a window that was just about chest-high. Quickly she looked around, then pulled the polo shirt over her head and held it, with her left hand, over the pane of glass. With her right hand she gently punched the shirt two or three times, gauging the tensile strength of the glass. Then she reared back and hit the glass hard, dead center in the shirt she held. The glass shattered. She waited a moment, listening for any alarms. Hearing none, she reached in and unbolted the window, and silently pushed the sash upward. She shook out the shirt and carefully put it back on, then climbed through the open window into the office.

246

She groped around in the dark, not daring to turn on a light, working her way to the front of the building, finally stumbling onto the owner's desk. She looked carefully, using the glow from the street, and her heart leaped for joy. There, on the desk, was a small flashlight, the kind dealers use to look at VIN numbers on cars. She snapped it on and found the batteries were fresh – the light glowed brightly. She played the beam about the office, across the walls and floor, not finding what she was looking for. Finally she shut the light off and gave the matter a bit of thought. After a moment, she slapped her forehead with the open flat of her hand. She reached down and tugged on the large bottom drawer of the desk. Her blood ran cold. It was locked.

Desperately looking around she saw little that could help her. She used the flashlight to guide her through the office to a door to one side of the desk. It was a rest room. She looked inside and was elated to see a tool box, but her elation was short-lived; the tool box was also locked.

She walked carefully to a table she had glimpsed on the other side of the office from the desk. It was a greasy table, with assorted oily auto parts strewn about on it. She noted that it could be hidden buy a collapsible curtain, apparently when the business owner had customers inside the office. On the table she found a hammer.

She glanced at her watch. Three and a half minutes had passed since she had turned on the flashlight – meaning it was about four minutes, perhaps a little more, since she had entered the office. The police should have caught on to her trick by now, and they would be doubling back checking all the parking lots. She was sure other cars had bottled up all the other ways out of this particular district of the city. She needed to hurry.

Back in the rest room she hit the lock on the tool box once, twice, three times, without success. Frustrated and getting scared, she reared back and two-handed the hammer, bringing it down onto the lock with all the strength left her body. She was rewarded by a snapping sound, and the padlock on the tool box was open. She removed it and threw it over her shoulder, opening the box and rummaging through its contents, the flashlight clutched in her teeth. Nothing in the top tray, so she removed it and picked her way through the bottom compartment. There she found what she needed; a flat crow bar.

She made the desk in five steps and knelt before the large bottom drawer, trying to force the bar's wedged end into the crack between the drawer and its frame. She tapped the other end with her hammer to make sure she had good purchase, and then eased her weight onto the top of the bar, pressing as hard as she could with even pressure.

It happened suddenly. There was a metallic sound, as though something had snapped, and then the drawer opened slightly. Throwing down the bar and hammer she yanked it open the rest of the way.

The sight was her reward.

There is the drawer was a fitted sheet of plywood on which there were hooks, four to the row. On the hooks were the keys to the cars for sale on the lot, each set of keys tagged with the description of the vehicle.

She took a moment and read several of the tags, finally selecting a set of keys to a Mitsubishi Spyder. She pocketed several other sets of keys, just in case, and left the building the same way she had come in, not bothering to close the window sash.

The Mitsubishi – mitsu-*bitchy*, she laughed to herself, was in the second row of cars, and fortunately, wasn't boxed in. She slid under the wheel and turned the key. The engine gunned to life. Carefully, she picked her way to the back of the lot with the lights off, and left the business. She then took the same route the police had, turning right passing the front of the dealership, and melted into the evening traffic.

Chapter Twenty-Nine

"That's the craziest, most convoluted story I've ever heard," Detective Armando Santos said, incredulously. He was sitting on the settee in the living room of the *North Bay Times* sweet in the Paramount Hotel. For the better part of 45 minutes, he was regaled with the entire story, from the 1946 murder to all that had happened on the present day.

"But it's all true," McDermott asserted, firmly.

Santos sighed.

"I know, that's what makes it so fantastic."

He sat back and crossed his legs.

"You didn't say why she was killing all these people," he mused. "That's the only think you haven't explained."

"That's the part we haven't figured out yet," Casio said. "The answer lies somewhere. I just think we're going to have to find her again and ask her."

"And hope some trigger-happy patrolman doesn't waste her before you can ask her anything," Santos said flatly.

"You think that might happen?" Pitcher asked, his eyes wide.

This is Baltimore," Santos said. "With the drug and crime problem this city has it's a flat miracle we don't have more police shootings than we do."

McDermott and Casio gnashed their teeth.

"So it's a good thing you didn't tell Eve about that floor safe, Mr. Pitcher."

Pitcher and McDermott looked at one another, as did Casio and Samantha Parker.

Santo's jaw dropped.

"Don't tell me..."

McDermott nodded, his mind a million miles away – or at least as far as Pitcher's apartment was. Casio and Pitcher nodded in perfect unison. Samantha Parker sat back with a blank look on her face.

Santos noticed their discomfiture.

"Don't tell me..."

McDermott grinned sheepishly.

"It's hard to know what to say when someone draws down on you," he said in a soft voice.

"But did you have to...?"

Pitcher's voice hardened just a touch.

"We're not action heroes, Detective," he said. "And a woman Mac's been dating just pulled a gun on us – and it's becoming evident that she may be behind all the killings in my family."

"You still haven't told me what it's all about," Santos said.

"We'll tell you..." McDermott began.

"...when we figure it out," Pitcher finished.

He turned to Parker.

"Sam, stay here and guard the chattels."

He looked at Casio and McDermott, and, as one, they rose and talked toward the hallway door.

"Hey," Santos protested. "Where do you think you're..."

They three turned left in the hallway and disappeared.

"...going?"

The mercury-vapor streetlights of Baltimore take about 90 minutes to reach their full intensity when the photoelectric cell recognizes oncoming darkness and clicks them on.

The Bondo Car sat against the curb at mid-block a couple of streets away from the Paramount Hotel. Eve Somers parked the stolen Mitsubishi five spaces behind the Bondo car, and got out, throwing the keys down a storm drain. She eased up, on the traffic side, and opened the unlocked door of the Bondo Car, pulling into the near lane.

Unconsciously, she drove a bit faster than she should have, but the one city police car, and the one sheriff's deputy she passed didn't pay her a second look. She maneuvered through the seedier parts of Baltimore, where the streets became progressively dirtier and filled with debris, stripped cars and human flotsam and jetsam.

As with the police officers she passed, the denizens of the night in lower Baltimore paid her scant attention. She drove through this part of the city as though she had an attitude, something that was essential for survival in this part of town.

Gradually, the culture changed as she drove toward the northern part of the city and the apartment complex where Rod Pitcher lived. At length, she left Skid Row behind and the streets widened to accommodate the middle-middle class families, work-a-day, two income families who lived in townhouses and mid-scale apartments. Pitcher fit that category. He had a ground floor apartment. It took her nearly thirty minutes to traverse the distance to the apartment complex Pitcher had lived in for several years. She pulled into the parking lot and took a space away from the building, and about three doors down from Pitcher's private entrance. In the glove compartment she found her flashlight, which she carried in her left hand, toting the Beretta in the waistband of her hotel pants. Leaving the car unlocked, she eased around the outside of the building and located the back window of Pitcher's apartment. She knew it was a window into the second bedroom, the one he used as his home office.

When she had visited the apartment a few days ago – the time she had trashed the place – she had checked all the windows in the place. The one in Pitch's office had a broken lock, and she had been able to shove the screen up, and then get a fingernail under the window sash and force it up a few inches. From that point it had been easy.

After she had destroyed most of Pitcher's possessions, she had closed the screen and returned the window as it had been when she found it. That time she had let herself out through the front door, leaving it open. She would do the same this time.

That was if, of course, no one had noticed the broken lock on the window, and repaired it, if all concerned had figured that the burglar, whoever it was, had entered as well as left through the front door. It was an easy enough assumption if the intruder had not left any obvious signs of alternate entry. She was careful to have left none.

She found the same window, noting the position of an air conditioning compressor and the media boxes for telephone, cable and internet. She had made a mark in the plastic the last time, and the beam of the flashlight easily found the mark. So she knew she was at the right place.

Gingerly, she pressed in on the aluminum frame of the screen, and inclined her arms upward. It moved. She continued to apply pressure until there was a crack at the bottom big enough to get her fingertips in. She did so, and applied more pressure, forcing the screen upward on unlubricated tracks. Finally it was open wide enough to let her body pass through.

Next was the window itself. She got a fingernail under the sash, hoping against hope that no one had noticed the broken lock – broken before she had ever visited this apartment – and she hoped it hadn't been repaired. If it had, her fingernail would probably snap down to the quick. It would be painful, but more painful would be the realization that she would have to find a less subtle way of getting into the apartment.

To her relief, it gave a little, and she was able to get a better grip on the underside of the window and force it higher and higher. In a short time it was as high as the screen she had lifted. She leaped up, hands on the sash, and pulled her body through the window into the darkened room.

Less than six minutes had elapsed since the moment she had stepped out of the car.

She went through the window head-first, landing in the fetal position on the floor three feet below. She pulled herself erect, and switched on the flashlight, cupping her hands over the light end to keep the beam as unobtrusive as possible as she made her way down the short hall to the master bedroom. She thought it was enormously funny that Pitcher had not yet replaced some of the destroyed furniture – that it had been lashed together with baling wire and duct tape.

In the second bedroom, the large bookcase against the far wall was the only piece of furniture. Pitcher's desk, which she had hacked to pieces, was gone, as were the computer stand and dresser which she had destroyed. Why she hadn't trashed the bookcase she could not remember, but she hadn't.

It was a very large case, the upper shelves were above her eye level. She wrapped her arms around it as much as she could and tried to move it, but it stayed where it was, seemingly with determination. She shifted her position and exerted pressure from right to left, and was surprised to find the chest move aside. It glided obliquely, the right side moving to the left, exposing a section of carpet beneath that was impressed with the legs of the large chest. Bending, she felt around the carpet inside the impressed marks until she found a flap, which she pulled aside easily. Beneath was a round metal door with a twelve-button keypad. She knew the next step was to find a combination. She looked around the nearly empty room, finding nothing that might carry the numbers she needed. So she headed back down the hallway to Pitcher's bedroom.

He had not repaired his bed. It was nothing more than smashed and splintered rubble. There were papers and envelopes strewed on the top and she held the flashlight under one arm as she riffled through them.

She finally found an old medical bill that she thought was probably in collection. His Social Security Number was on it, and she scribbled it down on a piece of foolscap and resumed looking. She noted that each of the pieces of mail had his four-digit address on them and she knew most safe combinations were four numbers, so she copied that down as well.

She also located his birth date – which was also four digits – and wrote that down. Satisfied, she carried the foolscap back to the second bedroom where she tried the birth date on the numeric pad. Nothing happened. The tiny LED light on the top of the door continued to glow red. She punched in his address numerical, and the light remained red. Crossing her fingers, she punched in the last four digits of his social security number. The red light turned green and she grasped the handle. The door swung upward, exposing the inside of the safe. She played the light into the abyss below and could see several folders and sheaves of papers. But at the very bottom was a small white box. As she started to reach for the box, she noticed something on the inside of the safe door.

There were six tiny switches on an inside panel, and a small display about one inch high by four inches long. Without warning the display lit, and displayed the words, "Counting Down." She stared at it, wondering what it meant, and then it changed.

"Signing on," it said, and she began looking about the safe, inside and around its edges for some inkling of what it was signing on to. Then it changed yet again

"Sending Intruder Alert," it said, and a moment later it changed yet again. "Alert Sent."

On impulse she tried to reach into the safe, but the display turned from green to red and displayed, "Closing Safe in 3... 2... 1."

Somers jerked her hand away from the safe opening just an eye blink before the heavy steel door slammed shut.

It dawned on her that the safe, itself, had just signed onto the internet and sent an intruder alert to police, which means a patrol car would be sent in a matter of minutes. She closed the screen and window, then ran the flashlight over the papers strewn about the room one last time. Sitting atop a pile of papers that had obviously been carefully sorted was a piece of personnalized notepaper she had not noticed before. The paper had some numbers and periods scribbled on it. Apparently Pitcher had felt it important enough to save from among the rubble of his home. Shrugging, she folded the paper and pocketed it, snapping off her flashlight as she walked unhurriedly down the hallway and through the living room. She helped herself to a banana on from a bowl on top of his tiny dining table, and let herself out through the front door, closing, but not locking it. She walked, again unhurriedly, across the parking lot where she found the Bondo car. She had backed out of the parking space and was driving toward the exit when a Baltimore police cruiser with its red lights ablaze passed her entering the parking lot. She stopped, signaled a left turn, and smiled as she entered the street and drove away.

The *North Bay Times* crew rolled into Pitcher's apartment complex parking lot perhaps 15 minutes after the first police car arrived. McDermott, Pitcher and Casio approached the open apartment door and found their way blocked by a burly, blue-clad Baltimore policeman.

"What do you want here?" the cop asked in what he thought was an authoritative tone.

"This is my apartment," Pitcher said, doing a bad imitation of the cop's severe tone.

Casio guffawed.

"Well let's break out some ID, then," the cop snarled, taking offense at being mimicked.

Pitcher hauled out his wallet and showed the officer his Maryland driver's license. The officer shined his flashlight on the license, and then sent the beam directly into Pitcher's eyes.

"OK," he said, jerking his thumb over his left shoulder.

Pitcher stepped into the lighted living room of his apartment, and McDermott and Casio tried to follow. But the uniform placed a beefy arm across the door frame and barred their way.

"And who might you be?" the cop asked, collectively

"I be his best friend and boss," McDermott said, again trying to mimic the officer's tone.

The cop ignored the attempt this time, probably because it wasn't as good as Pitcher's

"At the same time?" he found wit to ask. "Let's see some ID from you!"

McDermott showed the officer his license and his press card. The officer shined his light on the documents, and then into McDermott's face. While Mac counted the purple and magenta spots before his eyes, the officer looked expectantly at Casio. The detective smiled thinly and pulled his California driver's license and his detective's certificate, and had the foresight to close his eyes when the cop shined the flashlight in his face.

"OK, you can go in," the cop said, magnanimously. "Stay with your friend."

McDermott and Casio caught up with Pitcher in the apartment's second bedroom. Both men instantly noticed that the large wooden bookcase was moved aside and the carpet that had covered the floor safe had been disturbed. A crime scene technician was dusting the door of the safe for fingerprints. The door was closed. The technician lightly brushed a fine black powder across the face of the door, developing a print. He took an inch-wide piece of clear tape, peeled off the backing, and set the sticky side down on the powder. He pressed it smooth and carefully lifted, pulling up a clear, latent print, which he placed on a contrasting piece of cardboard, on which he wrote the location where it was found.

"That's it," the technician said, placing the cardboard and the fingerprint powder into a rigid kit box sitting next to him on the floor. He closed the lid and snapped the catches before standing and picking up the case.

"I'll run the print through the FBI files and see if we get a hit," he said.

The police detective, who had been leaning against the side of the bookcase nodded and clapped the CSI on the back. The detective wore a white shirt with a wilted, open collar, and a nondescript tie, open at the neck and pulled askew, plus brown baggy pants and wing-tips. His gold shield was clipped to his belt, which also held a pair of handcuffs, loose, with no case, and a snub-nosed revolver butt forward on his left hip.

"Somebody want to tell me what this is all about?" the detective asked.

"Not particularly," Pitcher murmured.

"What?"

"Detective Santos will be along in a few minutes," Casio interjected. "He will have the particulars for you."

"In the meantime, how about a preview?" the detective suggested, raising an eyebrow.

As an answer, Pitcher squatted before the closed door of the floor safe and looked up at the detective.

"OK to open this?" he asked.

The detective looked at the CSI, who was just leaving. The CSI nodded slightly, and the detective returned the gesture to Pitcher. The reporter punched the combination numbers into the keypad and swung the heavy door open. Inside the lid he moved the DIP switches, and the automatic alarm system disengaged.

255

As he did so, Detective Armando Santos eased silently into the room, watching with interest as Pitcher disabled the auto-notification alarm system.

"This is what alerted us?" the detective against the chest wanted to know.

Pitcher nodded.

"The landlord let me install this. It's the absolute latest thing," Pitcher bragged. "It uses electric power that comes in underneath the safe, so unless you know it's there you'd never look for it."

He pointed to the tiny switches on the inside of the door.

"This is the cool part," he said with a huge smile. "When you finish inside the safe, and before you close the door, you have to move these switches toward the top of the door in the correct order. That arms the system. When you later re-open the door, you must move them again, in reverse order, to disarm the system. If you don't, it counts down on a visual display, and if no action is taken, it signs onto the internet through a chip embedded in the metal of the bottom of the safe, and sends an email notification that shows up on the computer screens at Central Dispatch."

"Guess the crooks haven't figured that one out yet," Santos observed.

"That one didn't, anyway," Pitcher said. "And after it notifies Central Dispatch, it automatically slams the door closed after a short warning."

"I think Detective Santos meant no one has figured out how to circumvent this system yet," McDermott said.

"Even if they knew it was there," Pitcher said, "they would have to crawl under the floor to disconnect the power and they'd still never find the computer chip."

"What do you think the intruder was after?" asked the detective near the chest of drawers.

As if in answer, Pitcher reached deep into the safe and came out with a box that contained the courier watch. He opened the box and showed it to the detective.

"What is it?" the officer at the chest asked, staring.

Pitcher looked at him with a Bogart-like facial twitch.

"The, ah, stuff dreams are made of."

256

Chapter Thirty

The library branch was about ten blocks from rod Pitcher's apartment house, and it opened early. Eve Somers had driven around most of the night, afraid that someone had noticed her at the apartment complex, and, worse case, that someone had given the police a description of the Bondo Car. She knew that prudence dictated that she change cars sometime soon. But first, she would have to have some place to go.

She had spent the better part of an hour staring at a computer screen, inputting the numbers from the sheet she had stolen from pitcher's desk, but thus far, the computer had spat out nothing but gibberish.

Frustrated, she stopped the computer's program and sat back in her chair, thinking. She had chosen the last computer in a row that extended out from a wall, and had strategically moved a large artificial rubber tree into a position to partially obscure her computer position. It wouldn't hide her completely, but it would give her a heads-up when someone came in that appeared to be looking for her.

For the umpteenth time she looked at the numbers on the sheet she had filched from Pitcher's apartment office. She wasn't even sure that the numbers represented the contents of the watch she had sought for so long. In her mind she went through all that Mac told her about the quest for the killers of Pitcher's family. There wasn't much. Mac was notorious for not discussing the details of stories he and his staff were working on. But now that she thought about it, one name stood out in her mind.

Julian Peebles.

She knew where to find the pseudo-Englishman, having trailed Mac and Pitch to the North Baltimore mansion where he lived, though she had stayed in the car while they conducted their business. She had at that time merely wanted to dog them and see where they went so she could later keep track of their movements much easier.

She typed Peebles' name into the Google search field and clicked GO.

Peebles had been a successful businessman, having formed, built, and sold several companies, the last two to British concerns. It was while negotiating the sale of the first of those that he had developed his affected English accent – a fact noted in his Wikipedia entry on the internet. From that sale, and the sale of the second company, Julian Peebles had realized a fortune that had enabled him to move from his upper-middle-class neighborhood in Davidsonville to the Baltimore suburb where he now resided. It was there that his Anglophile ways hardened and increased. He had redone his mansion as an English manor house, and employed a British butler, and had spent considerable time amassing – and reading – a tremendous library. He had also developed a passion for looking abstract things up online, to the extent that he knew a little bit about a lot of things, which had, in his social circles, earned him the dubious title of PIHA. Pseudo-Intellectual Horse's Ass.

Did Julian Peebles know what the numbers meant?

Probably not. If he had, Mac and Pitcher would have known also, as Peebles would have told them.

Eve knew that Julian and Mac had known one another for some time and that they had developed a kind of friendship. Mac had once described it as a friendship involving a majestic collie (Peebles) who condescends to romp with a puppy (McDermott). And Peebles' condescension extended to being an informational source for a number of *Times* articles in which the foppish millionaire was attributed as a source. And being in the *Times* enhanced his already stellar prestige.

But it was his being a good friend of McDermott's that made up her mind which course she should steer.

The Delta shuttle from Kennedy International landed on time at Ronald Reagan National Airport on the outskirts of Washington. Charlie Hume was one of the first to deplane through the jet way. Peter McDermott and Rodney Pitcher were waiting for him. The three men exchanged handshakes as they walked toward the baggage claim area.

"I'm glad to be back," Hume said, irritated. "I didn't like the idea of being on Long Island when my staff was in jeopardy back here. You guys can't handle this fight alone."

"Who says we can't?" Pitcher demanded, indignantly.

258

Home extended his thumb and pointed it at his own chest.

"I do. Good enough?"

Pitcher studied his shoes.

"Yeah, I guess so," he said in a tiny, schoolboy voice.

The trio left the terminal and walked to the waiting area where McDermott's Jeep was waiting.

"I thought you said you'd have, you know, a car waiting for us," Hume whined.

"This is a car," McDermott pointed out. "It's got four wheels and a motor...

"And a ride that reduces my ass to sawdust."

"Harrumph!" McDermott barked, offended.

"Where do we want to go?" Pitcher asked in his best suck-up tone.

"Let's go to the hotel and pick up Casio, and then get someplace where we can compare notes and figure our next step."

"Great idea," McDermott said, genuinely.

"The four of us working together again," Hume thundered, raising a fist to the sky, which was immediately echoed by McDermott.

"We ride again," Pitcher said, grandiosely, thrusting his own fist aloft. "The Four Muscatels!"

The doorbell in the Peebles mansion was a soft chime reminiscent of, and loud enough to be, church bells, and every bit as melodic. The house master was seated in a high-backed, purple lounge chair in his high-ceilinged, cavernous living room perusing a just-delivered copy of that day's *London Times*.

Looking around, annoyed that his reading was being interrupted, he didn't see evidence of the lumbering, massive butler, so he set his paper on the table next to his table and went to the door himself.

Swinging open the massive, heavy wooden door, Peebles found himself face to face with a woman he didn't know a woman somewhat shorter than he, and he was no giant, with clearly defined features that were turned into a scowl. Without preamble she stepped off the porch and into the foyer, and from there, showed no inclination to stop. Annoyed even further, Peebles slammed the door and followed the woman.

"See here, you..." he began, but she didn't even pause in her gait until she reached the living room With a flair, she selected a chair across a large Medieval throw rug from the seat in which Peebles had clearly been sitting, and seated herself, a hard glint in her eyes and a thin, curled smile on her lips. Peebles strode purposefully to the center of the rug and planted himself, hands on hips, in front of the intruder.

"Would you please be so kind as to introduce yourself ...and explain what you are doing invading my house?"

She said nothing. Peebles set his face in an indignant mask and strode to the nearest bell-pull.

"I shall call my servant, young lady, and he will bodily eject you from the premises."

He reached up to pull the bell cord, but the effort ended abruptly in mid-tug, as a gun appeared in Eve's right hand, as though by magic.

"Please sit down, Mr. Peebles," she said is a soft casual voice that was belied by the rock-steady weapon that was currently aimed three feet from Julian Peebles' groin.

"It would be difficult for me to miss from this distance, Mr. Peebles,"

The Anglophile hesitated just a moment, then walked back to his chair next to his newspaper and sat. Eve Somers gave him a withering smile.

"Thank you, Mr. Peebles. I would now like to hear the story of the watch and what was found inside it. All of the story, please, Mr. Peebles."

Peebles pushed his head against the back of his chair.

"What do I get if I tell you?"

Eve Somers' eyes glinted, as she cocked the Beretta with its accompanying sounds.

"You get to stay in one piece," she said.

Peebles did his level best to maintain his hauteur and nonchalance.

"Well, then," he said, forcing a smile. "Consider me your friendly neighborhood story teller."

She lowered the gun slightly but did not take her finger out of the trigger guard.

"I want to know about the contents of the watch," she said, matter-of-factly.

"And what watch might that be?" Peebles asked, trying to sound casual.

Eve's eyes narrowed and she brought the weapon to bear again, with a special emphasis.

"Don't insult my intelligence, Mr. Peebles. I am here, I know about you, and just my mention of the watch should tell you that I know what it is and I know you have had some involvement with it. Now give me straight answers, unless you are prepared to be in a great deal of pain."

Peebles focused on the barrel of the weapon pointed directly at his belly button, and then looked up at the eyes of Eve Somers. They were clear, hard and unyielding, which told him that she would absolutely carry out her threat. He broke the eye contact with a quick glance at the gilded ceiling.

"Very well, then," Peebles said, surrendering. "Shall I start at the beginning with the history of the watch, or do you want the abridged version."

The gun lowered again, but was still in play.

"I know what the watch is. What I want to know is what was inside."

"You're quite certain, then, that the watch was safely opened?" Peebles asked, testing the waters.

"You're getting on my nerves, Mr. Peebles," Eve snarled, but she didn't move the gun.

"Very well. The watch was opened in my library in the presence of Mr. McDermott, Mr. Pitcher and Mr. Casio. I obtained the proper tool from a friend of mine in England by contacting him via email and the tool was sent to me FedEx standard overseas delivery."

He paused.

"You're doing fine, Mr. Peebles. Continue."

"The watch contained a small roll of thin tissue paper, about a half-inch high. It was very brittle and delicate. It was unrolled carefully and perused by all the men in this room."

"And what was on the paper, Mr. Peebles."

"Well, the writing was faded from all the years of being inside the watch..." Peebles began. But Eve waved him off with the fun.

"Won't wash," she said firmly. "McDermott's energy level has spiked since that watch was open. You found something inside that watch. I want to know what it is."

"You know Mr. McDermott?" Peebles asked, a little surprised.

"Very well," she said.

"Then why are you bothering me?" Peebles demanded. "Why not just ask him?"

She hesitated a moment.

"Let's just say that wouldn't be... appropriate ...and let it go at that, OK?"

Peebles got a knowing look in his eye and nodded, understanding.

"So what was written on that roll of paper?"

Peebles tried to evade the question.

"Well as I say, Miss, the writing was on old paper in old ink and it wasn't all that..."

The gun came up again. Without moving the rest of her body, Eve Somers leveled the pistol. Taking direct aim between Peebles' eyes.

"Mr. Peebles, if you bullshit me again, I'm going to shoot you in one of your knees. The next time, it will be in the other ankle, and the third time I'm going to turn you into a soprano. Are you reading me?"

Peebles seemed to shrink into the chair.

"Loud and clear," he said, weakly.

The gun lowered.

"I will ask you again, Mr. Peebles, and for the last time without a big noise. What was written on that paper in the watch?"

Peebles capitulated.

"Numbers," he said.

"Numbers?"

"Yes, numbers."

Barely moving, she pulled a folded piece of paper from her jeans and unfolded it with one hand.

"Were these the numbers?" she asked, extending it before her. It was the sheet of paper she had taken from Pitcher's apartment just hours before. Peebles leaned forward to look, but didn't leave his chair, not wanting to excite her.

"I believe so," he said, flatly, resuming his previous position.

"What what do these numbers mean?" she inquired.

Peebles shrugged.

"I haven't the foggiest notion," he said simply.

Again, the gun came up, but this time Peebles extended a restraining hand.

"That's the straight truth, my dear," he said hastily. "None of us know what the numbers mean. We've all been giving our computers numerical indigestion trying to figure it out."

Eve leaned forward slightly.

"Surely a man of your intelligence and resources could find an answer to this puzzle," she hissed. "Are you asking me to believe that you haven't found a thread that leads to the meaning?"

"To be perfectly candid," Peebles said, conversationally, "I really don't care what they mean. Mac asked me to help him with the watch and I did that. What happens after that is really none of my concern, is it?"

He smiled broadly.

"And please, don't call me Shirley."

Eve Somers smiled in spite of herself.

"So you have no idea..."

"None," Peebles asserted, shaking his head. "That is the simple truth, little lady. If you don't believe me, you might as well go ahead and squirt that thing. In terms of getting you the meaning of the numbers, it will make no difference."

"You don't believe I would really kill you, do you Mr. Peebles?" Somers inquired.

Peebles pointed at the gun.

"Your choice of hardware convinces me otherwise. That is not a weapon for threatening. That is a weapon for using."

"You know about such things, " she said, a statement, more than a question.

"I know of such things," he asserted, gravely. "To the extent that I don't wish to discuss it. So I'd ask of you to finish your business and leave my house."

"I have to say you're braver than I gave you credit for, Mr. Peebles," she said, a trace of admiration in her voice.

"You haven't seen my knees knocking together have you?" he asked with a thin smile.

"Nevertheless," she began...

"Hadn't you best be considering your escape?" Peebles asked. "I'd much prefer that you make your way out of here leaving me breathing, of course."

Eve Somers considered this.

"I only kill when I have a reason. And believe me Mr. Peebles, in the last few weeks I have had reasons. But I don't think I have a reason right now. I think you have been candid with me and have told me the truth. So if we can work out a way for me to leave here with some chance of a clean escape, we might be able to reach an accommodation."

"That would be nice," he said weakly, not believing her. "You realize, of course, that there is someone else in the house."

"A servant?" she asked.

Peebles nodded.

"And you realize," he continued, "that he is undoubtedly calling the police."

"Ummm. The thought did cross my mind," she said pensively.

"So an early flight would seem prudent from my point of view," Peebles said. "I'd be quite happy to hold the door open for you myself..."

She waved him off, and stood, holding out the empty hand, and leveling the gun with the other.

"Car keys," she said hotly.

Peebles hesitated, then reached into his pocket and handed her a set.

"Silver Jaguar convertible." He pointed off to one end of the room. "Through there and out the kitchen door. The car is in the driveway in front of the garage. There is a road that leads down an alley and out onto another street."

She closed her hands over the keys and looked at Julian Peebles for a long moment.

"You also realize," he said, as she turned in the direction he had indicated, "that my servant will also be calling McDermott about all this."

She stopped and turned to face him.

"I'm counting on it," she said.

Chapter Thirty-One

It's almost as though she's taunting us," McDermott said, a touch of apprehension in his voice. "She somehow seems to stay just one step ahead of us. We never seem to know where Eve is going to turn up next."

"I'd have been eternally grateful if you had figured that out before she knocked on my door," Peebles said, wistfully.

"You're a lucky man," Detective Armando Santos told Julian Peebles. "We believe this woman has killed three people already, maybe more."

Peebles sat in the same chair in which Eve Somers had threatened him, and stared goggle-eyed at the people in the room with him. There was Santos, and a female detective who was his partner, named Arlee Kelley. Along with them were a couple of uniformed officers, plus Casio, Hume, McDermott and Pitcher.

"She just strikes and then crawls back under her rock," Pitcher observed.

"And it's a damned mobile rock," Santos said, heatedly. "She stays on the move and doesn't give us a chance to catch up to her."

"Can't you put out a ...what is it you guys call it... an A.P.B.?" McDermott asked, looking at Santos.

Santos exhaled loudly

"An All Points Bulletin," he translated. And then his voice grew sharp. "Don't you think we've already done that?"

There was silence in the room for a long, awkward moment.

"At least she doesn't appear to be getting what she wants – whatever that is," Pitcher mused aloud.

"Oh, I wouldn't say that," Hume said sharply.

"You wouldn't?" Pitcher asked, surprised.

"No," Hume asserted. "She got numbers – apparently from your apartment, Pitch. And thanks to Mr. Peebles, here, she knows that those numbers were the ones in the watch, though under the circumstances I don't blame you, Julian, for telling her what she wanted to know."

Peebles smiled his thanks at the publisher.

"But at least she doesn't know what the numbers mean," Peebles offered.

Hume smiled.

"That's only because none of us know what the numbers mean," Hume answered.

"And that's what we have to figure out, and the sooner the better," McDermott said, seriously. "We know what we're looking for, the sooner we know where to look, the sooner we can bring this affair to a conclusion."

"And wind up with a hell of a story!" Pitcher said, elated. "I've been keeping notes..."

"Not now," Hume barked. "You got something in mind, Mac?"

"As it happens, I do," the editor replied. "What if all of us here, including Detective Santos and Detective Kelley, here, just sat around in a circle and started a word-association game?"

" Huh?" Pitcher and Casio blurted simultaneously.

"Think of every kind of number you can come up with – phone number, house number, and so on, and throw it out there. Maybe one of us will come up with the key."

Hume looked at Casio and both men shrugged.

"It's worth a try," Casio said.

"Let us begin," Hume ordered.

Eve Somers drove the silver Jaguar to the boat-launching ramp at Tolliver's Point in Eastport. She had taken the secondary roads; a longer drive than the Interstate and the Maryland State Highway System would have been, but less chance of meeting up with a police unit that knew what it was looking for. She drove the car down the ramp to the edge of the water and stopped. She opened the driver side door, and shifted into neutral, changing her position on the seat so her right foot was on the clutch pedal. Shoving the gear shift back into first, she let the clutch out and rolled out of the car, onto the concrete pavement. She came up to her feet with a single role, and watched as the expensive silver car splashed into the water. With the door open, the interior filled rapidly with water as the car kept moving, its engine not yet drowned. It finally disappeared, its headlights visible under the surface. Eve watched until they finally disappeared.

Satisfied, she walked the four blocks to the Eastport Marina, where she let herself into the security gate with the code McDermott had given her. She made her way silently to the pier where Mac's boat was moored, and stepped on board. She still had her key to the cabin. Letting herself in, she walked immediately to the starboard V-bunk. Inside she found a complete change of clothing, one she had left there as a sort of "hedging her bets" measure. She got the clothes out and laid them out on the port bunk, then turned on the breaker switch for the boat's water heater. She stripped to her bra and panties and sat down on the bunk, and let herself doze for perhaps half an hour. When she wakened she felt a little better. She entered the ship's head – or bathroom – and took a hot Navy shower. Toweling herself dry, she snapped on the television set and tuned it to a local station. The news wasn't on, but she sat down to watch anyway, not seeing or hearing what was on the screen. She switched off the water heater and considerately cleaned up the mess in the head before dressing in the jeans and tank top with the white socks, and the sneakers she came in with.

On deck, she shook out the second key on the boat key ring Mac had given her. Fitting it into the boat's ignition lock, she snapped the switch for the bilge blower. While it expelled any gas fumes in the engine room she singled up the lines, and disconnected the shore power cable, a bit more expertly than she had let on to McDermott. Turning off the blower, she turned the key and the boat's engine caught. Releasing the last mooring line, she shifted into "ahead," and eased the boat's throttle forward. The sleek craft nosed out of the slip. Eve turned right, and expertly guided the blue and white Bayliner across the harbor to the Set and Drift guest dock. She used the lines on the dock to secure the vessel.

She turned off the engine and climbed onto the pier, walking nonchalantly into the restaurant where she and Mac had met for meals so often during their on-again-off-again romance – a romance that was now over, she thought with more than a little regret.

She found a table near the back, rightly suspecting it was the table at which Mac always ate his breakfast on Friday mornings when he came to the posh restaurant in his grubbies, and was viewed askance by the Set and Drift management and staff. She ordered an expensive dinner and a single cocktail, a Tom Collins, again in remembrance of Mac who liked that particular drink, when he imbibed, which was rare.

She ate in silence then signed Mac's name to the dinner chit, along with his Yacht Club membership number. The staff, accustomed to seeing her in the place, accepted it without question. She ambled back to the pier, walking in an unhurried gait, and resumed her place on the main deck of the editor's boat.

Like a pro mariner in the bay, she conned the cruiser dead-slow through the no-wake zones near the piers at which many expensive boats were moored. She cleared the breakwater and opened the throttle and crossed the creek into the Severn River. She had no clear idea of where she was headed, but she knew something would occur. Once in the river, she slowly opened the throttle, pouring on the speed. The cruiser settled back astern and planed down, skimming across the water at a brisk pace. She noticed that the gas tank was full, so she had no worries about getting stranded.

After about twenty-five minutes she left the Severn River and entered Chesapeake Bay. The boat leaned into an easy turn to starboard, rounding Thomas Point light, pitching gently in the low swells.

There was no going back now, she knew that. She had known that since the night she had lured Reesa Lowenstein to that dusty old nightclub adjacent to the old Metropole Hotel. It had been OK, it had been reversible for the first few minutes. But when Reesa insisted that she didn't know anything about any Ziess Baden watch, and stuck with that story, she had become enraged. But it was still OK, her screaming at the hapless girl didn't mean anything, it could be forgotten after the tirade was over.

It had not been her intention to kill the girl, but she had done it anyway. She remembered in vivid detail the moment when she felt her finger tighten on the trigger. Even then, she could have averted the muzzle of the weapon, but no, she had gone to the trouble to seduce the property guardian at the Washington police department and obtain the weapon, so she might as well make it do what it was made to do, what it had done at least one other time at that point.

A bullet once fired cannot be recalled, she knew that. She heard the slug hit Reesa, she heard the tinkle as the ejected shell danced across the dusty stage; she heard the report of her second shot, not remembering having fired it. She saw Reesa Lowenstein grimace in pain and wonder, and then saw the look of agony in her eyes change to a blank, listless stare as she fell backward, already dead, her body's impact on the ancient stage kicking up a low cloud of dust before the dust mingled with the spreading puddle of red oozing from the cadaver on the deck.

At that moment there was no turning back. At that moment she changed, and her life was altered forever – shortened, she mused, her life was shortened, since her chances of completing her task and getting away alive were diminishing each and every day. All she could hope for is that she could use her wit and her feminine wiles to find a way out of what had already happened, and what was still to come.

Still to come.

Another turn to starboard, and the Bayliner entered South River. She passed the first channel marker then eased the helm to the left. The boat came to port in a graceful arc and left South River for a small inlet called Selby Bay. She kept to the left of the channel and aimed the bow at the Holiday Point Yacht Basin, a thousand yards ahead. As she approached the piers, she throttled back to steerage way and wove the boat through the various main piers and fingers until she found an empty slip. She parked the Bayliner there, hooked up the shore power line, and removed the keys from the floating fob before dropping them overboard. She walked up to the main pier and found her way to the parking lot gate. It opened with a combination, which obviously she did not have, so she stepped back, partially hiding herself behind a piling and waited. Eventually, a man and woman approached the gate and punched in the four numbers. She could hear the gate latch snap back and saw it swing open. As the man and woman entered, she sprang forward, nodding and smiling at the couple, and holding the gate for them. As they came in, she walked out.

"What about a VIN number?" McDermott asked, throwing that idea onto the conversational table.

"What?" Detective Kelley asked. "That's ridiculous."

"That's redundant," Pitcher interjected.

"That's what?" Casio asked.

"Redundant," Pitcher repeated. "V-I-N stands for 'Vehicle Identification Number.' So when you say VIN number, you're actually saying 'Vehicle Identification Number Number.'"

"You're getting on my nerves, Pitch," Hume growled.

"Yeah, but we don't know what might be important in this little game," McDermott asserted, since he had suggested the game. "All we need is one thread to sew a vest onto and we'll have a place to start."

"We we're certainly dead in the water right now," Detective Arlee Kelley said flatly.

"Did they have Vehicle Identification Numbers back during the Big War?" Pitcher asked.

McDermott shrugged.

"Search me."

"Don't tempt me," Santos shot back, his voice intimidating. "You guys are lucky I don't bust you for obstruction of justice right now."

"For what?" Casio demanded.

"Withholding information from the police, for starters," Santos barked. "You guys chose not to tell us everything about this nasty little affair, and without complete information we didn't know what we were looking for."

"And we did?" Casio demanded? "We gave you what we had as hard facts. We just kept the pieces that didn't add up to ourselves."

"You should know better than that, Casio," Kelley said, her voice developing a distinct cop's edge. "Holding back vital information can get your license revoked."

Casio sat back and clasped his hands around one knee, regarding the two police operatives with an ironic smile.

"Do you know how many times I've heard that?" Casio asked. "Every time I get ahead of a police investigation, some badge-carrier gets pissed and threatens my license." He shrugged. "If you guys think you can get my ticket lifted, hop to it. It's been tried for forty years, never successfully, and all it ever got the complainers was a good laugh.. I just thought you guys had a little more class."

Santos and Kelley visibly clouded over and seemed to shrink back into their seats. Peebles looked at the private detective admiringly.

"You don't intimidate, do you?" he asked.

Casio shook his head with a leaden smile.

"Are you guys going to continue with this cockamamie word association game?" Santos asked hotly.

Pitcher looked at McDermott who looked at Hume. All three were smiling.

"Don't you think we should keep playing until somebody wins the imitation Mardi Gras beads?"

"I could flash my boobs and get those," Kelly hissed under her breath.

Pitcher gave her chest an appraising look, then shook his head.

"Maybe not," he said, suppressing a grin. Kelley adopted a look of pure anger, pivoted, and strode toward the foyer and the door. Santos followed, a step or two behind.

"Don't worry about those clowns," Santos admonished his partner. "They're shooting at the moon."

"I was OK until Pitcher made that crack about my boobs. I can hold my own against anyone in that department.

Santos stopped long enough to fix his gaze as Pitcher had.

"Yean... OK," he stammered.

Kelley clouded over. Santos recovered quickly and returned his eyes to hers.

"Arlee I can't afford to think of you in those terms. Neither of us can. Now drop it, will you, and let's figure out what we're going to do next.

They had reached their brown police department Ford Crown Victoria. Santos slid under the wheel, and Arlee Kelly let herself into the passenger seat. She turned and put her left leg up on the bench seat, the better to face her partner, and waited expectantly.

"OK," Santos began. "If you were Eve Somers, what would you be doing right now?

"I'd be getting as far away from here as possible before the APB she must surely know is out for her, tips some traffic cop and she gets picked up on a tail light violation."

Santos leaned against the driver side door and regarded his partner. Santos was the senior of the two by seven years, Kelley having just made detective fifteen months before.

"You sure that's what you would do?" Santos asked.

Kelley raised her right eyebrow in a quizzical look.

"Aside from the possibility of being captured, why does she run? What has she accomplished?"

"She's killed three people, she's made two further attempts and she probably tossed an apartment and burned a car."

Santos nodded.

"Why?"

"Why?"

"Why?"

Kelley looked past Santos and out the window.

"Why did she do all those things?"

Santos nodded shallowly.

"She wanted whatever was in the watch," she said softly.

"Did she get it?"

"Yes."

Santos raised his own eyebrow.

"She did?"

Kelley didn't answer.

"She came to this house because she didn't know what the numbers from the watch mean."

"According to Peebles and McDermott, she still doesn't because they don't," Kelley said, disgusted.

271

"So she runs away before she finds out what the numbers are about?"

Kelley was mildly exasperated.

"You just said those guys inside didn't know either!"

Santos looked down.

"Yes," he said. "Now." But we might think those guys inside are clowns. But I shouldn't have called them that. Do you read the *North Bay Times*?"

She shrugged.

"I've seen it around."

"It's the most literate publication I've seen this side of *War and Peace*. It's solid and well written and put together so as to make it readable and useful. It takes smart people to put that newspaper together every week, and in the short time I've been around those three newspapermen, I've come to understand they are the smartest ones of the bunch."

He exhaled heavily and rubbed his eyes with the edges of his thumbs.

"They'll figure out what the numbers mean and they will act on what they learn."

Arlee Kelly thought a moment.

"So you're saying that Eve Somers is only going to get herself lost to throw off the cops – us. And she will eventually pick up the trail of these three guys, and she'll..."

"...stick to them like glue," Santos finished. "Whatever it is that they will find then they interpret those numbers, Eve Somers wants it, and she wants it bad enough to commit multiple murders to get it. She'll dog these guys' footsteps until they lead her where she wants to go."

"And we'll be there to nab her," Kelley asserted.

Santos nodded.

"And it won't surprise me if we save at least three lives when that happens."

He swung under the steering wheel and slid the key into the steering column slot, giving it a vicious twist. The engine fired on the first crank and settled down to a muted rumble.

"First thing to do is run this by the captain and make sure we have someone on their asses 24/7," Santos said, more to himself than to Kelley. He dropped the car into gear and drove off through the gate into the Baltimore traffic.

Lurch, the butler, brought another pot of hot coffee, and another Diet Pepsi for McDermott before withdrawing from the living room – the room that Peebles referred to as his "drawing room" – quietly. Peebles poured for his friends.

"I certainly hope the gendarmes have scared off that horrible woman," he said, with obvious relief in his voice. But his jaw dropped when he saw McDermott shake his head.

"Eve Somers doesn't scare," he declared. "Someday I'll tell you how she escaped from a speeding boat in the Atlantic on an inflatable boat with a fat pirate while being fired on by a large ship. She just doesn't scare."

"Then she'll be back?" Pitcher asked, shaking involuntarily.

"You can depend on it," Casio said firmly.

"So we'd better get our heads back together and figure out what these numbers mean," Hume said. "Who'd got a number we can kick around?"

"Nutrition numbers?" McDermott suggested.

Casio shook his head.

"No one was concerned with calories and carbs right after the Second World War," he said.

"Ah, you're probably right," McDermott said, waving at him.

"How about mileage," Peebles suggested."

"That's not bad, Julian," Hume replied. "But we've already run the mileage and traced it on a map, and it doesn't mean anything that way that we've been able to discern."

"Route numbers," Pitcher spat in disgust, "truck numbers, airplane numbers!" He rose and paced the floor flailing his arms in the air. "Those damned numbers have to mean *something*, don't they?"

"Calm down, Pitch," Hume admonished. "There's a clue here someplace and we'll find it, you just have to give yourself a little more latitude."

Pitcher stopped pacing and faced his publisher.

"I'm sorry, Charlie. It's just so frustrating – doubly for me because whatever this is about it's getting my family killed, not to mention the attacks on me..."

Pitcher stopped talking in mid-sentence and turned his attention to Peter McDermott. The editor had a blank expression on his face, his mouth was agape and there was a glow to his eyes.

"Mac?" Pitcher prodded.

"You got something, Mac?" Hume asked.

"Yes, come on Old Bean share with us," Peebles invited.

"Charlie," McDermott hissed, his voice barely above a whisper. "What was that you just said? What did you say to Pitch?"

"Huh?"

"What did you say to Pitch?" McDermott asked again, timbre returning to his voice, and it was now boulder firm.

Hume thought a moment, not immediately remember his exact words. In a moment he had it.

"I told Pitch he should give himself a little more latitude.

McDermott shook his fist in the air and looked at each person in the room in turn.

"That's it!"

Chapter Thirty-Two

Eve Somers sat at a picnic table just outside the Holiday Point marina gate, with her back to the table portion. She adjusted her tank top to show her cleavage and the tops of her breasts and leaned back to accentuate the effect, crossing her legs for extra measure. Several people came out the gate as she sat there, but most were couples, or two or more men together, and she smiled pleasantly at them as they scattered to their cars in the lot. At length, a man passed through the gate alone and turned toward the picnic table, giving Eve a long, appraising once-over look. She smiled and batted her eyes at him, and as she had hoped, he stopped to talk.

"Waiting for someone?"

It was a tired opening gambit for a guy, she thought, but it would serve her purpose.

"Not exactly," she said, pleasantly. "My boyfriend and I had a fight and he took off without me, so I'm stranded."

"Your boyfriend on one of the boats?"

She nodded.

"Yes, we were supposed to be the guests of a couple he knew."

"Which boat?" the man inquired.

She shrugged.

"We never got that far. We started the fight on the way down here, and after we arrived, I got out of the car and he just drove off."

The man narrowed his eyes, mentally cursing her non-existent boyfriend.

"Where do you need to go?" he asked.

"Annapolis," she replied, batting her eyes disarmingly.

"You're not some kind of ax murderer, are you?" he inquired with genuine mirth.

She almost choked, but managed to do little more than clear her throat. She could still feel the hard, cold metal of the Beretta sticking in the waistband at the back of her jeans.

"No I've never taken an ax to anyone," she said, truthfully.

"Well then let me at least take you into the city," he said, extending his hand. She took it, and allowed him to lead her to a white Hummer parked near the piers. He opened the door and helped her into the large vehicle, then got in and started the engine.

"Name's Jack Reece, by the way," he said.

"Eve," she replied, almost biting her lip for giving him her actual name.

"Nice," he said casually. "You got a last name?"

"Winters," she said, trying not to laugh.

"How long had you been with the boyfriend?" he asked, hoping he wasn't being too nosey.

"Not long enough for him to talk to me the way he did," Eve replied through clenched teeth, getting into the role.

The Hummer came out of the marina and turned right onto Highway 214, also known as Central Avenue, headed toward Mayo and Londontowne, as Eve and Jack exchanged meaningless conversation, Jack carefully gauging his talk against his chances of talking Eve into the back seat of the Hummer before she reached her destination, and Eve parrying with him trying to avoid such an entanglement. The Hummer turned right again, onto Route 2, Solomon's Island Road. By this time, Jack was getting the impression that his chances weren't too good, and Eve was aware that she was winning the sexual fencing match. They crossed the South River Bridge is silence.

"Would you care to stop somewhere for a meal or a drink?" Jack asked, trying to rekindle his campaign to find his way inside the tight jeans Eve wore.

She shook her head firmly.

"I really need to get home," she said. "Tomorrow morning comes really early."

"Where do you work?" he wanted to know.

"Turn right here," she said, and the Hummer made a right on red onto West Street.

This was an area well known to Eve Somers. For many years she had worked at the Maryland Historical Authority, whose offices were on this very street. Just last year she had been laid off in severe statewide budget cuts. It was then that she had hooked up with Willie Sykes, and by the time she disappeared, just minutes before Sykes was gunned down on Church Circle, she was already committed to a course that would preclude being rehired by any state agency.

West Street would take her to Church Circle, in whose center was St. Ann's Episcopal Church, one of the oldest churches in the United States. From there, a short, narrow brick road led to State Circle, a brick, circular drive that had the Maryland Statehouse as its center piece. Already the lit wooden black-and-white dome was visible ahead. For a moment, she looked at the dome and let her mind wander.

Construction on the building began in 1772, but thanks to the prosecution of the Revolutionary War, it was not completed until 1779. It is the oldest statehouse in continuous legislative use in the nation, and still houses Maryland's bicameral General Assembly consisting of a Senate and a House of Delegates, and the Office of the Governor. It is the only state capital to serve temporarily as the U.S. capital. It was in this house that George Washington resigned his commission as General of the Continental Army and left as a private citizen. And it was from the Old Senate Chamber that still exists in the building that the Congress, under the Articles of Confederation, called for a new constitutional convention that would result in the federal Constitution.

Eve shook her head to clear her thoughts. The Hummer was approaching a Crown filling station on the right.

"Pull in here," she said quickly, and Jack Reece cut the wheel and bounced into the parking lot.

"I'm going to get out here," she said quickly. "I'll call a girlfriend of mine who lives near here to come pick me up. I mean I don't know you, I can't very well let a total stranger know exactly where I live, can I?"

She leaned across the seat and gave Jack Reece a long, passionate, French kiss, then unceremoniously threw open the passenger side door and jumped to the ground.

"Thanks, Jack, you're a real life saver."

She slammed the door closed and stood back expectantly. Jack hesitated, trying to think of something to say. When nothing occurred to him, he accepted defeat, flipped her a wave, and accelerated back into traffic.

She watched until the tail lights of the Hummer disappeared down West Street toward State Circle. Satisfied, she walked two doors down, to a rental car agency. It was closed, which for her purposes was just as well.

She looked at the plate-glass window at the front of the agency, surmising, correctly, as it would turn out, that it had once been a gas station. She looked around. There was a late-model Lincoln Town Car on the lot along with a Toyota Camry and a Kia Sedona mini-van.

The front of the building was too public for her purposes. And besides the glass would be too thick, and would probably be wired with impact sensors. She stepped around to the side toward State Circle. There was another window there, this one apparently leading into the office of the agency. She looked, but it was too dark, by now, to tell whether there were any sensors on the window. She would have to try to get in without disturbing any of them if they were there, and she would have to take care of her business quickly.

She took off her tank top and turned it inside out. Standing next to the building in her bra and jeans, she placed the garment against the window pane and tapped it several times with her elbow. Finally, the frail glass cracked, and she was able to pull several large pieces of glass away from the frame. Reaching in, she unlocked the window. Looking around again, she stepped away from the building and shook her tank top to make sure no shards of fragments of glass were still in it, and then hastily put it back on. She hoisted her frame up the side of the building and through the broken window, waiting a moment for her eyes to adjust to the even darker environment inside the office. She made her way into the short hallway that was occupied only by two restrooms and another small office. In the front of the building, where most of the business took place, she quickly found a drawer with a key board. There were three sets of keys. She pocketed all three and let herself back out of the building the way she came in. First, she keyed open the door to the Lincoln town car. Snapping the key into the ignition, she turned it one click, to find that the car had not been serviced. The gas tank was only about one-quarter full. She got out and threw the keys into the street and moved over to the Toyota. The tank was full, but the car would not start. Again she threw the keys into the street, and pressed the Unlock button on the key fob belonging to the Kia. Sliding under the wheel she clicked the ignition once and found the car filled with gas. One more click and the engine quickly caught. She pulled the gear lever to Drive, and headed off in the same direction the Hummer did.

"I can see, now, that Uncle Albert was saying 'Eve,' not 'Even' when he gave me the watch," Pitcher was saying as the Four Muscatels sauntered into the large conference room at the *North Bay Times* offices.

"Agreed," Casio said, in a dejected tone. "And I see, now, that Harry Oglesby wasn't saying 'End Seize,' he was trying to say 'It's Eve.'"

Pitcher sat and slammed a fist on the table.

278

"Damn," he spat. "It was right in front of us all the time and we missed it."

"Trust me, it can happen to the best of us," Casio replied. "I'm supposed to be an expert in this kind of case. I had two chances, and I missed it both times."

"This isn't the time to assign blame," Hume barked, seating himself in his accustomed place at the head of the table.

"You'll take care of that later, right?" McDermott cracked, sitting to Hume's right.

"Damn right," the publisher growled.

The table being used by the Four Muscatels was diamond-shaped, with fourteen total places. Each place had a small computer screen, and a tiny keyboard, except the three places at the head, whose keyboards were standard sized and wireless. At the head of the room, behind Hume's head, was a large liquid-crystal display monitor. All the computer keyboards and monitors at the places on the table could either access the newspaper's server, or operate independently, and all had independent internet access.

All right, Mac," Hume began again. "You said 'that's it,' so tell. What's 'it?'"

"You said it, Charlie. You had the key."

"So what was it?" Hume demanded.

McDermott sat back in his seat and rocked, a huge smile on his face.

"I asked you to let me think it over all the way back from Julian's house," McDermott said, rocking still. "And I did, and the more I thought of it, the more I'm convinced that I'm right... you're right."

"About...?' Hume prompted, making circles in the air in front of him with his hands.

"About what the numbers mean," McDermott grinned, a smile which was echoed by Pitcher and Casio who were enjoying the exchange between the two men.

"Charlie, think," McDermott said, tapping the side of his head. Take another look at the numbers and remember what you said."

Hume looked askance at his Managing Editor, and pulled a folded sheet of foolscap out of his pocket. He scanned it, looking for perhaps the thousandth time at the numbers from the watch.

"OK I looked at them, and all I said that set you off was that Pitch should give himself more latitude."

At that second Hume's face changed radically, and it was as though a light bulb had suddenly been switched on above his head.

"My God," he breathed.

The same light bulb went on above the heads of everyone else in the room.

"Latitude," Pitcher whispered.

"And longitude," Hume finished.

Eve Somers slowed the Kia Sedona as it passed the offices of the Maryland Historical Authority. For a moment, about the time it took the white car to pass the building, she longed for the simpler days that office represented to her.

A block down the road she turned into a WaWa convenience store and parked. Hers was the only car in the lot at that moment, and she pulled into a space nearest the street. She turned on the radio to a soft music station and sat back, waiting.

It took awhile, perhaps fifteen or twenty minutes, but the parking lot suddenly filled up, with most of the cars pulling into spaces close to the store building. She waited a moment or two more until the store appeared to be crowded, and the lone clerk was very busy. Then she sauntered inside and looked around. Near the counter was a rack that contained prepaid cellular telephones. She grabbed two of them and made her way to the ladies room at the back of the store. There, she stripped away the hard clear plastic around the phones, found the prepaid cards that came with them and installed the minutes represented by the cards. She tested each phone by calling the weather service, pocketed both phones, and headed back into the store.

Even more people had come into WaWa in the few moments she was in the ladies room, and the clerk was far too busy to notice her leaving without buying anything. She deftly stole a pencil-sized flashlight and a couple of granola bars as she left the store, regained the Kia, and headed back onto West Street.

The Kia rounded Church Circle and turned right onto Duke of Gloucester Street. She drove all way down the street, past City Hall and the police station, and made a left turn onto Compromise Street, turning right and making her way to Eastport. She drove around the condominium parking lot for several minutes becoming convinced that Peter McDermott wasn't there. She was reasonably sure he had left the Peebles mansion with his friends, so if he wasn't at the condo, there was only one other place he could be. With her face clouding over, she backed into a parking space. She pulled one of her purloined cell phones out of her pocket and dialed.

280

"No, they haven't caught me yet," she snapped when the phone was answered. "And no I haven't found Mac and his cronies yet, they're not at the condo."

There was a pause.

"I know because I am sitting in the condo parking lot, and Mac's Jeep isn't here, that's how I know."

In a few quick sentences, Eve spoke into the phone, giving an account of all that happened the last few hours, concluding with her theft of the car from the rental agency.

"OK, OK," said the voice on the other end of the phone. "You must have an idea of where they are. Go there, find them and don't let them out of your sight. Call me when they're close and I'll join you."

Eve didn't reply, she just snapped the phone closed, pocketed it, and shifted the Kia into gear once again, heading out of Eastport and toward Baltimore.

McDermott and Hume took turns trying to ferret out the coordinates from the watch into a latitudinal and longitudinal position, but even McDermott, who had some navigational schooling, wasn't able to come up with a web site containing a chart that worked.

Sy Casio watched their feeble attempts with a look of amusement on his face, and Pitcher shifted his gaze from his bosses to the detective's mirthful expression.

"You guys ready to say Uncle?" Casio asked, casually.

"Just a few more minutes," McDermott said without breaking his concentration.

"I'm ready to give now," Hume said, shoving the keyboard from in front of him and looking up with a defeated look on his face. "Take over any time you want, Sy."

"Mac?"

McDermott fussed with the keyboard a few more times and finally looked up at the detective with a sheepish look.

"OK, Uncle," he said with a half-smile.

Sy motioned and McDermott ceded his chair in front of the large keyboard. Casio sat, signed onto the internet and consulted a notebook he kept in the pocket of his suit coat. Tapping a few characters into the browser, he then entered a user name and password. McDermott, who was looking over his shoulder, emitted a low whistle.

The screen in front of Casio – and the large one above the head of the table – showed the legend, "United States Department of Defense," and "U.S. Navy Coastal Navigation Material."

"My God, Sy, how do you get access to that? It's probably classified."

"No probably to it," Casio said. "These are the most detailed navigational charts in the world with a GPS database available to hook up from. This is what the GPS system was originally built for. It was never intended for release to the general public. It was a locator for the Military that could put anything anywhere, plus or minus six inches."

"So how is it that you have access to it?" McDermott demanded.

Casio turned to face him.

"I told you earlier in this caper that I have a way into a lot of internet places I'm not supposed to have access to.

"Suppose you get caught?" Hume inquired.

Casio shrugged.

"Foregone conclusion. I imagine their computers have tagged your server by now. You can count on a visit from a stone-faced guy from the National Security Agency. You know the one – charcoal suit, granite features, bug in his ear who talks to his sleeve?"

"That's all I need," Hume bawled.

"Don't' worry about it," Casio said. "I'll take care of it. No extra charge."

"Yippee," Hume said flatly.

"So where are the coordinates?" Pitcher asked, anxiously. "What's been the cause of all this?"

Casio smiled and turned back to his screen. He copied the numbers from the sheet of paper Hume left on the table into the appropriate fields on the web site and pressed Enter. A new window opened showing an overlay of Washington D.C. Casio clicked on the Map option, and looked at what the small flag on the screen showed.

"There's your answer," he said, pointing to the screen. The others in the room craned their necks to see.

"What is it?" Hume asked weakly.

Casio fiddled with the keyboard and mouse again for a few moments, and another new window opened on the screen. This one was a satellite image of a broad expanse of field with white marks evenly spaced, interspersed with gray ones of non-uniform shape and size.

"This is the beginning of the end of this caper," Casio said seriously. "This is the destination of whoever was supposed to get that watch."

The four men in the room stared at the large screen above the table head at the satellite image of the Congressional Cemetery.

Chapter Thirty-Three

"Well what are we waiting for?" Pitcher asked, incredulously. "We know where we're going – let's go!"

"I'm ready," McDermott chimed in. "I can run by my condo and get some shovels…"

"We can buy them on the way," Hume blustered. "They'll be on the paper's expense account."

Three jaws dropped. Compared to Hume, Ebenezer Scrooge spent money like a drunken sailor.

"Before you change your mind…" McDermott yelled, heading for the conference room door. Pitcher and Hume were a step behind him.

"Ahem!" coughed Casio.

As one, the three *North Bay Times* staffers stopped, turned, and assumed 'come on' faces.

"What's up, Sy?" Hume asked, his voice urging.

"Come on, let's go," Pitcher chided.

"Time's a-wastin'" McDermott added.

Casio leaned back in the low-backed swivel chair at the conference table.

"Where are you going?" He asked, like a professor addressing an errant student.

"To the Congressional Cemetery, of course," McDermott said, impatiently.

"Why?" Casio asked, folding his arms over his barrel chest.

"To find the diamonds," Pitcher said, stupidly.

"Where?" Casio demanded.

"In the Congressional Cemetery," Hume sputtered, losing his patience.

"*Where*, in the Congressional Cemetery?" Casio demanded.

"Right where the latitude line and longitude lines meet," McDermott explained, demonstrating his growing impatience.

"And you've got the idea that somewhere at those coordinates there's a sign," Casio began, then gesticulated with his arms, "Diamonds. Dig Here."

Again, as one, the shoulders of the three men drooped, their heads hung, and in a single movement, the three of them stepped forward and retook their seats at the table. Casio rose and paced the upper end of the room, beneath the large monitor, hands clasped behind his back.

"Gentlemen," he began. "In the first place we don't know precisely where to look once we get into the cemetery."

"I see that now," Hume said sheepishly.

"Secondly, if we walk into that cemetery with a bunch of shovels and start creating divots, someone is going to complain, and we'll have an opportunity to see the Washington City Jail from the inside."

"I hadn't thought of that," Pitcher said, shuddering.

"We need a plan," Casio said firmly.

"Definitely," Pitcher shouted.

"That's just what we need," Hume chimed in

"A plan!" McDermott yelled.

"Do you have one?" the three asked in perfect unison.

Casio sat at his place at the table and shook his head.

"Nope. And we're not going to formulate a usable one sitting here dead tired, hungry and needing to recharge. I'd suggest we all go home and get a few hours of sleep, and meet in the morning and come up with an idea. Of course you'll all be thinking about it tonight – we'll need all the thoughts you can muster in the morning."

McDermott nodded.

That's the best idea yet," he said, rising.

Pitcher rubbed his eyes and leaned back.

"Can't argue with that," he said, pulling his cell phone and punching Samantha Parker's number in speed dial.

The others followed him out of the room and out of the building.

Eve Somers was agreeably surprised by the Kia's brisk speed. She didn't know what to expect from the Korean mini-van, but she found it had a get-up-and-go beyond her expectations. The car was comfortable, once she figured out how to adjust the seat – the switches were on the door – and was fully instrumented, which meant little to her, but as long as the gauges pointed to the middle she was happy.

She chose the direct route, taking State Road 301 north through Pasadena and Glen Bernie, and onto Route 10, and on to 895. She took

284

the exit ramp for the Inner Harbor and drove unerringly to the *North Bay Times* offices.

She was surprised, and not a little nonplussed to find no cars in the parking lot of the converted warehouse that was home to the weekly newspaper. She parked the white Kia in a shadowy part of the lot and got out, approaching the door.

It was a simple electronic lock. After hours, a newspaper staff member had only to swipe the magnetic-striped side of his or her press card through the slot and the door would open. Of course during business hours, this door would be unlocked.

Using the pen light, she looked over the lock carefully, but quickly. She popped the plastic top off the mechanism, revealing the clock. It was a three-digit affair with thumb-wheels. She had seen Mac open it once when there had been a power failure, which had automatically locked the door and cut in a battery back-up. She knew disconnecting the power would not disengage the lock, but fooling the computer chip in the mechanism would. She used the point of a pen she found in the Kia to move a tiny switch to SET, and then moved the thumb wheels until the read 9:00A. Moving the switch back to RUN, she was rewarded with an audible click and the lock snapped back. Pushing open the door she walked up a flight of steps to the editorial offices on the second floor. Walking down the dark corridor she had traversed many times, peeked into Rod Pitcher's cubical. A perfunctory glance about the room, under the glow of the desk lamp Pitcher always left on, revealed nothing of use to her. Turning back to the hallway, she approached Peter McDermott's office and tried the door. It was locked. She toyed with the idea of picking the lock, but elected to keep moving instead. Now if she were holding a meeting with about four people, where would she hold it? McDermott's office? Probably not. His office had only one chair, and wasn't terribly comfortable once a lot of people got in there. Hume's office? A better idea, but maybe not. Main conference room? She nodded.

Eve Somers have been in the newspaper offices many times during the years she was part of an on-again-off-again romance with the paper's managing editor. She didn't need lights to navigate the editorial floor, and she walked unerringly to the conference room.

There were no lights on, but the glow from the large computer monitor gave a little illumination. Somers looked at the display on the big screen, the satellite picture of the Congressional Cemetery left up by Sy Casio as the crew made haste to the door for some rest before they went to find the diamonds.

"Can it be this easy?" she wondered?

She sat down at the computer, in the chair Casio had occupied, and printed the page on the screen. Then she checked to see what other pages then computer might have looked at and found the coordinate map that Casio had first used. She printed that, too, on the large printer in the room. She rolled the printouts and stuck them in the bag she was still carrying, returned the computer display as she found it, and made her way back down the hall.

Outside again, she reset the clock as she found it, and heard the lock bolt click back again. She replaced the plastic housing on the lock, gunned the Kia to life and headed for I-95 which would take her to the Beltway.

Peter McDermott stepped to the asphalt from his Jeep and carefully looked around. Satisfied that no one he didn't know was in the parking lot, he stepped to the curb and looked up and down the street – a second look, since he had done the same from the Jeep as he drove into the lot. Satisfied that no one untoward was in the lot or stalking him, he cautiously walked up the two steps to his porch, keyed open the door of his condo and stepped inside. He closed and locked the door, and dead-bolted it, then removed his sports jacket, dropping it to the floor as he walked. He traversed the entire condominium, checking windows, making sure they were securely locked. He checked his desk phone, finding no messages, a fact which caused his eyes to narrow a bit. Returning to the front door, dropping his shirt as he walked, he set the alarm system, then turned into his kitchen. From the fridge he pulled a carton of milk from which he drank deeply without bothering with a glass. He shoved the near-empty carton back into the fridge and pulled two boxes of raisins from a package next to his sink. Walking toward his bedroom, he ate the raisins out of the box, setting the empties on tables he found along his journey. His shoes came off halfway across the condo, followed immediately by his socks.

As he entered his bedroom he discarded his underwear on the floor in his path, and flipped on the light in his bathroom. He turned on the shower – hot only – and waited a moment while the water heated up. He stepped inside and leaned against the tile wall, letting the water from the massaging shower head beat down on his exhausted body.

He tried not to think, tried to allow his body to shut down, to give in to the ravages of the worst fatigue he had ever felt in his life.

But the events of the last couple of weeks had been nagging on his mind as they unfolded, each new event heating up the cauldron.

The deaths in Pitcher's family disturbed him quite enough. But then to find that a woman he cared about was behind those deaths was more than his mind could handle. Still, he had forced the resources in his mind and his emotions to digest all that was happening, and left room for the answers behind it – the watch, the numbers, and what they apparently meant, the death of Harry Oglesby almost right in front of him, the chases, the attempts – everything beat him down, wore him out. And now he was counting on the steaming water from the shower in his home to wash it all away.

Scarcely knowing where he found the strength, he lifted his arms to find the soap and wash cloth, and gave himself a good washing. He hoped that it would not only be a lavation, but would wash away the burden on his mind and his heart.

The shower worked in terms of cleaning his body. And it worked, not in throttling down his mind – there was very little that could do that. It worked in taking his body and mind past the point of no return. His mind would continue to work, but it would not keep his body awake to facilitate the thoughts.

He turned off the water and staggered out of the stall, grabbing a towel on the fly. He dried his body and hair, took a perfunctory look at his teeth, and deciding they could wait another day, he dropped the towel to the floor and reeled into his bedroom. There, he collapsed, naked, onto the bed, not bothering to turn it down. A half-second before his head hit the pillow, he was sound asleep.

Eve Somers parked the Kia a half-block from the entrance to the Metropole Hotel, locked the car, and melted into the shadows and she made her way to the side entrance of the long-abandoned hotel. The door opened at her touch, and she stepped inside, bolting it behind her as she looked across the dark, dusty lobby. From long practice she made her way to one side of the massive desk that had once welcomed everyone from presidential candidates to prostitutes' customers. She pressed the "up" button on the first bank of elevators and listened for the tell-tale sound of machinery starting up. Within a minute the elevator doors opened, bathing the filthy floor in a rectangle of light. She stepped inside and pressed the button for the third floor. The doors closed with a light click, and the machinery started up again, accompanied by the sensation of motion. It took less than a minute for the car to reach the third floor, and the doors to open.

It was not her first journey to the third floor, but the difference between it and the lobby below was still striking. Where the lobby was dark and dank, devoid of color, showing everything in black and white and gray, covered with dust and decay, the third floor was immaculately clean, well lit, and done in soothing, carefully chosen colors. Somers stopped for a moment to take it in, and then turn left, and made an immediate right, heading down the hallway. She stopped at the second-to-last door on the right, turned the knob and went in.

The room was softly lit, and her meager belongings were right where she left them. She shucked out of the cloths she had taken from the bunk in McDermott's boat and stepped into the shower. Like McDermott, thirty miles away, she let the water beat down on her, loosening her muscles and calming her down after a long chase and a long route to escape capture. At length, she came out of the shower, wrapped in a long, fluffy white towel, with another, smaller one, wrapped around her hair.

He was seated on the small divan when she came out of the bathroom. Somers was not perturbed at all to see a man in her room, seated casually across the room. The man was about fifty, sandy-haired and of medium build. He wore a suit over a polo shirt that didn't match, and he was sucking on the stub of a cold cigar.

About time you showed up," he observed, in a heavily accented voice. "Did you pick them up? Did you find them?"

She sat on the bed and removed the towel from her head and rubbed it briskly through her hair.

"They weren't at the newspaper office. And McDermott wasn't home when I ran by his place."

"You should have waited for him," the man growled.

Eve shrugged, and quickly redid the tuck that kept the towel around her.

"I had no way of knowing if he was even going to show up."

"Well you should have known," the man snapped.

"How?" she asked.

The man looked at the ceiling for a time.

"You were sleeping with him weren't you?" he demanded.

"There was a time," she said curtly. "But that didn't give me insight into his scheduling. He's a newspaperman, he works odd hours, and how did I even know he came back to Annapolis tonight?"

"Have you thought about calling his phone?"

"Many times," she said wistfully. "But right now I'm so tired I wouldn't know what to say."

"I can coach you," he said.

288

"Not tonight," she returned, shaking her head. "Tonight all I want is to get into that bed and sleep, sleep and then sleep some more."

"Harrumph," the man scoffed. "Then what?"

"Then we start again tomorrow," Somers said tiredly. "Tomorrow we pick them up and they lead us to the diamonds."

"How do you know where they're going to be?" he asked.

She stood and picked up her bag from the desk, and pulled from it, the print-outs from the newspaper office computer.

"That's where they'll be," she said. "I'd guess early evening."

"Where did you get this?" he asked.

"You don't have to know every move I make," she shot back. "That is where they will be."

"Why do you think late afternoon?"

Eve sighed impatiently.

"You have to know how Mac thinks," she said. "He knows you can't show up in a cemetery first thing in the morning and start digging things up. The neighbors will talk. I think Mac will show up in the late afternoon when the crews want to go home. He'll walk into the director's office, bamboozle him with some cockamamie story, and wind up getting permission to dig to China if he wants to."

"He's that good?"

She nodded.

"He's that good."

"I mean at bamboozling," he said in a conspiratorial voice.

She shot him a sharp look.

"You've got a sick mind," she snapped.

He pulled himself out of the chair and stood straight, stretching.

"OK," he said. "If you're sure they will show up at the Congressional Cemetery tomorrow, I'll leave it to you."

He stepped in front of her hands on hips.

"Just remember," he admonished. "Leave me out of it. I don't want my name to come to light, especially if something goes wrong."

"Nothing will go wrong," she promised. "And yes, I know, when I do this thing, you don't exist."

"But I start existing again as soon as you get the stones," he said, in an almost threatening voice.

She stood and turned down the bed, sitting on the top sheet and looking at him expectantly. He made no move to leave.

"Sure you don't want someone to share that with you?" he asked, indicating the bed.

"That's not in our agreement," she spat. "Try not to be such a damned pig,"

He shrugged and headed toward the door.

"Suit yourself," he said casually, stepping through the door into the hallway.

She walked to the door and snapped the dead-bolt. She was pretty sure the man wouldn't violate her bedroom while she slept, but the lock would make it certain, and would give her peace of mind – which she desperately wanted, and needed, if she was to sleep.

She dropped the towel and rummaged in her tote bag for a nightgown. Not finding one by feel, she stared at the bag for a moment, then hissed at it, climbed naked between the sheets and fell instantly to sleep not bothering to turn out the lights.

Chapter Thirty-Four

It was lunch time, and despite having slept in and not having done much during the morning hours, the *North Bay Times* quartet was hungry. By agreement, they arrived separately at the Rexall Drug Store a half-block from the old Metropole Hotel, where they would enjoy a convivial meal and some last minute planning before heading for the Congressional Cemetery.

The lunch counter at this ancient Rexall Drug Store was known throughout Washington for excellent, if not slightly greasy food. From time to time, Senators and Members of Congress sent aides to this place for take-out orders – and the more intrepid of them came themselves. The place was especially known for having the best hash browns in the city. All four of *the North Bay Times* team ordered those, along with other breakfast favorites. Thought it was lunch time in D.C., this lunch counter served breakfast twenty-four hours a day.

"I hate coming this close to the Metropole," McDermott said. "That place creeps me out."

"I know the feeling," Pitcher said fervently.

"I've had a major adventure in that old dump myself," Casio said softly, recalling the night in the hotel dining room when he had rescued his daughter from herself and from the terrorist group to which she had become affiliated. His adult daughter, who called herself Sasha Orstransky, had become one of the sect's leaders, and had assisted in using the offices of a corrupt U.S. Senator to make legal the purchase of all water systems in the U.S. Thus armed, the group had nearly brought the United States to its thirsty, stinky, unbathed knees.

"I was there," McDermott breathed.

"I was there more recently," Pitcher said, a little too loudly.

"Your story about the third floor is a little hard to swallow, Pitch," Hume said, spearing a forkful of scrambled egg.

"Nevertheless, it's true," Pitcher said flatly.

"Yes it is," McDermott said under his breath.

Casio looked at his watch.

"Let's check it out," he suggested, dropping some cash on the counter.

"I'm game," Hume responded, doing the same.

"Let's not," McDermott pleaded.

"Well for myself," Hume chimed in," I'd like to see this haven of hostelry Pitcher was babbling about. We may find more answers there."

Casio nodded speculatively.

"I agree," he said. "We might learn something important." He took the last bite of a piece of toast, drained his coffee, and signaled for his bill. Hume held up his arm, wanting the rail-skinny 19 year old waitress with alabaster skin, colorless hair and vacant eyes, to bring all the bills to him, which she did. McDermott and Pitcher looked at him in astonishment. Hume almost never picked up the check. But yes, it was no illusion; Hume collected all the paper tabs from the fragile waitress and pulled bills out of his wallet, sliding them across the table along with a generous tip – another astonishment to his co-workers. Casio grinned widely at their discomfiture. Each man locked eyes with the others for a moment, then as one, they turned and walked through the ancient drugstore and out into the street, turning resolutely and striding in unison down the sidewalk toward the decrepit corpse of a hotel.

The Four Muscatels.

The man was back in Eve Somers' room on the third floor of the Metropole, seated in the same chair as before, and with the same belligerent attitude, a frame of mind that gave Eve pause.

"You must have a plan," he said in a condescending voice. "This has gone on long enough. What's your plan?"

Somers was wearing jeans and a red buttoned dress shirt with short sleeves, adorned by a single gold chain and a rhinestone pendant, small and unobtrusive, with black patent leather mid-heeled boots. The Beretta was stuck in the belted waistband of her pants.

"I just need to pick up the trail of Mac and his fellow conspirators and let them lead me to the spot where the diamonds are hidden."

"Simple as that," he snorted.

"Simple as that," she snapped.

"And how do you intend to just pick up their trail?" he sneered.

"It's pretty obvious to me," Eve said. "We know they will go to the cemetery. I can pick them up there."

The man rose and faced the window.

"Simple as that?" he asked again.

"Simple as that," she said again.

The window out of which the man looked was a two-way glass. From the outside, it looked like ordinary glass rendered opaque by grime and disuse and dirt and time. From the inside, it was slightly tinted, but a useful portal to the street below. The man noted four men, walking in step toward the hotel. They seemed resolute, and their course was taking them toward the hotel entrance.

"Do you know those people?" he asked, pointing.

Somers rose and looked over his shoulder, then smiled.

"Well guess what!" she exclaimed. "It's them."

He turned to her.

"Them?" he asked, raising an eyebrow.

"Them," she said. "Hume, McDermott, Pitcher, and a private detective named Casio."

"Why are they coming here?" he demanded.

She looked daggers at him.

"What am I, a mind reader?" she spat. "I haven't the faintest notion!"

He thought a moment.

"Well," He speculated. "We could just let them come up here, grab them, and force them to tell us what we want to know."

"What if they don't know yet?" she asked.

"Huh?"

"Well suppose they know to go to the cemetery, but not what to do when they get there? Suppose they're just hoping the answer will become apparent once they get there?"

"Would they do that?" he asked her.

She nodded.

"Mac would," she said firmly. "He has uncanny luck at doing just that."

"What, then?" he inquired.

She turned back into the room and walked slowly toward the door.

"Seems to me if we capture them -- and they don't know exactly where to look – it would be counter-productive to our needs," she mused. "If on the other hand we discourage them from coming up here, and let them go on to the cemetery, it will be to our advantage."

"How?"

She turned back to him from halfway to the room door.

293

"If they're successful, we're successful," she snapped, tapping the side of her head with the flat of her hand. "God, how can you be so dense?"

"Then I would suggest we shut off the power to the elevator at once," he said declaratively.

Eve Somers have him a "no shit" look and continued to the door, which she opened, stepping out into the hallway. At the end of the hall near the elevator bank, she opened the metal door of a terminal box and yanked a large switch downward into the "off" position. She also moved another switch that dimmed the hallway lights on the third floor. With that, she sauntered back into the room.

"That ought to do it," she said, entering her room.

"Think they'll come up the stairs?" he asked.

She considered that for a moment.

"No, I don't think so."

The Four Muscatels made entrance to the hotel through the side door, which, curiously, they found unlocked. The entranceway took them into the hotel lobby, replete as always with dust and dirt and neglect. They approached the reservation desk and turned left and walked to the elevators. Pitcher pressed the button.

"You'll hear the machinery start up," he declared.

But nothing happened. They waited a minute, two, and no sound of starting motors greeted their ears. McDermott, Hume and Casio stared harshly at Pitcher. Sheepishly, Pitcher stabbed the button again, several times. When that didn't work, he walked to the other set of buttons about halfway down the wall and pushed again. Nothing. Defeated, he went back to his friends.

"I don't understand," he said quietly. "It worked when I was here just a few days ago."

McDermott gave Pitcher a shallow nod of faith and sympathy – since he, too, knew of the third floor but was prevented from agreeing with his reporter by a vow of silence.

"So what do we do now?" McDermott asked softly.

"Take the stairs," Hume thundered. "No sense in letting a little thing like a power failure, or whatever it is, prevent discovery."

"Not with my ankles," McDermott said.

"Nor my knees," Casio agreed.

"Let's not," Pitcher lamented. "This place is creeping me out."

"I'll second that," Casio asserted. "We have things to do, more important things than schlepping around a dusty old hotel."

"OK," Hume decided for the group. "Let's blow this pop stand."

Again, as one, they turned and walked in step toward the door from which they had entered. Once outside, their strides became more individualized as they headed for their cars.

"It doesn't make sense to take all the cars to the cemetery," Hume said. "Just two should do it. I have shovels and other tools in the trunk of my Lexus, so that will be one of them."

Let Sy go with you," McDermott suggested to Hume. "Pitch and I can ride out there in my Jeep."

Hume nodded.

"Agreed."

They split into teams as Mac had suggested. The Lexus and Jeep were parked, one in front of the other, in the same block as the drug store. They boarded as suggested and drove off in the same direction.

On the third floor of the Metropole, the man turned away from the tinted window with a satisfied smile on his face.

"How did you know?" he asked Eve.

"I know Mac," she replied. "And I know his boss, from having met him and from the way Mac talks about him – a mixture of friendship, disdain, and admiration."

He nodded.

"True of most bosses," the man said.

"But now," she said, pulling on a shirt cover-up that would hide the gun butt protruding from her waist band, "now I need to get on their trail and find out what they know."

She turned to him.

"Are you coming?"

He shook his head.

"I think it best that I stay behind. There are things that are in need of my care."

She assented with her eyes.

"Then I will go and take care of our outside business," she said, walking to the door. She put her hand on the knob, and then turned back to him, searching his eyes but not seeing anything she could recognize.

"Success," he said, fist upraised.

She merely nodded and closed the door silently as she left the room.

At the end of the hall, she restored power to the elevator and pressed the call button. The car doors opened within a minute, and she silently rode to the main level. By the time the elevator doors closed in the lobby, she had pushed open the entrance door and stepped into the street. She took a moment to allow her eyes to adjust to the early afternoon brightness, and then looked around carefully to see that her egress from the hotel had not been observed. Satisfied, she casually walked a block and a half to the stolen Kia. The button on the key fob unlocked the driver side door. She got in, gunned the engine to life, and drove off in the direction the Jeep and Lexus had gone.

The two cars containing the *North Bay Times* contingent were long out of sight, but she knew where they were going. All she needed to do was show up at the right time.

"The first thing we need to do is talk to the Cemetery caretaker," Hume said to Sy Casio. "He might know something we may find of value."

"That's a good thought," Casio said. "And we might need to prepare some kind of a diversion in case the caretaker is recalcitrant about letting us dig up his cemetery."

Hume unlimbered his cell phone.

"I'll tell Mac to interview the caretaker for a story in the paper. In the meantime, you and Pitch and I will try to figure out where to look in the cemetery for a load of diamonds that were worth two million dollars sixty years ago."

"Does Pitch have the watch with him?" Casio asked.

Hume shrugged.

"I'll ask when I call over there," he said, and thumbed a speed-dial number.

Three minutes later, he closed and holstered his phone, speaking to Casio while keeping an eye on his driving.

"Mac's got his shtick all set up. And Pitcher has the watch in his pocket."

"Does that make it a watch pocket?" Casio casually inquired.

Hume winced.

"Ha-ha," Hume chortled, sarcastically. "That's something I'd expect from Mac."

They rode in silence for the rest of the way, finally making the turn on to E Street Southeast. Hume watched the numbers, looking for the 1800 block, which he found, and turned in to a gated driveway with wrought iron gates in a twelve-foot brick fence. He stopped, and beckoned for the Jeep to pull up next to him, blocking the exit lane of the drive.

Before them stood the vast expanse of the cemetery,

The four men could see the roads leading around the various sections, each pock-marked with grave markers on various degrees of wear.

"I guess this is the place," Hume spoke out the open driver side window of his car.

"Unless you know of another Congressional Cemetery," Pitcher agreed from the passenger seat of McDermott's Jeep.

"This is the location where the coordinates from the watch meet," McDermott said, certainly.

"Then why don't you drop Pitch off here, and go on inside and start your diversion," Hume suggested.

Mac nodded and tapped Pitcher on the shoulder. The reporter stepped to the ground and opened the back driver side door of the Lexus and got in.

"You know what to do, Mac," Hume said.

McDermott nodded.

"I can handle it," he said.

"There's nobody better," Hume returned, as Mac drove toward the cemetery office.

Chapter Thirty-Five

The Congressional cemetery was founded by private citizens of the new District of Columbia and surrounding states in 1807, in the latter portion of the second term of President Thomas Jefferson. The cemetery is located on the banks of the Anacostia River, immediately south of the District of Columbia General Hospital – which is, itself, just south of the decaying RFK stadium. Just to its southwest is the Washington Navy Yard. It was given to the Christ Church, who named it the Washington Parish Burial Ground. By 1817, plots had been laid out for legislators and government officials. The markers in the cemetery include *cenotaphs*, or memorials for persons whose remains are interred elsewhere. Many members of the U.S. Congress, who died while Congress was in session, are buried here. It is the burial ground to 19 Senators and 71 Representatives, as well as power brokers, land owners, and many people who helped form the nation, and many of those who helped establish the District of Columbia as the federal city. Mayors of Washington as well as several Civil War veterans are buried there as well.

Among those buried there are Lincoln photographer Matthew Brady, and Lincoln assassination conspirator, David Herold, and lifelong FBI director J. Edgar Hoover.

Christ Church still owns the cemetery, but the grounds are managed by the nonprofit Association for the Preservation of the Historic Congressional Cemetery.

Christ Church is also known as Christ Church, Washington Parish, or Christ Church, Navy Yard, because of its proximity to the Washington Navy Yard. The church was also built in 1807 and is the historic church of Washington Parish, established by the Maryland General Assembly in 1794.

Today, a fund has been established that provides for grounds keeping in perpetuity, and fundraisers are ongoing to repair or replace the gothic-style buildings that date from the cemetery's beginnings. In addition, the cemetery is partially supported by its well-known "K-9 Corps," by which Association members, in addition to their dues, pay a small fee for permitting their dogs to roam unleashed on the cemetery grounds.

The four men parked their cars outside the gate and walked inside, stopping to marvel at the splendor of the rolling landscape.

"The first thing we have to do," Hume said, "is figure out where to look for what we want to find."

Casio nodded in agreement.

"Diamonds, even one representing that much money, aren't a huge amalgamation. They can be hidden in a relatively small place."

"And there's nothing to say that someone already found the diamonds and didn't bother to tell anyone about it," Pitcher said.

"Except his jeweler, or fence," Hume suggested.

The other three nodded.

"May I see the watch?" McDermott asked his ace reporter. Pitcher pulled a soft cloth from his pocket and passed it to the editor, who carefully unwrapped it and stared at the silver item. The others looked over his shoulders.

"There's something about this watch that keeps nagging at me," he said. "Even though we got the clue that was hidden inside, I don't think this watch is through talking with us yet."

"You may be right," observed Hume. "But we have a plan, and unless someone has a better one, it's best we stick to it."

"Right," Casio said. "We'll all stay here and look around and see if anything pops into sight for us. You go and interview the caretaker, and see if he spills anything."

McDermott sighed heavily and opened the driver side door of his Jeep.

"OK," he said, but his heart wasn't in it.

He swung into the driver seat and started the engine. Letting out the clutch, he waved at his fellow conspirators as he drove at idle speed to the office, a few hundred yards up the narrow paved road. He walked up the steps and into the unlocked door. Inside, there was a large counter that ran almost the width of the room. Behind it were a couple of desks and a copying machine. McDermott got the attention of the man seated at the desk toward the back of the room. He was pecking on the keyboard of a laptop computer when McDermott rang the tiny bell on the counter. He looked up and smiled, rising and walking toward the counter.

McDermott saw a small man with a slight pooch above his belt, but with powerful shoulders and sinewy arms. He walked with an ever-so-slight limp, yet an easy gait that went with the toothy smile he displayed above a pure-white Van Dyke beard and curly auburn hair. The stranger's blue-gray eyes appraised his visitor much as McDermott had appraised the stranger. The white-bearded man's hands set themselves on the counter palm down.

"May I help you, Sir?" he asked pleasantly.

"I am the Managing Editor of the *North Bay Times*," McDermott introduced himself.

"Heard of it," the stranger smiled.

McDermott grinned in return.

"I'm ashamed to say we have only recently become aware of this place, and my publisher thought I should check it out, and perhaps do a feature article on it in our paper."

The stranger scratched his bearded chin.

"I imagine that would help a bit with donations, wouldn't it, Mr. McDermott," he said

Mac nodded.

"Sure would. Can I talk to you for a few minutes?"

"Sure," the stranger said, brightly, indicating the end of the counter to McDermott's right.

The stranger returned to the desk and worked his keyboard for a few moments.

"Please sit down," he said. "I'm just saving what I was doing. Won't take a moment."

"Of course," McDermott responded flatly, pulling a narrow reporter's notebook out of his hip pocket as he seated himself. A moment later, the stranger closed his computer, sat back and clasped his hands across his middle and turned his attention to McDermott.

"Can we start with your name?" the editor asked, silver Cross pencil poised over the notebook page.

"You can call me Jay," the stranger said, still smiling."

McDermott smiled back.

"Thanks, Jay. I'll get your last name later. What kind of duties do you perform in your job here?"

Jay placed his fingers, palm in, over his mouth and sat up straight.

"Oh, I'm not the caretaker here," Jay said. "He's a good friend of mine, and sometimes when he has to run errands or go to the doctor or something, I sit here and keep the office open. If someone comes in, I can arrange a tour or give them literature for a burial here, but the caretaker has to finalize all those things. He's usually not gone very long, but today he'll be away most of the day."

"Oh," McDermott said lamely, his hands relaxing. He flipped his notebook closed and put the pencil back in his shirt pocket next to its mate. "Well it doesn't look there's much a story here today."

"No, not today," Jay grinned. "But if you want to look around the grounds, perhaps take some pictures, please feel free." Jay picked up a trifold brochure from a small pile on the desk and handed it to the editor.

McDermott took it an opened it.

"It's divided by ranges and sites," Jay said. "If there's a specific grave you want to find, you can check it in our card file, up at the front desk, or you can just call me from the grounds and I'll tell you where to find it."

"Thanks," McDermott said. "When will the caretaker be back?"

"Tomorrow morning," Jay said, pleasantly.

"What's his name?"

"Everyone calls him Digger," Jay said with an electric grin.

"A cemetery caretaker named Digger?" McDermott asked, incredulous.

Jay shrugged.

"Go figure."

McDermott rose and headed for the front of the room. He rounded the corner and put his hand on the front door handle. He stopped and turned to the man at the desk.

"Have we met before?"

Jay looked up and nodded shallowly.

"That's what I thought," McDermott said, and stepped through the door.

Five minutes later, McDermott stepped out of the Jeep and faced his three friends.

"Waterhaul," he said.

"What?" Casio asked.

"Journalese," Hume translated. "It means waste of time."

So what do we do now?" Pitcher demanded.

McDermott held out his hand, and Pitcher automatically dropped the watch into it, wrapping cloth and all. McDermott pocketed the cloth and held the watch in the sun so he could look it over carefully. For a moment he was unable to manipulate the watch. He had to put the brochure Jay had given him into his pocket before he had both hands free to study the watch. The others watched him as he turned the watch over in his hands again and again. Finally, bored, Pitcher tapped McDermott's shoulder.

"What was that you put in your pocket?" he asked.

Wordlessly, McDermott pulled out the brochure and handed it over, staring intently at the face of the watch and the hands.

"Hmmm," Pitcher mused aloud. "Ranges and Sites." It forms a grid, I guess, and that's how you find a grave in this place."

"It's like that in most cemeteries," Casio remarked.

"Damn, it's frustrating," McDermott blurted. "We are so close to finding the diamonds – but we're lacking a vital clue – and I'm certain that it's right in front of me and I'm not getting it."

"Happens to everyone who does detective work," Casio responded. "You just feel like you're looking right at it and you can't see it."

McDermott nodded enthusiastically.

"That's it exactly."

"It seems to me," Hume mused aloud," that the people who put the numbers in the watch wanted the diamonds to be found, right?"

"Of course," McDermott agreed.

"And they would want the clue to be obscure enough, that is not exactly latent, that if any of the Nazi collaborators got hold of it, they might not have the whole solution, right?"

McDermott was following Hume's thread and beginning to smile.

"Yes, that's right."

"So the clue is inside the watch – and once you take it out, you got a watch with no works," Pitcher chimed in.

"That's right, no works," McDermott repeated absently, staring again at the face of the timepiece.

"How about..." Casio began, but McDermott held up a restraining hand.

"Wait a minute," he exclaimed. "I'm getting something here, let me talk it out."

The others fell silent as McDermott stared with deep concentration at the face of the Ziess-Baden watch.

"If the watch has no works – and if it's worn on the right wrist – the bearer also wearing a conventional, working watch on his left wrist – why are there still hands on here?" he wondered.

"Probably to make it look 'normal' to whoever might casually see it," Pitcher suggested.

"Meaning if any German operative filched it, all he'd think he had was a broken watch," McDermott said, excitement building in his voice.

"That's right," Casio said."

"Seems to me I read something once," Hume said, stroking his chin. "Someone famous once said that if you want to hide something, hide it in plain sight."

"Oh my God," McDermott yelled.

"What?" Hume demanded.

"All this time we thought the position of the hands was completely random – like maybe where they were when the works were taken out of the back," McDermott said.

"Yeah," Pitcher agreed.

"But what if they weren't random," McDermott speculated, talking faster and faster. "What if they were deliberately set the way we found them? I've been looking at the hands, they haven't moved, why not? Why are they set as they are?"

He held up the watch face, close to the eyes of each man in turn.

"Pitch said it," he exclaimed, yanking the brochure out of his hands. "Range and Site. That's how cemeteries are laid out"

"So what?" Hume demanded.

"So this," McDermott said, triumphantly. "The watch was the complete clue. Inside, it gave us the latitude and longitude of the general location." He swept his hands across the landscape behind him. "Here is that place, generally. Now the hands of the watch give us the *specific* location. Don't you get it?"

"Get what?" Hume barked, impatiently.

But McDermott's enthusiasm was infectious, and the others, including a reluctant and impatient Hume were warming up to the editor's reasoning process.

"Get this," McDermott snapped. "The specific clue is right here, right in front of our noses and we missed it, just as the Resistance fighters meant the German operatives in Washington to do. We missed it because it was *too* plain, *too* obvious, *too* in our faces. Look at the watch again, and remember what Pitch said."

"The watch reads 4:20," Hume said softly.

"And Pitch said Range and Site..." Casio began, then he stopped, and his eyes got as big as saucers as the light bulb went on above his head.

"I think I get it now, Mac," he said, becoming even more exciting. "You're saying that if the watch brought us here with what was inside it, then the hands are the final clue and they tell us specifically where to look."

"Right," McDermott said.

"And the hands read 4:20," Hume repeated.

"So why couldn't it mean Range 4, Site 20?" McDermott asked, with a huge smile.

Pitcher consulted the map in his hand.

Only problem with that is there isn't a Range 4," he said, dejected.

McDermott looked again at the hands of the watch and pondered that statement for a moment. He was very close, of that he was certain. His theory couldn't be wrong, it just couldn't! He tore his eyes away from the watch face and looked up, taking a moment to let the blue sky over South east Washington clear his head.

He sighed heavily and returned his gaze to the watch. The others, also feeling that a solution was very close, didn't interrupt his reverie, not daring to talk unless he addressed them.

"Wait a minute," McDermott almost whispered. "It was a military operation. That's the key. It was military. So the hands, naturally, were intended to convey military time."

"How does that change things?" Pitcher asked, equally soft of voice.

"Military time follows a 24-hour clock," Casio explained. You begin at midnight and count hours as always, one, two, three AM and so forth, but you pronounce the two zeros at the top of the hour as 'hundred.' Thus, one AM becomes oh-one-hundred, oh one ten, and so on."

"OK I get that, but it still doesn't help, there's still no Range 4."

Casio continued." Yes, but don't you see? Once you get past twelve-noon, you don't go back to one again, not in military time. You just keep counting from twelve."

"You mean that one o'clock in the afternoon becomes thirteen hundred?"

"And so on," Casio said, clapping Pitcher on the back.

"Then my idea is the correct one," McDermott breathed. "It was right in front of us the whole time. The hands did it. The hands had the specific location clue all the time and we looked right past it."

"Then," Pitcher began, addressing Casio, "If we continue counting like you said, then 4:20 in the afternoon becomes..." he stopped to calculate the hours in his head, "...sixteen-twenty."

"That's it," McDermott yelled.

"Yes it is," Pitcher agreed. There *is* a Range 16 – and look, there's a Site 20 in that range."

"It can't be anything else," Hume bellowed. "That has to be it.

"Can it really be that simple?" McDermott wondered.

"It can," Hume whispered.

Chapter Thirty-Six

The four men followed the map to Range 16 Site 20. Before them was a rectangular stone whose top was above the ground by no more than one or two inches. It was a plain white stone perhaps three feet high by five feet wide. Just from its plain appearance it seemed out of place among the ornate markers and carvings in the vicinity. Even the stones on either side, also nearly flat to the ground, had intricate carvings and legends of endearment. The stone before them had only two lines.

Alvin Joseph Truscott
December 24, 1918 – January 12, 1944

That was it. The Four Muscatels looked at one another quizzically. Finally, Hume turned to his Managing Editor.

"Can you make head or tails of this?" he demanded.

McDermott stared slack-jawed at the stone and then back at Hume.

"No," he said, incredulously, shaking his head. "I don't know what I expected to find, but this isn't it."

"You didn't expect to find a sign with an arrow pointed down saying 'diamonds,' did you?" Casio asked.

McDermott looked at him askance.

"You've used that one before," he said laconically.

"Still holds," Casio said, bitingly.

Hume leaned against a large stone in the row behind the Truscott grave and regarded the back of his hand. It was lavishly carved, six-foot slab of marble with intricate filigree, with the legend, "Charletta Zuber, Congressional Page," and her dates of birth and death.

"So what do we do now?"

"Back up ten yards and punt," came a female voice from behind the stone.

Hume stood up straight, startled and not a little frightened, and the others tensed as they looked for the source of the voice.

Eve Somers stepped from behind the stone into view, and four jaws dropped in shock.

"Don't be so surprised, Gentlemen," she drawled. "I don't give up any easier than you do."

McDermott stepped toward a few feet.

"I wouldn't have believed you'd have the nerve to show up here."

She shook her head.

"Didn't take nerve, Mac. There's something here I want."

"And that would be...?" Casio prompted.

"Same as you," she said casually. "The diamonds."

Pitcher's face assumed a look of pure innocence.

"What diamonds?"

Eve's face hardened.

"Don't get cute with me, Pitcher, you know what I've done to get here!"

McDermott took a step closer to her.

"What I don't understand, Eve, is why! I'd really like to understand. What's this all about?"

Eve Somers sighed.

"You want the whole story, or the abridged one?" she asked.

McDermott studied her eyes for a moment, not liking what he saw.

"We might as well hear it all," he replied.

She nodded, satisfied.

"You're right," she said. "You'll live a few minutes longer that way."

"You going to do us like you did my family members?" Pitcher inquired.

She considered this for a moment.

"I am rather hoping not to have to do that," she said. "I have to say I am growing weary of all the killing."

"And it was all for nothing," Casio muttered.

Eve's face turned red.

"Nothing, Mr. Casio? Hardly!"

"Perhaps if you'd start at the beginning," Hume suggested, "then we will all be on the same page and maybe we can help one another."

She closed her eyes and vigorously shook her head.

"There's no room in this operation for any of you," she said firmly. "I'll tell you the whole story, but once I do you're going to have to turn around and drive out of here and not look back. I'll give you enough for

308

your newspaper stories, and Mac can have some more wood and plastic plaques to hang up on his wall. But that's all you get."

"And if we choose to continue the quest?" Mac challenged.

Eve Somers reached under her cover-up and pulled the Beretta. Casio saw it coming free and quickly reached for the Browning under his coat, but Eve caught the move and leveled her weapon at him.

"Ah. Ah, ah," she admonished. "Just for safety's sake, Mr. Casio, why don't you bring that cannon out with two fingers and throw it over here. You can retrieve it later – maybe – but let's keep from having an OK Corral-style shoot-out in the meantime, OK?"

Casio, looking sheepish, gingerly put two fingers inside his suit coat and pulled out the Browning by the back of the slide, and carefully tossed it in front of himself. It landed to McDermott's right, almost at his feet.

"You want to kick that over there, Mac?" she suggested, gesturing with the gun to an indeterminate spot farther to McDermott's right. Without looking he kicked at it, making contact with the weapon and sending it spinning about six feet from its original landing.

Eve Somers stuck the Beretta back into her waist band and hoisted herself up on to a nearby grave stone, which put her feet about twelve inches off the ground.

"You shouldn't sit there, it's disrespectful," Hume volunteered.

Somers made a show of looking around, then stared down at the inscription on the stone.

"She doesn't seem to mine," Somers said, shrugging.

"From the beginning, then?" McDermott prompted.

"From the beginning," she said.

McDermott reached carefully into his left hand pants pocket and came out with a small device about an inch wide, a half-inch deep, and four inches long.

"Mind if I record this?" he asked.

She shrugged.

"What do I care?"

McDermott moved a switch and pointed the device toward Eve.

"You're on," he said.

Somers took a deep breath.

"I always thought you were concerned that I was trying to maneuver you to the altar," Mac," she said softly.

"The thought crossed my mind," he confirmed.

"But did you know that wouldn't have been my first trip to the altar?"

309

McDermott shook his head.

"I got married right out of high school, to the co-captain of the football team. He never could keep his hands off me. We eloped. Maryland law allowed seventeen and eighteen year olds to do that then. Hell, maybe they still do, I don't know.

"Anyway, our parents had cumulative conniptions, and the marriage failed quickly. I got an annulment. Two years later, my ex-husband, Arvey Somers, was killed in a boating accident out on the bay."

McDermott was flabbergasted.

"So Somers isn't your maiden name."

She shook her head.

"Maybe the marriage lasted only a few months," she said sadly. "But I did love Arvey. So I kept his name. I dated, of course, but never seriously. Never, that is, until I met you."

"What has that to do with this?" McDermott inquired.

She shrugged, nearly sliding off the tombstone.

"Nothing, I guess," she said, laconically.

"That is the part that's relevant," she said. "My maiden name is Elmendorf."

"Elmandorf?" Casio exclaimed.

"Same name as…"

"Yes, as Karl Elmendorf, the man you heard about as Chance Caine, the trumpeter from the Blue Heron, a few blocks from here."

"You're related, of course," Pitcher said, a statement rather than a question.

"My grandfather," she said, simply."

"But what has that…," Pitcher began.

"Like Mac said, Pitch, let's start at the beginning.

"Ursula Spiedel shot him while he was performing onstage at the club. Ursula was an operative for the *Abwehr,* the German intelligence agency during the War. She took the watch off his wrist while his body was still warm, and left the club in the company of one Armand Wicht. Wicht was also reputed to be a Nazi counter-espionage agent, but as it turned out, he was paid by the British M-I-5 intelligence organization.

"Ursula's purpose was to prevent the shipment of a great number of machine guns to the German Resistance, thus keeping them under-armed. But there was a greater purpose. That was to bring Roag Arms to its knees."

"Why worry about the arms maker?" Hume wanted to know.

"Roag was the only maker of that particular machine gun," Somers continued. "If the Nazis could prevent the payment from going through on enough shipments, the company would suffer from the loss of a major customer and might have gone under – which did happen, but not until a bit later.

"But her friend Wicht, whom she trusted, was a double-agent. Once she had the watch, he took her to their rendezvous and met up with his contact, who killed her to get that messenger vessel."

"That was Oglesby," McDermott suggested.

She nodded.

"That was Oglesby. But Wicht didn't trust Oglesby either, and he managed to escape with the watch. Oglesby chased him for years even after the war ended. Two million dollars in uncut, untraceable diamonds was nothing to sneeze at."

"Indeed not," Casio breathed.

"Wicht transferred the watch to someone – he didn't say who until he was on his deathbed. The recipient was his nephew, Albert Lowenstein, himself a minor agent representing the American cooperative effort with the Resistance in Germany. Lowenstein wasn't privy to what the watch meant; his uncle merely told him to hang on to it as thought it was as valuable as life itself, which in a very real sense, it was."

"Considering that four people have died for it – five if you count Ursula Spiedel…," McDermott began.

"Six, if you count Oglesby himself," Casio pointed out.

"Yes," McDermott agreed, and turned back to Somers. "Considering those six deaths, that watch had a pretty high value placed on it, didn't it?"

Eve Somers clouded over.

"Apparently so," she agreed in a low voice.

"Do go on," Hume said. "You spin a good tale."

Eve Somers shook her head to clear it and get herself back on track, then relaxed in her seat on the tombstone.

"Be that as it may," she resumed, "Lowenstein held on to that watch, not telling anyone he had it, and treating it as a thing of great value. Wicht was supposed to return and claim the watch, or send him instructions on what to do with it. His last note, some six years after the war, stated that someone would come to get the watch, and would identify himself with Wicht's name. Lowenstein was to hang on to it no matter how long it took.

Wicht died less than six months after that final note to Lowenstein, but Lowenstein never knew that. Lowenstein held on to that watch for decades, keeping it hidden. When he died, his will sent it to his heirs with hidden instructions that they were to treat it as a thing of value, but were to tell no one why they did so. The first of the heirs to receive the watch was Reesa Lowenstein."

"Now maybe you'll explain how she managed to show up dead on the stage of that old nightclub," Pitcher barked.

"Gladly," Eve Somers retorted with equal fervor. "One of Reesa's interests was unsolved crime. She was a lab technician at one time..."

"Yes, that's right," Pitcher shouted. "But I never knew what kind of lab technician."

"She worked for the Maryland State Police Crime Lab as a technician, and in the course of her work, she shortened her name to Lowe. No one seemed to know why she did it."

Pitcher's facial expression indicated that he didn't know either. Somers went on.

"She inherited the watch. I knew that. I had word that Albert Lowenstein had it, and I attempted to make contact with him about it, but he refused to speak of it. This was only last year. You wondered, Mac, why I disappeared from Willie Sykes' hotel right before he was killed? I was trying to connect with that watch, but the elder Lowenstein was playing it cagey.

"When he died, I checked with probate, just as you did, Mac. I found that an undescribed batch of costume jewelry was specifically mentioned in the will, and it was to be divided among three of the heirs. Reesa was simply the first one I contacted. I won't tell you how I struck up a conversation with her, but she expressed an interest in the Blue Heron killing. I told her I would arrange to show her where it happened, and she was thrilled.

"She showed up and I demanded the watch. She said she had the watch, but had traded it to another of the heirs for some other things. I was infuriated. She demanded to know what the watch was all about. She said she was learning a lot from what I wasn't saying – that the watch had some hidden value so she would tell the relative she gave it to not to surrender it for anything, not until she found out what made it so valuable.

"As I said, that infuriated me. And I couldn't let her spread the word that the old watch had some importance. But she wouldn't listen to reason, so I shot her, I shot her more than once, and left her body on the stage. Someone must have heard the shots and called the police, thought I have to say I'm surprised that anyone in that neighborhood would even consider doing such a thing."

"And the others?" Hume asked with a sharp edge to his voice.

"I was pretty sure that Albert Lowe was the one who had the watch after Reesa," Somers continued. "I told him I represented a precious metal dealer that handled estates, and that he should meet me at 1801 E-Street Southeast and I'd make him a price on any Ziess Baden watch he might have in his possession."

"What address is that?" McDermott demanded.

Somers pointed at the ground.

"Right here. He showed up and the look on his face on seeing it was the Congressional Cemetery was priceless. He said he didn't have the watch, that there was nothing in his inheritance by Ziess-Baden, but that he had come out of curiosity about what kind of scam I thought I was running. He said the police were on their way."

She looked down at her feet.

"He might have walked away if he hadn't tried to physically hold me for the police. When he wouldn't let go, I let him have it. But I did take the time to search his pockets before I left. He didn't have it. That left one other heir and that one had to have it."

"Aunt Louisa's husband," Pitcher said through clenched teeth. Pitcher was amazed that Eve Somers could talk of the people she had killed in such a cavalier manner.

"Albert Lowenstein the Third," she nodded. "I caught up with him, but by that time the word was out. He was waiting for me, he confirmed that he had the Ziess-Baden, and he invited me into a taxi with him. He gave an address that turned out to be the local police precinct. I shoved him out of the taxi and we had a fist fight. He was winning. So I let him have it. He got back into the taxi, I couldn't believe he managed to do that, as shot up as he was. The taxi drove off. Now I know it went to your house, Rod, and that he gave the watch to you."

"There was no police report about a shot-up guy getting into a cab," Pitcher said. "I looked for one after he showed up at my place."

Somers snorted. "You think that camel jockey who was driving the cab was going to report such a thing? He'd have had a lot of explaining to do, assuming he was in this country legally. He cleaned the cab and apparently neglected to notify the authorities, and Al Lowenstein died at your apartment with no one knowing he got there."

"That clears up one mystery," Pitcher mused.

"And others will become clear," she said. "By now I knew that you had the watch, Rod. I made two attempts to rub you out and get it."

She turned to McDermott."

"Incidentally, Mac, that shot that went past you was meant for Pitcher. It was just plain bad shooting on my part."

"Thanks, I think," McDermott said.

"What about the Metropole?" Pitcher demanded. "That third floor that still has power, that's clean and looks like a Hilton?"

"That," she shot back, "is another part of this sordid affair that no one knows, no one but me, until now."

"Well, then..." McDermott prompted.

"I'll tell you," Somers said with a tiny smile as she pulled the Beretta from her waist band. "But then I'll have to kill you."

Chapter Thirty-Seven

Armando Santos and his partner consulted with Fred Mattingly of the Washington D.C. police at the Old Ebbetts, a pricy, upscale restaurant a half-block from the White House. Santos and Arlee Kelley didn't have bad news.

"I don't think they knew he was being followed," Santos said blankly to Mattingly. "We were conducting a loose tail – following about a half-block back – and they apparently double-turned on us. We know they were headed in the direction of Washington South East, but we don't know that area as well as your guys do."

"Well that means to me that your hot pursuit is over," Mattingly said, with a sympathetic tone in his voice. He knew how easy it could be for him to be on the other end of such a conversation sometime in the future. "We can put out a BOLO on your newspaper people. Now you're sure that Eve Somers will catch up with them?"

Santos nodded.

"If she hasn't already. They know where they're going, and whatever they are looking for, she wants. She wants it bad enough to kill three people for it, perhaps more than that. She will dog them to their last breath."

"Which may be what we're dealing with if we don't catch up to them," Mattingly thought out loud.

"Agreed," Arlee Kelley said, seriously.

"I'll call Dispatch and have all the South East Sector cars be on the prowl for McDermott's Jeep. That'll be the easiest way to find them. And we'll drive around the area south of RFK Stadium; maybe we'll be able to spot them.

"You deputizing us for D.C.?" Kelley asked.

Mattingly nodded.

"We've worked together before. And besides, this case has skipped all over the Chesapeake Watershed since the beginning, starting here

315

and moving into Baltimore. The more knowledge and experience we can get into the field the better. I've got an SUV outside. Let's head down the Anacostia and see what we can find."

Santos looked up, for the first time that day.

"Before you change your mine," he said firmly.

"Let's go!" Kelley exclaimed.

They drained their glasses, paid and headed for the door.

Eve Somers slipped off the tombstone she'd been using as a stool. She held her Beretta in a non-threatening way, but it was still in her hand. Casio touched each of his colleagues to caution them to make no sudden moves.

"You want to know about the Metropole?" she prompted.

"To be sure, if you don't mind," McDermott said, his voice slick with pompous hauteur.

"Let's go back to the deal for the machine guns," Eve began.

"Yes, let's," McDermott cooed.

Casio kicked him on the back of his leg.

Somers ignored both of them.

"I won't bore you the history of the old hotel. Suffice it to say it's been the headquarters for intrigue and double-dealing since the Capital was moved here."

All the men nodded in unison.

"About the machine gun deal," Pitcher promoted.

She winked at him.

"At least someone is staying on the thread, Rod," she grinned at him, tapping her head with her index finger. "Good job."

She slid back up onto the tombstone, but didn't put the gun away.

"Roag Arms agreed to supply machine guns to the German resistance. They agreed to the means of payment. And they sold the guns to the Resistance at a fraction over what it cost to make them. By the end of the war, the Resistance was the only contract Roag Arms had, and by that time they were in trouble. Their War Department contract had been cancelled and then freedom fighters in Germany were the only business on their books. The payments came – mostly – on time, but when the German agents got the better of the Resistance fighters' representative, there would be a long delay before payment was received. Payment was always in advance. But Roag Arms would manufacture the weapons in anticipation of the arrival of the money. The system worked well until the last order."

"That's the one Ursula Spiedel intercepted?" Hume asked.

"That's the one," Somers replied.

"What happened?" Hume wanted to know.

"By that time, Roag Arms was struggling, financially. That two million dollars in diamonds – even with the discount they'd have to pay to convert them to cash – would have saved the company. As it was, the company got by on small orders to the French, and the post-war Italians, but it was on its way to ruin, and when it finally came, the crash was devastating. All the jobs were lost and the company's founder lost his personal fortune in addition to his business. Martin Roag searched for that diamond shipment for years and years, to the exclusion of all else. He considered it his."

"What happened to him?" McDermott inquired.

"That's the sad part," she said. "The sins of the father were visited on the son. Martin Roag had a stroke fifteen years ago. It left him unable to function. His son, also Martin Roag, had been trying to rebuild the shattered family business, along with his father, but when the elder Martin was incapacitated, it turned him in ugly ways."

"Like…?" McDermott prompted.

"Like the obsessiveness of his father for finding that load of diamonds, but magnified ten times over. It's a singleness of purpose you have to see to believe."

"Do you have a connection to him?" Casio asked.

"You're getting ahead of me, here, Detective," she said casually. "At the heyday of the company, the elder Roag decided to try diversifying the business. I don't know, I guess he was either hedging his bets against the end of the war and the stopping of his arms contract, or he was going to try to make another business go. In any case, the Metropole came up in one of its frequent tax sales, and Martin Roag Senior bought it for a song. The hotel was operating at the time, but was losing money. Roag thought he could turn it around."

She shook her head sadly.

"Didn't happen. The hotel finally closed in 1945 and went to pot, as all of you know. But Roag and his son kept the third floor in good condition, and used it as a residence until his stroke. Now it's his residence, his nursing home, and will be his funeral home one day. One day pretty soon, I think."

She sighed.

"Go on," Hume prompted her.

"Martin Senior's obsession with finding those diamonds is nothing compared with the son. Martin Junior blames the watch and all who have touched it for the failure of his legacy and his fortune and for his father's infirmity.

"I'm the granddaughter of Karl Elmendorf. I don't know how Martin Junior tracked me down, but he did. I told him, truthfully, that I had never set eyes on the watch. And he convinced me to help him find it."

"I can just imagine how he did that," McDermott said, sarcastically.

"Don't you see, Mac?" she asked, plaintively. "The people who kept that watch and its contents secret all these years ruined countless lives. If they had just brought it forward and said, 'I have this thing and I want to give it back to whomever it belongs to.' But no one did that. It was taken from my grandfather's dead wrist by a woman who left my grandmother a widow with a son – my father. He spent his life wondering why other kids had a grandpa and he didn't. And Martin Junior, whom I didn't know from Adam until a few months ago – he had a father he adored, and that was taken from him – no, not even really taken, just... yes, taken from him, in the worse way imaginable. The shell is still there for him to see every day, but the Dad he knew and loved is gone."

She was close to breaking down, now. Tears were streaming down her cheeks and her eyes were welled up.

"Does Martin Junior know you killed those people?"

She nodded.

"He didn't bat an eye. He said those people who held the watch had done this to his father..."

"Eve, you know better than that," McDermott said, soothingly. "Pitch's family didn't know what was in the watch."

"They didn't have to, Mac," she said, crying openly now and wiping her eyes on her sleeve. "All they had to know was that they had something that was important to someone. And they did know that, but they did nothing to put their sin right. So they died in their sin, Mac."

"My God, Eve, you need help," Mac said, and stepped forward, extending his hands. Eve Somers jumped off the tombstone, her eyes suddenly clear, and raised the gun, pointing it rock steadily at McDermott's crotch.

"Stay back, Mr. McDermott." She yelled, sharply. "I think highly of you, but I've come too far to put sentiment before my duty."

"Duty?" McDermott asked, amazed

"My personal task is to find the diamonds and restore my grandfather's good name – and mine – and give Martin Roag Junior a good rest-of-his-life. Nothing else matters, Mac, not your life and certainly not mine."

McDermott took another baby step forward.

"Eve, there's a way out of this, there must be. Come on, now, let's work this out, the paper will..."

Eve Somers raised the gun threateningly.

"I've been here too long already. Thank you, Gentlemen, for showing me where the diamonds are," she said.

"We haven't found them yet," Pitcher pointed out.

"And you probably won't, for awhile yet," she retorted. "Mac, come over here, please."

McDermott hesitated.

"Come on, Mac," she cajoled, aiming the gun with apparent purpose.

McDermott approached her gingerly until he was just outside of arm's length, guessing her intention. She reached forward and grabbed his arm, pulling her to him. She pressed the Beretta's barrel against McDermott's temple.

"I know the police will be here soon," she said. "I'm pretty sure they will find me by finding you, and I'm not ready to be caught yet. So you and I are going for a little ride, Mac, and your friends are going to stand aside and allow us to leave here – temporarily."

"Oh that's all right, Eve, I don't really need to go for a ride, why don't you just..."

McDermott tried to pull himself out of her grasp, and almost made it. But she tightened her grip on his arm and pressed the gun against his head so tightly that it gouged the skin.

"Let's take a walk over to your Jeep, Mac," she suggested threateningly.

She pressed forward, her arm across his chest, pressing herself against him, gun still to his head, forcing him forward.

"You gentlemen don't need the usual admonition, do you?" she asked.

"You mean the one about, 'don't try anything or I'll scatter his brains back to the Lincoln Memorial,' that admonition?" Casio asked.

"That's the one," she said.

"Ok, gotcha," Casio responded, and moved to allow Mac and Eve through. The others followed suit. "We'll get in through the passenger door, Mac," she said. "You're driving."

"I'll have to climb over the parking brake and gear shift," he said.

"I know that," she growled, pulling open the door and shoving him against the frame of the black vehicle. Reluctantly, Mac climbed in and stepped over the gear shift, crouched low, and forced his frame into the driver seat. Eve stayed outside the Jeep for a moment, studying the faces of the men remaining. Then, with a thin smile on her face, she took careful aim and fired her Beretta twice. The passenger side tires hissed and flattened. She turned and climbed into the Jeep, placing the warm gun barrel against Mac's cheek.

"Drive," she ordered.

"Where?" he inquired, mashing in the clutch and starting the engine.

"Just drive, I'll tell you where."

McDermott drove out of the cemetery. Eve indicated with the gun barrel that he should turn right onto E-Street, and he did so.

"Head in the direction of RFK," she said.

Armando Santos, Arlee Kelley and Fred Mattingly arrived at Congressional Cemetery just moments after the Jeep left. The SUV stopped at the gate, noticed the Lexus a few hundred yards away and pulled up beside it. All three of the remaining men were on cell phones. Hume was calling the D.C. police, Casio was trying to convince a taxi company to send a car into that neighborhood, and Pitcher was trying to get in touch with Samantha Parker at the Maryland Historical Authority for a ride.

The North Bay Times crew flagged down the car, not knowing who was in it, but they were elated to find that it was the police.

"Somers was here and she took Mac," Hume bellowed as Santos rolled down the driver side window.

"They left just now," Pitcher screamed.

"They left about five minutes ago in McDermott's black Jeep Wrangler Unlimited. They turned right when they left the cemetery gate," Casio said in a calm voice.

Santos instantly grabbed the radio car's microphone and made a full report to Central Dispatch. Within minutes, patrol cars from all over the south side of Washington would converge on the area looking for the black Jeep.

Even as he did so, the three from the *North Bay Times* were clamoring into the back seat of the police SUV.

"Just exactly what do you guys think you're doing?" Santos demanded.

"We're here for the chase," Casio said.

"Let's go!" Pitcher shouted.

"Time's a-wastin'!" Hume thundered.

Resigned, Santos winked at his partner and dropped the car into gear. It headed for the gate leaving thirty feet of BPD rubber on the asphalt.

McDermott shifted the Jeep into fifth gear and aimed the nose northwest, away from the cemetery. He tried the old TV cop show ploys, crowding a stop light and driving a little too fast in the hopes of attracting the attention of a police cruiser. But the old adage – there's never a cop around when you need one – held true. McDermott was starting to get worried. Somehow he had to get word to his colleagues as to where his former girlfriend planned to take him. He had an idea of what she planned when they reached their destination. His chances of survival would depend on his own ingenuity and on the ability of his friends and the D.C. police to ferret out where they were headed. And he knew that he would need to give them a hint.

Carefully he worked his cell phone out of his pocket and transferred it to his left hand, out of site of Eve Somers who held the gun on him, but was watching where he was going. Looking down only furtively as he drove, McDermott flipped open the phone and pressed Menu, scrolling up an item at a time till he found "settings," which he OK'd and scrolled again. He found the GPS setting, and pressed it. The indicator changed from "off" to "on." He gently set the phone down on the floor between the seat frame and the door, then returned his left hand to the wheel – just in time because Eve Somers was now turning her attention to him.

"Turn into this parking lot," she ordered, pointing off to the left.

McDermott followed her point and saw the entrance to the stadium. He flicked on his turn signal and stopped, waiting for some traffic to clear, then made the turn onto the lot.

RFK Stadium opened in October of 1961, then called D.C. Stadium, home of the Washington Redskins, and the hapless American League Washington Senators baseball team. It was named for New York Senator, and former Attorney General Robert F. Kennedy in January of 1969 – six months after the Senator's assassination during his 1968 presidential primary campaign. It say, decaying, in the sight of the U.S. Capitol and the Washington Monument in a side of town rotting even faster than the stadium itself – now relegated to the D.C. United soccer team and rock concerts staged by a local radio station.

"Now what?" McDermott asked as he slowed the Jeep on the huge empty parking lot.

"Let's get to the stadium," she replied, pointing to the round edifice that was still half a mile away across the parking lot.

McDermott shifted to second gear and guided the vehicle to Gate 4 of the Capitol side of the building and stopped.

"Get out, Mac," she said, sharply .

321

McDermott opened the door, and deftly picked up the cell phone from the door well and sliding it into his pants pocket. Eve Somers also got out of the Jeep, her gun held in an unobtrusive way, but still evident to McDermott that she had the drop.

"What are we doing here?" McDermott demanded, rounding the vehicle and standing next to Eve.

"We're getting totally lost," she said, prodding him with the gun. "Inside."

The gate was open, and McDermott stepped through. He walked in the direction indicated by the gun barrel in the small of his back, following a wide concrete corridor. They passed the entranceways to several sections of seats. The hallways meandered upward, along the outside wall of the stadium. At the top of the pathways, they found the broadcast booth. It was locked.

"Open it," she snarled.

McDermott made a show of patting his pockets.

"I don't have the key," he said, casually.

She beckoned to the door with her head.

"Knock it down," she said.

McDermott shrugged. He bent low and launched himself at the door, hitting it with his right shoulder just above the knob. To his immense surprise, the door jamb splintered, and the booth lay open for his inspection. In the dim light coming through the large window at the front of the booth, McDermott could see the sound console, a twenty-four channel mixer, with two microphones on flex-stands, and other microphones lying atop the console. There was also a laptop computer and a tape cartridge machine, along with transmission equipment, and monitors for the cameras placed strategically around the ball park. Here, radio and television announcers called the action for those who tuned in.

McDermott recovered and turned to Eve, who was now holding the gun in plain sight and aimed at his middle.

"Get in there," Mac," she demanded, and poked McDermott with the gun. He stumbled backward over a step leading into the room that he hadn't noticed before.

"You should feel right at home in there, Mac," she said, sarcastically.

McDermott looked around.

"I've never been in here before," he said.

She stepped inside the room with him.

"Yeah, but all those years you spent as a broadcaster – you should understand all this equipment."

He turned to look again at the combination radio and television console, the monitors, the computers and the tape playback equipment.

"Yes," he said softly. "I'm familiar with it. It's a combination of the old and the new. The computers handle instant replays, and commercial cues. The old tape machines..."

Too late, his peripheral vision saw the gun coming at his head. He tried to duck but his reaction time was a tad slow, and Eve Somers had the jump on him.

The blue steel barrel of the Beretta connected with the right side of his head just above the temple. McDermott saw lights exploding outward and dancing on the walls and glass before him. He could feel himself sinking to his knees as he fought to stay awake, but the colors in the room, far from pronounced anyway, in the shadows of the stadium, faded from his vision. He battled against the blackness that was enveloping him, heedless of the blood running down his cheek and onto his shirt.

McDermott tried to look up at Eve Somers, but couldn't raise his head all the way. His eyes were cloudy, his mouth agape in pain and wonder.

He reached out to her as darkness overcame him.

Chapter Thirty-Eight

Eve Somers closed the door to the broadcast booth at RFK Stadium. Nearby, she found a loose conduit with sturdy wires exposed. She ripped some wires out of the pipe and secured door, trapping McDermott inside and unconscious. Satisfied that the editor was securely locked away, she returned to the wide concrete corridor and started making her way down, back to street level. She was on the second level high when she saw the SUV scream into the parking lot. Somers knew it would take some time for the people in what she took for a police car to find her, especially in the cavernous stadium – but the best way not to be found, she thought, was not to be there.

She left the stadium on the Capitol Avenue side, racing to the street where she hailed a convenient cab. She told the swarthy, bushy-browed driver to take her to the Metropole.

The driver let out an oscillating noise that was high pitched, somewhere between a yodel and a shriek.

"Oh no," he said in a high voice that trembled with fear. "I not go there, is bad place in town, bad place."

Somers snorted.

"I don't have time for this," she muttered, and she screwed the business end of the Beretta into the cab driver's right ear.

"Drive the car," she barked.

The cabbie let out that same shrill, ear-shattering noise again, his eyes wide with unmitigated fear. He dropped the car into Drive and pealed rubber into traffic.

Martin Roag Junior tapped on the door nearest to the elevator on the third floor of the Metropole Hotel. The knock was unnecessary; he knew he would receive neither an invitation to enter nor a bidding that he depart. He twisted the knob and stepped across the threshold into a room shrouded in semi-darkness. He stepped past the bathroom into the room's proper. It was identical in furnishing to the other rooms on this floor; the desk and luggage rack that always seemed like an afterthought in hotels. There was a large, high-backed, overstuffed chair next to the bed, and Rogue sat down in it.

The figure on the bed lay on his back, staring at the ceiling through colorless, unseeing, uncomprehending eyes. His gray hair was tousled and unkempt, his skin leather-like, with folds and wrinkles. The lips were faded and dry.

Roag took a glass of water from the night stand and bent to the old man in the bed, lifting the head. The man's eyes remained empty; he didn't blink, as the younger man let a few drops of water pas through the parched lips. Roag watched the elder man's Adam's apple. It bobbed. The water had been swallowed and retained. Gently, Roag lowered the man's head back onto the pillow and sat back in his chair, not taking his eyes off the face on the bed.

"It won't be long now," he said in a whisper.

He touched the waxen skin of the man's cheek with the tips of two fingers, then smoothed the short beard adorning an almost concave chin. Roag's expression softened.

"Eve will come through," he whispered with conviction. "We're close now." His voice hardened. "And all those who might lay claim to our property have been shoved aside. Hard."

He touched the man's cheek again and tried to smile.

"I know you don't like it here," he said, softening again. "Not so long, now, and I'll get you out of here and into a place where you can get proper care. I'll get rid of this place as soon as Eve comes up with the stones and we can be out of here, and you'll live like you want to live again," he said, and turned on his heel. Back in the hallway, he summoned the elevator and rode to the hotel's dusty, disused lobby. He made his way through the dust to the dining room and to the one-time kitchen, long devoid of appliances and equipment. At the back of the room was a set of stairs leading down. Roag pulled a flashlight from his pocket and gingerly made his way down.

At the bottom of the stairs was a utility room, with a huge kettle-like furnace dead center in the concrete floor, its ductwork snaking about like the tentacles of several octopi, stretching to all parts of the sinister building. Using the light to guide him, Roag carefully made his way through the room to yet another set of stairs.

These were much narrower, with no railing, and they led down into a black hole, a sub-basement from which numerous intrigues had been perpetrated through the long and checkered life of the hotel. Roag tiptoed down by the light of his flashlight, reaching the lower landing.

The room was rectangular, and concrete on the long sides, brick on the ends. Along one wall was a line of crates stacked, perhaps, eight feet high, the tops barely brushing the raftered ceiling above. Roag pulled his coat about his shoulders to stave off the cold of the tiny room and set to work.

From his coat pocket, Roag took the second of two cell phones Eve Somers had shoplifted from the WaWa store. He switched the phone on and waited for the display to come up. While he waited he pulled another object, about the size of a ring-box, from his other pocket, along with a short length of wire with a mini-plug at each end. He connected the cell phone's charging plug to the small box and set them on the edge of one of the crates whose rim extended outward from the others a bit. From his pants pocket he pulled yet another cord, this one thinner and longer, with a mini plug on one end and a metal shaft, perhaps three inches long and an eighth of an inch thick. He connected the mini plug to the small box, and then pulled a pen knife from his pocket. With it, he cut away the outside cardboard from one of the crates exposing a gray, clay-like substance filling the inside. He shoved the other end of the cord into the clay and pressed hard, to make sure it seated.

His work finished, he turned and sat heavily on the floor. Despite the cold, he was sweating, but it was done, now. Turning, he checked his work.

The cell phone could be called from anywhere, and he was sure the battery was charged enough to last for about two days. Once the phone rang, a tiny spark would go to the charging jack, and would be transmitted on the cord from the phone to the small box. That box was a distribution amplifier. It would take the tiny spark, perhaps half a mili volt, and step it up, perhaps double what it was. It wouldn't last long with the step-up, but it wouldn't have to. The enhanced spark would travel down the wire and into the clay-like substances in the crate – which was, in reality, C-4 explosive. The same stuff was in all the crates that lined one wall of the sub-basement, they had been there for about a year, left behind by another group of insurgents who weren't able to get their job done.

The spark would explode the crate in the center of the pile and it, in turn, would set off all the others, reducing the Metropole – and two city blocks around it – to a smoking pile of rubble.

He would do it – he would call the number of the prepaid cell phone as soon as he and his father – the old man in the third floor room – were safely away, with the diamonds both men believed were the rightful property of the former Roag Arms. And that would be after he had dealt with the likes of Eve Somers, the granddaughter of that blackguard Chance Caine, or whatever he chose to call himself. It would be done. The hotel would be gone, his father would get proper care, and he could give both of them a good life – what was left of it.

Carefully he programmed the number of the triggering cell phone into his own unit, double-checking it for accuracy. He holstered his own phone and made his way back to the kitchen of the ancient hotel. The elevator took him back to the third floor where, again, he looked in on the old man in the first room down the hall. It was all of a long hour before he returned to his own room.

A wave of pain replaced a sense of nothingness in Peter McDermott's head. He tried opening his eyes but it hurt too much, so he remained still, hoping the pounding in his head and the ache in every joint would subside. He tried to lift his right arm, but quickly abandoned the idea as a stabbing sensation coursed through his entire body. But because of the direction his arm lifted, albeit only a few inches, he knew he was lying on his back. That thought alone convinced him that he was alive, and that he was coming back to consciousness. He lay motionless, giving himself a little time to recover. Finally he opened his eyes. It took a moment for them to adjust to the light inside his prison, but once they did, he recognized the broadcast booth, and remembered where he was.

"RFK," he whispered, surprised for a moment at the sound of his own voice, low though it was. He lay a little longer, waiting for the pounding in his head to subside. When the paid reduced to a somewhat manageable level, he flailed his right arm about with eyes closed, groping for a handhold. His fingers grasped something solid and he willed them to close tight onto whatever it was. Using his back muscles and his arm he pulled himself into a semi-sitting position and forced his eyes open.

"Broadcast booth," he said, his voice louder and firmer this time.

He looked to see that his hand was gripping the thin sides of an earphone amplifier that was mounted under the console of the producer's station in the massive booth. He tried to haul himself up into a squat, but found that too ambitious at this point. But he did notice something jabbing him on his right side. He released his hold on the amplifier and ran his hand down to his waist to find the intrusion. The result made him force a smile through cracked lips. It was his cell phone.

He eased his body around and leaned against the booths outside wall and unholstered the phone. Flipping it open, he was gratified to see the display screen light up. It was working. In fact, Pitcher's speed-dial number was on the screen as being among the last numbers he had called. But before he could press "redial," there came a banging on the door that tortured his pain-wracked brain and forced his eyes closed in a tight wince.

"Mac are you in there?" bellowed the voice of Charlie Hume.

McDermott tried to answer, but found he couldn't speak. Reaching over with his left hand, he banged on the door's lower panel to signal him. A moment later the door was violently thrown open and Hume and Pitcher tumbled into the room.

"Mac, are you OK?" Hume demanded, looking at the crumpled and disheveled form of his editor. He lunged forward and helped McDermott into a position where he could begin pulling himself to his feet. Pitcher came into the room and moved in to assist as well.

"It's all right, he's in here!" Pitcher yelled out the door as he and Hume helped the struggling McDermott to s standing position. Santos, Kelley and Casio, all three out of breath, stumbled into the room.

"We were looking around for Eve Somers out there," Santos puffed.

"We were listening, really," Kelly interjected. "We were trying to hear her footfalls somewhere in the stadium."

Casio shook his head.

"What's your problem?" Santos asked, indignantly, noticing Casio's gesture.

"This is a big stadium," Casio said softly. "You think you're going to hear the footfalls of one woman in a place this size?"

"Well she locked Mac in here, so she was probably on this side of the stadium," Kelley pouted.

"It was worth a try, wasn't it?" Mattingly asked."

Casio shrugged.

"I guess so," he said flatly. When Mattingly looked away, Casio shook his head ever so slightly to Hume, who grinned.

"Unnnhh!" McDermott moaned.

Hume and Pitcher looked carefully at him, Hume concentrating on McDermott's eyes. McDermott himself reached his left hand up and stroked the painful back of his head. Hume noted the gesture.

"You don't have to worry about that head of yours," Hume said with a smirk. "It's hard as granite. Nothing, but nothing, could hurt it."

McDermott massaged the back of his skull and winced at Hume.

"I don't know which is worse," he said through clenched teeth. "Feeling the way I do or waking up and listening to you again!"

Hume and Pitcher relaxed. McDermott's sarcastic remark had clinched it. The editor was unhurt, aside from a massive headache that would stay with him for weeks. At least, thought Hume, no permanent damage was done.

"How did you guys find me?" McDermott asked.

Mattingly held up a small box with a computer screen on one side.

"We followed the GPS signal you set off on your phone," he said, with a smile.

"What's that?" McDermott indicated the little monitor.

"It's a GPS device that seeks out a particular signal being sent to the satellite from a specific phone," Kelley said.

"All we had to do was program in your phone number and the satellite found your signal and sent the location to us," Santos continued.

"It even gave us turn-by-turn directions on how to find the location," Mattingly chimed in.

McDermott shook his head trying to clear it.

"I remember, now," he said. "When I was in the jeep with Eve, I switched on the GPS locator in my phone."

"That's what we followed," Santos smiled.

"Let's get Mac to a Doc-In-The-Box and have him checked out," Hume said, firmly.

Mattingly scoffed.

"In this neighborhood? You've got to be kidding!"

"Let's call an ambulance and take him to Sibly Hospital for a check-up," Santos suggested.

"That's the thing to do," Hume thundered.

"Now wait a minute…" McDermott began.

"Wait a minute nothing," Pitcher barked. "You got conked on the noggin pretty good, there. We need to make sure there's no concussion."

McDermott pulled himself up straight and placed a placating hand on Pitcher's shoulder, looking at Hume as he did so.

"Charlie… Pitch… I'm not going to the hospital now. I'm going to see this thing through to the end."

"You think we're at the end?" Hume asked.

McDermott nodded firmly.

"I think we've got a lot of the answers, and it's time to get the rest of them. Then we can find the diamonds that Pitcher's family has been dying for and see that they get to the proper owners."

"If any," Pitcher chimed.

"If any," McDermott agreed.

"Well if that's the case," Arlee Kelley began, "the next thing on the agenda is to look for Eve Somers before she gets involved in some other mischief."

McDermott thought a moment, the thinking activity aggravating a severe headache. Finally he stepped to one side with his back against the broadcast console.

"If you stop and think about it," he said, "we really don't have to look for her."

"We don't?" Santos asked

McDermott shook his head.

"There's only one place she will go now."

There was a moment of silence. Then, eight voices chorused as one.

"The Metropole!"

The Diamond cab pulled up in front of a shabby Rexall drug store a half block from the imposing red brick edifice that made the entire city block seem creepy. Eve Somers sat in the back, behind the driver with her gun barrel still screwed into the Mideastern man's ear.

"You get off here, yes?" he said, his voice nearly a shriek.

"I get off here, yes," Somers affirmed, pulling the gun away and dropping three twenty dollar bills on the front seat next to the man. The meter read $49.20. She eased out of the car and stood straight on the sidewalk. The cab wasted no time in pealing rubber into a screeching U-turn before it roared off into the night. Somers replaced the gun in the back of her waistband. With a furtive look around, which found the street deserted, she began a fast walk toward the stygian old building.

In a room on the third floor, Martin Roag Jr. peered through a deliberately dirty pane of glass, shaded by black-out curtains. He had been waiting. He saw Somers get out of the cab and watched carefully as she walked toward the building. Her gait told him everything he needed to know. She didn't have the diamonds and hadn't extracted the information from the newspaper crew as to where they would be found. Anger welled in his gut and moved its way up.

He sat in the cloth chair near his bed, seething, and waiting for the telltale sound of the elevator machinery as it brought the girl up to the third floor.

It took several minutes, during each of which Martin Roag was getting madder. By the time she pecked tentatively on his door steam was figuratively coming out of his ears.

331

"Come in!" he snapped, and the door swung open instantly. She was framed in the lights from the hallway and the semidarkness of the inside of the room. Carefully she stepped into the room and closed the door.

"You have no good news for me, do you?" he asked, in a controlled voice.

"Did you get the place rigged?" she asked, sidestepping his question.

He nodded and indicated the cell phone sitting on the desk near the bathroom door.

"It's ready," he said flatly, then he stood and faced her.

"No information? You come back here with no information, no diamonds, no way to make my father rest comfortably as he is now? How could you even show your face back here with no information and no stones?"

She backed against the door, feet apart, fists on her hips.

"I don't see you out there trying to fish out information from people who know how to keep secrets Marty..."

"Martin!" he corrected

She wagged her head at him.

"Well you're 'Marty' to me right now while you're acting like a jerk!"

Martin Roag Junior exploded.

"There is a matter of degree here, Ms. Somers. For you it is a matter of family honor. For me it is my father's life and my family's legacy. *Do you get that?*"

The last four words were a clenched-teeth bellow.

"This is the last chance for my family to save face, for my father to die vindicated from having received those stones. That's why all those people had to be killed, because they interfered with my quest."

He swept his arms around the room.

"I don't want my father to die in this place, a dump we happened to get stuck with when the war ended. I want him to die in a place where he can have some dignity and comfort. And I want the legacy and quality of life for myself after he's gone that he worked for decades to get for his family. Do you get that Somers? Do you get that?"

"Yes, I get it, you self-centered prick," she hissed. "I also get that you think your family is the only one here that matters. I got into this because you looked me up and convinced me that *my* family name also needed to be vindicated, and finding the package that my grandfather died so publicly for, the mystery of the watch, would give his death meaning it didn't have. Didn't you say that, *Marty*?"

She spat the last word, before penetrating more deeply into the room, shouting at Roag from across the queen-sized bed.

332

"And you think you're the only one who has something to lose?"

She pulled her cell phone – the first of the two she stole from the WaWa store and touched a couple of buttons then turned the phone so he could see the display.

"You think you're the only one who wants this over? I can make it over right now, you supercilious jackass! Do you recognize the phone number here?"

He looked. It was the same number he had programmed into his phone, the number of the cell phone five floors below, the one that was connected to several crates of C-4. He nodded.

"Well all I have to do is hit SEND right now, and you and your father die failures. So are you going to calm down and be reasonable, or do I send us to heaven?"

Martin Roag Junior stared at her with unconcealed hate. He was sorely tempted to grab the phone from her and hit the button and end it all himself, giving him the satisfaction of taking her with him. But too much had happened, too many lives, too much water over the dam for him to stop now.

"They'll be here soon," he muttered.

"Who?" she asked

"The police and probably your newspaper buddies," he said. "We have to move fast. You go and get a car. I'll get Father ready to travel and we'll get out of here. They'll take the hotel, and we need to be away from here."

He started gathering up his belongings and shoving them into a plastic tote bag.

"We have the watch numbers. We'll take Father somewhere so he can get some treatment, and we'll regroup and figure out the numbers ourselves. Hurry."

Her eyes narrowed.

"What are you planning?" she demanded.

He stopped and looked at her, reaching for his own cell phone.

"We're going to wait until they all get inside the building – give them a chance to get up here – and then… BOOM!"

Chapter Thirty-Nine

They walked like the Earps headed for the OK Corral. Peter McDermott, Charlie Hume Rod Pitcher and Sy Casio walked side by side and in perfect step from their parking space near the Rexall Drug Store. Their lips were pulled into thin, determined lines, their eyes were glinting, hard, and grim, narrowed against the early sunlight. Their hands swung to and fro in perfect rhythm as they walked unerringly, in a wide gait.

They were followed, perhaps two steps behind, by Arlee Kelley, flanked by Armando Santos and Fred Mattingly, each brushing the butt of powerful weapons with his and her hands in time with the steps.

There was no talking; there was nothing to say. Each had his and her own errand.

Rod Pitcher was determined that this would be the moment of reckoning for the deaths of his family members, and for the attempts on him.

Peter McDermott was there to back-up his friend, and perhaps to try to calm him down, or even bodily restrain him if he got out of hand – and while he knew Pitcher as one of the most even-tempered people he had ever known, he also knew the reporter had had quite enough, and was capable of just about anything.

Charlie Hume was angry on several fronts. First and foremost, the lives of his friends had been threatened. McDermott and Pitcher were more than employees to him. They were family. And they were key people in the success of his newspaper venture, and to the future of his organization. He was not going to take such a threat without putting himself on the front lines with them, to do whatever was required to resolve the situation and protect his friends. He had demonstrated that on more than one occasion – and on one of those occasions he had nearly been killed.

Sy Casio tapped the left side of his overcoat for the hundredth time since getting out of the car, making sure, time after time, that the Browning was there, right where he wanted it, in a place where he could get to it quickly and draw it into line and fire accurately.

The officers walking resolutely behind had their own agendas, and yet they were eerily similar, perhaps even identical. All were mentally ticking off the charges they would file once they arrested. Murder was the grand prize – multiple counts of it, perhaps three, perhaps more. Attempted murder. Multiple counts of automobile theft. One count of car-jacking. Several counts of breaking and entering, which would cover the car dealership and Pitcher's apartment. And each officer was trying to figure out what other charges might be tailored up for her. What if she was telling the truth about Martin Roag? Had she discussed the killings and other things with him? That constituted conspiracy.

All three officers were mentally rehearsing their remarks that would be made when they received their promotions.

And all of those making the Tombstone walk this day were resolute, determined, and charged with conviction, determined to do what they came to do without regards to the possible consequences. They were determined that nothing would stop them.

The seven figures had been spotted. On the third floor of the decrepit building, Martin Roag Junior stood to one side of the tinted window camouflaged with dirt and disuse. He stood to one side so that even a shadow, an accidently glimmer of light at just the right angle wouldn't reveal his presence above them.

"Here they come," he murmured to no one in particular.

"You can't be serious about this," Eve Somers spat at him from the other side of the room.

He turned to face her, a look if surprise on his face.

"Listen to you!" he spat back. "You killed four people and then started making a botch of killing the others, and all for the same cause as me. You killed like you enjoyed it, and now you get squeamish about seven more?"

"There are police officers in that coterie," she said, flatly.

A light bulb seemed to go on over Roag's head.

"And McDermott."

"McDermott is nothing to me," she scoffed.

Roag guffawed.

"Tell that to someone who would believe it, Eve. I won't."

"He was a source of information," she said affirmatively.

"He was your lover," Roag returned.

336

She nodded involuntarily, her mind wandering momentarily.

"Of course I had to seduce him," she said harshly, "to get the information I needed out of him."

Roag gave an open-mouthed nod, surrendering the argument but not the point.

"Of course," he said, barely above a whisper. "Dad's in his wheelchair in his room. As soon as they get into the building we'll disable them and lock them in the room across the hall. Then we'll get Dad down the elevator and into a car, and we'll blow the joint as we leave."

She nodded shallowly and stepped out of the room, taking a quick, but speculative look at Martin Roag Junior as she left.

She ambled down the hallway, taking her time, touching the room doors idly with her left hand as she walked. With her right hand, she unclipped her own cell phone and held it away from her, alternately looking at the doors as she touched them, and looking at the cell phone. Finally she stopped, and hesitated a few moments in the hallway before coming to a decision. She turned on her heel and marched purposefully in the opposite direction, opening the door to her own room. She bolted it from the inside and stepped into the bathroom, closing and locking that door as well. She closed the lid on the toilet and sat down, dialing a number from memory on her cell. It was answered on the fourth ring.

"McDermott."

"Mac, don't come in here. You and your friends stay out there, I'm serious, don't some in here," she bleated.

"Eve?" he asked, incredulously

"Yes, she hissed into the phone, trying not to yell, knowing a loud voice would penetrate the walls and Martin Roag might hear her. "Don't come in here."

"By 'here' I am taking it to mean you are in the hotel," he said, matter-of-factly. "We have a couple of police officers with us who would like to ask you a few questions. And I have to admit, I have one or two myself. So we're coming in."

"Please, Mac," she pleaded. "Stay out of here. Put as much real estate as you can between you and here. Please don't come in here."

On the street below, McDermott stopped walking, and his compatriots gathered in a circle around him straining to hear.

On the third floor, Even Somers burst from the bathroom and her hotel suite and ran down the hallway toward the stairs.

"I can't do that, Eve. Too much water as rolled over the dam. There are questions and you have to answer them. Now," said McDermott.

337

"Mac...?" she pleaded again as she ran down the stairs, her voice echoing and enhancing the tears that now rolled from her eyes.

"We're coming in," McDermott said, affirmatively.

Her eyes and her voice hardened as she made it to the second landing.

"I don't think so," she said, flatly.

"What do you mean by that?" demanded McDermott.

She reached the ground floor landing.

"Mac," she said, her voice cracking.

"What?" he asked.

"Take cover," she said loudly, and broke the connection.

Instantly she called up a number from the phone's internal directory, a number she had put into the phone herself. It was the only number in her personal directory. For a long moment she stared at the number on the digital display, again trying hard to make a decision. Then she pressed SEND.

Two floors below, the cell phone lying on the edge of one of the crates in the sub-basement rang. In that instant, the receiving of the signal and the activation of the ringer sent a tiny spark into the charging jack, and thence down the wire Martin Roag had plugged into it. The spark was intercepted by the small transformer in the box next to the phone, and stepped up before being sent out the other side in yet another wire, whose bitter end was stuck in the clay-like brick of C-4. That crate exploded. In the wink of an eye, before the expanding gasses from the first crate completed their reach from origin to ebb, the other crates, almost as one, exploded together.

The explosion blew out the ceiling in the sub-basement, and the furnace fell into the hole. As the other crates joined in the explosion, the force moved upward and shattered the lobby floor. Once the floor was out of the way, the shock wave rushed into the vacated space and expanded outward, bending or uprooting the upright supports even as it blew out the side walls, scattering bricks for blocks in all directions.

As the first floor disappeared, the second floor collapsed into the same space, in a cloud of dust illuminated by flames from the exploding C-4 far below.

The third floor followed the second, and so on, until the building fell in on itself, crashing to the ground in a choking cloud of brick dust, concrete dust and dust dust.

McDermott saw a momentary flash of light ahead of him a split second before the rumble of multiple explosions picked him up and slammed him against the brick wall of the nondescript building to his left. The force of the blast did the same thing to the other six men, they landed together in a confused mish-mash of arms and legs and torsos, all akimbo as they tried to sort out who belonged to whom. Bricks were added to the equation, hundreds of them, landing around and on top of the pile of humanity on the crumbling sidewalk. Bricks that raised welts, bumped heads and tore clothing already turning color from layer upon layer of dust and debris.

McDermott was the first to regain his feet, followed almost immediately by Hume.

"Eve!" he shouted and tried to run toward the settling wreckage. But Hume grabbed him by the tail of his jacket and hauled him back, throwing him back to the ground without meaning to.

"You stay here!" Hume barked. "That's too dangerous."

Casio had pulled his cell phone and dialed 9-1-1.

"D.C Police, this is Sy Casio. The Metropole Hotel has just exploded. Yes, I'm sure, I've been battered by falling bricks and they are still coming down. I am less than a block away, myself and six others. Yes, we think there was someone inside. Thank you."

He holstered his phone and hauled himself from his sitting position into a crouching stand, doing his best to brush off his clothes, ignoring, for the moment, the dust that was turning his face and hair chalk-white.

"The police dispatcher wanted to know how I knew the Metropole was exploding."

He turned his eyes skyward.

"Sheesh! Have things gotten so bad on this side of town that you can't even get the police to cover an explosion?"

Sirens could be heard in the distance, getting closer.

"Apparently not," growled Mattingly, painfully pulling himself out of a pile of bricks. "D.C.'s Finest is on the way"

Mattingly was bleeding from a cut on his cheek, and his shirt was discolored by a spreading red stain. Arlee Kelley, also bleeding from impacts with bricks, was using a handkerchief from her purse trying to stop the flow of blood on Mattingly, heedless of her own. Armando Santos had taken a brick hit to the head and was supine and unconscious. Pitcher, who was barely conscious himself, was crawling to the policeman trying to rouse him.

McDermott struggled against Hume's unrelenting grip on his coat tail.

"Charlie, Eve called, she's in the building, let me go!"

"Mac," Hume bellowed, yanking hard on McDermott's coat and pulling him to the ground once again. "There is no building! It's blown up, collapsed, destroyed. Whoever is in that building is probably dead. People are on the way that have the equipment and skills to find that out. Now sit down and let them do their jobs."

McDermott forced himself to relax, and Hume released his coat. It was then that McDermott noticed that both he and Hume were also bleeding, and Hume had a great big egg on his forehead from a collision with a flying brick.

The first police cars were arriving with an ambulance close behind. A paramedic peeled out of the box-like vehicle and approached the group on the ground.

"We'll keep," McDermott yelled. "There's someone in that building."

The paramedic looked around.

"What building?"

McDermott could no longer speak. He merely pointed to the dusty pile of bricks a bit less than a half-block distant. The paramedic keyed the microphone clipped the epaulet of his jacket.

"Two-mike-twenty-one, need additional ambulances and heavy equipment at the Metropole, the building has been destroyed and an eyewitness says there is someone inside."

"10-4, units are rolling," came the response.

The second paramedic from the unit was working on Armando Santos, taking his vitals, and then applying smelling salts. In a moment Santos came moaning back to consciousness, but he continued to complain of double vision.

"We need to take this fellow to Sibly," the second paramedic said to all and sundry. "I suspect he has a concussion and he needs immediate treatment."

His partner nodded.

Police units screeched to halts next to the band on the ground, and uniformed officers tumbled out, hands on their guns. They relaxed when they say the paramedics and ascertained that the group on the ground was fairly harmless.

"What happened here?" asked a blue-clad cop with sergeant stripes on his shoulder. Sy Casio struggled to his feet and took the officer aside, displaying his private detective's credentials as required by city ordinance, and calmly explained to the officer what had happened in the last few minutes.

"I want to take them all to Sibly and have them checked," the first paramedic said to the ranking cop. "Some of them might have internal injuries that need quick attention."

The sergeant considered for a moment, then nodded.

"That will make it easier for us to get statements from all of them. You take those who need ambulances. I'll have the uniformed units take the rest of them."

The paramedic nodded in agreement and began the process of getting Armando Santos, Arlee Kelley and Fred Mattingly into ambulances. Their sirens cleared the way through the midday traffic.

Hume, McDermott, Pitcher and Casio squeezed into the back seat of a blue and white Crown Victoria which accelerated into traffic with its blue lights on, but no siren.

As they left, crews began the laborious job of rummaging through the still-smoldering wreckage of the Metropole Hotel.

The building lay in a jumbled heap, smoke from the powerful detonation of pounds upon pounds of C-4 mingling with the cloud of dust that still had not settled. It looked like a victim building in a combat zone, which, in a way, it was. Its long history of intrigue had finally caught up with it.

The ancient hotel had been burned several times in a history that dated back to the plotting of the Federal District in the closing years of the 18th century. At the request of his ally and former army confidante and friend, Lafayette, President Washington agreed to appoint Pierre Charles L'Enfant to design the federal city, and to designate a plot of land for French occupation. The government in Paris built the hotel and called it the Metropole. Through more than two centuries of its existence it had had many owners, it had burned and been rebuilt several times, it caused bankruptcies and business failures and death, but it was always called the Metropole.

Throughout its life, the hotel had been a scene of intrigue, of espionage, of black ops and treason. While the French had been an ally of the Colonies in the Revolutionary War, they certainly were not after that. Espionage agents of the French regime used the hotel as their headquarters until the Civil War when it was sold to Southern interests.

The new owners tried to make the Metropole Washington's premiere hostelry. They made much being a vantage point from which to see the newly elected president as he made his way from Illinois to Washington in secret, under threat of assassination – which could have taken place from many of the hotel's windows. From 1861 to 1865 it served as a headquarters for Southern patriots in the Capital. By that time it had been given a fourth floor and a hidden mezzanine, plus an attached tavern next door frequented by many who worked for the gray – and at least one, who thought he did. The tavern was a frequent stop for John Wilkes Booth. Its ball room became an armed camp, its secret mezzanine a hidden place for Confederate and Federal agents to meet and negotiate. Confederate spies, suppliers and sympathizers came and went with impunity through the hotel's doors. In its lobby, deals were made for wool, cotton, gunpowder, raw metals, rifles, side arms, ammunition, cannon and food – all the trappings of a nation at war. Couriers carried messages between the hotel and the telegraph office two blocks away, under the noses of Federal agents who knew what was happening, but did little to arrest the activity.

Fire destroyed the hotel in 1888, along with most of the two surrounding blocks. New owners, using insurance money, took two years to rebuild, and then re-opened the surviving pub next door to great fanfare. It failed quickly.

For years, the hotel sat empty and became more and more forlorn. When it opened again in 1902, it quickly became an afternoon and evening hang-out for the second and third echelon of government officials, and the mid-priced prostitutes who were increasingly migrating to this section of the city. Rarely did guests stay overnight, and the hotel kept maids on hand around the clock to make up rooms when short-term guests left. The Metropole became the place in Washington *not* to be seen, where hours kept to one's self could be spent with no questions asked.

In 1906 a second fire leveled the building, and killed thirty-one people, mostly prostitutes and some of their customers. Their names sparked a scandal that resulted in the indictment of a deputy sheriff who was tried and convicted of starting the fire. A year after his execution in the electric chair, his innocence was conclusively proven.

Rebuilt again, the hotel enjoyed a new popularity in the city. Its restaurant was always filled with of more genteel diners than had ever ventured there before, and its nightspot next door, expanded into a fully fledged nightclub, boasting among its patrons the likes of Eddie Foy, A.L Erlanger and George M. Cohan.

In 1912, Wannamaker's Department Store put a telegraph shack on the roof of the Metropole. It was a "keeping-up-with-the-Jones" move, since arch-rival Macy's had one on another building up north. It was a device for communicating between stores, speeding the exchange of merchandise and ad matter. Had the Washington station been listening on the air in the predawn hours of a cold April night that year, they, and not the New York store, might have picked from the air the faint signal that heralded the greatest of all sea disasters of the 20th century as the *Titanic* took fifteen hundred souls to a frigid grave.

The hotel and its telegraph office closed in 1916 and stood empty as World War I raged in Europe. In the 1920's it became a particularly notorious speakeasy during Prohibition and despite several Treasury raids, few knew that the second and third floor rooms of the hotel were stacked high with casks of alcohol. Speakeasy patrons had sex among the barrels until a carelessly discarded cigar caught some leaking alcohol afire, which in turn lit a guest room curtain, and then the rest of the floor. Patrons scurried into the Washington night wrapped in towels and tablecloths.

Rebuilt again, the hotel languished, all but unused until World War II when the War Department took it over as a bachelor officer's quarters for the nearby Washington Navy Yard. When the war ended, so did the use of the hapless building which went dark yet again.

In 1961 the hotel was sold again, but to whom was cloaked in mystery. The true owners were cloaked in such a tangle of corporate holding companies and blind agents that no one cared to follow the paper trail and hunt them down. Some believed that the hotel was in fact, sold several times during that period, which is how it apparently wound up in the hands of the Roag Arms Corporation.

Emergency workers summoned a bulldozer and crane, plus a fleet of dump trucks to carry away the debris. They worked through the day. By early evening they had found the body of Martin Roag Senior, still in his wheel chair, having dropped four stories into the sub-basement.

Early the next morning, rescuers recovered the body of Martin Roag Junior, but his remains were badly mangled by bricks and the effects of the explosion.

A day later, the last of the remains were carted away to be used as rip-rap along the Anacostia River. No other bodies were found in the rubble

After 200 years, the Metropole Hotel had ceased to exist.

No trace of Eve Somers was found.

Chapter Forty

A jogger found the body that same evening, beneath the supports of the South Capitol Street S.E. bridge, a hundred yards or so from the end of Water Street. The body was half in and half out of the water of the Anacostia River, with only the waist and legs sticking out of the water; the head and torso were submerged. Most of the clothing appeared to be burned away; what remained was singed and scorched, and damaged beyond repair. The shoes were gone, the bare feet covered with blackened, cooked skin, the meat of the arches plainly visible. The exposed skin was battered, bruised and cut to ribbons, dried blood caking the charred tissue.

The jogger took a moment to recover from his shock before pulling his cell phone out of an elastic band clinging to the bicep of his left arm. A call to 9-1-1 brought the D.C. police and an ambulance, but there was nothing any of them could do. The police foliated the area with yellow crime scene tape and searched for clues, but aside from some blood-spattered footprints leading to the body's position, there was precious little to find. By and bye, the police allowed the remains to be taken to the morgue across the river in Maryland.

Dr. Aridan Ooscadoo was the pathologist catching the night shift. It was he who supervised the removal of the remains from the plastic body bag, onto a stainless steel table in the middle of a well-lighted room lined with surgical tile on the walls and flooring. He was cutting away the fragmented remains of the clothing when Detective Fred Mattingly ambled into the operating theater.

"Hi, Dan," he greeted, using the Americanization of the doctor's given name.

Ooscadoo grunted a reply and continued the work his surgical scissors through the clothing that was falling away at his touch.

"Whatcha got?" Mattingly asked, looking over the doctor's shoulders at the corpse on the table.

"I'm just starting," the doctor replied in a heavily accented voice. "Appears to be a white female about 35 or 36, dark hair, what's left of it, and she's been battered and burned."

"Which is the worst of it?" Mattingly wanted to know. "The burning or the battering?"

Ooscadoo shook his head and faced the detective for the first time.

"As I said, I am just getting started."

Ooscadoo continued his preliminary probe of the battered, bruised body, cutting away the tattered clothes as he went. Mattingly watched with detached interest. The doctor slowly and carefully palpated the damaged corpse, cutting away the tattered and scorched clothing as he went.

When he reached the sports bra, the only thing she wore on the top of her torso, he stopped. Something looked awry. A mass where none should be. The doctor's eyes narrowed as he moved the scissors to the fabric and snipped. As the fabric opened, a small plastic lump fell into his other hand. Mattingly strained over the doctor's shoulder hoping to see.

Ooscadoo sat heavily on the stainless steel stool near the table and gingerly spread the plastic out on the vacant table next to that which held the body. Carefully, he unfolded the plastic, hoping to identify it, and perhaps the woman who had held it to her breast.

Ooscadoo examined the plastic with a practiced eye. It was white, and milled thin, with some blue markings on the inside. He leaned back, caught himself before he toppled over, then looked hard at Mattingly.

"It's part of a Wal Mart bag," he said, incredulously.

Mattingly pulled up another stool and leaned into see for himself, then nodded his agreement.

"A piece of one, anyway," the doctor mused half to himself.

"Anything in it?" Mattingly wondered aloud.

"Indeed there is," the doctor. "There's a paper – looks like a hot dog wrapper from a streetside trash can."

Mattingly waved his hand. "Is that all?"

Ooscadoo shook his head absently, concentrating on what he was seeing in his hand.

"There's some writing on it.

"Advertizing for a particular brand of mustard?" Mattingly asked sarcastically.

Again, Ooscadoo shook his head.

"No, it's writing all over one side, but there's a flap folded down at the top with something writing on the outside of the flap."

"What?" Mattingly demanded.

Ooscadoo passed him the paper.

Written on the flap were the words, *"Get this to Peter McDermott, North Bay Times."*

Mattingly folded the flap up and read the writing on the paper. It covered both sides, in a small, rounded, feminine hand that somehow seemed strained across the paper. He read it all carefully then began to go through it a second time, stealing an occasional glance at the corpse on the table as he read. When he finished, he handed the paper back to Dr. Ooscadoo, and the doctor noticed there was a tear in the hardened detective's eye.

Peter McDermott limped into the *North Bay Times* offices promptly at eight o'clock the next morning. He was obviously in pain as he forced his battered body to move down the newsroom corridor to his corner office. He keyed open the door and snapped the light switch, rounding his desk and turning on his computer in one practiced, fluid motion.

McDermott looked quite a bit different that the purposeful, confident editor who came into the office every day. He was stooped and slow-moving. His eye was black. His nose was smashed and red. There was a large bandage on his head extending from just above his left eye and into the hair line. His cheeks were red and scratched, and his hair was tousled. The eyes themselves were distant, nearly vacant. He dropped heavily into his chair and leaned back heavily, closing his eyes. After a moment, he re-opened them and leaned to his computer keyboard, checking his messages, and then calling up the stories for the next edition that had been filed since late the previous day. There weren't many. He was reading through one story from his financial writer when a shadow fell across his desk. He looked up.

Charlie Hume, easily as bashed-in as McDermott, stood in a pained crouch in front of his editor's desk.

"We need you in the conference, room," he said softly.

"Who's 'we?'" he asked.

Hume said nothing, but beckoned with his head toward the corridor, before ambling out of the room.

McDermott felt every bone, every muscle, as he pulled himself up from his chair. Hating every step, he hobbled across the newsroom and through the door to the editorial conference room. There he stopped. Fred Mattingly and Rod Pitcher sat at chairs near the middle of one side of the massive table. Hume motioned to chairs across from them, and

347

they sat, doing so like men twice their ages. McDermott looked at the Washington D.C. police detective with a quizzical eye.

"We have the answers," Mattingly said flatly. "To all of it."

McDermott blinked several times.

"To all of what, Fred?" he asked in a voice near a whisper.

"To all the killings," Pitcher rasped, his voice breaking. "To the murders in my family."

"And the diamonds?"

"Yes," Pitcher spat. "Yes, and the damned diamonds, too."

McDermott put a softened conciliatory look on his face.

"I'm sorry, Pitch," he said in a semblance of his normal voice. "What have you found out?"

"Nothing yet," the reporter said, indicating Mattingly with his head. "This bird said he'd tie up all the loose ends."

McDermott's expression hardened.

"Tie away, Fred."

Mattingly looked pained, as pained as the beaten-up men sitting around him.

"Eve Somers is dead, Mac," Mattingly said quickly.

McDermott acted as though someone had hit him. He recoiled into his seat with a blank expression on his face, his mouth set in a bewildered "O." His eyes pleaded with the detective for more information.

"Her body was found along the Anacostia River last evening by a jogger. He clothes were singed and ripped and her body was pretty badly beaten – like you and Pitcher and Hume, but more so."

"Did she say anything?" Pitcher asked.

"A very great deal, actually," Mattingly began.

"But you said her *body* was found," McDermott interrupted.

Mattingly nodded and passed a manila folder across the table to McDermott

"We read this, Mac, but it was addressed to you. Sorry about that."

McDermott nodded in silent forgiveness, opened the folder to the hot dog wrapper, and began to read.

Dear Mac,

There isn't much time, and I need to clear up a few things for you in the hopes that you will understand all this and some day you will find it in your heart to forgive me. This wrapper is all I could find to write on.

Karl Elmandorf, the man you knew as Chance Caine, was my grandfather. He was murdered in public by a woman in the company of a

guy named Wicht, who had that watch until he died, and it went to a nephew, Albert Lowenstein. That was Pitcher's relative. How ironic that when I met Pitcher through you I never realized that his relatives were responsible for the murder of my grandfather.

I always thought my family deserved those diamonds. Karl's wife and children were deprived of his life – yes, he knew what he was getting into, but still, he didn't deserve to die as he did at that evil man's hands. And so, the sins of the father were visited upon the son – or the uncle and nephew in this case.

It was when I met Martin Roag Junior that all this started. I came across him as I researched the Resistance and the courier watch that Pitcher finally got hold of. He felt HIS family should have the stones, since they were meant for their company – and could have kept the Roag Arms Company out of bankruptcy as the war ended. I won't kid you – I had intended to enlist his help in finding the stones and then double-cross him and keep them for myself and the rest of my family, what's left of them, which isn't many.

Now for the confessions.

I lured Reesa Lowenstein to the old club. I had hoped to enlist her aid in finding the watch, and then the diamonds, but she wasn't cooperative and that's what started the killing. You know what a temper I have. I worked a little seduction on a police property guy and found the gun that killed my grandfather. It was such a rush to threaten Reesa with that self-same gun. When she defied me I shot her in a blind rage, shot her more than once. That started it. The others got easier, each one easier. The tough one was Pitcher. I knew him, through you, and I didn't really want to kill him – I let my emotions get mixed up with it and I missed him. Oh, and that shot you thought was aimed at you, well, I can't decide even now if it was you or Pitcher I was aiming at.

It felt strange becoming a criminal, but you know how it is, Mac, you can get used to anything.

Just to keep the record straight, it was Roag who killed Oglesby, not me. And it was me who blew the Metropole, not him, even though he was the one who set up the detonator in the explosive that was already there – from where I haven't the faintest idea. All the other stuff, the way I stole the cars and that sort of thing, well, I've always been able to think on my feet. The Willie Sykes incident should have shown you that. And it should also have shown you that I have no conscience at all. Never did.

And yet now, since I know I will never see you again, I get to thinking about what we might have been together. What if I have been able to keep my nose to the grindstone and be a "good girl." What if I hadn't been

349

attracted to the "bad boy" type like Willie? I guess I never would have gone off with him, not for long anyway. When I disappeared from his hotel room in Annapolis all those months ago – at the very moment he was being murdered, I found out later, I had intended to square myself with the authorities and come back to you. But it seemed the squaring was going to be more costly than I wanted to face, so I spent some time in Canada, and just wandering around until the heat was off. Then I came back to see you.

You were right to be suspicious of me. Your gut always told you the right things, and it was correct this time as well. I know what a good reporter you are, I knew that once Pitcher's family started getting knocked off you'd start nosing into it, and you'd find out about the watch, and then the numbers. I was counting on that. I figured if I stayed close enough to you, you'd do most of the work in leading me to the diamonds. I could kiss you and bed you and make off with the stones before you knew what happened. Despite your good instincts I could always blind-side you, Mac, and I used that.

I suppose if I'm capable of loving – which I don't for a moment concede – I probably did love you. I never gave any thought to a future with Willie Sykes or with anyone else until you. With you I could see the house with the picket fence and whatever we might have done in terms of a family even though neither of us are spring chickens.

Sitting here along the Anacostia, thinking about you and waiting for the end to come is the roughest part of the entire ordeal. I didn't make it all the way out of the hotel when it went up, and I caught a load of bricks and mortar all over my body. I know I'm bleeding on the inside so it's only a matter of time. And not too much time, either.

I know the police will read this before you do. This will close the books on a lot of things they've been worrying about.

I'm running out of wrapper, here, Mac, so it's time to say our farewells. This seems a strange way to do it, on something I picked out of a trash can, but since there's no way for me to find you and say goodbye in person, this will have to do.

Think of me, Mac, but instead of thinking of me for the lives I took and the lives I ruined out of misspent familial loyalty, think of what I might have been – of what WE might have been. I know you can find it in your heart to forgive me, I just know you can, and that thought is by far the most comforting thought I take with me into the next world.

Good bye, Mac.

Eve.

McDermott returned the hot dog wrapper to the manila folder and passed it to Rod Pitcher. Without a word he stood, not looking at anyone else in the room.

McDermott moved like a very old man, trudging out of the conference room, his head sunk between his shoulder blades, his feet shuffling in the carpet. He pulled the door as he passed it, but it didn't shut all the way. Charlie Hume rose and started to follow his editor, but thought better of it, and sat back down, watching Mac until he was lost to sight in the newsroom bustle.

McDermott saw and heard nothing as he moved through the noisy editorial bull-pen and passed the threshold of his own office. He pushed the door closed with a resounding slam and collapsed on the tiny couch against one wall of the room. He picked up a pillow from one side of the couch and buried his face in it.

He didn't remember ever crying as an adult, but now he did, in long, hacking, unstifled heaving sobs, with long streaks of tears staining his face. He cried for long minutes, doing as Eve had asked, thinking of her for what she – and they – could have been. He thought, and bawled for nearly an hour before finally collecting himself and returning to his personal calm. He put the pillow aside and returned to his desk, staring at, but not seeing his computer screen. By and by, Charlie Hume bounded into his office.

"I'm sorry, Mac," he said softly.

McDermott smiled his thanks and nodded.

"We can relax now," Hume continued. "It's over."

"Over?" McDermott asked, with a granite look.

Hume nodded, but McDermott shook his head.

"Not quite."

The editor bounded from his chair and beckoned to Hume. He strode to the conference room and grabbed Pitcher by his open collar, urging him on toward the office door. McDermott was punching a number into his cell phone as the outside door closed behind the trio.

Chapter Forty-One

The walked single file and in perfect step, their shovels and picks right-shouldered, their left arms swinging in rhythm. Their course took them from the road where they had parked their cars, to a slightly downward slope leading to a tract of the Congressional Cemetery. Their silent, uncadenced march took them unerringly to Range 16 Site 20, the final resting place of Alvin Joseph Truscott. Arriving, they fell out of step and brought their shovels to Order Arms, each man staring at the grassy ground before the plain, unadorned stone marker identifying the eternal home of an obscure Congressional page. Each man hoped the other would be the first one to penetrate the earth, but no one moved.

"Well," began McDermott in an uncharacteristically soft voice, "if no one else will begin, I will."

The editor raised his shovel, preparing to slam the blade into the ground, but the tool came down softly, without even cutting a blade of grass. He looked at Charlie Hume and Rod Pitcher sheepishly. He sighed deeply.

"Ok," he said, frustrated, "I can't do it either. So what's the problem here? Why can't I? Why can't *you*?"

As one, the other members of the Four Muscatels shrugged their shoulders. Rod Pitcher looked longingly at his best friend and boss. Charlie Hume studied his wing tips. Sy Casio looked straight ahead, a glassy, blank look in his eyes.

"What's with us today?" McDermott demanded, to no one in particular. "We were all ready to do this a few days ago."

"A lot of water has gone over the dam since then, Mac," Hume said laconically.

McDermott nodded to his boss in appreciation of the point and shifted his gaze to his ace reporter.

"Pitch?" he said, questioningly.

The reporter dropped his pick and sat down on the loam, his back against the stone. He stared ahead for a moment, then set his jaw and looked up at McDermott.

"I guess I'm not the only one having second thoughts about this, am I?"

"About what, Pitch?" Hume asked sympathetically.

"About the end of this mystery. About the final scene of the play that took the lives of a number of my family members."

He turned a bit and pulled one leg underneath himself, stroking the wooden handle of his pick with his hand.

"We're looking at the climax of a plot that started playing out more than 60 years ago," he said. "Think about that. The Resistance buys guns from a company by exchanging gems for them – their courier is murdered in the full view of the people in that nightclub a few blocks from here – just a few blocks from here."

He looked down at the pick and followed his hands with his eyes as he caressed the handle.

"I guess what's bothering me is that this thing has come full circle."

Casio squatted down like a catcher behind the plate, and laid his shovel next to Pitcher's pick.

"I think I see what he means," the detective said dryly.

Pitcher threw Casio an angry look that melted away instantly.

"What I mean is that it all started those many years ago. It was war. Somehow Eve Somers' family and my family came cross to one another, and it festered for more than half a century. And in the last few weeks, the war came back here, and what started all those decades ago seemed to pick up where it left off – except the people who offended one another are all dead, so it started to play out with those people's descendants."

"The sins of the father..." murmured McDermott.

Pitcher nodded to his editor with a thin smile.

"My exact point, Mac. For some reason known only to people who can't speak for themselves any more, all this, which should have ended sixty years ago, slammed itself into present day – and members of my family as yet unthought-of when it all began, had to pay the price for the mistakes of those who lived then."

"Aren't you rambling a bit here, Pitch?" McDermott asked, soothingly.

Again, Pitcher smiled at his editor and friend.

"I'm rambling a lot, Mac. So much has happened, now and way back during the war. So many lives have been ruined – I guess that's the point I'm trying to get to."

"What point?" Hume asked.

Pitcher hesitated, suddenly looking very tired.

"My point," he said in a voice that was almost whiny, "is that it should have stopped all those years ago. And now the only people who can bring this vicious cycle to a stop are right here on this tiny plot of earth."

He struggled to his feet.

"So why don't we?"

"Why don't we?" Hume demanded.

"Why don't' we just walk away. Why don't we just march out of here and leave the mystery unsolved."

Charlie Hume pulled a tape measure from his pocket and regarded it for a long moment.

"Pitch, with apologies to your family... I gotta know!" he almost whispered. "I've watched all this come out, in what's happened, in what you and Mac have written in the paper about it. I just can't stand to leave a mystery unsolved."

"I have to agree with that," Casio chimed in. "It's an occupational disease."

The detective thrust his shovel down, breaking the earth for the first time since their arrival. Pitcher watched as the California sleuth placed his foot on the spade's flat side and pressed the blade into the ground, turning a shovelful of grass and loam.

"Yeah," said Pitch, almost to himself. "I gotta know, too!"

He picked up his pick and raised it over his shoulder, bringing it down with all the force in his body near where Casio was digging.

McDermott looked at the two of them for a moment, then dug his owl shovel into the ground, turning more and more earth. Charlie Hume used his tape measure to mark out the approximate diameter of the grave, then he, too, grabbed his shovel and started digging.

Each man gave thought to Pitchers soliloquy as he put his shoulders into the digging. There were fleeting thoughts of how sore they would be by the end of the day, using, as they were, muscles normally dormant in their backs and upper torsos. There would certainly be a price to pay.

But they also considered Pitcher's words, and weighed again, over and over, his suggestion that they simply stop what they were doing, replace their divot, drop their tools and walk back to their cars, forever leaving the final act of the war drama unplayed. But none of them could give the matter further voice, because each had his own reasons for wanting the mystery put to rest once and for all. Even Pitcher who had the most to gain and the most to lose, thought similarly as he swung his pick again and again, loosening up the hard clay for his partners to scoop out into the increasingly large pile at one side of the grave.

At length they took a break, resting against the pile of dirt sipping soft drinks McDermott had thoughtfully brought with him in a small ice chest kept in the back seat of his Jeep.

"Have you noticed," McDermott mentioned, being the first to break the long silence, "that the color of the dirt has changed?"

The other three studied the dirt they were leaning against. Mac was right. They had begun digging through brown clay, but for the few minutes before their break, they had encountered loose, black, spongy dirt. Pitcher, who was standing, ambled over and looked into the hole.

"What's that?" he asked casually, pointing into the opening.

"What's what?" Casio replied, pulling himself erect with a grunt of pain and following Pitcher's gaze.

"The sun glinted on something for a moment," he said. "There it is," he concluded, pointing.

By that time the other two men had joined Casio and Pitcher at the rim of their hole and were looking for what Pitcher was pointing at.

It wasn't hard to spot. It was a small object with a shiny side, catching the sun's rays just right. McDermott dropped into the abyss and dug it out with his fingers. He held it up for the others to see, brushing the loose dirt away.

"I'm not sure, but I think this is a diamond," he said to no one in particular.

"There's another one," Pitcher said, excitedly pointing to McDermott's left.

"And another," Hume barked, dropping into the hole and squatting.

"Hand me a shovel," McDermott demanded, and one was supplied to him instantly by Casio. McDermott gingerly scooped the soft dirt into the bowl of the shovel head and brought it up to his face, blowing and flicking away the dirt. Two shining stones remained in the shovel. In addition, Pitcher and Hume and discovered two others each.

Ingenius," McDermott breathed as the men climbed back out of the hole. He picked up one of the stones and brushed it on his shirt, then turned it in his fingers, holding it aloft so the sun could find its facets. "How beautiful," he whispered.

"What's genius?" Hume asked from the edge.

McDermott palmed the stone and turned to face his editor.

"Suppose we'd used a backhoe to dig out this grave. What would we be looking for?"

Hume shrugged. "A container with the diamonds in it."

"Exactly," McDermott affirmed.

"Except in this case the container apparently sprung a leak," mused Casio.

McDermott shook his head.

"There isn't any container, Sy," McDermott declared.

Casio screwed up his face. Hume and Pitcher looked at the editor, perplexed.

"That's was the genius," he said. Whoever did the burying of the gems simply put a layer of potting soil or something in the hole and embedded the gems, loose, in that. That's why the dirt changed colors – it was to show someone doing the digging that here is where the diamonds were. Someone not knowing the shtick would just keep digging until they found the coffin, and probably would open it looking for the gems and finding only old bones. With no container to find..."

Hume's face lit up.

"Yes..." he said. "Pure genius."

"So..." Pitcher began.

The other three looked at him.

"Now what," he asked, flatly.

"Pardon?" Hume asked, shifting his gaze to the reporter. Pitcher's face was set in granite as he fixed each of his companions with a cold stare.

"Now what?" he repeated, with a bit more emphasis.

"What do you mean, Pitch?" McDermott inquired, pulling himself out of the hole and sitting on the grass near his friend.

"I mean," Pitcher said, his voice nearing a yell, "now that we've found the stones, what do we do with them? Who do they belong to? Who do we turn them over to?"

The three men paused a moment then each looked at the other. All of them shrugged, then turned their attention back to Pitcher.

"You got a suggestion, Pitch?" McDermott asked, soothingly.

Pitcher spread his arms out over the hole.

"Leave them there," he said.

McDermott's left eyebrow raised.

"I'm serious," Pitcher barked. "Leave them here. How many lives have been lost, how many graves like this one have been filled with the bodies of people who wanted these stones? Never mind that some of them were entitled to have them, such as Roag Arms – but not Roag Junior, he just wanted them for – whatever reason – Roag Arms has been gone for a long time. No business, no payment, that's the way it is."

The other three were staring, open-mouthed, at the reporter during what for him was an oration.

"I think it's appropriate that these diamonds are being found in a grave. They've certainly filled enough of them."

Pitcher looked at the two stones in his hand. He flipped one of them up into the air a few times, catching it without looking. After a moment of doing that, he tossed both stones back into the hole and turned away, but the other three noted that his eyes were filling with tears. For a moment his blurred gaze fell on McDermott.

"Let the dead bury the dead, Mac," he said, his voice cracking.

Rubbing his eyes he walked back to the road and past the car he had arrived in, and through the gate of the Congressional Cemetery to the main road, where he hailed a cab that appeared seemingly out of nowhere. The other three men watched silently until the cab disappeared.

Long moments after Pitcher's abrupt departure, the three remaining Muscatels turned and stared for long, silent moments, at one another, and then at the three-foot-deep hole they had worked so laboriously to dig.

In a single motion, they turned to with their shovels, and in a moment, brown clay was slapping against black loam in the bottom of the fissure. In an hour, they patted the sod back into place, and the grave of Alvin Joseph Truscott looked much as it had before their arrival – just a few wide seams betrayed their labors. The men stowed their shovels in the truck of Charlie Hume's Lexus, and they drove through the brick arch and iron gates and back into the mid-morning Washington traffic.

Chapter Forty-Two

Peter McDermott arrived at the *North Bay Times* offices the next morning with the sense of emptiness that always portends the climax of a major story. Accompanying that feeling was a deep sympathy for the emotional stress and familial tragedy being suffered by his best friend and top reporter. As he swiped his press card in the outside door lock, and heard the familiar click as the bolt threw back, he resolved to call Pitcher, and tell him to take a few days – as long as he needed – to shake off the effects of all that had happened. He knew that Pitcher would never entirely get over it – just as he wouldn't, for different reasons.

McDermott ascended the stone stairs to his office level and passed through the glass doors, into the office on the newsroom side. He nodded to the receptionist, who always arrived before he did, no matter how early he came in, and ambled down the dimly lit corridor toward his office.

"Mac!"

McDermott heard that voice, calling out that word several times a day. It was Charlie Hume, who was, as usual, sticking his head through the door at the far end of the newsroom that led to the "sales" side of the building.

McDermott looked up. Hume's head disappeared as quickly as it had poked through the door, but there was a clear indication of what Mac was to do. He turned right next to his own, dark office, and passed through the portal. He always felt it was something like passing through Alice's looking glass, away from the analytical, relatively sane (so he perceived it) atmosphere of the newsroom, into the mad, mad, mad tea party of sales. And in his mind's eye, he often saw Charlie Hume with an oversized hat on his head, with the size in the hatband, yelling "Move down, move down, clean cups, clean cups." Because of that vision, McDermott could never look a cup of tea in the eye.

The editor stepped into Hume's large, wood-paneled office and dropped onto the couch along the right-hand wall. Hume turned his oversized computer monitor around and joined his editor.

"I couldn't stand it, Mac, I Googled Alvin Joseph Truscott and then visited the web sites we use to find people's vital stats. You know what?"

McDermott lifted an eyebrow.

"There never was an Alvin Joseph Truscott," Hume said. The resistance agents in the U.S. buried a coffin filled with sacks of cement, just to convince the cemetery officials that there was a body in there. It was a blind for hiding the diamonds. Isn't that something?"

McDermott's eyes dilated and he seemed for a moment to be a million miles away.

He was, in fact, not miles away, but years, as his thoughts took him into the past. For a moment it was he, digging into the soft earth in the dead of night to hide raw stones. It was he who came to the cemetery to recover the stones, and then transfer needed weapons and ammunition to a group of Germans who knew what a monster their *Fuehrer* was.

"Very interesting, Charlie," he said softly. Without a word or a glance at the publisher, McDermott rose and sauntered out of the office and back into the newsroom.

"Be sure to use that when you write your article," Hume called after him.

McDermott gave no acknowledgement as he crossed the newsroom and keyed open the door of his own office. It was a corner room, overly large, and the wall that faced the newsroom was mostly glass – capable of being made opaque by a series of blinds that went from ceiling to floor. The blinds were closed now, as they were every day when McDermott left the office for home.

He turned on his desk light and his computer in about the same motion and dropped into the high-backed, leather swivel chair behind his desk. He riffled through the stack of pink phone message slips and selected a few he wanted to answer personally. The rest he would staff out. It took him a few moments to notice the envelope and the cloth bag with a string closure sitting on his desk. He mentally went through his list of the few people who had a key to his office, trying to determine who had left them, as he rasped the envelope open with a mean-looking letter opener. The note was from Pitcher, who was one of those who had a key. Inside the envelope was a handwritten note on Pitcher's personal stationery. He spread the paper out on the desk, popped the top on a can of Diet Pepsi from his office fridge, and began to read.

Dear Mac,

I won't be in to work today, nor for the rest of the week, but I will be back on Monday. I know we have to write articles and sidebars and follow-ups to all that has happened the last few weeks – and we have to do it in the midst of our own grief. I want you to know I'm sorry about Eve. You never said so, probably not even to her, but I know you loved her. That's enough about that.

As you no doubt know, I will be dealing with my own grief, even as I help the remnants of my family sort out estates and arrangements for the people killed in this sad affair. I need to take the rest of the week to begin that process – and to spend some quality time with Samantha, who will try her best to make me feel better. She will be successful.

Next week I'll do all the writing you want me to do about all this. But once I've done that, I'd be grateful to you if we never discussed this episode again.

And just to bribe you into submission with my wishes in this matter, I'm leaving you a present.

See you Monday.

As ever,

Pitch.

McDermott reread the note. He read it four times. Then he turned his attention to the cloth bag.

It was a small tote, much like the ones Crown Royal whiskey comes in, closed at the top with a tiny leather draw-string. He loosened the string and pulled the top of the bag open, upending it and letting the contents spill out onto his desk. There was only one thing in the bag. It clattered across the desk top, bounced off the base of his flat-screen computer monitor, and came to rest on top of Pitcher's note.

The smooth sides of the diamond picked up the beam of light from McDermott's desk lamp, refracting it, and manifesting with rainbow shards of light bouncing hither and yon across the editorial desk.

Peter McDermott stared numbly at the stone for a long moment, then laid his head on his arms atop the desk and sobbed. He let the tears come until they would come no more – oblivious to the two people who came to his open door, witnessed his discomfiture and departed.

He cried for Reesa Lowenstein, for the three Albert Lowensteins who never saw it coming. He cried for Martin Roag, and Martin Roag Junior who died not for what they believed in, but for what they felt life owed them. He cried for Harry Oglesby. He cried for Eve, who took a wrong turn and couldn't reverse course.

And when at last tears would no longer come, McDermott walked across the hall to the men's room where he washed his face and took a moment to collect his thoughts. Ambling back to his office, he sat down, opened a new MS Word page, and began to write.

Post Hoc, Ergo Propter Hoc

Peter McDermott disobeyed Charlie Hume's order to write about the non-existent Alvin Joseph Truscott. His reasoning, which he easily sold to Hume, was that he didn't want people to run out to the cemetery and dig it up looking for the diamonds – which he was sure would happen. Hume agreed.

The story occupied three editions of the weekly *North Bay Times*, beginning with the long piece McDermott wrote the day after leaving Congressional Cemetery. The following week, McDermott, Hume and a returned Pitcher collaborated on a multiple part series that occupied most of the paper's pages for the next three weeks.

The piece won several major awards and was chosen for the Library of Congress's exhibit on clandestine operations of World War II.

True to his word, Rod Pitcher returned to the office the Monday after the cemetery debacle, put together and ready to return to work. His prose on the aspects of the plot that involved him and his family members were handsome pieces of writing that drew the attention of major publications that sought his services. Aside from accepting a few freelance assignments – and a handsome raise from the *Times* – Pitcher elected to stay where he was, working for his best friend.

Charlie Hume had entered into a deal to buy a small newspaper on North Carolina's Outer Banks, but the seller backed out of the deal right before it closed. Bitten by the bug to increase his journalistic holdings, Hume finished his part of the diamond story and left McDermott in charge. He was out of the office more than he was in over the next few months, looking at the multitude of small and metropolitan papers, many with their own print shops that a sour economy had put on the 'for sale' block

Fred Mattingly continued as a detective with the Washington D.C. Police Department for three more years. On the day he was promoted to Captain, he was shot in the leg after walking in on an armed robbery in progress at a S.E. Washington convenience store. He was given a desk job overseeing the overnight shift in the Detective Division's bunko unit. He retired at the age of 59, and moved with his family to Maryland's Eastern Shore. He was defeated in two runs for town council of Easton, Maryland, and died of pneumonia in that settlement, at the age of 80.

Ballistics expert Marv Bent was forced into retirement at the age of 60. For the first few years he wrote books on unusual weapons and their unique characteristics. But inactivity drove him crazy. At this writing, he lives in Los Angeles, and serves as a technical advisor for a television crime drama.

Pitcher's Aunt Louisa became a recluse after her husband's murder, and those of other family members. She gradually stopped attending family events and retired to her room in her home where she died of natural causes at the age of 93.

The body of Eve Somers was held by the D.C. District Coroner as long as it could be, then was cremated. The ashes were sent to the family of Arvey Somers, her ex-husband, who returned them to the morgue. The ashes were placed in a funeral home vault where they are, at this writing, unclaimed.

Julian Peebles wrote scholarly articles for historical magazines about the German Resistance Movement, and their use of the watch for courier duty. Peebles was lauded by the intelligentia and was invited to take the entrance test for Mensa, which, to his embarrassment, he failed.

Peebles' butler, the one McDermott and Pitcher called "Lurch," continued in the Peebles household. No one, not even Peebles, seems to know his name or age.

Sy Casio returned to California long enough to close his agency. The detective told his secretary, Madelyn, that he was tired of years with no changes of season, and he moved his entire practice to Washington D.C. Madelyn came with him, and they opened an office in a downtrodden building about three blocks from the former site of the Metropole. Casio's agency did so well that he hired a couple of young detectives to help him.

Investigators from the U.S. Bureau of Alcohol, Tobacco and Firearms spent two weeks poking through the rubble of the Metropole Hotel. Six months later they issued their report, and Peter McDermott was the only one on the mailing list to receive a copy. The report called the explosion "the work of a nefarious machine, placed in service by person or persons unknown." Despite the testimony of McDermott and others at various hearings, the ATF report didn't mention Eve Somers or Martin Roag Junior. The report did, however, make copious reference to the manner of the explosion – a large cache of C-4 plastique set up in the hotel sub-basement and detonated remotely by a cell phone.

The day after the second long installment of the diamond story hit the stands in the *North Bay Times*, a Komatsu power shovel and a fleet of dump trucks sidled up to the Metropole. The shovel began scooping up the remaining pile of bricks that once made up the hotel edifice, assisted after the third day by a bulldozer.

In the hotel's storied past, numerous fires had damaged or destroyed it, but rebuilding always followed, fueled by insurance money. Not this time.

D.C. City officials were unable to find out who actually owned the hotel, though they did trace it as far as Roag Arms Corporation. Evidence showed there were others who carried title or were investors in the property, but each of those wisely decided the best course of action would be to quietly crawl away from the investment.

Peter McDermott wrote about the final demolition of the bombed-out hotel, rehashing both of his experiences in its walls. In the weeks to come he would advise Charlie Hume on his intended purchase of another Maryland newspaper, this one with its own print house. He would also have his boat returned to him from its temporary berth at Holiday Point Marina in Edgewater where Eve Somers hid it. McDermott would enjoy many weekends on that boat, to the extent that he would go for weeks at a time without pulling his grubby-clothes joke on the hapless staff of the Set and Drift.

McDermott was in S.E. Washington three days after the shovel and dump trucks arrived. He was there with his camera and his laptop computer when the last of the bricks were scooped up, dropped into a truck, and hauled to the Anacostia where they would become rip-rap, and eventually be carried downstream to the Potomac.

McDermott watched the bulldozer level the lot, then drive onto a flatbed truck to be driven away along with the power shovel. He was struck by the eerie silence of the intersection now, and the strange look of the end of the block, like an evil smile in a mouth with a tooth missing.

More than two hundred years after the French built it, after centuries of fires and killings and intrigue, the Metropole Hotel ceased to exist.

THE END

Peter McDermott will return in *The Color of Dark*

About The Author:

Jay Zimmer is a full time freelance writer and novelist following 40 years of award-winning work as a professional broadcast and print journalist. Born and raised in Indianapolis, Indiana, Jay spent his summers in the Annapolis, Maryland area and fell in love with the Chesapeake Bay. He lives in Evansville, Indiana. Visit him on the web at: **www.jayzimmer.com**